Jo Thomas worked for many years as a reporter and

The Olive Branch

Real Reader Reviews

'[A] wonderfully vivid, beautifully written, entertaining and colourful journey into the heart of Italy. It was literally like going on holiday in my Kindle. I finished it with a smile on my face, which for me is one of the best ways to end an adventure that I have taken within the pages of a book'

'*The Olive Branch* is a "sunshine" read. It's a book that would be best read whilst sipping a glass of wine, with a plate of focaccia so the reader can fully immerse themselves into the story'

'I have just this minute put down *The Olive Branch* by Jo Thomas after finishing it in one sitting – and I absolutely LOVED it!! It is SO my kind of book – full of olive groves, Italian magic . . . pure escapism!'

'Another fabulous read from this very talented author . . . Jo Thomas has a wonderful gift not only for bringing her characters alive but also for describing the surrounding scenery of the land so well I could almost smell the lemons, plus the odd goat . . . Ruthie is the perfect flat mate!'

'This book had it all – full of emotion, laughter and even more tears, plus a lot of glasses of wine, mixed with the beautiful food Italy is famous for'

'This is a lovely story, well written and beautifully put together. I loved it and have to admit that I shed a few tears in places'

'Warm, romantic and frothy fiction perfect for a holiday read . . . There's always a market for a bit of fun and *The Olive Branch* is exactly that: a bit of well-written fun set in a beautiful location, and ultimately uplifting'

'*The Olive Branch* is a refreshing read with attractive characters and a wonderful setting. The narrative evokes the atmosphere of rural Italy, and mouth-watering descriptions of food and drink will bring back memories to those who know Italy and it will tempt those who don't'

'Perfect for a day on the lounger with a glass of wine on one side and some nibbles on the other'

'You feel the delicious warmth of the summer sun on your back and the taste of olive oil on your lips. Read this book, you won't be disappointed!'

'I read this book in one gulp travelling from Bordeaux up to Paris by train and loved every minute of it – the descriptions of Puglia, the food, the olive oil tasting, the slow burn of the relationship, the family dynamics, the friendships that Ruthie makes, her sheer persistence – everything'

'Jo Thomas has yet again satisfied the romantic in me. A gorgeous story of life in Italy, coupled with the inner struggle of belonging. Wow, it makes me want to sell up and ship out to Italy'

By Jo Thomas

The Oyster Catcher
The Olive Branch

Digital Novella
The Chestnut Tree

The Olive Branch

JO THOMAS

headline
review

First published in paperback in 2015 by HEADLINE REVIEW
An imprint of HEADLINE PUBLISHING GROUP

6

Cataloguing in Publication Data is available from the British Library

ISBN 978 1 4722 2370 8

Typeset in Caslon by Avon DataSet Ltd, Bidford-on-Avon, Warwickshire

Printed and bound in Great Britain by Clays Ltd, Elcograf S.p.A.

Headline's policy is to use papers that are natural, renewable and
recyclable products and made from wood grown in well-managed
forests and other controlled sources. The logging and manufacturing
processes are expected to conform to the environmental regulations
of the country of origin.

HEADLINE PUBLISHING GROUP
An Hachette UK Company
Carmelite House
50 Victoria Embankment
London EC4Y 0DZ

www.headline.co.uk
www.hachette.co.uk

*For Richard. Thank you for the inspiration and help,
and for being my bro and a top uncle.*

Prologue

My hand hovers over the mouse. My heart is pumping and I'm not sure if it's the Prosecco we've drunk or pure madness racing through my veins.

I take in the bare room around me. It's soulless, empty of furniture and feelings.

I look at my friend Morag, her eyes bright with excitement.

The clock is ticking, and with every passing second my heart beats louder.

'Ten, nine . . .' The timer clicks down. My mouth is dry.

'Eight, seven . . .' I feel sick, again not sure if it's due to Prosecco or tension. This is insane.

'Six, five . . .' I look around the place I once called home – now an empty shell, like me.

'Four, three . . .' I consider my options. There's only one as far as I'm concerned.

'Two . . .' And it's utterly reckless.

'One.' I glance at Morag, who looks as though she might burst, and I don't know if I do it intentionally, or if my finger just twitches involuntarily. But I press the button, and we fall giggling into a Prosecco-fuelled slumber on the lumpy settees.

The next morning, after paracetamol and gallons of water have started to take effect, a slow realisation creeps over me like cold custard. I rush to the computer and check my emails. There it is, in black and white, bringing back my moment of madness and reminding me of why it should be compulsory to take a breathalyser test before using the internet late at night.

Congratulations! You were the successful bidder! My heart jumps into my mouth and bangs noisily against my ears. Now what am I going to do?

My panicked thoughts are interrupted by a knock at the door, and as I stumble across the room to open it, my heart thunders some more.

'Hi, we've come for the sofas,' says the bright, well-spoken young woman who is standing there with her eager boyfriend. I look at the couch where Morag is still sleeping.

'We'll just be a moment. I'm nearly done here,' I say as the young couple start lifting the sofa that was my bed until a few minutes ago.

There's only one thing I can do, says the mad, impetuous voice in my head. And I realise it's mine.

Chapter One

As I watch the goat marching up and down the courtyard, like a foot guard at Buckingham Palace, I wonder if I've bitten off more than I can chew.

'Recalculating! Recalculating!' My sole companion for the entire journey continues shouting, her voice cutting through me like a dentist's drill. I switch her off firmly, with pleasure, before turning off the engine of my little Ford Ka. The windscreen wipers let out an exhausted whine and the screen is a whiteout of water in seconds, like fake rain in a low-budget film. Only this is not fake, it's very real, I remind myself, as the water drums noisily on the car roof.

I take a deep breath. It's been like this ever since I left Bari, the sprawling port at the top of Italy's heel, where I stopped off to do a quick shop in Ikea for essentials and lunch. This is another thing I wasn't expecting, aside from the goat: torrential rain in summer in southern Italy.

I gaze out of the car window and pull my lightweight hoodie closer around me. A collection of silver bangles jangles on my wrist and I look down at my Rolling Stones T-shirt, which I've cut into a crop top, and my paint-splattered cut-off Levi's. I'm definitely underdressed.

Grabbing my favourite vintage leather jacket from the seat beside me, I pull it on and shiver. I should be in waterproofs and wellies.

Taking another deep breath, I pull the handle and push the car door open against the driving rain. I straighten up, holding one hand over my eyes, and shiver again as I look down at the envelope in my hand.

The rain lashes against the paper, making the ink run, and I have to keep shutting my eyes against the deluge. The goat glances in my direction and I'm sure I hear it snort.

I use one hand to shield my eyes and strain to look at the house in front of me, then back at the long, potholed drive I've just driven down. I can hardly see the big stone pillars and red metal gates at the entrance. I shove the envelope back in my pocket and pull out a printed picture of the house. The image is papier mâché in seconds, disintegrating and landing on the wet stones at my feet. If I'm not quick, my canvas slip-ons will go the same way. This has to be the right place; there's nowhere similar nearby.

I passed a couple of small houses on the way in, as the narrow road led me up and down and round and round like a fairground ride, with occasional potholes for added fear factor. Some of the houses had curved roofs, while others were modern and flat-roofed. I also spotted the occasional collection of dilapidated *trulli* – small circular houses with conical roofs, like clusters of field mushrooms. But I'm not looking for a *trullo*. The house in front of me now is like something from a film set. It's old, weather-worn, faded pink and big – much bigger than I imagined. There's nothing else like it on the lane. This must be it.

I hold my hand up against the punishing rain, and half wonder whether a plague of locusts is going to follow next. Perhaps this is a sign . . . I push the silly thought away, along with the memory of my mum's despairing phone messages and Ed's disapproving emails.

My T-shirt is stuck to my skin and the rain is dripping down my short hair and on to my face, running off round my nose stud like a little waterfall. There's no point in rummaging in the boot for my raincoat now, so I sling on my lavender leather satchel and wonder what I've let myself in for. I could get back in the car, drive away from here as quickly as possible and email Ed to tell him he was right all along: I am daft, impetuous and irresponsible.

But then again, at least I'm not boring and stuck in my ways. There's only one way to go: forwards! I bow my head, pull my bag tighter to me and run towards the listing veranda groaning with an unruly and neglected bougainvillea.

With my chin tucked into my chest, I spot a large pothole and sidestep it, slipping and skidding on the worn cobbles. I'm startlingly close to the cross-looking goat, which is now standing across the front door. I am in the middle of my worst nightmare.

'Maah,' the goat bleats, making me jump. God, that was loud. I stare at the goat and it stares back at me. Its eyes are different colours: one scarily yellow, the other blue. For the first time in weeks, I have no idea what to do. Guard goats were not on my list of essential information.

I wonder whether 'shoo' has the same meaning in Italian as it does in English. It's not something I can remember covering in my evening classes. But I need to do something. I'm freezing out here.

'Shoo, shoo!' I say, waving my hands in the goat's direction and backing away at the same time. I don't want it to run at me with its horns, which look pointy and sharp. You don't get goats standing in the way of your front door back in Tooting. The odd drunk camping out for the night, maybe, but somehow they seem easier to overcome than this.

'Shoo, shoo!' I try again, this time with more hand-waving. The goat flinches, as do the terrified butterflies in my stomach, but still it doesn't move from its position in front of the big, dark wooden door. Even the three-day drive down through France and Italy, with stop-offs in lay-bys to catch forty winks and only an irritating, indecisive satnav for company, is nothing compared to this.

I've spent the past six weeks dealing with estate agents, flat viewings and solicitors, packing up and dividing the belongings Ed and I shared. I separated everything out and gave over custody of our joint retro record collection and the player I found on eBay. I sold off redundant furniture, oversaw its collection and moved myself out of our flat. It all went without a hitch; nothing fazed me. But territorial goats? No idea! I throw my hands up and turn my back on it.

Opening up my satchel, I search around for some kind of magic bean that will help me out here. Then I spot it: a half-eaten Kit Kat I bought in a service station somewhere outside Rome. I thought the sugar boost might get me round the greater ring road – that and Dolly Parton on the CD player. It sort of worked. I got round on a wing and a prayer, nerves jangling, heart in mouth, high on energy drinks and with a lot of hand gestures and horn honking – not necessarily mine. I pull out the Kit Kat and wave it at the goat. It steadfastly ignores me, looking the other way from its sheltered position. I quickly pull back the wrapper.

'Come on. It's chocolate.' I wave it, immediately feeling like the Child Catcher in *Chitty Chitty Bang Bang*, and break off a piece to toss in front of the goat. As it backs away, I think I'm going to have to give up and look for somewhere else to stay tonight until I can find the owner. Then it sniffs at the taster and snaffles it up with appreciative noises, walking towards me, no doubt hoping for more.

'See, it's good.' I break off another bit, tossing it in front of the goat, which is now moving faster and faster. I walk backwards, getting quicker all the time. I feel like I'm in a scene from *You've Been Framed*. I'm miles away from home, in the heaviest rain I've ever seen, with my worldly possessions in a Ford Ka, trying to tempt a goat away from a front door with half a Kit Kat. I'm beginning to understand how Noah felt, and I'm debating whether there would be room for goats on my ark.

This is all Ed's fault! I think irrationally. And my mum's. The goat keeps hoovering up the Kit Kat and I'm nearly at the edge of the slippery forecourt. I step back and my heel hits a low stone wall, giving me a reality check.

I step up on to the wall and my phone springs into life. I pull it out, hoping for some kind of encouraging words. Two text messages and some missed calls. I don't bother to check the calls. The texts are from Ed and my mum. That's all I need. If Ed knew that at this moment I was trying to bribe a territorial goat, he'd start by saying 'I told you so,' with lowering eyebrows. It's his reaction to everything I do – he thinks I'm impulsive; 'hot-headed', he calls it. He's forever telling me I always leap before I look. He, on the other hand, doesn't do anything without consulting Google or Facebook first. We're total opposites. At first, that was the fun part about it. But now he thinks I knee-jerk-react to everything. I think he thinks too long and hard about things and doesn't take risks. It could've been the perfect combination. But it wasn't.

If Ed had been here, it would be a whole different story. He wouldn't have stepped out of the car without a team of health and safety officers inspecting the place first, and he'd've employed Bear Grylls himself to get rid of the goat.

No, I can't fall at the first hurdle now, even if this goat does have the guarding instincts of a Rottweiler. It pushes its face up towards my hands and I can't move. I do the only thing I can: reach out a tentative hand and scratch it between the eyes. It seems to like it. But I'm stuck here now. If I stop, it nudges me, hard. There's nothing for it, it's now or never.

I throw the last piece of Kit Kat as far as I can, beyond the uneven cobbles. The goat turns and nearly topples over in its excitement to get to it, slipping, sliding and clattering across the stones before leaping on the tasty treat. I throw myself towards the front door. My hands shake as I pull out the big, rusting key and push it into the lock, whilst trying to keep one eye on the goat. In the process, I drop the envelope on the wet floor. I pick it up and push really hard against the door. It doesn't budge. The goat is trotting back towards me. I pull away, dip my shoulder and give the door an almighty shove; it flies open just as there is a huge crash of thunder and a silver sliver cracks across the sky. I fall through the front door, desperate to escape the elements, into a cavernous room, along with the goat.

'Maah,' it says loudly, dripping all over the floor. A great wave of despair washes over me. What on earth have I let myself in for?

Chapter Two

I grapple up and down the sides of the door frame in the dim light of the farmhouse, looking for the light switch. I find it. I flick it down with a clunk and glance round the room, but nothing happens. I pull the door open wider to let in more light and in the hope that the goat will find its way out. There's a damp, musty smell. I'm not sure if it's the house or the goat. I give the animal a wide berth and go to the first window I can see. I open it, then pull back the stiff bolt on the wooden shutters and push them open.

There's another huge clap of thunder. The goat doesn't move, possibly hoping I haven't noticed it standing by the front door.

I go round the room and open every shutter I can see. Some are stiffer than others, and I make a mental note to give the bolts a spray with WD40 as soon as I can get to the shops. I'm sure I passed an ironmonger in town.

The windows are small and the room is still dark, but when I get to the glass doors at the end of the room and push open their shutters, it really makes a difference. My eyes begin to take in everything, and as they do, they're drawn upwards. The light cream stones make pointed dome shapes that cross in the high ceiling, creating a star shape. It's amazing. I turn round, taking it all in – breathtaking – then promptly trip over a plastic table piled high with boxes of junk in the middle of the room.

Whilst the ceiling may be breathtaking, the rest of the room is in need of some real TLC, I think, looking at the patchy paintwork. My mind starts racing with all sorts of ideas for how to show off its best features. It was the same when Ed and I first saw our flat. I could see all the possibilities and the ideas just kept coming: how we could turn the kitchen into a kitchen diner, make the fireplace the feature in the room again, bring in light. Ed saw the investment potential, I saw the design possibilities. It's the same here. My mind won't stop whirring with ideas.

The stone wall above the fireplace is blackened and could definitely do with repainting. I'd keep the walls white, of course. There are bare bulbs in the sockets on the walls; some terracotta roof tiles would work well as uplighters.

It's all fixable. I mean, I knew the place would need work, and the scope is fantastic. But I'm going to have to find the local tip to start with, I can see that.

I'm freezing and hug myself. Maybe I should try and light the big woodburner. But I want to explore some more first. There's no point trying to bring my stuff in from the car while it's still raining out there. I go to the stone archway where three stone steps lead to another room. I take the steps and look round for wooden shutters to open.

Wow! A domed roof. Lower than the other room but actually curved. This was probably the *lamia*, used for animals at one time. There's a semicircular stone arch on one wall. Set into it is a collapsing sink unit, crooked cupboard doors and a crusty cooker. But I'm sure I'll be able to put those cupboard doors back on, and paint them up, too. Maybe do some tiling behind the sink.

I once went on an evening course back home to learn how to do tiling. I was self-taught with the carpentry on the skirting and the window seat I made in the flat. I suppose that's the thing about working from home: I always had those DIY programmes on in the background and I guess I just got hooked. I was hoping to do a plumbing course too, but took Italian instead in a moment of madness, seduced by a glass of cheap Prosecco and a square of pizza at the open evening. Luckily Ed and I never needed the plumbing sorting. We bought the flat knowing it needed work but that it would make us a tidy profit if it was done up. And Ed was delighted that I'd be able to do most of it. His skills were in numbers, investments, book-balancing, and he certainly invested well when we bought the flat. Still, the work needed on it was nothing compared to this place.

There are more boxes spewing junk in this room: cables and cord, bottles, plastic funnels and redundant overalls. I definitely need to find the tip as soon as possible! In fact, first things first, best find out what they call it. I pull out my phone to look it up on my translation app. Typical! No internet access here. Looks like the stone wall at the front of the house is the best place for a signal so far.

I rummage in my bag for a pen and the black Moleskine notebook I bought at the ferry port. It's my 'change my life' notebook. I take a deep breath. I'll show everyone I'm not just going to roll over and disappear into a pit of misery or put up with another night on a sofa. My back's still aching.

Our big sleigh bed went weeks ago. It felt like it was barely cold. After Ed and I split up, it took just six weeks for the flat and its entire contents to be sold. I was sleeping in the empty flat on one of our big squashy sofas until the new owner could come to pick it up. That was the thing that did it, I think. I didn't even have my own bed any more. That, and the thought of going to my mum's and having to see her partner Colin in his vest every morning, belching and scratching himself whilst watching *Lorraine* at full volume. Mum and Colin got together when I went to college. Not long after I moved out, he moved in. It was like my place at home had been filled. There was no going back, no vacancies. I was on my own.

I open the new notebook. My last one had been full of electricity readings, Post Office redirection reference numbers and skip hire details. The pages of this one are stiff and have that wonderful 'new book' smell. This is an important page. The first page of the rest of my life.

1. I put a firm full stop after it. *Tip.*

Then I cross it out and write: *1. Internet. 2. Tip. 3. Goat owner!*

I must find out who owns that goat.

I go to pull back the greying net curtains over the sink and they fall down in my hand, dusty and smelly. I sigh. They probably needed replacing anyway.

4. Kitchen nets. And the list starts to grow.

I go back down the stone steps, running my hands along the cold stone walls. There's another doorway opposite, to one side of the fireplace, and a stone staircase disappearing into the thick wall on the other.

Through the doorway, which is more like a corridor, I'm in the living room. There's an empty fireplace and another couple of small windows. I open up the shutters. More rubbish. But that's okay. Rubbish can be got rid of. It's not like it's anything major. After another look around, I can see myself sitting here, armchairs in front of the fire. Maybe even use it for B&B guests if I can get the bedrooms painted up. I'll keep it all white in here too. I touch the lime-washed wall. It's cool, and my teeth are beginning to chatter. There's a door leading out to an overgrown courtyard.

I look out of the window to the front and can just about make out my car parked beyond the stone forecourt. The rain must be easing. I'll get my clothes in once I've had a quick look round the rest of the house. It should've stopped by then, or at least be lighter, and hopefully the goat will have gone too.

I suddenly remember something, and add it to my list: *48. Electricity box.* I don't want to be stuck here in the dark tonight. That could be a step too far.

As I head through to the next room, towards the back of the house, I stand stock still in the doorway. I can't believe what I'm seeing. There are only tiny high-up windows, so I hold up my phone's torch. It's a high-ceilinged room again, though not as high as the first, and all white. There's an arch in the wall at the far end, and set into it, a stone statue of Jesus on the cross with a red curtain below. There's a table in front of it covered with a deep red cloth, and eight chairs set out in front of the table. It's an altar! A church!

I wasn't expecting this at all. It's amazing, and so cool and peaceful. It's a great space, but I have no idea what I'll use it for yet. I turn around, wondering about the family gatherings that must have taken place in here. A place for christenings, marriages and funerals. All that history, now just abandoned and gone. I take it all in as I turn around, and then, like a child who's just got everything on their Christmas wish list, I run through the other rooms, making more and more additions to my list.

There are stone stairs down to the cellar that I take two at a time. It's another dome-shaped ceiling, and there are even one or two dusty bottles left behind in a corner, and a couple of large steel barrels that actually look quite new. I run back past the goat, who's now at least looking out through the open door. I'm tempted to give it a shove, but think it's more likely to go if I ignore it. This time I take the stone stairs going up, running my hand along the wall, getting more excited about everything I could do. I can't believe I'm here, or that this place is actually mine. I'm desperate now to see what's upstairs.

It's dark at the top of the stairs. I pull out my phone again and use the torch, just avoiding tripping over more rubbish piled high. I poke my head into each of the three rooms, wondering which is the most habitable. The floor is bare boards and the walls need something doing to them. I decide to go for the room at the back as my bedroom. It's the smallest, but it looks like I can move straight in. I've got a blow-up mattress; Elinor, one of my Italian night-class gang, lent it to me. That'll do for the time being. It'll be like camping, I tell myself, fun! And at least it's in southern Italy, not south London. I think back to the day my bed was carried out of the flat.

Coming out of the bedroom, I go straight to the long window on the landing at the back of the house. It takes all my force to open the shutters, but my God! I catch my breath. There is a small wrought-iron barrier that I hold on to in order to steady myself, and I wonder if it's safe. But what a view! Despite the mist and the steady rain, I can see for miles: olive trees, with the occasional house snuggled amongst them. And you only know they're there because of the smoke rising from the chimneys.

Fires? I think suddenly. At the end of August? Then I remember, it's probably the *fornos* being lit, the outdoor ovens. It is Sunday after all. I remember that from my last trip here, when I fell in love with the area and everything about it, including a young art student called Francis. I smile at the memory. He wasn't the love of my life; I was only seventeen. He was lovely and fun, but I didn't feel any urge to come back and find him. What I did fall in love with was Italy. I always said I'd return.

Ed didn't get it. He liked all-inclusive holidays in Sharm el-Sheikh, or skiing holidays in January. He didn't like the food or anything about Puglia when we visited last year, before 'we' became 'I'.

I wanted to move here there and then. I thought it would give us a joint interest, help to put us back together, but Ed just wanted to find Wi-Fi so he could check the household account and his pension fund. He would never have done something like this. When we met in the university bar in our final year of college, it was an 'opposites attract' thing, I think. He was there with his business studies mates and me with my art buddies. We'd all come to see a band play. It was one of the few things we did have in common, our taste in music. We went to lots of gigs. They were fun times.

During our early days in rented flats, we'd scour markets and boot fairs for furniture and bric-a-brac. That's when we started seriously collecting the eighties albums. It became our weekend hobby. We'd travel all over the place, eating fish and chips on the way home on a Sunday night. That was eight years ago now. But as Ed started to climb the corporate ladder, his tastes began to change and second-hand bric-a-brac became a thing of the past. Ed wanted new, apart from the retro record collection, which had risen in value. He thinks I'm mad now. Maybe I am.

I turn and look at the big landing. I still can't believe I own all of this. In Tooting we had a two-bedroom flat. Okay, it was a nice flat, and as Ed predicted, it was a great investment. We had loads of interest when it went on the market, selling it in days for twice what we paid for it, but it was nothing compared to this.

I go to the other long window at the far end of the corridor and push open the shutters. I look down on my car, parked at an angle like it's been abandoned. The rain definitely seems to be easing up to a light shower. I want to go and explore the courtyard to the side of the house now, where there's a *trullo*, and an open-sided barn that I just know will be full of junk. I smile. My own *trullo*. An old single-storey, conical-roofed stone building. When I first came out here, I was fascinated by them. I'd read somewhere that they looked like the Smurfs' houses, and they do!

I run back downstairs to the front door. I'll bring in my case now as well, and find some dry clothes. I step outside. It's warmer than inside, and guess what? It's stopped raining. The wet and battered bougainvillea is giving off the most wonderful scent after the storm. I look back at the house. *My* house. I would never have believed I could own something like this, not on my own, not without Ed. There's a flicker of excitement in my tummy, like fairy lights being switched on and lighting me from the inside.

'The only regrets you have in life are the things you didn't do,' my grandfather used to tell me. So I took him at his word. Now my mum thinks I'm certifiable. But it was just a window of opportunity. I didn't do it to horrify Ed, although that helped me make my decision. A part of me had always wanted to break out and do something like this, buy a wreck and do it up. I didn't mind where, but I had thought it more likely to be some run-down part of London or maybe Kent. I was never going to be able to afford something on my own in London, though, and now I own all this!

My mind starts to run off into a fantasy world as I go through the archway at the side of the house and look beyond the overgrown brambles. There's the open barn on one side of the courtyard, and yes, it is brimming with rubbish. But it would make wonderful B&B accommodation. I couldn't do it now, obviously, but one day, who knows? For now, I have plans for the little *trullo*.

I try the door. It's not locked. I pull out my list again and scribble: *74. Lock for trullo*. Then I push open the door and bend down to go in, like Alice in Wonderland after she's had the 'Eat Me' cake.

I stop. I hear it before I can see it. Once inside, I stand up straight and listen again. There's a dripping noise. I pull out my phone and use the torch. There's some furniture here: a dark set of drawers that will do for one of the bedrooms in the house, and a small table and chairs. Then I look up, and up and up at the white plaster ceiling – like the inside of a gnome's hat, I think to myself, and smile just as a plop of water hits me in the eye and my phone dies. Ah, so that's where the dripping noise is coming from.

With an old paint bucket in place, I take a final look round. This will make the perfect rental cottage, bringing in a little bit of money to top up what I earn with the online greeting card designs.

101, I write in my notebook. *Internet connection*. I underline it a lot and then make a very firm full stop. I look back at the *trullo*. I'll put a bed in, a table and chairs, and cushions along the alcove by the fire. I'll post pictures on Facebook. I know Ed'll see them. Then I look down at my list and some of the fairy lights in my tummy flicker out. There's a lot to do, and suddenly I shiver as though someone's walked over my grave. I distract myself quickly with thoughts of unpacking and lighting a fire. I'm presuming that without the fire there won't be any hot water, unless there's some super-duper brand-new water tank I've missed somewhere. But I don't think so. Like I say, it'll be like camping: fun!

I dodge the large puddles of water in the courtyard and the clumps of grass growing up through the worn cobbles, and grab my case from the car along with a black bag of clothes. Then I head back to the front door. The goat has gone, thank God, and I shut the door firmly with my bottom. My front door! Not Ed's, or the communal door to the flats; all mine. I smile, and some of the fairy lights come back on.

Upstairs, I peel off my damp clothes, hang them over the window frame and change into some lightweight dungarees I picked up from one of the charity shops on the high street. I pull on my vintage floral waist-length cardigan from a boot fair and flip-flops from Primark. I like to mix up my wardrobe. I wonder where my new shop of choice will be. Maybe the local market, which is on a Monday – tomorrow! Now all the fairy lights come back on and I give myself a little squeeze. I've done it. This is all mine! I think about my mum, my brother Lance, and Ed. I'll show them all. I lean out of the window to take in the view and my phone pings into life, as if by telepathic communication.

Make sure you drink bottled water, texts Mum.

There's also a message from Ed: *Have you got the electricity bill receipts from last year?*

Electricity receipts? Really? I have so much more to think about than last year's electricity bills. Even now we've gone our separate ways Ed is still considering things like how best to divide the final electricity bill seeing as he wasn't there for the last six weeks. He has been practical about the break-up, moving out and moving straight in with Annabel, his colleague from work, who was there, ready and waiting with a shoulder to cry on and a spare room to sleep in. Whereas I spent nights wondering what the hell I'd done and crying into the boxes as I was packing up. That's not to say Ed doesn't keep texting me every few hours. He may have moved on physically but he hasn't quite grasped the fact that I'm not at the end of a phone whenever he wants me.

Annabel is a quick worker indeed. She'd had her eye on Ed for some time. She made no secret of it and told me at their office Christmas party that she was surprised that Ed was with 'someone like you'. I was too surprised to ask her what she meant. But looking around at everyone in their suits while I was in my straight-from-evening-class dungarees, I think I got it. When I finally plucked up the courage to tell Ed that wet afternoon in June that it really wasn't working any more, Annabel had already cleared her spare bedroom and had the Kleenex waiting.

Not long afterwards, the hand of friendship turned into the vice-like grip of a woman who'd got her man and wasn't going to let go. Some might call her smug. I certainly wasn't going to give her the satisfaction of thinking I'd made a completely foolhardy decision. She already thought I'd done that when I finished with Ed.

Looking at my surroundings now, I know that if I think too much about the amount of work needed, it will become too daunting. I have to break it down into bite-sized pieces. But my mind is buzzing. What if I have just taken on too much? What if I can't do it? I try and push the little demons out of my head.

A clatter downstairs breaks into my thoughts. Oh not the goat again! I turn to run downstairs. This time I really will give it a shove out of the door.

Just then a bleat comes from outside the landing window. I lean out and look down into the courtyard. It's the goat. He's still here. I roll my eyes and turn to go downstairs. I must have left the door open. Maybe it doesn't catch properly. I must add it to the list.

I reach the bottom of the stairs and freeze. My heart jumps into my mouth, which is suddenly as dry as the desert. The front door is shut. I feel myself go cold, very cold indeed. Another clatter from the living room makes me jump, and my heart beats so hard it feels it's going to burst out of my chest. Because if the goat's outside, who's in my house?

Chapter Three

'Aargh!' I hear myself yell.

'Aargh!' yells the stranger emerging from the corridor to the living room. Boxes of papers and other junk hit the floor as the man jumps back in surprise. We both stare at each other. Wide-eyed, he runs his hand across his dark curly hair. He's tall, clean-shaven, with olive skin. In fact he's surprisingly attractive. I wonder if he's going to make a run for it. He looks at me as if I'm going to. When neither of us moves, he looks down at the boxes that have spilled their guts across the floor, blocking his path, and then back at me. He obviously wasn't expecting to find anyone here. The place does look as if it's been abandoned for some time. Perfect for someone on the rob. But maybe he's new to this. He doesn't look dressed for the job, that's for sure. I'd have thought trainers, gloves and sunglasses would have been better. Instead he's wearing a cream linen suit, with chestnut-brown shiny pointed shoes. He's not going to run very far or fast in those. In fact, he doesn't make any attempt to run at all.

'*Che cazzo . . . chi diavolo sei?*' he says, still obviously startled, and although I can't exactly understand him, I get the gist of what he's saying.

'Who am I?' My hand flies to my chest. All the Italian words I spent months at evening class learning seem to have left me along with my regular heartbeat. I may not have been fluent but I could hold a sensible conversation back then.

'You scared me!' I say crossly, still unable to form the sentence in Italian. And then I suddenly realise. He must be the goat's owner! 'Is that your goat?'

'*Scusi?*' He frowns at me like I'm the village idiot.

'You really need to tie it up. *Legarlo?*' I attempt, doing a rope-around-the-neck action and pulling at it, which may look like a noose action I realise. His frown deepens. He probably thinks I'm threatening to kill myself. I drop my hands to my sides and sigh.

'*Ah, Inglese, si?*'

'*Si.*' I nod expansively, pleased that he's understood me. 'Tie it up! The goat!' I point towards the door, feeling like an amateur-dramatic pantomime dame and cross with myself that all those hours in the car with my really expensive Learn Italian refresher course have been wasted. I have no idea what the word for goat is. I really need to get online as soon as possible; at least then I'll be able to access my dictionary.

To my surprise, he tosses his head back slightly and laughs. I'm not sure if he's laughing at my lack of Italian or the fact that I've found his goat.

All my fear leaves me and is replaced by annoyance. I'm fed up of being laughed at. I march crossly over and open the door wide for him to leave.

'*Legarlo!*' I repeat, pointing at the goat and make the

choking action again. He laughs again. Maybe he thinks I'm asking him to kill the goat.

'Not . . .' I draw a finger across my throat and make a noise in my cheek like a lisping raspberry. 'Just . . .' I make a tying action with my hands, like I'm teaching a child to tie a bow. He's still shaking his head with what looks like disbelief and now he folds his arms.

'*Capra*? The goat?' he asks in English, clearly but with an Italian accent so it sounds like something much more exotic.

'*Si*, the *capra*.' I nod and smile. We're understanding each other, which is good. But what I don't understand is what this man is doing in my house. I make a mental note for my list: *122. Bolts for front door*.

The thought of the list suddenly makes me feel absolutely exhausted, and all the doubts come flooding in at once. Am I really going to stay out here, in rural Italy, where strange men just wander into the house? I don't even know if I could phone the police if I wanted to. And it's not just that. Am I going to be able to tackle all the work this house needs and deserves? Can I do it justice on my small amount of savings and what I earn? Am I really mad? I can't even deal with a goat on my own.

'The goat, he lives here,' says the Italian flatly, breaking into my thoughts. For a moment I'm speechless.

'He what? *Cosa? Scusi?*' I ask, and he repeats himself exactly the same as before.

'The goat, he lives here.'

I thought that's what he said.

'But not any more,' I say firmly, not bothering with my

pigeon Italian when this man clearly speaks perfectly good English and I just want this sorted out and him gone. I hold the door open a little further. The sun is attempting to push through and is reflecting in the puddles outside.

The man frowns again and looks down. The boxes are still scattered at his feet. I look down at them too. There's not much there worth stealing, to be honest, just junk he seems to be helping himself to.

'*Scusi*,' he says politely but with a puzzled look back at me. For a moment I wonder if he's apologising for the mess or his bungled burglary, but then he says, looking straight at me, making my heart start to pound again, 'What exactly are you doing here?'

I'm a bit thrown and find myself answering as though I'm being interviewed for the position of new owner. Bizarre, considering I should be asking him the same question. Maybe it's tiredness, or the shock.

'I'm . . . well, I'm an online greeting card designer actually,' I start to explain. 'I design cards for birthdays, Christmas, retirement, moving house,' I emphasise. 'And I'll be, um . . .' I clear my throat, as if saying it for the first time makes it all seem real. 'I'll be doing some holiday lets,' I finish, feeling like a complete fraud.

He smiles again and refolds his arms, which just irritates me even more. Why isn't he leaving? I've been polite, I haven't called the police. What more does he want? My CV? And actually, that's *my* junk he's helping himself to. This place may have been neglected and abandoned, but as of a week ago, it's mine.

I raise my eyebrows, hold the door back and make a

gently sweeping gesture with my hand towards the goat. I don't want to get off on the wrong foot with this person – he's obviously local, although he doesn't look dressed for rescuing a goat or burgling a house – but really I think his interest has gone far enough.

'That's very good,' he smiles, 'but what are you doing in my house?'

There's an awkward moment as I try and work out if this man is seriously deranged or just annoying.

'Um . . .' I smile and then say slowly and clearly, 'Actually, *you're* in *my* house.' I smile again kindly, but there's an incoming wave of doubt in my voice.

He frowns, his thick brows coming together and his eyes narrowing. He puts his finger to the corner of his mouth and his linen jacket rises up, puckering around the armpits and elbows. His hand is soft and smooth, with neat nails. Definitely not someone used to working outside. He gives a hollow laugh.

'I think you are mistaken,' he says, still frowning. 'You're not from round here, no?' He looks at me, tilting his head and raising one eyebrow, suddenly making my firm stand disappear like quicksand beneath my feet.

I shake my head. He couldn't be right, could he?

'This is my family's home,' he says evenly. 'It's not for sale.' He bends down and starts putting papers and small ornaments back into the boxes, then glances up at me. 'I think you must be in the wrong house.' He stands again, juggling the boxes in his arms, distributing the contents evenly. My mouth's gone dry and I feel like someone's poured cold custard all over me.

'The wrong house?' I try and say through a mouth full of cotton wool and a heart beating so loudly it's drowning out my own words.

'It's an easy mistake to make. These roads are confusing if you don't know the area.' He nods briefly towards the potholed lane that I took from town this morning. He's right, if a little haughty: they do all look the same, and the signposting is so unclear. But I thought I'd followed the landmarks to the letter.

'And the weather is terrible. It's understandable,' though he looks like he doesn't find it understandable at all, making me feel like a foolish child. Here he is, dressed as if he's come from the office – of course he isn't a burglar! I feel a total idiot. He'll have a story to tell his wife and family this evening, laughing at the foolish English lady. I feel like crying. I want to curl up and die of exhaustion and an extreme case of stupidity. I could never have afforded this. Who was I kidding? And the work here – I puff air out through my lips – really, way too much for one person. This needs an army of trained professionals. It's a money pit. Money I don't have.

'Here, let me help you with your things. I'll just dump these in the car. If you've got the name of the place you're looking for, I can give you directions, but I can't think it's near here. I don't know any houses for sale close by,' he says, obviously keen to send me on my way so he can get on with whatever he's doing. I bet he has a large family, and probably a good job. He looks like the sort of person who has made all the right steps in life. Not like me. I seem to keep missing the steps and falling through the gaps in between. I mean, how many people move into someone else's house and tell the owner to hang his goat?

My eyes itch and redden and I swallow hard. He turns and carries the boxes across the cobbles, instinctively dodging the potholes, and over to the smart red car blocking mine in. The goat has gone back to trotting up and down.

The goat lives here, I repeat in my head. Of course he does! The goat lives here. I don't! Idiot me!

I turn to the plastic table in the big dining room and gather up my notebook and satchel, realising I am actually relieved. I mean, this place is beautiful, but there is so much of it. I don't know what I thought I'd got for my money, but it couldn't be this. There must be a much smaller version nearby. They all look alike online. I mean, I know I'm looking for a *masseria*, but that just means a fortified farmhouse. There must be loads of those around here.

As I sling my bag over my shoulder, the envelope I was holding earlier slips off the table and on to the floor. I stop, bend and pick it up. I stare at the smeared name on the front: *Masseria Bellanuovo*, it says. Although admittedly it's a bit harder to read now after its drenching, that's definitely the envelope I arrived with . . . the one with the key in it! The key that fitted the door.

Stupid doesn't come close to how I'd describe myself right now. I grip the envelope, scoop up the key and go to the door, where I try it again, just to make sure. Like Cinderella's foot in the glass slipper, it fits. Now I'm furious. Who does this con artist think he is? Breaking in, trying to convince me I'm in the wrong house and stealing my junk!

I watch him walking back from his car. He pats the goat's hindquarters and practically skips towards the front door. This time I'm standing in the doorway, arms folded.

'Masseria Bellanuovo?' I ask, pulling myself up to my full height of five foot three and a half inches.

'That's right,' he says. 'This is Masseria Bellanuovo. My family's home.'

'In that case, sorry, I should have introduced myself. I'm Ruthie Collins, from London, England. And you are?'

'Marco, Marco Bellanuovo.' He accepts my extended hand and shakes it with a slightly unnerved look about him now.

'Well, Mr Bellanuovo, I think you'll find this is *my* house. Masseria Bellanuovo. I bought it,' and I swing the key in front of him in a rather childish but effectively dramatic manner.

He looks at it and then explodes.

'*Che cazzo?*' he roars, and I take a step back. I'm beginning to understand what that means.

'It can't be! This house is not for sale. It belongs to my family, my grandfather.'

He stares at the key, and I show him the envelope too. The colour drains from his face and he seems genuinely shocked. He holds out a hand and uses the door frame to support himself.

'Look, how about a sit-down,' I say, thinking I could have done this without the dramatic effects, and stand aside to let him back in. 'I'll find some water.'

'No, really. Thank you.' He holds up his hand. 'I need to find out what's going on.' He's thinking, and my brain too is whirring faster than my thoughts can keep up with.

'Please, could you tell me, who did you do your business with? Who sold this to you?'

'Giovanni Bellanuovo,' I say, a lot less triumphantly. Judging by the dark look on his face, he obviously had no idea.

'My grandfather,' he says quietly, and turns away.

I don't think I'll bother asking for the junk back. It's probably his by rights.

'*Merda!*' he says very suddenly, and slaps his hand on his thigh. He holds his head as he walks away.

'Look,' I say, hoping my thoughts will organise themselves quickly. The sun is coming out and I can sense it on my face, and it feels good. I follow him and touch his elbow. 'I . . . I didn't know that I was buying a family home. Why don't you go and see your grandfather? Get him to explain.' My voice is getting higher and higher, as are my shoulders in a Mediterranean shrug.

He looks at me and then says, 'It'll be a job. He died a week ago.'

My hand flies over my mouth. 'I'm so sorry,' I say with automatic sympathy.

'The funeral is tomorrow. That's why I'm here, why we're all here. The family.'

I can't think of anything sensible to say, so I say nothing. The only thing I know for sure is that I really do own a large house that needs lots of work, and I've already upset the locals.

'You'd better come with me,' he instructs, like a teacher marching a naughty pupil to the headmaster's office.

'Where to?' I frown.

'Mama's. The family are all there. My cousin on my mother's side, she is married to a lawyer. He'll know what to do.' He turns and marches towards his car, and I find myself following with quick little footsteps, having locked the front door, hoping I can settle this once and for all.

'What about the goat?' I say to his back as he points his key fob at the car and it bleeps into life.

'I told you. The goat lives here. Now get in,' he says, flinging open the car door and starting the engine with a roar. Without question, I do as I'm told.

Chapter Four

Arriving outside a big white villa with red and white canopy awnings, I feel like I've just been on a monster fairground ride. A bit like the time I took Ed to Alton Towers, only he refused to go on any rides, and I ended up feeling like I'd been shaken upside down and put back with bits in the wrong places.

We took off in Marco's car at full speed, rattling down the drive and through the gates, and then into the next-door drive, stopping with a body-bracing screech behind the many other cars abandoned at various angles on the gravel. My heart races and I clutch the dashboard so hard I wonder if my fingers are actually embedded in it. Marco gets out and slams the door. As I peel my fingers from the dashboard, I hope that his family – my new neighbours – are more welcoming and understanding than he is.

He turns to check I'm following, locks the car and then takes the marble steps two at a time to the stone-built veranda with three arches across it. There is a swing seat there, and a lemon tree in a pot. Suddenly a cacophony of barking stops me in my tracks and a gang of dogs comes tearing round the corner towards us. Marco stops and says something to a small cream and white mutt by way of greeting before turning back to me abruptly, beckoning with his head. I pull my cardigan around me and follow. It's early evening now, and I really need to sort this out before it gets too late. Part of me is reluctant to follow him, to be summoned like this, but another part knows I'm going to have to meet the neighbours at some point. I just wish it could've been under better circumstances.

I skirt the now quiet dogs and join Marco as he reaches for the front door. He instructs the little cream dog to stay, and it sits obediently, staring at him as he pushes the door open. A wall of noise and heat hits me as we enter. There are people all around: a couple sitting at a table, one holding a baby while another fusses over it; others talking in a group, sipping drinks and nibbling on small breadstick-type biscuits.

'Ah, Marco!' I hear a woman's voice, and then an older one, and suddenly there are lots of different voices. I can't really understand them, but I can sort of understand their hand gestures. The first woman, who I presume is Marco's *mamma*, is waving her hands and pointing to an older woman wearing black and gently sniffing into a tissue. I think she's asking where he's been and telling him that Nonna needs him.

There is a younger woman working with Marco's *mamma* in the kitchen. I hear a reference to 'Rosa', and they all look at the clock. Marco's *mamma* taps her wrist. There's obviously a time issue here.

I feel like a sausage at a bar mitzvah, standing out but also totally ignored. They're all talking so quickly, and I can pick out occasional words but nothing that makes any sense. I'm finding it hard to concentrate. If they could just speak one at a time, maybe that would help, like back in my Italian classes. I feel very uncomfortable and wish I could just slide back out again. In fact, maybe I could. I take a step towards the door.

'*Chi e questo?*' His mother finally waves at me, and I stop mid backwards step.

'Maybe now's not the time,' I say. I look around at the large family dressed in dark colours, the weeping old lady, the table laid for a meal, and the steaming pots and pans. I put up my hand by way of a hello and a goodbye. '*Un altra voltra*,' I say, 'Another time,' and take the step back.

'Eh?' Mamma puts her hands on her hips.

'A visitor,' Marco says, as much for my benefit as theirs, implying that I'm not staying around.

The chatter stops and everyone turns to look at me. It's like I'm staring back at a painting, like time has stopped. It's a big room, with a large gilt-framed mirror on the wall at one end, a shiny marble-topped kitchen with a long table running the length of the house. There are chairs and a gold-legged coffee table in front of the patio doors at the front. A marble-effect staircase leads upwards, and the open-plan theme continues to the back of the house, where there is more seating looking out on to another veranda. From here I can see it's a covered area, with lots of bleached white stone and a tall statue of a semi-naked woman holding an urn.

The woman I'm assuming is Marco's mother is dressed in black, with big gold earrings, thick gold chains around her neck and an eclectic mix of costume jewellery on her wrists and fingers. Her hair is tied back into a tight bun with a flower clip and she's holding a wooden spoon like a conductor's baton. The older woman is sitting at the end of the table, shelling peas. There is steam curling its way along the ceiling, and the smell of hot, home-made food suddenly makes my stomach rumble loudly, breaking the spell.

'*Chi e questo?*' Marco's *mamma* waves the wooden spoon at me and smiles, her bingo wings flapping under her thin black lace cardigan. Then she turns back to Marco, demanding to know where he's been and what's going on.

'This is . . .' He looks at me like an actor asking for a prompt, raising an eyebrow and holding his hands out, palms upwards.

'Ruthie Collins, *dall'Inghilterra*,' I say slowly, smiling as I am finally able to answer in perfect Italian, and go to hold out my hand.

'*Cosa?*' She frowns and looks around at the others in the crowded kitchen, who all shrug.

'Ruthie Collins . . . *Inglese*,' Marco says with an exasperated sigh.

'*Ah! Inglese!*' she says, and they all smile and nod, understanding.

'This is my *mamma*, Anna-Maria Bellanuovo.' Marco extends a hand by way of introduction. Anna-Maria just looks puzzled. 'And this is my family.' He begins to introduce each one by name, like he's calling out the register, and I try to keep up. His sister; a husband, I think; his cousin and somebody's baby. I turn and shake hands with as many of them as possible and ask how they all are, but they just stare at me as if they don't understand a word of what I'm saying. The names fly in one ear and out the other until eventually he stops at the old lady.

'My *nonna*, grandmother,' he explains, 'Serefina.' I try and move forward to shake her bony, knobbly hand. She stares at me, hard, and I step back and squish a pea underfoot. Marco looks around. 'That seems to be everyone. My other cousins are still travelling. They'll arrive later. But not here.' He sounds awkward. 'And Filippo . . . my brother. He's coming too.'

I'm ushered to sit down on the bench next to the bowl of peas. Anna-Maria fires out instructions and another place is laid in front of me – plate, knife and fork and a glass. I say that I'm not staying to eat, but my protests are waved away like ineffectual flies. It's been a long time since lunch in Bari; another lifetime ago, it feels like.

'*Posso?*' Marco speaks to the man holding the baby and nods towards the room at the back of the house. The man hands the baby over to his wife and stands to follow. This must be the lawyer, I realise. The women look puzzled but start to bring out little dishes of food and put them in front of me. There are red and yellow peppers glistening in olive oil, warm and soft in a blanket of golden breadcrumbs; small mozzarella balls in little knots; tiny tomatoes; deep-fried crispy balls of pork; a plate of celery, carrot and peppers in vivid green oil; a green and white mash of broad beans, peas and broccoli; cold meats, thinly sliced and laid out in a fan; small rolls of aubergine in white sauce with cocktail sticks holding the ham in the middle. My stomach roars loudly again. I blush and am encouraged to eat. My wine glass is filled with red wine. I take a sip. It's thick, rich Primitivo.

'I think I should explain,' I say in English. The family look blankly at me. They obviously don't understand, so I try again in Italian. 'I'm Ruthie Collins from England . . .' Still they look blankly at me. I don't get it. They don't seem to speak English, but they don't understand my Italian either.

Suddenly the front door flies open and in comes a younger version of Marco, in his early twenties, his smile brightening the room.

'Hey! *Ciao!*' He embraces Serefina, who hugs his face to hers, then kisses the other women and men and shakes hands all at the same time.

'*Siamo qui?*' he asks, looking at me and smiling.

Behind him is a woman in dark glasses. This must be Rosa, and what looks to be her parents. Rosa is tall, slim, dark-haired and olive-skinned. She is in her late twenties. Her mother is short and round and has a face like a prune, but with a huge smile. Rosa is wearing black jeans, high-heeled silver trainers and a black T-shirt with a sparkling rose motif on the front. Despite her casual clothes, she looks effortlessly stylish as she pushes her large sunglasses up on to her head. She's beautiful, despite wearing hardly any make-up and looking like she's sucking a lemon. She is constantly glancing around, searching for someone. I'm guessing it's Marco.

They all greet each other, and Anna-Maria does the same routine about the time, pointing to Nonna – who is sniffing and has peas in her white hankie – and tutting about Marco's disappearance

'*Inglese!*' She nods to me and shrugs.

'English, eh?' says the young man, Marco's mini-me, and he sits down next to me, straddling the bench. 'I'm very pleased to meet you. I'm Filippo Bellanuovo. Welcome to my family.' He puts out his hand and makes me smile. Finally, someone I can speak to! So this is Marco's brother, but it's a big age gap. Marco must be mid thirties.

'You have a very good accent,' I say warmly.

'I learnt English at school. I hope to go and work there one day.' He smiles again. 'They have jobs there for good barmen. I'm a good barman. But here there aren't that many jobs, especially as the summer season is ending. I am working in Alberobello at the moment, but that will end soon.'

'*Mangiare! Mangiare!*' instructs Nonna, pushing little plates of tasty morsels towards me. The juices in my mouth gush at the sight and smell of them. The yellow and red peppers look gorgeous, but eating them will involve putting them on my plate and looking as though I'm staying, and I'm not. Eventually I take a bright red tomato and in the other hand a fried pork ball. Filippo takes one too and pops it in his mouth. The rest of the family seem to be watching me and talking amongst themselves. I haven't a clue what they're saying. It's like they're speaking another language, nothing like the Italian I learnt in my evening classes. I'm guessing they're wondering what on earth I'm doing there. Rosa and her parents sit down.

Rosa glares down the table, looking right through me. I wouldn't like to cross her.

'My name—' I start to tell Filippo.

'Ruthie Collins, *Inglese*,' Anna-Maria finishes for me and puts some bread in front of me. The smell is to die for, hot and doughy, and my mouth waters all the more. I can't resist taking a slice, breathing in its comforting smell. I really need to explain who I am, but I'll just try a corner of this bread first. It's fantastic. I try to ask whether it's from the bakery at the end of the lane.

'Forno Sophia?'

'Pah!' Anna-Maria turns her mouth down in disgust and turns her back on me. I wonder what I've said wrong. Did I misuse a word? I didn't expect it to be so hard to use my Italian.

'My aunt Sophia,' Filippo explains, 'By marriage. My aunt and my mother . . .' He shakes his head and pulls his mouth down into a grimace. Then he grins widely again, making me smile, and changes the subject quickly.

'So you're a friend of Marco's?'

'No, not a friend,' I say, popping the tomato into my mouth to try and free up a hand. I bite into it and it explodes, shooting into the corners of my mouth, filling it with wonderful flavour, tangy and sweet. I haven't tasted a tomato like that in . . . I don't know when. Nonna pushes a pot of smelly cheese towards me and I recoil slightly.

'Try it with the tomato. It's strong ricotta,' Filippo says. I'm pretty sure they're winding me up and the joke's going to be on me. 'Try,' he insists, and it feels rude not to. Filippo takes the lead. I tentatively take a small spoonful and follow his example as he puts the cheese on the tomato and then eats them together in one mouthful. My hand rises to my mouth, as does the smell of the cheese, like stinking socks. They're all looking at me. I do it. Chew quickly and swallow. Then I look at Filippo in surprise. The flavours together are amazing, like the most unlikely marriage (other than Ed and me, I think wryly). I smile broadly, forgetting for a moment that I'm some kind of fly in the ointment here. He smiles and nods back. I look round for a serviette and wipe my hands. Everyone is still looking at me and talking amongst themselves, waiting to hear who I am.

'Why can't I understand what anyone is saying?' I say in a low, frustrated voice to Filippo. 'I've done loads of Italian classes.'

'Oh, they're not speaking Italian.' He smiles. 'They're speaking Della Terra. We all have our own local languages in Italy.'

I sigh and catch a glimpse of Marco outside, talking very animatedly to the lawyer. I wonder if I should be there too.

A short, fat man in working clothes appears, pulling off his flat cap. He shakes Marco's hand and they exchange a few words. There is a tall young man behind him, holding his hands together. He leans forward respectfully and shakes Marco's hand too. Rosa, I notice, suddenly stands as if to join them but is told otherwise by her father. She sits back down sulkily as the two newcomers turn and leave, the younger man throwing a glance our way over his shoulder as he goes.

'So, where are you staying?' Filippo asks.

Thin rings of squid in light golden batter appear in front of me. I dab my mouth with the serviette and look away, wishing I could try it but knowing I have to put the record straight.

'Here,' I tell Filippo. 'I'm staying here.' There, I've done it.

'Here?' He looks confused and glances at his mother.

'No.' I shake my head and give a nervous little laugh. 'At Masseria Bellanuovo,' I finally manage to say. Filippo's face drops, as does Anna-Maria's and those around her.

'Masseria Bellanuovo?' Anna-Maria stretches round to look for Marco, then turns back to Filippo and says something to him.

'How?' he asks, his eyebrows dipping inwards.

'Because I bought it,' I reply.

There is a deathly silence.

'*Ha comprato,*' says Filippo, looking round at the family's stunned faces.

'Marco!' Anna-Maria calls urgently to her son. Suddenly the family go into overdrive, asking questions of Marco and the cousin's husband as they come to the table shoulder to shoulder. I take another cherry tomato. It has been a long time since lunch.

'My mother wants to know how you came to buy it.'

Anna-Maria fires something else at Filippo, waving an arm towards me. He sighs, and Nonna sobs.

'She wants to know if you are a lover?' he translates, and Anna-Maria nods and waves her spoon around, making her bingo wings flap even more. I choke on the cherry tomato.

'No, I'm not a lover,' I say when I have recovered, and Filippo informs the family to sighs of relief.

'They want to know where it happened. Where did you exchange the paperwork?' he says kindly, not translating his *mamma*'s words quite accurately.

'In Bari. I flew over last week.'

The lawyer starts texting and waving his phone around looking for a signal.

'I can phone my solicitor in the morning if you want proof,' I offer.

'Did you come and see the house?' Nonna wants to know. I swallow and wonder whether to lie. But I can't.

'No, I didn't.' I take a fortifying sip of wine. 'There was . . . some kind of incident.' I blush and shrug, feeling dafter by the moment. I can just hear Ed tutting in my head. I take a deep breath and begin to explain what happened on that day, and I realise I'm retelling it more for my own benefit than for the expectant faces all looking at me.

'I flew into Bari and went to the solicitor's office, where I met Giovanni Bellanuovo.' He looked frail, I remember. Filippo translates and Nonna gives a sob.

'My grandfather,' Filippo adds for my benefit. I nod, understanding, and carry on with my story.

'I asked to see the house before I signed, but the road was blocked. There'd been a mudslide.' They all suddenly start 'aahing', obviously remembering the day it happened. They're pointing to the road and to each other, recounting it. I sit for a minute until they turn back to me, expectantly. 'I couldn't see the house that day. I had to make a decision there and then. I was just flying in and out. I'd left enough time to see the house and sign. It was a case of sign now or lose the whole thing. Someone held a pen out to me and asked if I wanted the house or not. I had to choose.'

I think back to that day. It was so hot in that tiny office, and so full of people. I remember the smart silver pen being offered to me. Of course I knew I should say that I couldn't sign. That I would have to come back again. But how could I? Someone poured me a glass of water, I can't remember who. It may have been my solicitor, an English-speaking woman. She had big black hair and very red lipstick. I remember the smell of her hairspray in that hot little office. Giovanni was sitting on one side of the big wooden desk with his solicitor; I was on the other with mine. I took the water and drank it. I had to be back in the UK the following morning to hand over the keys to the new owners of our flat. I thought about texting Ed and telling him to do it whilst I stayed on.

I pulled out my phone and ran my fingers over the keypad. What would I tell him? *Sorry I can't be there, I'm in Italy buying a run-down farmhouse.* I could just imagine what he'd say. He'd make me feel I was leaping without looking and would talk me out of it. I didn't want that to happen.

I finished the water and put the glass on the table. I took the pen being held out to me. My hands were hot and shaking a little. Was I really going to do this? Was I really going to sign for a house I hadn't seen?

Suddenly my phone chirped, telling me I'd got a message. I dropped the pen and scrabbled around on the floor for it whilst grabbing hold of my phone from the desk with my other hand. I sat back up, pen in one hand, phone in the other. The gathered group shifted impatiently. I looked at them and then slowly at the screen of my phone. The message was from Ed. I caught my breath. How could he know? Was he telling me to stop and think? Not to be so impetuous? He used that word about me a lot. Like the time I offered to look after the neighbour's plants when he went away for a bit, and it turned out I was watering his cannabis farm. I didn't, of course. I told him I'd had to go away and they'd died. He played Metallica at full volume for days afterwards, and through the night.

I swallowed and opened the message, holding my breath. I felt like a naughty schoolgirl.

I've got some post here for you, copies of the final bills. Shall I send them to your mother's? Is that your new address?

And that was it. That *was* my new address: Cynthia Collins' settee, Flat 49 . . . If I didn't sign, I was going to be moving back in with my mum for the foreseeable future. And my mum had hardly been sympathetic to my situation. She couldn't see why I was splitting up with Ed at all. Not when I had such a comfortable life. She was constantly telling me to stop being so daft, and that it was perfectly natural to go through a rough patch. You just got on with it. But I couldn't. I was comfortable with Ed, but I knew we weren't in love with each other. There had to be something more. But what?

I was coming up to my thirtieth birthday and I was going back to live with my mother . . . and Colin, in his vest. And I knew I had to do something, I had to strike out on my own. So I signed.

I look up at the amazed faces staring at me around the table, hanging on my every word.

'I should go,' I say quickly, standing up. 'Leave you to your . . . family time.' I've introduced myself and I think it's pretty clear that I've bought the house fair and square, whether they like it or not.

'The thing is . . .' The lawyer starts to talk and Filippo translates. 'Here in Italy, after the exchange of money and signatures, it can take some time for things to be finalised.'

I take a moment to absorb what he's saying.

'But they agreed I could move in!' Oh God, don't tell me I've messed this up too. Rushing in, desperate to get away from Ed and Annabel, Mum and Colin. That would be just typical of me. But they *did* say I could move in straight away, I remember.

'Yes, but it doesn't always mean you fully own it yet.'

Marco is talking quietly and intently to the lawyer. One arm is across his body and the other hand is teasing at his bottom lip. Anna-Maria says something quickly, waving her hands at the two men, and Filippo translates.

'My *mamma* says we must get this sorted. You must stay until it is cleared up. You must eat with us, she says.'

I look at Anna-Maria, who is staring back at me, nostrils flaring. I get the impression she doesn't want to let me out of her sight. I sit back down reluctantly. I feel like the mouse having tea with the Gruffalo, neither of us sure who is going to swallow the other one up. Rosa is still glaring at me. Nonna keeps handing me more bowls of food, which I eat, politely, until I'm so full I can't bear the thought of another mouthful. Food is passed up and down the table, wine is poured. Arms are waved and the conversation keeps going in fast and furious Italian, but I still don't understand a word of it.

'They want to know if you will put a pool in. Will you rent it out this summer? Wouldn't you be better where there are more ex-pats living? Ostuni is nice. Or more tourists? Alberobello.' Filippo is passing on the questions from various family members. All the time I can tell they are hoping the paperwork hasn't been completed. And frankly, I'm beginning to feel the same way. Maybe I *would* be better off in Alberobello or Ostuni; maybe there I could understand what people are saying. I'm never going to fit in here, obviously.

I'm exhausted, and so full of food I fear I may have to be rolled home. This is turning out to be one of the longest days of my life.

'My grandmother thinks it isn't a very good house for holiday rentals. There's nothing around but olives,' says Filippo, who is also flagging a bit now.

'Oh, I'm not going to rent it out,' I say, slowly and clearly. 'I'm going to live in it.'

There is a communal blowing-out of cheeks.

'It's far too big for one person to live in!'

I think Nonna may be saying something along the lines of how a woman my age should have a husband and a family, but I'm not sure. The lawyer's phone suddenly trills into life and he speaks quickly and quietly to the person on the other end. Finishing his call, he puts his hand on Marco's shoulder and gives it a sympathetic squeeze. Marco's face darkens. He's hardly touched his food.

'The contracts were completed straight away. Just before he died.' Filippo drops his head.

So that's it. The house is mine for definite, but instead of being elated, I realise that I feel strangely disappointed.

It's eleven o'clock when I finally get to leave, after the pasta course, the meat, the panna cotta and the coffee. Outside, I feel like a fly that's escaped from a spider's web, and take great gulps of air. Marco drives me back to the *masseria* in silence and at speed, although I insist there really is no need. When we pull up outside the house, the goat is lying by the front door.

'I'm sorry for your loss,' is all I can think of saying to Marco. But I get the feeling he blames me for his loss right now. Although the sale has gone through, this is far from over.

I get out of the car. He doesn't move. I'm going to have to be bold with the goat. I don't want to look totally foolish. I point my phone torch ahead of me and march towards the door, unlocking it quickly as the goat scrabbles to its feet. I push the door open and step inside, shutting it firmly behind me and reaching for the light switch. Nothing.

'Marco!' I shout, yanking the door open just as his tail lights disappear down the drive. I can't go after him. That really would make me look like the daft Englishwoman he thinks I am. I'm very much on my own now. I've made my bed and I'm going to have to lie in it.

*

Lying on my blow-up bed, I pull my duvet up around me. I'm cold despite it being August. I certainly wasn't expecting weather like this. I wasn't really expecting any of this. I'm exhausted and I'm feeling, well, like I'm looking down at myself from the corner of the room. A woman the wrong side of twenty-nine, single and having blown her entire nest egg on a run-down house that she can't even afford to furnish. And then of course there was that meal. The whole family arguing and shouting, but cooking and eating and gathering together. Not like my family. When I split up with Ed, they were nowhere to be seen, apart from my mum, who told me grudgingly that I could stay with her just until I sorted myself out. Meaning until I went back to Ed or found a flatshare. I think about the family that must have once filled this house; now, it's just me.

I feel I've had a moment like Gwyneth Paltrow in that film *Sliding Doors* that shows her parallel lives: one when she manages to make it through a set of Tube doors before they shut, and the other when she doesn't. I saw it with Morag and Elinor from my Italian class one evening in February. My *Sliding Doors* moment happened back home in Tooting. If I hadn't hit the 'buy' button that fateful night, I'd be on my mum's lumpy sofa right now looking at flatshares on SpareRoom.com and worrying about dodgy flatmates. The Ruthie who did hit the button is lying on a lumpy blow-up bed wondering about dodgy neighbours. So not much in it then. Only here I have my own front door, if not my own kettle yet.

I mean, it's not like I haven't had to start over before. Back when my dad left, I was just beginning secondary school. Everyone else was busy making friends and going out; I was having to dash home, coax my mum out of bed, cook tea for my brother and then pack up the house ready for moving. I didn't think about it, just got on with it. We moved into the flat and did our best to make it homely. It was just the three of us then: me, my mum and my brother.

This time, I am thinking outside the box, being my own woman. I'm not mad; I'm being brave, I tell myself. But that little doubting voice somewhere within me says, 'Really?' And it sounds a lot like Marco Bellonuovo's.

Chapter Five

Having spent the night tossing and turning on a sagging blow-up bed, in a strange country, in a strange house, with no electricity and hearing every creak and groan, I'm up with the lark, literally. The birdsong is so loud it's like one of those free CDs you get in the Sunday newspaper. I stand up, keeping my duvet wrapped around me – more for its comforting smell of home than for warmth – and pull open the window.

I left my shutters open all night, and despite it being pitch black, far blacker than back home, the moon shone like a silver disco ball, brightly and straight into my room.

There's a low mist creeping through the olive trees now. But the sun is coming up slowly but surely. The rain has passed. There's nothing but the sound of birds, singing like they're opera singers, but then we are in Italy. Back home I'd be waking to the sound of buses, car alarms and the rumble of commuters. This is why people do this, right? This is what it's supposed to be about. They come for a better life, or in my case because it couldn't get any worse. I look around at the cracked plaster walls and the bare boards. So why do I still feel so . . . homesick? There's nothing back there for me. Briefly I wonder what Ed's doing. Getting up in his smart flat and probably cycling to work. Maybe he and Annabel have matching bikes. If they knew what I was doing, I'd be the talk of the breakfast table. Granola for two and a side order of jokes about Ruthie's moment of madness. I cringe and push the image aside by focusing on the mist, like cigarette smoke twisting through the trees.

Of course Morag and Elinor would love this place. I miss them, actually. They'll be so envious when I Facebook them. I first met them on my women's tiling course. Morag is from the Highlands, with thick red hair and an accent to match that gets more impenetrable the more she drinks. Elinor is fairly recently widowed and signed up for every evening class she could. It was her suggestion that we try Italian. I smile fondly and imagine them sitting round a table in a Tooting pub wishing they could do it too, live out their dreams. If only they knew how far I am from living the dream right now.

My fresh starts always seem to be a slide back down the snake in a game of snakes and ladders. I wanted this one to be different. I wanted to leave behind the feeling of being adrift that I felt when the flat was sold. I wanted this to feel like home, but it doesn't. My mind starts turning over again. But it's not Tooting that's playing there now; it's the Bellanuovos.

I spent the night going over my dinner with them. I still can't help but wonder why Giovanni Bellanuovo would sell this house without telling his family. I also worked out that I'm surrounded by the Bellanuovo family here – there's no escape. Marco's mother Anna-Maria, is next door in her mini-Southfork; his sister and her husband live on the other side of her in a plain, simple villa; his brother and grandmother live with Anna-Maria. I actually have no idea where Marco lives, but from what I could gather last night, it's Bellanuovo land all around. I'm completely surrounded by a family who now think I've stolen their inheritance.

I sigh. I can't let that stop me being here. After all, I have no choice. I've bought it and it's not like I've got anything to go back to.

I feel a lump in my throat and a mixture of self-pity and tiredness swirls around my thumping head and stings my eyes. I give them a quick brush with the back of my hands and then slap my palms on to the peeling paint of the wooden window frame.

'Right, that's enough of that, Ruthie Collins,' I say out loud with a sniff, pushing back my shoulders. It's this or my mother's lumpy settee. I take another look at the view. No contest! 'Now . . .' I turn from the window and look at my makeshift bedroom. I need to get busy. And busy is something this place is going to give me in bucketloads. I grab my list from the floor beside my bed, next to the clothes I dumped there by torchlight last night. Busy is just what I need right now.

First things first: I have to bring in the rest of my belongings from the car, and find the electricity box. I make my bed so you can't see the saggy mattress, and find a clean T-shirt and some cut-off shorts to put on. For breakfast I grab the last of my Diet Cokes and a handful of Jaffa Cakes from the journey, then bring in the remainder of the boxes and black bags from the car and dump them in the dining room. After that, I explore the house from the cellar up to the flat roof that I didn't get to see yesterday and that will make a great terrace. The mist is clearing and in the field next to mine I spot a *trullo* with three cones, surrounded by olive trees. It looks like it's been allowed to go to rack and ruin. With the sun pushing through the clouds, everything looks different. Today is a whole new day, I tell myself.

Pushing open the stiff doors off the living room that are kept shut by the brambles growing on the other side, I find myself in the overgrown courtyard. In the far corner, even more overgrown, is the orangery. Obviously this is a bit of a suntrap and vegetation has thrived here. I fight my way to the barn, stuffed with rubbish. There, surrounded by boxes, bags and metal drums, is a large stone circle like an old press, with a corkscrew in the middle. It'll be some job to move that and it certainly isn't high up on my list of things to do now, but who knows, one day.

I find an old pair of rusting secateurs and with a bit of elbow grease get them opening and closing. Armed, I fight my way through the brambles to the archway leading out to the olive trees. As I try and release myself from the clutches of a particularly vicious bramble trying to wrap itself around me, I wonder where on earth you hide an electricity box. Throwing my hands up I turn and look back at the house. Where could it be? I can't do anything until I've got electricity.

The only people I can think who might help are my

solicitors. It's not like I bought the place through an estate agent that I could ask, as sensible people would! I give myself a metaphorical kick. I don't know anyone else apart from Marco and his family. So the solicitors it is, and I pull out my phone, covering my eyes against the bright warm sunshine that feels like it's massaging my neck. As I squint at the screen, it flashes up a message telling me to connect to charger, and promptly dies.

My heart sinks. So now there really is only one person I can ask, and I can't do anything else until I've done it.

Round the front of the house, the goat appears from nowhere with a rustle and a snort and trots up to me, nudging me, nearly knocking me off my feet. I stumble back, hemmed in by the wall behind me and with no Kit Kat! Then I remember the rubbing between the horns. As I reach out my hand, the goat looks up and sniffs for snacks, and for a moment I draw back but then try again, this time going straight for between the ears. It seems to like it. I wonder who feeds it. Maybe it's hungry. I'll talk to Marco about it. I don't want to be accused of killing their grandfather's goat on top of everything else.

I turn and march purposefully down the long drive, taking in the mix of olive and what I think are almond trees; one with dark green leaves, the other light. The sun is really quite warm now, even though it's only . . . I look down at my watch . . . ten o'clock. I twist the button to move it on an hour. The smell is fantastic as the soil warms up, earthy and even a hint of pine in the air too. This is when you know you're somewhere different, not just

Clapham Common on a hot day. In London, the smell would be hot tar and petrol fumes. Here it's pines, the flowers that are everywhere and the deep terracotta-coloured soil.

I dodge clumps of grass and watery craters up the long drive. It's shady under the huge trees with their big twisted trunks. Some of the roots reach up from the ground, making little archways at the foot of the trees. The ground is rocky in parts, despite the rich soil around it, and it's a wonder anything grows there at all. But these trees do. Now that's resilience. They don't seem deterred by their hostile surroundings and neither should I!

Lifting my head a little higher, I reach the red-painted gates, drag open the sagging left-hand one and pull it back. As I do, I see Marco standing at the bottom of his mother's drive. Her gates are black and have gold eagles on the top. My spirits lift. He's on his own. I might be able to do this without the entire family watching my every move. I must grab the moment while I can.

'Marco! *Scusi!*' I say loudly and wave. I don't want him to disappear inside before I reach the gates. When he doesn't respond, I call more loudly, determined not to let him ignore me. I'm not going to feel on the back foot just because he doesn't want me here.

'Could you tell me where the electricity box is? I've no electricity,' I say in my best Italian. 'And about the goat . . .'

But he's blanking me! I can't believe it. That is so petty. I reach out and tap him on the shoulder. '*Scusi*, Marco,' I say firmly.

He turns slowly to look at me over the shoulder I've just tapped. His face is stony and I take a step back. He's not pleased to see me, that's for sure. But I won't be put off.

'I bought the house, just the house, not a house with a goat! Look, I'm sorry it was your grandfather's and he sold it without telling you, but that really isn't my fault . . .'

He's wearing a very smart black suit, a crisp white shirt and dark tie, and I shock myself by thinking how attractive he looks. Clean-cut. I can smell his citrus aftershave from here. He steps away from the gates and turns to face me. As he does, I see the cars that have gathered on the drive, engines running . . . the funeral cars! Oh God! My toes curl upwards, blood rushes into my cheeks and makes them burn and I feel frankly quite sick, not helped by the taste of stale Jaffa Cakes in my mouth.

'Oh God, I'm so—' But before I've even attempted a respectful apology, he turns and marches past me.

'Follow me,' he instructs, and I don't argue. He strides towards my gates and I have to run to keep up, whilst trying to say that it really doesn't matter, perhaps later. He stops abruptly and I brake suddenly so as not to go crashing into him and his very smart suit. Without saying a word, he opens a small metal box in the stone gatepost to reveal an electricity meter and a large switch, which he flicks down with a *thunk*. Still saying nothing, he shuts the box, turns and walks back to the gates where the large black cars are beginning to make their way out on to the road.

'*Grazie*,' I say through my burning embarrassment, and then '*Scusi*,' and give a dry cough. I want to run back to the house and hide, but don't want to look disrespectful or, worse still, like I'm gloating, I definitely don't want to look like I'm gloating. I have to live here. I need to make friends with my neighbours. And after all, I may not know the man who's died or why he sold the house to me rather than leaving it to his family, but I do owe him my respect at least. I decide the best thing to do is to stand still, hands folded, and wait for the cortège to pass.

A big silver Mercedes hearse heads the procession. Inside, a bunch of olive branches and red roses, tied beautifully with raffia ribbon, sits on top of a shiny deep brown wooden coffin with large gold handles. Then the first of the cars with passengers in it pulls out in front of me. Anna-Maria and Marco's Nonna turn to look at me through an open window. Anna-Maria is in large black sunglasses with bling trim to match her black outfit and gold jewellery. Nonna is wiping her eyes under her glasses with a large white hankie. I can feel the burn of their stares and wince at their thunderous faces. The window goes up with a disparaging whirr.

I wonder for a moment what they would think of a funeral back in London. They look so different from the mourners at my grandad's funeral. His mates from the pub were in mismatched and ill-fitting suits; my brother's girlfriend wobbled down the crematorium path trying to keep control of her stilettos after too many pre-funeral Bacardi Breezers; and my mum's M&S funeral skirt was actually her work uniform skirt too. I miss my grandad. We were close after my nan died. I would buy food at the market in Tooting and then go round and cook for him.

He seemed to like it. Thought I should enter *MasterChef.* I enjoyed cooking for him. My mum and my brother didn't let me try out stuff on them. They preferred food that came out of a box, ready meals, not the 'muck' I'd make. But I kept cooking round at grandad's until he died.

It wasn't long afterwards that I met Ed. He liked my cooking too. Life with Ed was great to begin with. I slipped happily into his world. We were good at different things. I was more practical; he was more . . . well, good at figures. My brother used to say that I'd only got anywhere in life because of Ed and his good job. He thought I should get a proper job. Going to art college and designing cards was just a hobby in his book. Even though it was me who used to rewire the plugs on his music system and make signs for his home-made sweets and doughnuts market stall.

Grandad used to understand me, though, when I went round to cook for him and do the occasional little DIY job. He gave me my first drill. Said it was more use to me than him and showed me how to put up shelves.

As the next car leaves, more heads turn to me. I'm not used to being in the limelight at the best of times and this attention is very unwanted. I'm cringing inside. It's hot now, really hot, and my head feels quite light, as if this is all unreal. Beside me the electricity box is buzzing. This is the longest couple of minutes of my life. Well, apart from the ones when I finally decided to buy this house. And I'm beginning to think Ed was right: I am irresponsible and rash.

The final car stops and Marco gets in. He pulls his

wraparound glasses down from his forehead. While the rest of the Bellanuovo family have turned their heads, their grief and their frustration to me, Marco looks straight ahead.

I stand there until the final car has disappeared down the lane, swaying this way and that over the potholes. Further down the road, an elderly couple stop as the cortège passes, paying their respects, and then look at me before getting in their little three-wheeled Ape truck to follow. I turn quickly, pushing open the listing gate by lifting it back on to the hinge and letting it drop again once it's closed. Then I run back to the house, keen to shut the front door on the outside world.

Bare bulbs are buzzing away brightly and lighting up the high stone ceiling with its crossover star shapes. I run round and turn a few lights off, adrenalin pumping, then start unpacking the bags and boxes in the dining room, furiously and in no particular order, just feeling the need to make my mark on the place. I pull out books and CDs. The only thing missing is my vintage record collection and my record player. Those records were part of me, who I was. Each of them meant something to me. But Ed insisted on keeping them. It was the only thing we really disagreed about. I gave in in the end. But now I've had time to think about it, I should have been firmer.

I pull out my painting box and the canvases that were covered in dust when I brought them out of the attic. I stop manically unpacking stuff and look at them. I was half tempted just to throw them out before I left, but I'm glad now I didn't. They are pictures I did back in college, when I first met my best friend Beth. We both met our partners while at college. She hooked up with another art student, Theo, and I got together with Ed. She moved to Cornwall to be a full-time painter when we left; I moved into a run-down flat in London, agreed to pay half a huge mortgage and had to start doing design work to meet my bills before I eventually moved on to the greeting cards.

Beth and I are still in touch, but less and less often these days. I'm not even sure she knows I've moved. I look from the canvases through the dining room doors. It really would be amazing to paint this place, I surprise myself by thinking. It's been ages since I've actually painted anything for fun. Maybe I will again. But first I have jobs to do. I must get in touch with Brandon, my boss. He's the one I design the cards for. He'll be wondering if I've disappeared from the human race . . . and frankly, it feels a bit like that.

It's Monday, market day. I'll go into town, pick up some groceries, a kettle now that I have electricity, some WD40 and maybe some goat food. It's probably not high on the Bellanuovos' list of priorities at the moment, and it might actually build a few bridges if I take care of the goat for a few days, just until the dust settles. Wonder what its name is?

But first I need to find an internet café. That way I can start organising internet for the house and start working again. I can at least pretend this is home.

Chapter Six

There are sheep all across the road and I have to slow and stop. A young man with very dark olive skin is herding them from one side of the road to the other whilst looking down at his mobile phone, and I wonder if he's got reception. He looks up at me, and I realise it's the young man I saw last night at the Bellanuovos', outside on the patio. He looks at me as if hopeful I might be someone he knows, but when he realises I'm not, he goes back to looking at his phone, slowly guiding the sheep across the road. He's in no hurry.

I, on the other hand, am desperate to get news from home. Some small crumbs from Morag or Elinor, who is a whizz on Facebook, or a message from Beth might help the gnawing homesickness in the pit of my stomach. Even one of my mum's texts asking if I've come to my senses would do. But not one from Ed. I really don't want to find any more emails from Ed asking about my plans. I don't have any plans! Well, no bigger than getting the internet sorted and buying a kettle, anyway.

I watch as the last of the sheep trots off the road into pastures new. They have long tails and bigger ears than the sheep back home. Not that I'm used to seeing sheep in

Tooting. And then I get to wondering when I would have last seen a sheep up close and personal.

The sun is hot and bright and I make a mental note to buy sunglasses at the market. I pull down the visor. The young man with the sheep looks up from his phone as I start to move again. I wave in thanks. He frowns and peers in at my window as if he should know me. I raise a hand again and then put my foot down and shoot off.

I manage to get to the end of the lane with no other real problems. It's a couple of miles of slim road and thankfully I don't meet any cars coming the other way. And when I get to the crossroads, I understand why. Everyone's already here. There are cars parked up on the verges and in any spare bit of kerb space. There are three-wheeled Ape vans, Vespa-type scooters and Fiats everywhere. In front of me is a playground, with pine trees throwing shade down on the children playing on the swings, being pushed by their mums. Old men are sitting under the trees playing cards. There are also men playing *bocce*, which is like the *boules* we used to play on the beach in Cornwall when I visited Beth and Theo.

Beyond the *bocce* and the playground is the market. There are sun-faded red-and-white-covered stalls and women with baskets moving in between them. Many are dressed in black, and I wonder if they will be going to the funeral. Piles of green offcuts litter the ground around the stalls and crates of vegetables. There are drop-sided stalls selling cheese and salami and flowers. The baker's shop, Forno Sophia, has blackout blinds across the window: closed for the day by the looks of it. There are cars crossing every which way. In front of me, the road starts to climb the hill towards the old town. There are blocks of flats either side of this square, a new addition to the town. Across from the playground is the school, a single-storey grey building with just a few tissue-paper butterflies in the windows.

I edge out, not knowing which road to take to find a parking space.

Parp! Parp! I jump as a car pulls out in front of me when I was sure it was my right of way. My heart starts beating faster and I know I can't wimp out. I have to do this. I follow another car and hope they know where they're going. The roads all look the same and the junctions just tie me up in knots. The only way I know where I am is because I've now driven past the ironmonger's three times. I decide that, like a maze, if I keep turning left I'll eventually get there . . . or is it right? I know I've passed this little square with the clock tower and the *cantina*, where you buy wine, three times. I turn left down a street with square flat-roofed buildings and past a bar with a green and white floral awning and signs for ice cream. For an area with beautiful buildings like the *trulli* and the church I can see at the top of the town, it's surprising that these houses are so depressing. Not that different from any other town really.

I want to just park up and then walk around the market and up to the plaza and the church. It seems to be straight up the hill from here. I'm stuck at lights. All the other cars are taking a short cut through the car park to avoid them. I decide to go Italian and do the same. But heaven knows which way I'm supposed to go now. I stick with the keep-turning-left theory and narrowly miss another car coming from my right, but they don't seem to notice. Then I see it, a parking space. I turn left again.

'Shit!'

I think I've just gone down a one-way street. I turn to look and see if I can reverse. But the traffic has stopped. I'll have to keep going. I put my foot down, but suddenly I'm faced with what looks to be a brass band playing soulful jazz music, like something from New Orleans. They're coming straight towards me. I look round to reverse again.

Parp! A car pulls out of the parking space in front of me and is coming towards me. I try to move to one side to let it pass, but there isn't enough room, not with that parking barrier there.

Parp! The driver waves his arms at me and is clearly using some really colourful language. The band are getting closer and I can hear the brass and the bass reverberating through the footwell of my car.

I try to reverse again, and two women, arm in arm, step out behind me. I slam on the brakes and they too gesticulate at me, shaking their heads. I wipe away the wetness on my top lip. My heart's now banging to the beat of the jazz. Why on earth would a band be coming through town on a busy day like today? That's when they come fully into view, all of them in dark suits and glasses . . . followed by a big silver Mercedes. It's the funeral procession, the Bellanuovos' funeral procession, and I'm blocking the road!

The band is now in front of me. They stop, as do the

cars behind them. The band keeps playing and I can hardly hear myself think. In fact I may just get out of the car and walk away. Someone climbs out of one of the funeral cars and is walking towards me. It's Marco. He's come to see what the holdup is. There is absolutely no way I'm going to let him see me. There is only one thing for it. Now I have to finally drive like an Italian. I shove the gearstick into first, spin the steering wheel, mount the kerb and skim past the other car. I hear the scratch of metal down the side of my car from the parking barrier. The other driver screeches off with more gesticulating hands and the band moves past.

As soon as they've gone, I drive on, without the same fear as before, because it really couldn't get any worse than that. I abandon my car outside the ironmonger's, right in front of a group of old men gathered on the pavement, in flat caps and rain jackets despite the heat. They're all looking at me and talking in a low, fast way. Their language might be different, but there's no denying the universal signs. They're talking about me, nodding towards me and shaking their heads, having obviously spotted the English number plate. One of them throws his brown cigarette butt to the ground and stands on it, then the three of them head off in the direction of the church, giving me a stiff nod as they pass.

I turn and look up at the church. The bells are ringing and I think I'll do my shopping first before walking that way. I'm sure I'm the last person the Bellanuovos want to see right now.

I walk up the steps of the ironmonger's. *Ferramenta* is

written in seventies-style red lettering over the heavy glass doors. There are big silver vats outside, hosepipes like sleeping snakes, watering cans, rolls of table coverings, and rakes with funny-looking heads. Inside, it's an Aladdin's cave. It's surprisingly cool, too. That may have something to do with the pile of free-standing fans for sale, with one or two blowing out cool air on to the customers. There is a man in overalls standing at the counter, and a shorter, fatter man behind it, dressed in a checked shirt that barely fits over his bulging belly.

The man in overalls holds up a hand in a wave and smiles. He's about my age, with bleached blond hair. He's also incredibly good-looking, in a laid-back surfer kind of way. To say he looks out of place compared to the other men standing outside is an understatement. His overalls are tied low around his waist by the sleeves, and his tanned forearms and hands are covered in dark grease or oil streaks.

'*Buongiorno,*' says bulging belly man behind the counter.

'*Buongiorno,*' I reply, slightly nervously. I nod to the man in overalls, too. He beams and nods back. I start to look around. The shop is full to bursting. There is an aisle for every kitchen accessory you could want: sausage-making machines, pasta machines, corking machines, scales, griddles for the open fire, chestnut pans. There's a pet aisle and one for post boxes. There are tools, drills and work benches and then another section that I have no idea about, with more of the funny-shaped rakes and cones. I can't imagine what they're used for.

'*Cosa stai cercando?* What are you looking for?' the man

behind the counter asks. I'm obviously not hiding my Englishness very well, despite trying to drive like a local.

'Um, WD40? Spray, tsh, tsh,' I mime and feel ridiculous as soon as I've done it. Nearly a year of Italian and I come up with 'tsh, tsh', I think crossly. The other man laughs and the shopkeeper shrugs. 'For shutters. The bolts are stiff.' I keep burbling while he crouches down looking through his shelves of stock.

'For where? Which house? You're on holiday, *si*?' he asks from behind the shelves.

I swallow. Here goes. This is where I have to start telling people.

'Masseria Bellanuovo. And no, not holiday. I've bought it. *Ho comprato.*'

The shopkeeper stands up slowly from behind the shelves and the man in overalls suddenly drops his lazy smile and his eyebrows shoot up.

'Ah, you're the one they're all talking about.'

I nod and try to smile.

'*Si, si* . . . I'm the one.' I roll my eyes and try to pretend I don't care.

'So you're going to rent out the *masseria*?'

'No,' I say slowly. Why does everyone think I'm going to do it up and rent it out? Because that's what normal people would do! I hear my mum's voice saying. She's already suggested it. 'I'm not renting out Masseria Bellanuovo.' I take a deep breath and wait for the laughter. 'I'm going to live in it.'

The two men look at each other and raise their eyebrows even higher.

'With your family?' asks the big-bellied bloke.

'On my own,' I say firmly and turn to look at the shelves of gloves and boots. I decide to treat myself to a pair of really thick gloves to tackle my thorny problems back at the *masseria* – well, the brambles anyway.

'I'm Ryan,' says the man in overalls as he holds out a hand, smiling warmly. This time it's the turn of my eyebrows to shoot up.

'Australian?' I sound surprised and quietly delighted at the same time. Someone who understands me!

'That's right. And no, I'm not on holiday either. I work here.' He smiles again, and it's a very welcoming smile. I feel an unexpected rush of relief that I'm here talking to someone who might just know how I'm feeling. I'm ridiculously pleased to meet him. I smile back at him and he looks down at his overalls.

'Sorry about the mess. Tractor broke down.' We shake hands lightly and I get a little tingle of pleasure as we touch hands. 'I heard you'd moved in. Well, I heard someone had moved in. They didn't say it was a good-looking girl.' I find myself blushing at his bold comments. Anywhere else, in another time and another place, I'd've told him to sod off. But right now, he's made my day.

'Looks like word's got around. Oh, not about the good-looking girl.' I blush again, ridiculously. 'I mean about me moving in.'

'News travels fast around here. That and the cars. Apart from that, for a country that is so keen to get everywhere quickly, everything else moves very slow.'

I can't help but laugh at his dreadful generalisations,

but it feels like some sort of release. In fact, it feels really good and I keep smiling.

'Look, if you need any help, give me a call.' He hands me his card. 'I can call in sometime if you like. I can turn my hand to most things. I do mostly olives, but I'm a pretty good builder too. It's a nice place, eh? A lot of work for one person, though. Maybe I could show you around, take you for dinner one night.'

'Thanks, I'll bear it in mind. I mean the help, not the dinner.' I laugh, embarrassed this time, and take the card.

'Well, the offer's there,' he says cheekily and then turns to say something to the shopkeeper. A word I don't know.

'Ah,' says the keeper and disappears under the counter again.

Turning to go, Ryan slaps the counter in a friendly way and says, '*Ciao*,' then raises a hand to me and heads for the door.

'*Ciao*,' calls the shopkeeper, appearing from under the counter with a can of spray that looks just like WD40, and a wide, toothless smile.

'*Ciao*,' I say. Ryan turns back at the door, and smiles a wicked smile, then winks, which makes me laugh again. I feel better than I have for days, and I turn the card over in my hand, wondering if dinner with someone warm and friendly who speaks the same language as me would really be such a bad idea. In fact, it sounds like a very nice idea indeed.

Chapter Seven

The market is just how I expected it to be. Busy with chatter, bustling with sales and people taking the time to stop and talk to their neighbours and friends in small groups. I walk through the stall-lined streets. There's a queue of customers outside what looks to be just another shop doorway, and it turns out to be a flour mill. On the streets there are tables of cheap gold jewellery; brightly coloured scarves next door to a stall of dark nylon trousers. The flower and plant stalls make me want to take up gardening, but I wouldn't know where to start. I watch a woman picking up plants, inspecting them and settling on the one she thinks is best. The smell is wonderful, and there are even lemon trees with lemons like big gold cricket balls dripping from their branches. There are settees and second-hand furniture, which I should definitely come back for, and of course there are the food stalls.

Ed and I came to Puglia not long before we finally agreed to split up. Just after his dog, Dudley the pug, died. I loved the markets then. Ed didn't. I think it was then we started to realise we were totally incompatible in the long term. Without Dudley (named after Dudley Moore in

Arthur, Ed's favourite film) to walk and fuss over, we had nothing in common any more. I had hoped the Italian trip would bring us closer together, but it just left us wanting different things and even further apart.

I wanted to smell, touch and buy everything in sight. Ed couldn't see the point when we could just eat at the hotel. We ended up going to Torre Canne for the rest of the day, and lay on sunbeds miles apart, in our own little Kindle worlds, both wishing we were somewhere else. So today, I'm determined to shop local. If this is my new home, I need to start trying to fit in.

The sun is now really hot, and I quickly buy some large gold-trimmed sunglasses and don't feel in the least bit daft. Everyone is wearing them. I'm determined to prove to Ed that he's wrong. This wasn't just a moment of madness. This is what I dreamed life would be like, and I throw myself into the food stalls. Red, orange, green and white, the colours are fantastic. The perfume from the fennel fills the air. The oranges are like footballs and the tomatoes like little pumpkins.

I stop at one vegetable stall and the dark-skinned stallholder in flat cap and holey jumper opens up a bag. I look at the other woman picking up the vegetables, smelling them and squeezing them. I'm determined to be just like them. But what I notice is that more and more of the buyers are staring at me. I don't want to be the outsider; I want to fit in, and I start to try in my best Italian to ask about the food I'm buying. There's a certain amount of miscommunication, I think is the best way to describe it. In my efforts to fit in, I just nod and point a lot. The other women talk amongst themselves and I can hear their shared humour.

I end up with kilos of tomatoes, onions, cauliflower and green beans, fennel, broccoli and chillies, a huge lump of cheese, which cost me an arm and a leg, and enough focaccia to feed a family of ten. I can't work out if it was my Italian or my gullible face, but I strongly suspect it was the latter. I've handed over huge amounts of money and am now being stared at even more as I struggle away from the food stalls, blue carrier bags bashing at my calves. I feel like I'm doing the walk of shame back through the market: the Englishwoman who had no idea what she was buying.

I head for the shade of the older streets up the hill, away from the groups of gossiping stallholders and their customers. The coolness is welcome, and it's quieter here too. To the left and right are narrow cobbled streets with washing hanging from windows and square street lights strung across from building to building. Steep steps lead up to archways over front doors and there are red geraniums in window boxes. As I reach the top, it opens on to a square and a church with huge stone steps leading up to it. The view from here is amazing. You can see right across the valley and the neighbouring small hilltop towns, forming a blanket of green olive trees with *trulli* scattered across it like little clusters of white mushrooms.

The church bells start to ring out and suddenly the big wooden double doors at the top of the stone steps swing open. I stand and watch from a distance, intrigued, as the priest, in purple robes trimmed with gold, steps out, followed by two altar boys also in robes, heads dipped. Not being a churchgoer, I'm fascinated by the pomp and ceremony of it all.

I'm suddenly taken aback to see Marco Bellanuovo stepping out behind them, his grandmother on his arm, small, bent and visibly weeping. Of course, the funeral, I'd almost forgotten. And now the very last person I want to see is there, in his black suit, pulling down his sunglasses. I can't let him see me. I step back into the shadows but don't move away just yet. I'll watch from a distance for a minute.

Marco stands to one side of the doorway. He's joined by his mother and other members of his family that I met last night. From the shadows, I'm fascinated as another woman, about the same age as Anna-Maria, steps out and purposefully stands on the other side of the doorway. Anna-Maria lifts her chin and turns her head away from the woman, who mirrors the action. Hands clasped in front of their bodies, holding clutch bags, they look like bookends, both ignoring the other's presence.

The other woman is joined and surrounded by what looks to be her family. They group together around her as Marco's family groups around Anna-Maria, shuffling and standing shoulder to shoulder, chins lifted on both sides. Neither of the two women looks at each other. Their faces are set. The two families talk low and conspiratorially amongst themselves, but neither side speaks to the other across the dividing line that is the coffin as it's brought out. I'm wondering if this is the Aunt Sophia of Forno Sophia that Filippo told me about.

As the coffin passes by, the two women slowly turn to look at each other and then simultaneously lift their chins and flick their heads away again. Despite the heat of the day, the frostiness is almost palpable as they dismiss each other with disdain. The coffin is carried to the waiting hearse at the foot of the steps and loaded in. Then, snappily, the two women motion to their supporters, who fall into line, throwing looks over their shoulders and down their noses at the family on the other side of the steps. The formalities here done with, the two groups move away from each other as quickly as possible, making for their cars in opposite directions. I'm wondering if they're now going to the mausoleum – the huge stone burial building on the way into town.

Marco is still supporting Nonna. She holds his arm with one hand; the other clutches a big white hankie as they take the steps slowly, and I can't help but feel guilty that I have added to this old lady's grief. It's time to go before I'm seen, and I turn and slip away, back towards the market, where hopefully the audience I entertained earlier with my vegetable-buying will have dispersed.

I walk back in the direction of my car. I'm feeling hot. And I still have to go to the supermarket on the way back to the *masseria* to pick up all the essentials I didn't get at the market. But as I'm heading back through the square blocks of flats, I spot the café, the one with the butterfly awning. There are people outside, on their laptops, drinking coffee. It's busy here. They have Wi-Fi! Suddenly I'm desperate for any contact with home.

The smell of coffee is just wonderful, drawing me closer.

My whole body suddenly craves caffeine. I guide my bags in, knocking some of the chairs, drawing attention to myself, although I could be starting to get a bit paranoid. I head straight for the covered terrace outside. Beyond the awning, large square parasols create a huge area of shade. A man gets up and leaves. I don't hesitate, and sit down at the table he's vacated. It's a table for four, but I really need a coffee now.

I put some of my shopping next to me and some on the floor, letting go of the handles and having to herd the bags up again as they fall this way and that like startled cats.

Eventually they're still. I rub my hands together where the bags have left their marks and pull my laptop from my satchel. Just as I do, a waitress comes and stands next to me with a small round tray and a cloth. I order a coffee and a glass of water, and a panini. I look at the other tables: a mix of Italian families out shopping and tourists in shorts and brightly coloured T-shirts, baseball caps and sun block. I live here! I think, as the tourists ooh and aah at the green valley of olive trees beyond the blocks of flats. This is how it was meant to work out.

I smile as I open up my laptop. It feels like I'm welcoming back an old friend as it flicks into life. It feels like I can touch home.

The first message to greet me is from eBay: *How would you rate your recent transaction?* I dismiss it with a quick click, not wanting to think about it.

I go to my inbox, and my heart and spirits lift to see lots of new emails and Facebook messages from friends back home wanting to know how I'm doing. They're mostly from Morag and Elinor, worrying that they haven't heard anything. But there's one from our Italian teacher, and one from 'Jammy Jane', as we used to call her, looking for a holiday invite. Maybe I'll post some pictures of what I'm up to on Facebook later, so the rest of my evening class can see. Though I don't know if I'd want absolutely everyone to see. When I think about it, a lot of my friends on Facebook are really Ed's friends; apart from my evening class mates, and Beth, of course. But as Ed and I grew to be a couple, it was usually his friends that we spent time with. They became my friends too, sort of. And when we split, I guess he got custody of them.

Morag and Elinor have been fantastic. They've been there for me all the way. Especially as the move happened so quickly. Only the two of them and my boss Brandon are aware of it so far. There are several messages from Brandon, and they seem to be getting more and more irate, wanting Christmas designs from me and demanding to know why I haven't been in touch. I've started to type a reply when I spot a message from Beth. I feel terrible that I haven't even told her about the move. I've been meaning to email her but somehow I never really believed it was happening myself, until now. I mean, she knows about me and Ed splitting up and the flat sale, but I just haven't been in touch since the night everything changed. I haven't told her what I've actually gone and done.

I usually try and visit Beth and Theo twice a year, but what with me working all hours to still pay my half of the mortgage, even though we were selling, I just haven't had time recently. Ed made it clear that we might be in a relationship but I still had to pay my half of everything, to the penny. Some months I ended up robbing Peter to pay Paul, with the help of a few credit cards. They were the first things I had to sort out when we finally completed on the flat.

I can see there's an email from Ed too, probably asking if I've come to my senses yet, and when will I be coming home. I open it quickly, saving my email from Beth to savour and enjoy afterwards. He says he's been to see my mother and they both agree that I've acted rashly and the best thing for me to do is to rent the place out and come home! Grrrr! How dare he go talking to my mum about me? Then he asks for forwarding details in case in needs to contact me. Why would he need to contact me? We're not together any more! I hit the button, closing his email with more force than necessary out of frustration. Ed needs to move on and stop contacting me. He's with Annabel now. But I can't tell him that now. I want to read my email from Beth. She was always saying I was living in Ed's shadow and that I should strike out and do something on my own; well now I have and I can't wait to tell her. I open her email.

Hi hon, where are you? Been trying to phone but I just keep getting a strange ringtone. Are you at your mum's? Been thinking about you. Something's come up I think you might be interested in. In fact, I know you will be. There's a new art gallery setting up down here. Theo's been helping them source artists, etc., and they're looking for a manager. Thought it could be right up your street, especially what with you looking for a fresh start right now. Money's okayish but there's a flat with the job and I reckon you'd be able to see the sea from your bedroom. Let me know if you're interested. Who knows, coming down here might even start you painting again! The sea air does funny things to people. Wouldn't it be fab! Love as always Beth (and Theo and Lulu the Labrador)

Oh God! It sounds so perfect I could weep . . . and I nearly do. Why didn't I just hang on? I put my head in my hands. My rising spirits plummet. I could've been living near friends, in a flat that I might actually have been able to afford furniture for, and back in the art world instead of trying to work out how to do up a house that I don't even feel I belong in. A great dollop of self-pity falls on me from on high.

'*Scusi.*' I jump and look up. '*C'e qualcuno seduto qui?*' says the smart-looking woman about my age, in wonderfully clear Italian that I understand every word of.

'*Per favore.*' I hold out a hand to show that the other seats aren't taken and start gathering up my bags.

'Ah, English?' she says in a clear Welsh accent. I'm taken aback and try and think of something to say quickly so as not to appear rude.

'Yes,' I say, stuffing the tomatoes under my chair with my foot and grabbing the bag of cheese and trying to hide it on my lap.

'Ah, tourist cheese!' She points to it and I get the impression she's laughing at me too. I feel affronted and frankly fed up of being made fun of.

'Actually I live here,' I say a bit too haughtily.

'It was the same when I first arrived.' She takes in the rest of my shopping. 'Took a while for me to realise it wasn't my bad Italian that was to blame.'

She sits down and orders a coffee and a salad and pushes her sunglasses on top of her head.

'Been here long?' she asks, crossing long legs in white jeans.

I sigh and relax a bit, pleased to have someone to talk to.

'About forty-eight hours,' I say, and then look at the cheese and laugh too.

'Lou Antonelli.' She puts out a hand. 'From Porthcawl but now Puglia.'

'Ruthie Collins, Tooting but now Puglia.' We shake hands and smile at each other.

'Did you meet someone out here then?' Lou asks as her coffee arrives and she thanks the young waitress with a smile. 'Do you want another?'

I nod. 'That would be great. But I'm not sure the waitress understands me.'

Lou waves a dismissive hand and gestures to the girl. 'Probably understands more than she lets on.' She rolls her eyes. 'S'okay, I'm in with the boss. It's my husband's café.'

'Oh,' is all I can think of saying.

'We live here.' Lou helps me out and points to the flats above. 'What about you? You move here with family?'

'Actually, I moved here on my own,' I say, wondering if she's going to think I'm as daft as everyone else seems to think.

She picks up her coffee, sips and nods. 'Cool,' she says, putting down the cup. 'Why not? If you're going to move anywhere, might as well make it somewhere fab.' She nods at the view beyond the town.

'Exactly!' I find myself smiling as the waitress puts the cup down in front of me and I quickly take a sip. A salad of tomatoes, mozzarella and basil with dark green olive oil drizzled over it arrives for Lou, with a basket of crusty bread. I have to be careful not to unload my worries on this woman. I don't want her to think I'm some loner who's latched on to her for being British too.

'So, you met someone and moved out here?' I ask, feeling that I can. She puts her fork into the tomatoes and takes a mouthful, nodding and smiling as she chews.

'Holiday romance,' she finally replies.

'No? Really?' I'm agog. 'That's really . . . brave,' I say lamely. 'And what? You moved over here?'

'Well, we met in London. I was on a hen weekend. He was the barman in TGI Fridays. Then his father fell ill and he had to come and take over the business and I'd gone and got pregnant and I thought, why not? Where would I rather be? Sometimes in life you just have to take a chance.'

It's true, but it looks like I took the wrong chance. My chance is waiting for me in Cornwall!

'You? Any kids?' she asks. I hoped she wouldn't, but people always do.

I shake my head. 'No, no kids.' I try not to dwell on it. It's probably the thing that makes me saddest about splitting from Ed, knowing I won't have a family of my own. I add more brightly, 'But I have a house to pour my time and money into now.'

She laughs, and I do too, grateful for her understanding. I like this woman.

'So, where are you living?' She tucks into the mozzarella and breaks a slice of bread. 'In town?'

I take a big mouthful of my panini, wishing I'd been more adventurous and ordered the salad. When I've chewed and swallowed, I say, 'Masseria Bellanuovo. It's just on the road out of town.'

She nods, her eyes wide. 'Yes, I know it. I work near there, at the school. Wow! That's a lot to take on.' She frowns. 'And what with the family, too. I bet they're none too happy.'

My happy, brave bubble is burst and I put down the panini and wipe my hands.

'You could say that,' I say carefully. After all, I'm not really sure who this woman is, as much as I like her.

'How did you come to live there?'

'Well . . .' Despite telling myself I'm not going to spill my guts, I find myself about to launch into the whole story.

'Oh.' She holds up a hand, looking at her watch. 'Look, I have to go. Got to catch the post office before it shuts. A care package for my dad.' She gestures to a bag with a brown paper parcel in it. 'Olive oil and honey. He loves it. And I have to pick my son up from his grandparents.' She stands. 'Looks like we'll have to do this another time, over a glass of rosato. What d'you say?'

I nod. 'I'd like that.' I take a big breath, as if sucking back in the thoughts I was about to spill. She looks at her watch again.

'How are you getting on with the language?'

I hold up a hand and wave it this way and that and grimace. She laughs.

'Ah, local dialect. Don't worry, you'll get the hang of it.'
We both laugh. I wish I could be as sure as she is.

'So, let's meet up some time. Actually,' she turns back and lowers her voice, 'this is really cheeky, but I'd love to see inside the house some time, the *masseria*. People say it's gorgeous, but no one's been in there for years.'

I smile. I like her up-frontness.

'Sure,' I say. 'Come for lunch. Any day. I have plenty of cheese.' I waggle the bag and we both laugh again and swap numbers on our phones.

'Nice to meet you, Ruthie. *Ciao*,' says Lou. She bends and kisses me like an Italian woman, and I feel I've made a friend.

'*Ciao*,' I reply with a smile, and watch her go, pulling down her sunglasses, head held high, hair swishing, bag over her shoulder. I wonder if in time, if I stay, I'll develop the Italian walk too.

If you stay? Stick it out more like! says a little voice in my head.

It's true, there's a huge amount to do and the Bellanuovos really don't want me there. Yes, if I stay, I say to myself, and reread Beth's email.

Sometimes in life you just have to take a chance . . . Lou's words come back to me, and I wonder if there's any way, any way at all, I could go home.

Chapter Eight

'Oh no, that's all I need,' I mutter under my breath as I leave the café with my bags. Marco Bellanuovo is walking this way, from the direction of the mausoleum, but he doesn't seem to see me. He's talking into his mobile. I bend down, pretending to look for something in my bags. He's getting closer. A smartly dressed woman, also talking on the phone, is coming in the other direction, a small Bichon Frisé trotting at her side in a diamanté collar and lead. The dog stops just by my bags and starts snuffling. The woman continues to talk very quickly into her phone, ignoring her pet. I give the dog a nudge with my hand, pushing it away from the bags. It sniffs indignantly at me and turns a circle. Marco is stepping out into the road, skirting the woman and me. It looks like he hasn't seen me. I realise I'm holding my breath. I've no idea why, but I just don't want another difficult conversation right now. Nor do I want him to see the ridiculous shopping I've come back with, as if I've got *tourist* tattooed on my forehead.

He's passed me, thank goodness, and I breathe again.

I can't understand what he's saying, but I'm sure I hear the word *masseria*. My senses are suddenly alerted. What?

My *masseria*? This would all be so much easier if he'd just bought the place off his grandfather in the first place.

I straighten up and watch his broad back in his dark suit. He seems out of place in the market. Taller than the locals who stop him to kiss both cheeks and shake his hand. And not dressed like the locals I've seen. Here it's all orange and red trousers, lurid T-shirts and expensive trainers. Marco stands out in his smart and understated suit. Mind you, he is dressed for a funeral, and you'd think he'd be at the wake by now, if that's what they do in Italy. All I know is that after my grandad's funeral, it was back to the pub for ham sandwiches and sweet sherry. First come, first served.

I go to pick up my bags just as the little dog lifts its leg as if to pee.

'Hey!' I shout and make a grab for them. The dog turns and yaps noisily at me. As I jump back, scooping up the bags, the smartly dressed woman turns and snaps at me in Italian whilst not taking her phone from her ear. I wish I could think of something witty to respond with, but instead I spin and turn to walk away, and as I do, red tomatoes tumble out of their bag and roll all over the pavement and into the gutter. Passers-by turn to look but carry on walking. The woman tuts, then gives the dog's lead a tug and struts off. The dog squeaks indignantly but struts off too, head held high.

I attempt to hide my embarrassment by bending over and grappling around in the gutter for my tomatoes. I'm picking them up and tossing them back into the bag when someone joins me and puts three in at once.

'*Grazie*,' I say, and look up. My cheeks burn with embarrassment.

'*Prego*,' says Marco as he picks up the last couple and I straighten up. Neither of us says anything for a moment.

We're both uncomfortable. I want to say that I hope the funeral went okay, but right now, I'm not sure he'll want to hear that from me.

'It's warm,' I say finally.

'Of course,' he replies, still not moving away, and I bristle.

'I . . . I hope the funeral . . . went as well as it could.' I move a bag into my other hand and feel balanced.

'It's a difficult time,' he says.

'Of course.' I don't know what else to say. I want to get back to my car and out of town.

'We need answers. We have no idea why our family home has been sold to a complete stranger. If that is what you are?' He raises an eyebrow and I feel a sudden surge of indignation rush through me.

'Of course I'm a stranger. How could I have possibly known your grandfather?' I say as people pass us and stare.

Marco shrugs. 'We just need answers. Why did he sell it? And . . . where has the money gone?'

'I have to go.' I don't want to get into this speculation.

'Yes, I have a meeting to attend.' He turns away.

I'm about to strut off like the Italian woman, but then I turn back and say, 'Is the meeting about the *masseria*?' It's out of my mouth before I know it. See, Ed was right: I am hot-headed and impetuous.

'Masseria Bellanuovo?' He nods. '*Sì*. It is. Like I say, we need answers.'

'I should come with you. Look, perhaps we could sort something out between us. Perhaps you could just buy the house back off me.'

He stops and turns to look at me, and I wonder if he's thinking about it.

'I mean, you could just give me my money back. I could go.'

'You would do that? I thought you were one of those who wanted to live the good life.' He uses his fingers to emphasise the words like speech marks.

I ignore the childish gesture.

'It could work for both of us.'

He says nothing, and then, 'Maybe.' He looks at his phone. 'I have to go.'

'If it's my house you're talking about, I should be there too!' I blurt out, and start to follow him, trying to keep up with his long strides.

'No, this is family business,' he says, as if talking to a child.

'If it's about my house . . .'

'Which you don't seem to want now.'

I'm passing my car and I can finally drop off my purchases. Marco is stopped by a group of short ladies who are obviously talking to him about his grandfather. I load up my boot and then turn back to see him starting to walk off again, without me.

It's still my house that I bought fair and square! I want to know exactly what's going on. I slam down the boot, shove my keys into my bag and follow him.

He heads back up the hill and I see him disappear into a tiny bar on the corner of two streets. There's just a single table and chair outside. I follow him into the darkness.

It takes a moment or two for my eyes to adjust. The place smells of strong coffee and cigarette smoke, despite the smoking ban. There is a man behind the counter and two other men standing drinking coffee. A large, whirring fridge holds cold drinks. There's an ancient-looking computer where someone seems to be checking their lottery ticket, and three fruit machines next to it.

All four men turn to look at me. I look around for Marco but can't see him at all. Is this a wind-up? Has he left through another door? I turn to leave, cross at myself for not being faster and sticking to him like glue.

'*Si?*' the man behind the bar says abruptly.

I hesitate. I can't just walk out.

'I'm looking for someone . . . *Alla ricerca di qualcuno*,' I dredge up from my lessons back in Tooting.

The men at the bar talk in a low rumble amongst themselves.

'Who?' asks the barman in English.

'Um . . .' What do I say? A friend? He's certainly not that. 'A neighbour,' I reply.

'Where? Where you live?' he says.

I take a deep breath. 'Masseria Bellanuovo.' They stare at me for a moment, and then laugh.

'There's no one here,' says the barman, shaking his head, cleaning a glass.

I'm not going to get any help here. I turn to go, but

then hear raised voices. I recognise Marco's. I can't make out much, but once again I hear the word '*masseria*', and then 'Giovanni'. I turn back, fed up of being made to feel a fool. Behind the two men drinking coffee is a faded curtain. And behind it . . . my business! Something in me just sees red, like the time Catherine Tanner and her friends laughed at me in school when I proudly told her that Jamie Darren had asked me out after months of me fancying him. They laughed and laughed, and then Jamie joined in and told me it was a dare. Eventually I could stand the laughter no more and punched Catherine on the nose. She didn't laugh at me again. And I didn't care about the two hundred lines I had to write. It was worth it.

I march past the two men drinking coffee and dismiss the protestations from the barman by holding up one hand and yanking back the curtain with the other.

Marco is standing over a table, his palms slapped down on it. Opposite him, one man is standing and another is sitting. The barman follows me and I gather from all the gesticulating that he is apologising for my intrusion.

The seated man holds up his hand to silence the barman. He is clean-shaven, dressed in pink chinos and a light-pink shirt. Something gives me an uneasy feeling. What have I just walked in on?

'*E tu sei?*'

'Ruthie Collins,' I stammer, wishing I hadn't been quite so quick to be part of this. 'I own Masseria Bellanuovo.'

He switches to English seamlessly. 'Then come in. You've saved me a visit. I was going to drop by and introduce myself. I am Franco Pugliese. I am a local businessman. I help . . .' He thinks for a moment. 'I help life to run smoothly round here.' He stands up to shake my hand, then gestures to me to sit down. 'I like to think I can be of assistance when my friends need me,' he says with a smile. A coffee appears in front of me, but the way my heart is racing, I decide not to drink it. 'And I hope we can be friends.'

Marco tuts and turns away. Franco sits back down.

'Marco and I are just discussing his grandfather's property. He has come to me to look for answers: why he sold it and where the money is.'

Marco is looking furious: his fists clench, his jawline is taut. He's obviously distressed, but I'm going to put that right. I'm going to tell him now. He can have the house, I'll agree to it. It obviously means a great deal to him. His smooth jawline twitches again.

I'm not sure who this guy Pugliese is and why he should have all the answers, but there is some kind of Mafia alert going on in my head. Ridiculous, I know. I laugh nervously to myself. Probably been watching too many films. I'm not going to be bullied out of the house, but I do know how I can sort this out.

'Look, I bought Masseria Bellanuovo. It's all above board and anything that needs to be discussed about it should be discussed with me,' I say. I sound bold, but inside I'm shaking. It's something I've done since I was a kid. After my dad left with one of the mums from the school gate, there was loads of teasing. My brother couldn't take it and I couldn't have that. I managed to stand up to them, told them what I'd do if they didn't back off, but inside I was terrified, and when I was on my own, my knees and hands shook like they had a life of their own. And now here I am doing it again, letting my mouth run off before consulting my brain. What am I doing here? What on earth have I got myself into?

'Quite right,' says Pugliese in perfect English again.

I take a deep breath and try and speak steadily. 'But I have decided that if the Bellanuovos really want the house, I'm happy to sell it back to them.'

He raises an eyebrow and puffs on an electronic cigarette that looks like an old-fashioned cigarette holder.

'They get the house, I get my money back, we're all happy!' I beam, thinking about the email I can send to Beth telling her to hold the job for me, and scan Marco's face for a reaction. 'We all win!' I say brightly, thinking he's misunderstood me. But he doesn't respond. It's Pugliese who speaks first. 'Marco, I can only tell you what I know, the truth. I know it's not what you want to hear, and I'm sorry for that.'

'What? That there is no money? I have to go back to my family and tell them the house has gone and so has the money?'

I suddenly feel very uncomfortable. This isn't my business at all. What was I thinking of, barging in here, invading this man's privacy and his grief? I feel I've made things ten times worse.

'Look, maybe I should . . . You were right.' I stand up to go. Pugliese holds up his hand and I sit again.

'You're right to be cross.' I listen carefully to him talking to Marco. 'But your grandfather was a good man.

He wanted what was best for you. There were debts. After your father and your uncle argued, the family started to fall apart. He tried to hold it together, but with your father dying, and then your uncle, he had to work hard to keep the estate going. He tried, but once it started to get carved up, there was less and less for him to make a living from. He ran up debts.'

'The fool! Why didn't he come to me?' Marco practically spits, like he's forgotten I'm there at all.

'He didn't want the family left with the debts when he died. If he hadn't paid them off, if he'd left you the house, you would have been liable. As it is, the slate is wiped clean. The sale of the house has left you with no debts.'

'And no heritage,' Marco says, squeezing his fist into a ball. 'And now it belongs to not just a stranger, but someone who knows nothing about the area, the land. Someone who thinks they can run away from their problems at home, and that a bit of sunshine and dolce vita is going to make everything all right.'

'Excuse me!' I blurt out.

'Please, please.' Pugliese puts out his hands to calm things.

'And the debts?' Marco leans towards him.

'An accumulator bet. He tried to pay off what he owed. West Ham lost . . .' There's a moment's silence. 'Marco, I'm sorry I can't give you better news. But you have your grandfather's good name to cherish. Miss Collins, you have a house that is clear of debt too. Look after it, and if you think I can be of help at any time, please call on me. So, you're going to rent it out?'

'No,' I say patiently, wishing I didn't have to, 'I'm going to live in it.'

He raises his eyebrows. 'In that case, you will need to pay me your local tax.'

'Local tax? What local tax?'

'We like to call it security,' and the man standing steps forward with a card machine.

Many euros lighter, I follow Marco out through the curtain and into the bright sunshine. I take a deep breath.

'Who the hell is that?' I demand.

'Like he said. He's the businessman who makes things run smoothly round here. It's how things are done.' Marco turns to walk away, pushing his hands into his pockets. His shoulders have dropped. It seems the answers he's got are not the ones he wanted to hear.

'Look, Marco.' I try and catch up with him. It's afternoon and not as hot, but I'm boiling, infuriated by his rudeness. 'Just for the record, I wasn't running away!' I shout after him, but he keeps walking and I know in my heart of hearts that he's right. That's exactly what I was doing. Running away from the ashes of disaster that were my life. Feeling I didn't belong any more because I didn't have a home of my own, feeling like a failure after Ed and I split. Well, I'm certainly never going to belong here!

I start walking back to my car, my heart still racing as if I've drunk fifteen espressos, and I don't know if it's the meeting or the way Marco made me feel when he looked at me, hurt etched in his eyes as he realised there was nothing more that could be done. That's it. Even if I wanted to tear up the paperwork and hand the *masseria* back, the money's gone. And with it any chance of a small flat over an art gallery and a fabulous new beginning in Cornwall.

The market has packed up when I get back to the car, and I stop off in the café and post on Facebook telling anyone who'll read it about my fabulous, mad new life. I describe the olive trees, the house and the courtyard; the orangery, the sun and the views. I don't tell them about the bare rooms, the crumbling walls, the hostile goat or the even more hostile neighbours. And all the time I'm trying to work out in my head how I can leave.

Back at the *masseria*, there are cars everywhere, presumably for the wake; on the grass verges, up the lane and across my drive.

Finally it's time to be honest with myself. Ed, my mum, my brother, they were all right. Even Morag and Elinor thought I was mad. I've made a mistake, a big fat spur-of-the-moment mistake, and I'm stuck with it. There's no way out. I grip the steering wheel with both hands, put my forehead to the hot plastic and give in to big gulping sobs.

Chapter Nine

I can hear the noise from Anna-Maria's villa as soon as I'm out of the car, feeling worn out and eyes still stinging. I don't want anyone to see me. There is a huge gathering there, spilling out on to the verandas at front and back. All around the house people are standing talking; some are smoking, with drinks in their hands, and I can see Anna-Maria waving her arms, directing Marco's sister and cousin as they pass through with trays of food to be laid on the long tables at the back of the house. Men with sunglasses on their heads are helping themselves to the bite-sized morsels as they pass. Children are running in and out of the bushes down the side of the house and the olive trees at the back, and up towards the three-coned *trullo*. People are talking fast and expansively, children are laughing, and parents are calling them to mind their clothes in the dirt and to come and eat.

I turn back to the *masseria*, silent and empty. Apart from the goat, that is, who is strutting up and down outside the front door. This time I'm ready for it and from my satchel pull out a paper napkin with the leftovers from my lunch that I saved for just this situation. I toss the food as far as I can, and as the goat's hooves skitter on the worn flags towards the tasty treat, I unlock the front door and start to unload my shopping. When the goat trots back, I rub it between the ears and then give it a friendly shoo. It follows me to the car, where I'm pulling out a bag of goat feed I bought in the ironmonger's. I find a bucket in the open-sided barn and pour the grain in for . . . her, I think I've established, judging by her teats.

She's kicking and knocking over the bucket in her excitement, and I wonder who's been feeding her before now. Giovanni Bellanuovo, I suppose, but he's been gone for nearly a week. Mind you, if you had to live off the land, this is the place to do it. I look around. There's a vegetable plot to the side of the house, very overgrown and I have no idea what's in it. And there are bushes and trees that I don't recognise. I know the olives, and the almonds dotted in between them. But I haven't a clue about any of the rest. The most I had in the flat was some herbs I bought from the supermarket and put into pretty pots on the windowsill. There wasn't much room for anything else in the places I grew up in either. Although I did once notice some green plants on our neighbour's balcony, I realise they weren't to enhance his cooking.

I always fancied an allotment, though Ed said I'd get bored of it and move on to something else before I even made it to the top of the waiting list. But I bought books on what I was going to grow, and I'd get them out every now and again and dream about what I could plant. Maybe I'd dig them out now, see if I could work out what was growing here.

But first I had to try and sort out the leak in the *trullo* or I'd never be able to get that up and running. I needed the money it would bring in if I was going to do any of the other repairs and start buying furniture. After Brandon's feisty emails about not being able to rely on me and having to look for other designers, I really needed to get something to him, and fast.

Brandon and I go back years. He'd come to the college and leave business cards around, looking for young art students to work on a freelance basis for him. In other words, cheap labour. When Ed and I decided to buy our flat, we knew we could make money if I did it up and sold it on, but I'd still have to work to cover my half of the bills. Working part-time in Pizza Palace wasn't going to pay enough, so I rang Brandon. I only ever meant it to be temporary. Just until the flat was finished and I could start to paint again, maybe get an exhibition together. But there was always something to do on the flat. And the temporary work became more permanent. It just sort of happened. There was never a time when I could stop working for Brandon and do what I'd trained to do: paint. I still rely on him. If I didn't work for Brandon, I'd have no income at all. Painting is something I used to do in another lifetime.

I look around the barn. The goat is now lying down on the veranda, looking quite content, and I can't help but think she should have somewhere to sleep at night. I start to shift some of the junk and in no time I've created a pen out of some crates stacked on their sides, an old door and a large plastic tub that looks as if it might once have had an olive tree in it. I'm pleased with my work and open the door a couple of times, like a gate. She can sleep in here. I can just imagine the consequences if anything happened to her whilst she was in my care!

I add a couple more handfuls of food to her bucket and shake it. 'Come on, goat,' and she trots happily into the home-made pen. I leave the door open; I'll only shut her in at night. Ha! Wait till I tell Beth I'm looking after a goat. But I can't keep referring to her as 'goat', even if she isn't mine. Her jaws are moving like she's chewing gum. Her long beard bobbing up and down reminds me of Ed's mother's hairy chin. Ed's mother is called Daphne. We never got on. In fact, when Ed and I moved in together, she made it very clear that she didn't think I was good enough for her son, and told me so. Told me she'd been to a clairvoyant and that Ed was going to marry and have two beautiful sons, but sadly it wasn't with me. Every Christmas she bought me the same gift, a scarf and some Turkish delight, and then gave Ed a big cheque to get himself something. I still have the scarves. They're mostly pastel colours, where I'm more of a bold colours person. I've never been quite sure what to do with them. I don't like Turkish delight and always gave it to the food bank. That was Daphne. Daphne, I think, looking at the goat. That'll do. Daphne the goat. It makes me smile anyway.

As I turn to go, something moves in the corner of the barn, making me jump. Oh God! Not rats! Two shiny eyes peer out at me. I take a step forward. It looks like a really big rat, judging by the size of its head. I pick up a long stick that's leaning against the wall. Why? I have no idea. What good is a stick going to do me? The rat's going to run. But it doesn't run, and as I get closer, I can see it's not a rat, but a cat. A small grey cat. It's not moving and I wonder if it's hurt. I step forward, and it hisses and spits and shows its teeth. I back off. It's feisty all right. I slowly put down the stick, and turn back to the cat. Then I see it . . . or should I say them. Three little kittens feeding from her. That's why she's not moving. She's made herself a bed in amongst the netting that's rolled up in here. I decide the best thing I can do is step away and go and find her something to eat. There must be something among all that stuff I bought today.

Returning with some milk and eggs, I put the dish on the floor a little distance from her so as not to disturb her. I don't think she's going to come anywhere near it while I'm still here. She needs to do this in her own time. I get the impression she's feeling a bit like me, trapped and backed into a corner, terrified and scared but spitting and hissing on the outside.

I step back, kicking a box of glass jars and bottles, making her hiss again. 'Sorry, sorry,' I say, as I back away with my hands out, careful not to upset her any more.

I take my shopping into the kitchen. It's no good. I can't make myself at home here until I've begun moving the rubbish out. And that's what I'm going to have to do. I start sliding, lifting and dragging the boxes to the front door and form a huge pile there. It looks like someone started the job but never actually got round to finishing it. Giovanni Bellanuovo was obviously a man trying to get his affairs in order in his own way. Looks like he just ran out of time on this one.

I think once again of my grandad, who always believed I could do anything I turned my hand to. And thinking of him makes me want to cook. I go to my pile of books on the kitchen floor and put them on the windowsill. Now it's starting to feel like I live here. I flick through one of my well-thumbed recipe books. There's nothing else for it, I think, looking at my shopping and back at the book: piccalilli! Grandad loved piccalilli.

I run back to the shed and grab the box of jars I almost fell over, then pull the vegetables from their blue carrier bags. I wash them and chop them, the perfume of the fennel filling the room, comforting me already. Then the green beans, the broccoli and cauliflower, the chillies and the shallots. I put them all in a big bowl, cover them in water and add salt. Then I chop the onions, and when my eyes start to prickle, I don't wipe away the tears that fall.

Once I've had a good sob, I pull out my biggest saucepan and add oil. I find the box of spices I've brought from home, and line the jars up on the windowsill. I throw in mustard seeds, cumin, turmeric and nutmeg, just as I remember from Jamie Oliver's best piccalilli recipe. Then I turn down the heat and add mustard powder, flour and a splash of vinegar. The mixture starts to thicken, just as it's supposed to, and I take comfort from having control over something, even if it is only piccalilli. I top up the vinegar and add water. The smell hits my nostrils as the liquid hits the pan, sizzling and spitting with glorious sounds and a spicy aroma. When I used to make this back home, all the flats around where Grandad lived would be full of the smell and I'd have to deliver extra jars to the neighbours to keep them happy.

Whilst the piccalilli is bubbling away, I grab a bottle of water and start to put my other books on the mantelpiece in the living room.

'Ah ha!' I pick up a book triumphantly. I knew it was here somewhere. I give the cover a wipe with my hand and blow off the dust, then sit on the cool flagstone floor, sipping from my bottle. Outside I can still hear the voices from the family get-together next door. Most of the neighbours seem to be there. Although I did notice that there was a similar gathering, with everyone dressed in black, going on at Forno Sophia at the end of the lane. And if I'm not mistaken, it was the other family I'd seen standing on the church steps. One funeral, two wakes by the looks of it. Unusual, I think as I flick through my gardening book, trying to identify anything I've seen in the vegetable plot at the side of the house. What about that big prickly bush that looks like something from *The Jungle Book*? Could it be that? I look at a picture of a bush that's apparently a rhododendron. Maybe this book is only for British plants. I don't have a clue. It's pretty, though, the bush; I wonder if it would make a nice picture for a Mother's Day card.

I think back to the emails from Brandon. I really need to start work on something for him this evening. I can't afford to cheese him off any more. And the quicker I get something out to him, the quicker I'll get some money in. I decide to take my camera outside and photograph a few plants to put into a design.

I scramble to my feet and grab my camera and the book. I push open the big glass doors at the back of the house, and pick my way tentatively through the undergrowth and out to the vegetable plot. I just hope there aren't any snakes in this long grass.

Marco leaned back against the trunk of the big olive tree and let out a huge sigh, allowing his shoulders to drop and his hands to fall to his sides. His head tipped back to touch the bark of the tree too. He stared at the big house. The walls that had once been terracotta red were now faded and peeling. He couldn't believe how much it had deteriorated since the last time he'd been here. But when had that been? Months turned to years so quickly. All the time he'd been away, he hadn't had to think about this place. But now that he was back, it brought it all home as if it was yesterday.

He didn't have time to come back. His life in Naples was so busy. When he wasn't teaching and working hands-on in the research laboratories, there were lectures to give on tastings and growing patterns, not to mention the articles he wrote for British food magazines. The British seemed obsessed with the Italian way of life. But he wasn't complaining: there was plenty of work for an English-speaking olive oil expert. And now he'd had an offer to write a whole book on the subject. He ran his fingers through his hair. He just needed the time to do it. At the moment, he barely saw the inside of his apartment.

He needed to find a way to put things right for his

family. Once this was settled, he'd be able to go back to his work, his life in Naples, with peace of mind. They deserved to have something from the old man's estate after everything that had happened.

Everyone had been affected by what Marco's father had done, his grandfather more than most. He'd had to watch his own family divide and fall apart. He had died knowing that his life's work, the estate where they'd all grown up, had been carved up and sold off. If only his father hadn't been such a greedy man. Marco rolled his hands into fists. The estate had been making a name for itself, but Marco's father hadn't been content to let things grow slowly; he'd wanted change, and fast. New house, new car. Maybe he'd thought his family would love him more if he could give them those things. He'd forgotten what was really important in life: his family and this place. Marco felt the familiar stirrings of anger as he remembered the day it had all come to an end. The local businessmen and their men had turned up. They'd found out about his father selling the watered-down oil, sending it abroad, making fast money for a fake product, cheapening the name of the area and its good reputation.

He didn't know who his father had been more worried about, the authorities, the local Mafia or the business contacts he'd conned. It certainly wasn't his family. Marco remembered the look on his grandfather's face, the look of disbelief that his son could do this to the family name. His brother had stopped speaking to him there and then. And then he'd disappeared, leaving his family to face the shame. Filippo had only been a baby then. Their father had died some years later in a road traffic accident in the north. Marco, an angry teenager, hadn't shed a tear. Not like his grandfather, who had wept for everything that had been lost.

Marco, like his cousins, who were strangers to him, had moved away at the first opportunity. He had helped his grandfather on the farm up until that point, but when an opening at the college came up, he fled too. He loved his family but he had a life to live. His grandfather, desperate to keep the family together, gave all his grand-children parcels of land in an effort to keep them in Della Terra, but as the estate became more and more divided, so did the family.

It was never going to put right what had gone on, but maybe if the house was back in the family they could all decide what to do with it, how it should be divided, and then get on with their lives, finally move on. His sister could move into town, even start up her own restaurant. Filippo could go to England as he'd always wanted to. Marco was sure the cousins would want to sever ties with this place too. But first he had to get the *masseria* back into the family, for all their sakes. He wished he'd seen his grandfather before he died. He shouldn't have left it so long between visits. He would visit Nonna and Mamma more often from now on.

He felt that anger rise in him again. If only his grandfather had told him he was in trouble. He could've helped. After all, it was because of his father that the trouble had started in the first place. He should've been given the chance to try and put it right. He clenched and unclenched his fists, looking up into the boughs of the silver and green olive tree.

As for this Ruthie Collins, he couldn't make her out at all. He felt bad. Maybe he'd been a bit hard on her. But she didn't look like she'd come here to turn the place back into an olive business again. Most of the tourists who bought here thought that a bit of sun and good food would put right all their problems, but problems had a habit of following you wherever you went.

The little fawn dog crept up behind him and lay down at his feet. He smiled and bent to stroke her head.

Having said that, there weren't many people he knew who would do what she'd done: take on a house like this, in a country they didn't know. She was either very brave or as mad as they came. He straightened up and watched her coming out of the house, tiptoeing through the long grass with a camera and a book. He found himself smiling. Either brave or mad, and he still had no idea which.

She was definitely intriguing, he thought, and attractive. He liked her spirit. She excited him. She was determined and feisty. In another time, another place, he would have liked to ask her to dinner, find out more. With a thud, he realised this was the first woman he had actually found attractive in a very long time. Maybe it was grief playing tricks with his mind. He shook his head. He needed to get this business sorted quickly. There was no way he could let her get under his skin, no way at all. Much as he'd like to find out more about what made Ruthie Collins tick, he needed to keep her at arm's length.

He could hear his mother calling him. He turned

towards the house. She probably didn't need him; she just liked the fact he was here. She wanted them all to live here, but life just wasn't like that. He'd stay until the business with the *masseria* was sorted, then he'd have to go back to Naples. He would need to raise some money, but no one was giving out loans these days. He had to try, though. After all, hadn't Ruthie Collins said today that she was happy for him to buy it back from her? She'd obviously realised she'd made a mistake. She'd be pleased to go. He'd go round and sort it in the morning.

He watched her with her book again, trying to sort out what was what in the vegetable plot. She didn't even know one type from another. How did someone like that ever think they could manage an olive grove? He shook his head. Definitely madness, he thought. A smile tugged at the corners of his mouth, surprising him. Then he shook his head again, reminding himself: *Arm's length. Remember: arm's length*. Life was complicated enough already. But what was she up to? He couldn't help but wonder. She was obviously oblivious to him being there. The last thing he wanted was to scare her by moving suddenly. He'd just wait until she spotted him, make polite conversation and then move away quickly. Like the voice in his head kept saying: *Arm's length*.

From the back door here I can see my land . . . *my land*, I repeat slowly in my head. To the left of the *masseria* there's some scrubland and then another olive grove even more overgrown than mine. On the right there is a falling-down stone wall and on the other side of it more olive trees, only here there's not a weed or bramble in sight. The ground is deep reddish brown, like the colour of hennaed hair, and has little grooves in it like someone's carefully combed it. The party next door is in full swing. The guests have moved from standing around with glasses of Prosecco to sitting outside the back of the house at tables laid with white cloths. The *forno* is chugging out smoke and the smell of aromatic herbs and cooking meat makes my mouth water. Every now and again I hear Anna-Maria's voice giving out instructions, and I relish the sound of the language that I fell in love with on that college trip.

I look back out to my land. I can just see a table and chairs under the big listing olive tree right in front of me, offering shade with its big branches. I might even hang a hammock there. Because as lovely as they are to look at, I don't think I'll be doing much with the olive trees. I certainly won't be combing the ground around them. I've got enough to do with the house.

I hear a noise behind me and turn.

'Hey, Daphne,' I say, and she trots up behind me and tentatively nudges me. I rub her in between the ears, then turn back to the vegetable plot. It's very overgrown, but I manage to walk round it, stumbling in parts over brambles and divots. I spot what I think might be onions, and peppers, though I'm not advanced enough to be able to identify types. But I have no idea what these bushes are, especially that one from *The Jungle Book*. I'm flicking to and fro in the book.

'Prickly pear.' A voice startles me and makes me jump, and then my heart sinks. I'd recognise that deep, disapproving tone anywhere. Marco Bellanuovo has a very strange effect on me; a bit like coffee. It smells nice and is fine in small doses, but otherwise it makes me sweat and my heart race and gives me a headache. He's on the other side of the wall, his hands in his pockets, leaning on an olive tree, looking up at the house.

'Sorry?' I bristle and stiffen. I probably shouldn't even get into conversation with him, but I can't help it. How dare he? 'Are you talking to me? What did you call me? Excuse me!' I persist as he stares up at the *masseria*. Honestly, it's like being back in school. Well, I didn't like being bullied then, and I'm not going to start now.

He pulls his gaze away from the house and stares straight at me, like he's wondering whether to say it again. Then he straightens up, lazily, as though I'm dragging him away from his favourite TV programme, keeping one hand in his pocket. He walks towards me and I have to remember he's grieving. At my grandfather's funeral there was a punch-up between his best mate and his son over the darts score. I'm thinking that maybe I should just walk away when suddenly he points to the bush.

'It's a prickly pear,' he repeats. 'The tree.'

I look at him blankly, suddenly embarrassed that I was so ready for a row and that I have no idea what a prickly pear is. He takes a hankie from his pocket and reaches over and pulls one of the round purplish fruits from the tree. With a small penknife, he peels away the outer skin and then slices the fruit open and into segments. He holds it out to me.

'Try it,' he says. He's not smiling and I daren't say no.

He takes a slice and bites into it. Hesitantly, I do the same. Then he wipes his chin with the back of his hand. I do the same. He has very blue eyes and he's looking at me as if he's trying to suss me out. I can't blame him for being suspicious. I mean, I rock up here on my own with no obvious skills and a bucketload of foolhardiness. But what about him? What is it about this house that's got him so riled? We stare at each other as we finish sucking on the prickly pear and wiping the juice from our chins. Neither of us letting the other in on what we really want to know.

'Prickly pear,' I confirm. So, not me then, the fruit. 'It's good,' I say. He nods in agreement. I wonder if this is him trying to be neighbourly, and think I should do the same. 'Um, look . . . I know this hasn't turned out the way—'

'Marco!' Anna-Maria calls. He turns.

'Excuse me, I'm needed to help with the cooking,' he says, and is gone.

Well, really! That man is so infuriating, and rude! He wanted to do the neighbourly bit and now I feel like I've been left hanging.

Feeling ruffled, I slam my book shut and head back to the house for my toolkit. That's the last time I try and make small talk with Marco Bellanuovo. I have a ceiling to sort out.

I stalk round to the *trullo*, checking the barn as I go. I notice that the milk and egg has gone from the dish, and *mamma* cat is licking her paws contentedly in her bed in the nets. But she hisses at me anyway.

The sound of chatter from next door is very much muted on this side of the house. At least I won't be able to hear the laughter as Marco tells them how I was trying to immerse myself in Italian life with the help of a Dr David Hessayon self-help book and a camera. I find an old wooden fruit-picking ladder in the barn and take it to the *trullo* along with the toolbox, determined to lose myself in work and not think about the flat above the gallery with the view of the sea where I wrote my name in the sand in my mind and now am watching it being washed away by the rising tide.

That night, after an afternoon of rubbing down and filling in the cracks in the *trullo* roof, I open my laptop and start work on some designs for Brandon. But while seagulls and white weatherboarded cottages play out in my mind, on paper I'm doodling *trulli* and prickly pears.

Chapter Ten

Judging by the cool air and the mist rising off the olive trees when I push open the shutters early in the morning, it must have rained again in the night, leaving puddles of water everywhere. August has turned to September and this is an unwelcome reminder that autumn is waiting just around the corner.

It's been two weeks since the funeral, and I'm beginning to find my way around. I've dragged an old iron bed into my makeshift bedroom, and I'm using a wooden barrel from the barn as a living room table, complete with a small lamp. I've bought a three-piece suite off the man in the market, at tourist prices no doubt, and have even treated myself to a new mattress. I've barely seen anyone except for when the delivery truck got stuck in the lane and Anna-Maria and Nonna and the little sheep herder up the road and his son came to offer help, waving hands and shouting directions.

I yawn and stretch, breathing in the wonderful fresh air, and head downstairs for coffee and a slice of focaccia. Sophia at the bakery may be sour-faced, but she makes great focaccia and it is the closest shop to me. Who said food has to be made with love, eh? Certainly not in this case.

I've got into a routine of going into town to pick up bread from Sophia's shop at the end of the lane. The smell in the place is amazing, warm, inviting, like a big cashmere sweater covering you in comfort, which is more than can be said for Sophia. Hard as I try to make conversation, telling her how much I love the small, soft milk rolls I buy for breakfast, or the potato bread that I slice and toast, she never responds. There are jars and jars of brightly coloured sugared almonds behind the counter too. Everything about this shop should shout joy. But Sophia never raises a smile.

I was beginning to think it's just me she doesn't like. Until the other day – market day – when I was standing at the big vegetable stall trying to work out how to order just one punnet of strawberries, *fragola*. It was busy; there were people jostling all around me, talking loudly and shouting their orders. The smell from the strawberries was amazing and sweet. There were only three punnets left, and I knew that the stall owner would make me take all three, bundling them into a bag before I had a chance to tell him I just wanted one. I still hadn't managed to stop him doing that.

I decided to pick up a punnet and have the right money in my hand. That way, he had to understand me. I dug into my bag for my purse, but I only had a ten-euro note. I was going to have to *show* him I only wanted the one. I reached out to pick one up, but as I did, a long arm stretched practically over me and made a grab for all three, calling to the stallholder. I looked at the gold-bangled wrist and knew instantly who it was. That jewellery, those big dark-skinned arms, that perfume, thick, strong and cloying. Anna-Maria. Oh God, now what was I going to do? Was I going to have to fight her off with a cucumber? There had obviously been a run on strawberries that day, and now there was a chance I wouldn't get any.

Almost as soon as her hands were on the punnets, however, another hand came in from the other side, right across my body, making a claim on the same strawberries. I looked down at the fat fingers claiming victory.

'*Scusi!*' I said loudly, waving my ten-euro note at the stallholder, not wanting to be bullied out. I live here too, I thought, and I need to start behaving like I do, rather than like the new girl in the school playground. I could feel the tension around me and looked up to see Anna-Maria's set face. Eyeing me, her expression became more determined than ever, and suddenly I wasn't sure I could fight her. I already had something she wanted: the *masseria*. I stepped sideways to let her through, but as I did, I was blocked by the woman on the other side of me. I turned to see Sophia from the bakery. Her face was set too. I wondered if letting her have the strawberries would encourage her to be more friendly when I next went to her shop.

I looked from one woman to the other. The air around us chilled and I was now completely invisible. The two women glared at each other and I realised it wasn't just me that Sophia had a problem with. It was Anna-Maria as well by the look of it. Then I suddenly remembered the meal at Anna-Maria's, and the funeral. Oh God! Of course, Sophia was Filippo's aunt and Anna-Maria's sister-in-law, and from the face Filippo had pulled and their behaviour at the funeral, they didn't get on.

The cheeky stallholder for once looked uncertain, glancing from Anna-Maria to Sophia. His palms were held out, his shoulders up. He looked like a rabbit caught in the headlights; clearly, both women expected his undivided loyalty. I felt caught in the crossfire and wanted to hold my hands over my head and crouch down until it all passed. But I was stuck. Trapped between two large sets of intimidating bosoms. There was only one thing I could think of doing, and it might have been rash but I wasn't sure of any other way to escape the situation unscathed. I threw my ten-euro note in the direction of the stallholder, who scooped it up gratefully before stuffing all three punnets into a blue bag and handing it to me. '*Grazie, mille grazie,*' I heard him say as I hurried away. I couldn't see the two women, but I knew that their fury was now directed at my back rather than each other as I moved swiftly out of the market and back to my car.

Well, at least I knew why Sophia was so off with me now. If Anna-Maria was incandescent that I'd bought the *masseria*, I'm guessing Sophia was too. It had thrown a hand grenade right into the middle of an already raging war.

I give a little shiver at the memory of 'strawberry-gate' and wonder whether to try and light the fire again. I'm going to have to get to grips with it soon for heat and hot water. I'd give anything for a bath. I wash and wash up with water boiled in the kettle, but that keeps making my hand go funny every time I use it, sort of numb.

I take my breakfast outside and put it down on the

barrel I'm using as a table. The seat is wet from the overnight rain, so I dry it off with a tea towel and sit and enjoy the rising sun on my face. The quiet is breathtaking.

Most days after I've got my groceries I walk to the café to use the internet. Brandon has gone very quiet on me, despite me sending through some Italian designs and lots of cheery emails. I'm starting to worry they're not what he wants at all. Maybe I should take some more pictures today.

Then, the shattering noise of a drill sears through the early-morning peace. I look around, trying to work out where it's coming from. I don't have any close neighbours apart from the Bellanuovos, and I've barely seen any of them since the funeral.

I stand up and strain to see in the direction of the noise, over the overgrown veg patch. It's him, Marco Bellanuovo, at the *trullo* on the other side of the stone wall. I thought he'd gone. He's dressed in jeans and a T-shirt, old ones. The T-shirt is rippling at the back in the tiny hint of a breeze that makes this September morning just gorgeous. Well, it would be if he wasn't taking off the *trullo* door with a large drill and a hammer; and it's not even eight in the morning. I daren't say anything. Instead I march back into the house. He might have a three-coned *trullo*, but I have a single one of my own to be working on, and it's really coming on.

Pulling on light dungarees, and a plain white shirt , I grab my toolbox and my bag of odds and ends from the ironmonger's and head out of the front door. I let Daphne out of her pen and she nearly topples me over with a run and a butt of her head.

'Oomph! Hello to you too!' I laugh once the shock subsides. I rub the top of her head, put down the toolbox and go to feed her. In the corner of the shed, the little grey cat stretches and stands, hoping to be fed too. Her little ones stay tucked behind her as I put some cat food in her bowl.

'At least someone's pleased to see me,' I say, setting down the bucket of feed for Daphne. I run my hand along her back and rub her wiry fur, then pat her behind. She snorts and throws back her head, showering grain everywhere. I step away from her, still not entirely used to her eccentric ways. As I pick up the toolbox and head for my *trullo* to start work, there is still the sound of drilling from next door.

I spent yesterday evening working up some new cards for Brandon and a wedding invitation for a couple getting married next summer. It won't pay much. I need the rental income this *trullo* could bring me from holiday-makers. I'm pleased with how it's looking already, and actually I've loved doing it. The *masseria*'s a big job, but the *trullo* is a perfect project. It's like playing dolls' houses. I can see all the potential. It's like I'm painting a picture and it's turning out just how I wanted it to be.

I'm up a ladder with the overhead lights on full. I adjust my head torch – a Valentine's present from Ed last year when I was thinking of doing a plumbing course. Shame he didn't cook an Italian meal when I went for Italian instead. My arms are aching as I reach up and fill the crack. Thankfully it isn't too high; I've already filled it once and smoothed it over. I'm just going back over it now, really working in the filler. I want to do the best job I can. Then I'll give it another lick of paint.

I decide to take a breather and a slug of water. Outside, the day is warming up, but inside the *trullo* it's really cool. I've got the windows and door open, trying to get rid of the smell of paint and damp. I'm sure it just needs a good airing. I sit on the little plastic chair by the table and look around proudly.

There is a kitchenette on the left as you walk in through the front door, and I've polished up the sink and washed and ironed the curtains over the cupboard below it. Behind that there's a shower. I've regrouted the tiles and put up a new shower curtain. In the main room there's a fireplace, and an alcove beside it like a dome that just fits a bed. I bought a new mattress for here too, and a table and chairs. I'm going to take out the chest of drawers and use it in my bedroom for now. It'll make more space.

It's a perfect little love nest for two, I think. I must get it on to Owners Direct. Trullo Bellanuovo. *Bellanuovo* means beautiful and new. New beginnings! Perhaps I could advertise it as the perfect honeymooners' cottage. I'll plant up some window boxes, and make an outdoor dining area in the courtyard, though first I'm going to have to get it cleared of the overgrown brambles.

I stand up and climb the ladder again, switching my head torch back on. I reach up and press at the filler to see if it's dry. I'm standing on tiptoes, and it occurs to me that if I had an accident, no one would know. It's not as if anyone's going to drop by and check how I'm doing, after all.

Suddenly there's a sharp rap on the front door.

'Hello! *Ciao!*' and a large figure is bending to come into the *trullo*. I jump and grab hold of the ladder. My heart starts its caffeine-style racing and I grip the rung tightly.

'Marco!' I look down at him and blow out a long sigh of relief.

'*Scusi*, I didn't mean to scare you.' He holds up his arm against the glare of my head torch.

'You didn't scare me. I'm just . . . not used to people walking into my house,' I say, bluffing.

'I see you're doing some repairs.' He nods at my handiwork and I feel myself swell a little, pleased that I've made a good job of it and pleased that he's noticed. Not just the silly Englishwoman now, eh?

'Yes, and I hear you've started some of your own,' I reply more sharply than I intended. I'm still on my guard with him. I'm not going to start chatting just for him to wander off again.

'Look, I wonder if I might talk to you,' he says, ignoring my comment.

'I don't think we have anything left to say, do you? You don't like the fact that I bought your family's *masseria*. There's nothing we can do about it, even if we wanted to. The deal has been done and the money has gone.' I spell it out.

He doesn't say anything, and he doesn't move either.

I sigh and turn off the light on my forehead. He slowly lowers his arm. He's holding something in one hand. It looks like a tin. He sees me looking at it and holds it out.

'A peace offering.' He smiles, and it changes his whole

face. He is a very attractive man. I wipe my brow and realise how rough I must look: hot, shiny and not a lick of make-up. Not that it matters, I think quickly. The last thing I want people to think is that I'm looking for a man. Especially after the scowling look I got from Rosa the other night. She's obviously quite possessive over Marco.

I have a red and white spotted bandanna round my head, and I pull it off and wipe my face and hands as I'm coming down the ladder.

'My mother made it.' Marco pushes the tin towards me.

'Leftovers, is it?' I laugh before watching his face fall and realising I've put my foot in it again. 'Sorry,' I mutter. 'British humour.'

He waves away my comment and smiles again.

'It's lemon cake. I thought perhaps we could have coffee and a slice.' He points towards the *masseria*.

I'm on my guard but I don't want to refuse the hand of friendship. I accept the tin.

'*Grazie*,' I say, trying to start over in a more civilised manner. I point the way out of the *trullo*, where he seems to take up a lot of space. He's also holding a bottle. It's deep green in colour. The colour of moss. 'And this,' he holds it out to me, 'is Nonna's secret recipe. A digestif, made with bay.'

'*Grazie*,' I say again, and lead the way back out into the bright sunshine and to the house. I put the tin down on the work surface and try and quickly flick the switch on the kettle so it doesn't make my fingers buzz. This time it does more than make my fingers buzz. It gives me a huge kick and sends me reeling back across the kitchen.

'Shit!'

'*Che cozza?*' Marco is there and grabs my hand. I'm shaking and I feel sick but we both know what's happened.

'Sit, sit. I will get you water,' he says.

I shake my head. 'I'll be fine.'

'You need to get the electrics looked at,' Marco says firmly, still holding my hand. 'I know someone. I'll send him this afternoon. Are you sure you're okay?'

I nod, but I'm not sure if I am actually nodding or just turning my head around.

'Come and sit down. We will have Nonna's digestif instead.' Marco starts to lay up a tray with glasses and the lemon cake. 'Let's take it outside,' he says, and I follow obediently.

'I see you paint,' he says, looking at my work on the big plastic table as we pass.

'Well, I did,' I say, feeling like someone's filled my head with cotton wool. 'I trained as an artist. But these days . . . well, like I said the other day, it's mostly commercial stuff. Design work.' I skim over the fact that actually giving up painting was one of the hardest decisions of my life.

I follow Marco out through the long glass door to my wooden barrel table, under the shade of an old bamboo lean-to roof.

'Are you sure you're okay?' he asks, concerned. I nod again.

'Really, just a bit of a shock,' I say, wondering whether to explain about British humour again.

'So, how are you finding things around here?' he asks, pouring the green gloop.

'Starting to find my way around, thank you.' I sip my water.

'You've started doing the place up. Do you have anyone to help you? Is there a Mr Ruthie Collins following on?' He hands me a slice of cake and a drink and smiles.

'No,' I say simply. 'It's just me.' Briefly I think about Ryan from the ironmonger's and his offer of dinner. I take a sip of the green drink and nearly choke. It's disgusting, the colour and texture of duck poo. I put it down and try the cake, hoping the sugar might help the shock my body's just had.

'It's a lot of work for one person. The olive grove alone . . .' He nods towards the trees.

'Oh, I'm going to get the house sorted first,' I cut in, keen to show him that I have plans and I'm not just here to sunbathe. 'I'll rent out the *trullo* as soon as it's done. This is a beautiful part of the world,' I continue, worried that we're running out of conversation.

'It is. I've been away too long,' he says, crossing his long legs. 'I grew up here, in this house. The olive grove was my playground. It is sad to see it in such a state.'

I bristle, but then realise this is the most we've spoken to each other, ever.

'I should've done something about it ages ago.' He does genuinely look full of regret. His blue eyes are wistful. His jaw twitches under his dark olive skin, just below the little scar on his chin.

'Where have you been?' I ask quickly, keen to keep things on safe ground until the cake and drink are finished and the hand of neighbourliness has been shaken. I bite into the cake. Crikey! It's very dry. I take another sip of the awful green sludge.

'This is really good.' I smile and try, '*Molto bene!*' then wish I hadn't. I don't want to give him another reason to laugh at me. As if reading my thoughts, he hides a chuckle.

'My sister's is better. She uses more olive oil in it.' He nods, and I realise he's laughing not at my Italian, but at the cake. Finally we have something we can agree on.

Marco seems tense. Like he wants to relax but something's stopping him. Well, I'm not stopping him. In fact the sooner he tells me why he's here and leaves, the better. After a little consideration, he answers my question.

'I'm away, teaching. In a college of gastronomy. It's like a food college,' he explains, 'the science of food, for food professionals. From how it is grown to the business of food. I teach about tasting and grading olive oil.'

'What, like a sommelier for olive oil?' I smile, not wanting to but trying the drink again. God, it's awful.

'Exactly that.' He doesn't taste his drink. 'But I'm having some time off, for research. I write for a lot of magazines in the UK, but I have a book to start. And I need to be here for a while, to keep an eye on things, my family . . .' He shrugs.

'So you're staying around for the time being.' My heart sinks even further, maybe partly due to Nonna's awful concoction, that or the electric shock. Now he'll be here watching my efforts with a keen eye. I'll feel like he's waiting for me to mess up.

'I'm doing up the *trullo* . . . it's a good place to work. And to keep an eye on things.' The corner of his mouth twitches, and I think it's an attempt at a smile. See, I knew it! He's going to be watching my every move as I try and find my way around the vegetable patch or get to grips with the goat. He'll be there, laughing at me. I'm not sure I can live like that, knowing he's just the other side of the wall.

As if reading my thoughts he says, 'Actually, I have a suggestion, something that might interest you.'

'Go on, try me,' I say, intrigued.

'Well, I . . .' He hesitates, trying to read me. 'I want to make you an offer, to buy this place from you.'

Without warning, the images of seagulls and Cornish beaches come rushing back into my head.

'You want to buy this place? But I thought . . .'

'The money from the sale of this property has gone. My grandfather should've come to me to help sort out the debts.' His eyes darken. 'It was my debt to pay. I could've helped, got the people he owed off his back. But he was a proud man. Too proud to realise when he'd got himself into trouble, bitten off more than he could chew.' He stares out at the olive grove, obviously finding it very difficult to talk about himself and his family to a stranger. Then he turns back to me, his eyes the colour of the Puglian sky in September. His voice is low, slow and just a tiny bit seductive when he says, 'Would you be interested if I were to make you an offer?'

It must be the sun, the shock or the green digestif; something has suddenly got me all excited. Or maybe it's the prospect of putting this ridiculous blip behind me without having to admit to my mum and Ed that I've made one huge fat mistake and go running home with my tail between my legs. I'm going to Cornwall after all! I must email Beth!

I suddenly feel as if I'm on holiday and enjoying every minute of my time here, rather than stuck here trying to work out how I can make this house my home. Everything looks different. Even Marco looks as though, in a different time and place, he could be a rather appealing prospect.

'To new beginnings,' I say, holding my glass up and clinking it with his. I'm leaving, and I won't ever have to see Marco Bellanuovo again.

Chapter Eleven

'How much?' I splutter into my glass of Nonna's green concoction while holding the cheque he's just handed me with the amount he's offering to pay for the *masseria* in the other hand. I choke, cough and swallow quickly, trying to cover up my embarrassment with my bandanna. The last thing I want is for Marco Bellanuovo to have to perform the Heimlich manoeuvre on me.

He waits until I've finished choking and then says calmly and evenly, 'It's a fair price,' with a flick of his left shoulder. I bang the glass down with more force than I intended, and I'm not sure if he's slightly embarrassed or surprised at my reaction.

'But that's half what I paid for it!'

'I'm sorry it's not more, but I'm afraid I think that's what it's worth,' he says politely. 'In its current state and, well . . . its position.'

'The position is amazing!' I stand up, clearing away the remnants of the lemon cake and signalling the end of our discussion. I should've known it wasn't going to be that simple. I let myself think for a moment that there was a way out of this mess. This house is stunning, its location is stunning. It's just not where I should be. It's a family home with no internet connection, not for one person and their internet business. But of course I'm not selling for that price.

'Just because I'm a single woman, just because I bought the house . . . like I did, it doesn't mean I'm stupid or desperate,' I blurt out, whisking up my glass of duck poo and putting it on the tray to take in.

'I didn't think either of those things.' Marco spreads his hands to emphasise his calmness. But I'm seething. How dare he? First of all he tries to question the validity of my contract, then he tries to track the money down in the hope I'll take it back, and now he's offering to buy the house from me for half what I paid for it. Honestly, this is the end. He's worse than my brother Lance, who'd try and tuck you up as soon as look at you if he thought there was a tenner in it for him. Lance can't wait to hear that I've messed up. He was always taking the mickey out of me for going to college. He'll be delighted when he finds out I've bought a house and been offered half its value within weeks.

'No, I'm sorry, no way,' I say, turning to take the tray into the house. 'I'd rather put it back on the market than take that low offer.'

'There will be very few people interested in buying it, like I say, with its current position.' Marco stands too and looks around at the overgrown land in front of us.

'What are you talking about? It's a fabulous position!' I repeat, hoping he'll take the hint and leave, and then I'm going to get out here with my gardening book and prune all this back. I look at the overgrown veg patch. I'll show him.

'My sister is that way, and my brother and mother . . . and of course then there's the rest of the family, my cousins, they all have pieces of land round and about.'

Oh I wish he'd just go now.

'Look, you may not be the friendliest neighbour I've ever met, and I've met a few. We once had our TV nicked as we were moving into a flat on the second floor. The lift was broken and a lad on our landing was looking for his next fix, but he did apologise later.' I take a deep breath and try and get businesslike again. 'But this is still a fabulous location and, I'm sorry, worth an awful lot more than you're offering,' I say firmly and finally. Our eyes lock on to each other's, his as determined as mine. Neither of us wants to back down.

'Take time to consider my offer,' he says, still staring right at me, his eyes framed by dark lashes and furrowed brows. For a moment neither of us says anything, both standing our ground. The sun feels hot on the back of my neck; it's hitting the ground around us, drying out the overnight rain.

Suddenly there is an almighty crack, like thunder, followed by several more of them. I wonder if it's a *festa* nearby, with fireworks. Very nearby. The noise cuts right through me, making my heart thump. I look around, but there wouldn't be fireworks in the middle of the day. The cracks turn into rips and tears, then a low, deep rumble that keeps rolling and rolling. I look up and Marco looks around. But there's not a cloud in the sky. We both stand up, knocking over the crates that were our seats, and run in the direction of the noise, round the side of the house.

When we reach the doorway to the courtyard, we stand stock still, staring. I catch my breath. Marco is right behind me. His hand touches my forearm. I can feel his breath on my neck and his body up against mine as I block the doorway, holding on to the frame to steady myself. My stomach squeezes and squeezes and a hotness travels up my chest, my neck and into my face. I go to run towards the plumes of dust that are rising from where the *trullo* roof has collapsed, but the large hand grabs the top of my arm and pulls me back.

'Stop! There's nothing you can do. You have to let it finish. It happens round here. The *trulli* roofs are made to collapse. It's an old way of avoiding the taxman. You had window tax, we had property tax. The story goes that when the taxman rode into town, the keystone in the top of the roof was pulled and the roof collapsed. No roof, no tax. Then later on, the *trullo* was rebuilt. It happens. These are old buildings now. Maybe it was the rain that caused the damage. It was very heavy.'

I turn and glare at him and shake him off, my whole body trembling with shock, but I don't try and run towards it again. Instead I stand and watch the plumes of dust and wait until the tumbling and rumbling has stopped. My *trullo* roof has collapsed, and with it all the dreams I had of it being a honeymoon hideaway.

Marco breathes out: 'Phoof!' He leaves a short pause before saying tentatively, 'You might want to reconsider my offer. It's a specialised job getting a *trullo* roof rebuilt.'

I swing round to him, my eyes searching and full of suspicion. What if someone's done this deliberately? It wouldn't have taken much to pull the keystone at the top of the roof. Someone who really wants me out.

'Well how convenient!' I blurt out childishly, tears brimming behind my angry eyes. This can't be happening!

'You can't think I did this.' He holds his hands to his chest and shakes his head. 'It was the rain. The *trullo*'s needed fixing for ages. But then if you'd had a proper inspection done, you'd've known!'

That stings, and my eyes are full and blurry. He's right. I'm an idiot! Everyone told me I was. I just didn't want to hear it.

'Maybe it was the repair work on the ceiling inside,' he continues. 'Like I say, they are skilled craftsmen, the *trulli* men. And expensive unless you know someone who can do it.'

I feel totally beaten. I tried. I tried to make a new life for myself. Take a bold step, strike out on my own, step out from Ed's shadow, but I blew it. I completely blew it.

'It would make sense to do a deal,' he says quietly and actually quite kindly. 'The house now, it's worth even less. Do you want to shake on it?'

So that's it. He wins. He wants my house and now he's going to get it, because if I have to have that roof repaired, it will take every bit of my savings. I'll have nothing left to live on.

'Take your time, think about it,' I hear him say as I turn and push past him into the house. I slam the door shut with him on the outside and then promptly run through the house to the table outside where he's left his untouched green sludge. I pick it up and take a huge gulp, and then another. It's still disgusting, but it's no more than I deserve. Ed's words are ringing in my head: 'You'll never be able to do it. It's just a dream. That's your problem: you always were a dreamer.'

Chapter Twelve

I ignore the first couple of knocks on the front door and then finally on the third knock I yank it open, ready to tell Marco to leave me alone and stop harassing me.

'I really hope you don't mind me popping over like this. I tried to ring . . .'

'Oh, um . . . no signal,' I say, trying to recover myself and waving the phone from my pocket weakly at Lou. 'Only out the front on the wall, or on the balcony upstairs. Come in,' I add. Lou's standing on my front doorstep with armfuls of goodies. She comes into the big dining room and goes straight to the pictures on the table.

'Oh, you're a painter?'

'Not really. I design greeting cards – well, I hope I still do. My boss is finding it hard getting hold of me and I may just have burnt my last bridge.'

'It can't be very easy not having good internet access, what with you needing to work. It's pretty shocking round here. The café's your best bet, but I don't know how much longer we'll be there.'

'No! Why? What happened?'

She takes a deep breath as if this is the first time she's said it. 'The tourists are going home,' then she chokes a little, 'and the landlord has put the rent up.' Another big breath. 'My husband can't afford it.'

'That's terrible,' I say, feeling bad about my own worries. These people have a child to support. I can go home and sleep on my mum's settee if need be. What will they do?

'We still have my job at the school, but it's only part time.' She looks different from last time. Worried.

Today is just getting worse. I want to hug her, but we really don't know each other that well. I put my hand on her forearm.

'Look, I won't stay if you're . . .' she looks at me and she must notice my swollen eyes, 'busy,' she says tactfully. She runs her eyes up and over the ceiling, taking in the fabulous stonework and maybe distracting herself from her own worries. Then she looks back at the table, my computer, and the few designs I've produced. I was sure they would've been perfect for Brandon, but apparently he wants gondolas and Tuscan landscapes. I'm nowhere near gondolas or Tuscany!

'Look, I'll just leave these and go.' She unloads the contents of her arms and puts the gifts on the table. 'Just some lavender soap I made, sun-dried tomatoes and some of our olive oil, of course. Just to get you started,' she says quickly, looking like she's feeling she's imposing.

'Gosh, that's so kind! No, please do stay,' I say quickly. 'In fact, you'd be doing me a very big favour.' It's my turn to take a deep breath. 'I'm beginning to think I haven't seen a friendly face for what seems like forever.' My mind flicks back to Marco's determined one when I told him his offer was too low. I push it out of my mind and smile at Lou.

'Well, only if you're sure,' she says, putting her basket on the floor.

'Absolutely. I'm really sorry about . . . when you got here. I thought it was someone else,' I say, rubbing nervously at the tiny diamond stud in my left nostril.

'Been a bit tough, has it?' Lou looks as if she can feel my pain. I nod and don't trust myself to speak.

'Look, you grab the glasses and the cheese and show me the bottle opener,' she says, waving a bottle of rosé and the jar of sun-dried tomatoes at me and scooping up a loaf from her basket. 'This way?' She points to the shaded patio out the back and I smile widely and nod, happy to let her organise us. I run into the kitchen to grab a tray with cutlery, plates and glasses.

'Oh wow! This is fabu— What is that noise?' she says as a whining and drilling shatters the peace again.

I point in next door's direction as I put the cheese on the tray and follow Lou outside.

'I'm not sure what's going on. He's doing something to the old *trullo* in the olive grove over there.' I nod in the direction of our adjoining wall.

'What? The Bellanuovos?'

I nod, putting down the tray and nipping back in for a bottle of water.

'I didn't think any of them were interested in doing anything on the land. They were all too busy waiting for the old man to die so they could take their inheritance and leave, like the other side of the family have done.' She sits down on the crate where Marco was earlier and I sit opposite, laying out cheese, glasses, plates and a sharp knife. The sun is hotter now, but underneath the bamboo covering it's lovely and shaded.

'It's Marco. I'm not sure what he's doing over there.'

'Hmm,' says Lou, opening the wine and pouring while I cut the bread. The smell rises up and somehow makes the stresses of the day just a little bit easier. I breathe in the warm, comforting aroma.

'Oh wow! Sophia's?' I ask as I open my eyes.

'Of course.' Lou smiles and helps herself to a hunk of cheese.

'I don't think Sophia approves of me being here. I think it's the only thing she and Anna-Maria have in common.' We both laugh. 'But Sophia's bread is the best around.' I sniff the rosemary and black olive focaccia again and my mouth waters.

'Ah, so you've worked out that Sophia is Anna-Maria's sister-in-law. They don't speak. The families haven't spoken since I moved here.' Lou fills me in matter-of-factly.

'That's why they had two wakes on the day of the funeral?' I'm loading my plate with cheese and tomatoes.

Lou nods and drizzles the olive oil she brought over her tomatoes.

'So what caused that?' I ask. 'Must have been something pretty big.'

'No idea.' Lou shakes her head. 'No one talks about it, not to me anyway. Some family fall-out. All I know is that there were two brothers: Marco's father and his brother. They've both died now, but whatever the argument was about, it's been going on for years.' She takes a big bite of bread. 'But Sophia's focaccia is the best.'

I tear off a corner of the bread. 'Oh yes,' I agree and sink my teeth through the salty crust. Then I try the spicy cheese, which makes my gums tingle. I take a slug of wine.

'So, what's been happening with you and the Bellanuovos?' Lou asks, topping up my wine.

I let out a long sigh. 'Marco came round to offer to buy the place from me this morning,' I say, suddenly feeling so much better for just sharing with someone.

Lou shrugs in an Italian way.

'And do you want to sell?'

I falter and put my bread down on my plate.

'Well, not to him . . . I mean, not for what he offered anyway,' I gabble. She says nothing. 'He offered me half what I paid for it.'

'Would you have taken it if he'd offered you a good price?'

'I . . . I . . .' I know that if I let out anything of what's going on in my head right now, it could all come tumbling out.

'Oh, wait.' I run into the house and come back out with a jar of my piccalilli.

'Piccalilli!' Lou squeals. 'I haven't had that in ages!'

'Here, there's a jar to take home too,' I say, putting the piccalilli in front of her and then settling back ready to tell her my thoughts. 'I got offered a job, a good one. I love this place,' I hold a hand out to the house, 'but, well, it's a good job. It would've suited me. Put it like this, I think I may have rushed at this. And frankly, I want to go home.'

'But it's beautiful, there's so much you could do here.' Lou looks around, her passion rising, and I'm delighted she gets it and can see why I came. 'I mean, out here is gorgeous, but the house itself is to die for, and then you've got the *trullo* and the olives . . .'

'Ah, the *trullo*. Well that's what I was depending on,' I shuffle on my crate, 'but the roof collapsed this morning.'

'Oh,' she says, and pours more wine. 'We have a *trullo*, six cones, up the lane here, next to Luigi's place.'

'Who's Luigi?'

'He has the *trullo* next to us but lives in town. He's the local goat man. Him and his son, Young Luigi. They look after the sheep and goats out this way and some of the land for people too.'

'Yours is the one for sale?' I realise, and Lou nods.

'I'd love to do what you're doing, but we just don't have the money or the time to renovate it at the moment. *Trullo* roofs are a skilled job.' She sips her wine thoughtfully.

'So how do you find it being here? Would you ever go home?' I ask, wanting to put off thinking about the *trullo* roof.

'No.' She shakes her head. 'My boy's Italian now. I won't go back to the UK. Not unless we have to. Everything changes. Nothing's how it used to be when you left it. Of course his mother's a nightmare, even checks to see if I've ironed his underpants, but at least they're great with our son and I can work. Like I say, I won't go back unless . . .' she takes a breath and a sip of wine, 'unless we have to.'

'That's great that you teach in the school. So brave.'

'I don't know about brave,' she laughs, 'but it fits in well with family life, and I love working with the kids. But what about you? How did you end up here? You never said,' she says, stabbing her fork into the piccalilli. 'Do you have friends or family here?'

I dip my bread into the glistening green pool of olive oil around the tomatoes.

'No, no one,' I say, and suddenly it feels very real and really quite lonely.

'So how did you end up buying the Bellanuovos' *masseria*? I didn't think they'd ever sell it. Oh,' she holds up her hands, 'tell me to shut up, I'm too nosy for my own good. Really, don't let me come round here asking questions. It's none of my business.'

'No, it's fine,' I say, pouring more wine. 'The thing is, well, Ed and I, my partner, we split up. After his pug died, we realised we didn't have much in common really. We never did, I don't think.'

'His pug?' Lou looks incredulous. I realise now that it does sound bizzare.

'Uh-huh,' I nod. 'Dudley.'

'Dudley the pug?' Lou asks.

I nod again. 'We'd both known it for a long time before that. But somehow we just sort of limped on. Taking the dog out together was part of our daily routine. Like everything else we did together. Which side of the bed we slept on, which cereal bowl he ate out of, what we bought in the supermarket and how we divided the bills.'

Lou sits back in her chair and listens.

'Once Dudley was gone, everything else seemed to collapse with it. Suddenly I couldn't stand the way he always ate his cereal from the same bowl. I didn't want to sleep on the left of the bed and I was fed up with the same shopping and the same bills. It was all pointless. When he talked about getting another dog, I knew I had to leave before we started the cycle all over again.'

'*That* was brave,' she bats back at me. 'I mean, it's easier to take risks when you have nothing to lose.'

'No, I'd been a coward for too long. I should have ended it sooner.'

'How did Ed take it?' Lou picks up her glass and leans back again.

'It took him a while to accept it. He went very silent for a couple of weeks, but really he knew it was over too. Once we agreed that things weren't working any more, he packed a bag and moved in with his work colleague Annabel, at first just as a lodger. But it wasn't long before I realised they were starting to become more of an item. That hurt. The fact that he could move on so quickly. Soon after that, he put the flat on the market.'

'Blimey, it does seem a bit quick.'

'Well, Ed likes things straightforward and filed in their place.'

'So, you had to move out?'

'Yes, pack up, sell up and move out. Ed didn't want anything from the flat. Annabel's place is in Canary Wharf. Doubt they have room for a full-size fridge there, let alone all the furniture we'd bought for the Tooting place.'

'Couldn't you have kept it and moved into another flat?'

I shake my head, brushing crumbs from my lap. I catch a glimpse of the small grey cat tiptoeing through the grass.

The sun is hot and high now, and the building noise from next door has stopped.

'Prices in London are just so high. There was no way I'd've been able to buy another place. And frankly, the thought of going back to renting a room in a flatshare just left me cold.'

'So . . .' Lou's still trying to put the story together.

'So once the flat was sold, not only was I single, but I was, well . . . homeless. And I didn't have the sort of job where I needed to go to the office every day. I didn't have any roots. My best friend lives miles away, and my other friends are great but they've got jobs of their own, and families. I just didn't feel I belonged anywhere, even though I've lived in south London all my life. I felt as if I'd been cut adrift.'

I sigh and cup my hands around my glass.

'On my last night in the flat, my friend Morag was staying with me. That's when I decided to do it, to buy this place. The next day, I moved into my mum's. That's why I needed the sale to happen quickly, and so did the seller.'

'But it was never on the market. We'd've all known . . .' Lou is becoming more and more intrigued. I might as well tell her, I think, because it's not like I'm going to be staying. I've decided. As lovely as this lunch is, I certainly don't feel I belong here, and I'm never going to fit in. I know what I'm going to do now.

'I bought it on eBay,' I say, and sit back and watch Lou's jaw drop.

Finally she says, 'On eBay!'

'Yup,' I say, and smile, holding my glass to my lips. 'I bought it on eBay,' and my smile turns to a laugh.

'That's bonkers!' Lou shrieks hysterically, not looking at all Italian now, but like a girl from Cardiff when Wales have scored the winning try. Her accent has got stronger and stronger with each sip that's slipped down.

Now it's my turn to shrug. It didn't seem that mad at the time.

'I couldn't afford a place to live in London, but I could afford one here. I'd been selling our furniture on eBay, the three-piece suite, the fridge freezer, even the bed. And then I saw it . . . It came up as an advert and I just clicked on it.'

'What? And you just thought "I'll buy that"?'

'No.' I shake my head, feeling a wonderful sense of release. 'It reminded me of when I came out here as a student. I was happy then. I thought anything was possible. I thought I'd feel the same if I came back. So I just thought I'd put in a bid, see what happened . . .' I trail off.

Lou looks at me and narrows her eyes.

'Had you been drinking?'

Not for the first time today I nearly choke on my drink, but this time it's with a full-blown laugh.

'You had, hadn't you?'

'Okay, okay.' I put up my hand. 'I'd been out with Morag and our friend Elinor. It was Morag's birthday. When we got in, I was checking my eBay account to see who'd won the wide-screen TV and the tropical fish tank, because I'd have to arrange the delivery.'

'Tropical fish tank?' She screws up her nose.

'It was Ed's. I bought it for him when Dudley died.'

At that moment Daphne strolls round and lies down on the terrace beside us as if it's the most natural thing in the world to have a pet goat at your feet. Suddenly a fish tank doesn't seem so strange.

'We'd had a meal at the local Italian. Morag came back with me and stayed over instead of catching the night bus home. We were finishing up the peach brandy, and there it was.'

Lou has her hand over her mouth, like she's never heard anything so mad or impetuous.

'It was either that or a long stretch on my mum's couch. At the time it seemed like a good idea.'

'So you just bid on it?'

'Uh-huh.' I nod, picking at the crumbs around the cheese.

Lou suddenly stands up and goes across to a vine growing over a tumbledown pergola. She picks a bunch of grapes, pours some water over them and puts them by the cheese.

'It was a bit of fun really. We were just wondering if it would be possible to change your life with a click of the button.'

'And you did, oh my God!'

'We went to bed. I forgot about it. Then the next morning I went to check the computer and there it was: "Congratulations! You were the successful bidder!"'

'You didn't think about trying to get out of it?'

'I did. But I wanted to show Ed, and my mum, that I could do something on my own.'

For a moment Lou is speechless, then she says, 'And what are you going to do now?'

'I'm going to sell it, just not to Marco Bellanuovo. But he did give me the idea. If I saw it and bought it, there must be plenty more people out there who are looking for a property like this. Who knows, I might even make a profit.' I smile. 'I'm going to put it back on the market, on eBay even.'

Lou's face drops.

'But what about the *trullo* roof? That could put a dampener on the sale. People might want to rent it out, like you did.'

She's right. 'I'll have to see about getting it repaired.' It'll mean all of my savings, every bit of money from the sale of the furniture from the flat. But if it gets me to back to the UK . . . so be it.

To my surprise, just as we're finishing lunch, an electrician turns up. Marco rang him and instructed him to check all the electrics in the house. He works in the ironmonger's and does odd jobs in his spare time. He inspects the wiring, sucks air through his teeth, apparently a universal language, and starts work. There's no way I can sell this house knowing the electrics are faulty. When he leaves, he tells me he'll be back, and I thank him and hand him some piccalilli, much to his consternation. I have to get rid of it all before I go. Because I'm selling up and moving on, and Marco Bellanuovo and his family will be someone else's problem.

Chapter Thirteen

Fuelled by friendship, laughter and rosé wine, and by being able to make a coffee without electrocuting myself, I march down the drive towards the Bellanuovos' with Marco's cheque in my hand. I also need to find out how much I owe the electrician. It's my house, my problem.

It's cooler now. Lou has gone, and I feel a huge weight has been lifted off my shoulders and gone with her.

I lift and pull back the heavy iron gates, still listing on their hinges, and make a mental note to put them on my list of things to repair. Then I take a deep breath and set off down Anna-Maria's drive, along the side of the house and towards the olive grove at the back. Daphne is trotting up and down on the other side of the wall, looking indignant that she's not privy to what's going on. A small cream and white dog comes hurtling round the corner, followed by her crew. Big, small, really small. They all stand and bark at me, and I freeze. Maybe this wasn't such a good idea. Daphne seems intent on getting in on the act and is pawing at the wall. I take a couple of steps back – yes, one step forward and two back; the irony of it isn't lost on me. It's a bit like my life right now. The only way out seems to be to sidestep the dogs and jump over the wall. There's a bit of a drop the other side, but I think it may be my only option.

I shuffle sideways, the dogs still barking. As I stretch out my hand, I can feel Daphne's nose snuffling in my palm. I put a foot up on the wall, and stones tumble and fall. I don't want to take my eyes off the pack getting closer and closer to me.

Suddenly there's a whistle and a shout. The dogs stop barking just like that and turn and run back from where they came. My heart's racing even though they've gone. Maybe I should just leave anyway. I put the cheque in my pocket, but then look back at the *trullo* where the noise has been coming from all day. Anna-Maria is standing looking out of the window of the house, beneath the red and white awning. Daphne bleats. I look back at Anna-Maria, who turns away, and I swear there's a tiny smile in the corner of her mouth. That's it. I decide I won't be scared off by a gang threatening a sharp bite. Not the dogs, not the Bellanuovos.

I straighten up and march towards the *trullo*, but when I reach the end of the drive, there's no path, just earth. Looks like my cream deck shoes aren't going to last long. But this is no time to be faint-hearted. I take a first bold step, and my foot sinks into the damp, thick, heavy reddish-brown earth, the colour of dark terracotta. It smells, but not in a bad way: earthy, rich and full of minerals. The sort of thing I could see Beth getting all animated over and wanting to run her hands through and inhale.

After the first step, there's only one way to do this. I

stomp across the earth, clumps gathering round my feet, which are getting heavier and heavier. By the time I reach the low doorway of the *trullo*, I feel like Bigfoot, the yeti. I hold on to the crumbling door frame and bang my heels, and tiny bits of stone fall away from the wall. I immediately let go of the frame and try and scrape the mud away instead. Given my current record for property falling down when I touch it, I don't want anything else to collapse around me.

'*Ciao!*' I call into the dark room. Then I try 'Hello!' because it just seems a more natural thing to go hand in hand with walking into someone's home unannounced.

The *trullo* has three cones. The walls are uneven. On one side there is a stone stairway up the outside of the building, leading to the roof. Unlike mine, these roofs are still intact. There is a solid white surround round the front door. The tops of the cones are grey concrete but may have once been painted white. They have decorative balls on the top too. Across the doorway there's a piece of wood, presumably to stop any dogs or goats wandering in. I step over it, dropping lumps of soil from my shoes as I do.

'Hello!' I try again, and just like when I first arrived at the *masseria*, my eyes are immediately drawn upwards to the unique ceiling. The cream stones are exposed here, unlike in mine, which was plastered – 'was' being the operative word. They form perfect lines, working their way round and up to the tip of the cone. I turn around as I stare and marvel at the craftsmanship. To one side of this main room is a wide archway and to the other side a low corridor. The floor is rough rubble and there are alcoves in each of the walls of various sizes.

'Hello?' I try again and duck down through the corridor, running my hand along the cool stone wall. I feel like Alice disappearing down the rabbit hole, and wonder what I'll find at the other end. There's another conical roof, this time smaller, with an archway, a deep one, just big enough for a double mattress. There are tools and cut stone on the floor, and by the looks of it a new doorway has been knocked through. I poke my head through the opening, wondering if Marco is here. But I can't see him anywhere, just a large pile of rubble and a small dome-shaped room with small windows but no frames.

'*Buongiorno, posso aiutarla?*' I recognise the voice behind me but it still makes me jump and bang my head as I quickly turn back into the room, feeling like a snooper.

'Oh, um, *buongiorno*, um, I was just . . .' and I have no idea why I'm feeling quite so tongue-tied. I have come to find him, after all. 'I, er . . .' I clear my throat and straighten myself up, giving my head a quick rub. 'I was looking for you.'

'And you've found me,' he says, looking vaguely amused. He's looking very different as well, in combat trousers and lace-up boots splattered with whitewash. His loose T-shirt is covered in stone dust. His dark wavy hair has a light dusting in it too.

He puts his hands on his hips.

'This is becoming a habit, me finding you in my family's property. You're not going to tell me you own this one too, are you?' he says, amused, and I'm furious that he seems to make me feel like a silly schoolgirl.

'No, sorry, I . . . knocked. I thought maybe you couldn't hear me.' I put out a hand to lean against something and knock over a sweeping brush. 'Sorry, sorry . . .' I tail off. What on earth is wrong with me? I look around. I can't help myself, I have to say something.

'This place is really amazing,' I tell him. 'But then you probably know that already. People must say it all the time.' He shrugs, with what I assume to be indifference. I'm stunned. 'You do think it's amazing, don't you?'

'I suppose we're just used to having them here. Tourists are fascinated by them. We seem to forget what we have.' He wipes his hands on a cloth. 'It needs work, but it'll do me for now.'

'For now? People pay a fortune to stay in something like this.' I look around again, imagining it finished, in soft whites and greys.

'What, people like you?' He raises a dark eyebrow.

'Sorry?' My back suddenly stiffens up and I'm not tongue-tied any more. In fact, I'm quite clear about what I want to say. 'What do you mean, people like me?'

'People who think the sun and wine will solve all their problems.'

'No! I came here because I always wanted to live in Italy and I . . . saw a window of opportunity and went for it.'

'And now? Maybe you're not so pleased you "went for it"?'

'Like I say, I realise there might be somewhere else I should be.'

'What? Home?' He raises that eyebrow again.

We stare at each other stubbornly. I know I should just back down and tell him he's right. That's always been my problem. It's the reason Ed and I stayed together so long. I was too stubborn to admit we just weren't right for each other. I thought I could just keep working at it and it would finally come good.

'Have you always loved old houses?' He suddenly breaks the moment.

'I'm not sure.' I'm thrown for a moment but regain my composure. 'I've only ever lived in flats, purpose-built blocks, y'know. Even the last one was an ex-local-authority flat, just in a good location, for London. But I guess I've always wanted to renovate a house, make it a home again.'

'Put the heart back into it, you mean.' Those intense blue eyes look straight at me again, and my heart starts banging, riled. I have no idea why this man has this effect on me.

'I just meant that I wanted to take something that had been neglected and turn it back into a home. This place came up and I thought I could do it . . . until my roof collapsed, that is.'

'But a home isn't a home just by its decoration. A home is a home because of the heart that's in it.'

Oh now he wants to argue about my use of the word 'home'. He really is too much.

'I've come to tell you that—'

'You're going to accept my offer.' He folds his arms across his chest and a smile tugs at the corner of his mouth.

'That I've decided to sell after all.' I cross my arms pointedly too.

'Well, that is good news. Please let's discuss it over a

drink.' He leads the way back through the low corridor, and I watch as the top of his head brushes the low roof.

'No, I don't think you understand,' I explain as I duck through after him.

'Mamma will be delighted. And Nonna. I believe this is the right thing for all of us, especially now the *trullo* roof needs repairing, and of course with its position.'

There he goes again, banging on about the position. He's gathering up dust sheets from a table and chairs and carrying them out into the sunshine.

'Wait, please, you don't understand,' I say again.

He stops suddenly and turns to me, still holding the table.

'I think I do. You said you will sell; you'll accept my offer, no?'

'No.' I shake my head, frowning and squinting in the sudden sunlight now that I'm outside. This is harder than I thought it was going to be.

'First I need to get the *trullo* roof fixed, and then I'm going to sell the *masseria*.' I hold my hand up against the sun's rays as I explain.

He puts the table down. 'I'm perfectly capable of fixing the roof. I've been looking after *trulli* since I was a boy. I'll get on to my cousin's husband, the lawyer, and get the paperwork sorted. You've made a very sensible decision, really.'

I *am* being sensible. I'm selling up and going home. But I can't help but feel very, very flat. I take a deep breath, determined to get it out this time.

'I am going to have the roof fixed and then I'm going

to sell the *masseria*, but not to you. Not for that price.'
I hold out the cheque.

He looks at it and then back at me. This time it's his turn to frown.

'Then who are you going to sell it to?'

'I'm going to put it back on the market. If I wanted it, someone else will. I have a friend who knows someone who helps British buyers find holiday homes. She's contacting him for me.' I hope Lou's been able to speak to him like she said she would after our lunch, and that he's agreed to take my place on.

Marco looks down at the cheque. I notice there's a faint shake in my hand. Then he looks back at me. He smiles suddenly, a lopsided, lazy smile in the corner of his mouth, and then his shoulders shudder. He's laughing!

'I don't think you heard me right. I am selling, but not to you, Marco,' I repeat, confused by his reaction. I glare at him as if trying to prove to Ed and my family that I'm not going down without a fight. 'No deal!'

'I tell you what,' he replies quietly and oddly gently, 'hang on to that cheque until you're ready to sell.'

What! What's wrong with this man? I bang the cheque down furiously on the table and march away. I'm not accepting his offer! No way! I'd rather sell to anyone other than Marco Bellanuovo. I slip and slide across the field, thick clods of earth clinging to my feet, slowing me down, and leave red footprints on Anna-Maria's white stone drive, giving her yet another reason to hate me.

Chapter Fourteen

I stomp back up my drive, shaking off the rest of the thick soil clinging to my shoes, which are now dyed henna red. There's a truck parked outside the house and Daphne is marching up and down, her radar on full alert. It's early evening and the sun is beginning to sink in the sky, taking the heat out of the day.

I squint at the van and hope it's not the local business-man and his mate again, looking for more taxes. I look around but can't see anyone. I speed up, breaking into a jog. Not easy with lead weights on my feet.

'Hello?' I call out. '*Ciao?*'

What on earth can be happening now? Not someone else who wants to tell me I shouldn't be living in my own house? Well I certainly wish I'd never bought the bloody place. This is the very last time I will be impulsive and silly and led by my heart. Ed and my mum were right. There, I've said it, even if it is just to myself. They were right and I was wrong. This is a bloody nightmare, not some sodding romantic dream.

'*Ciao!* Who's there?' I call out.

'Hey! *Ciao!*' A head pokes out of the door of my *trullo* and I jump before breathing a sigh of relief and finding myself breaking into a smile. It's Ryan, from the ironmonger's.

'Hello,' I say inquisitively. 'What are you doing here?'

'Hi.' He waves a hand. 'Still odd speaking English. Maybe I'll actually give my family a call.' He comes out of the *trullo* and straightens up.

'Don't you speak to them then?' I put a hand over my eyes to shield them from the sun again. He shakes his head.

'Na. Left years ago. Didn't get on with them. Thought it was best to get out of there.' Marco's words about people thinking that a bit of sun and dolce vita will make their problems disappear play over in my head. Ryan turns and looks back at the *trullo* roof. 'But then if you're hiding out in rural Puglia, you're probably running away from something too,' he says, as if reading my mind.

'I'm not . . .' I reply, and he turns and gives me a big smile, which helps shoo away all the agitation I was feeling leaving Marco's.

'Just joking,' he says. 'Anyway, I heard your roof needed looking at. I was in Bar Antonio earlier.'

I look blank.

'Lou's husband? He told me about your roof.'

'Ah. Yes, of course.' The penny drops.

'I can fix that for you.' He nods towards the roof, his bleached blond curls bobbing brightly.

'Can you?' I ask.

'Sure.' His curls bob again. 'I did some work for a guy in Alberobello. Showed me how to do it.'

Finally, something's going my way. I smile widely now. This man has a habit of making me feel so much better about my day.

'That's great. When could you start?' I clap my hands together.

'Tomorrow if you like. I can clear some space.'

I brighten even more.

'This is a big job.' He suddenly gets a lot more serious.

'Is it?' and I suddenly get a lot more worried.

'Yes, it'll be worth me putting the other stuff on hold. Just some olive tree maintenance.' He's smiling again and walking round the *trullo*. 'Looks like you've got a lot of work on here. I can turn my hand to most things if you need help. I mostly look after olive trees for other people, but I'm happy to have a go at anything. '

'When you say big job,' I swallow, 'how much are we talking exactly?'

'Well . . . I do have a lot on.' He wavers and I realise he wants to get his money's worth here.

'Oh no, please, I'd be really grateful if you could help me out,' I say quickly, because right now this man is my ticket out of here. I have to grab this chance.

'Tell you what, let's have an *aperitivo* and I'll see what I can work out for you,' he says, grabbing a pad and pen from the dashboard of his dusty van. He smiles again and I know that I should feel happy that I've found someone to help me out until I can sell, especially someone as lovely as Ryan. He's friendly, he speaks the same language as me, he understands what I'm going through. He's very attractive. And he's doing me a favour by pushing other work out of the way.

'Absolutely,' I say.

That evening, I'm still in shock about the amount of money it's going to cost to repair the roof. I've been into town to see if Brandon has any work for me, but it seems he's found a couple of graduates from my old college who he's 'bringing on'. More like employing them for half what he pays me. I'm furious with myself. If I hadn't moved out here, I'd still have a steady stream of work, as well as the chance of the job in Cornwall. This is all my own fault. I can't even afford to have the internet installed, especially not now the *trullo* roof needs repairing. According to the electrician who looked into it for me, I would need a huge booster on the roof and it would cost a fortune. Furiously I drive back to the *masseria* at speed and start to clear out some of the rubble in the *trullo*, trying to work out my frustration. Hopefully, too, it'll make my final bill with Ryan cheaper if I've done the donkey work.

Having pulled out some of the bigger stones, I drag out the chest of drawers. Not only is it covered in dust, but it's damaged where a stone has hit the left-hand side leaving a large chunk of wood missing. I drag it across the courtyard. It'll still do for my bedroom if I clean it up. Might as well use it. It'll look better when I show viewers round the place, rather than having my clothes still in black bin bags on the floor.

I dust it down in the dining room and start dragging it up to my bedroom. I'm about halfway up when I stop, out of breath and arms aching, wondering if I'm going to make it to the top, and what will happen if I don't. I have to do it, that's all there is to it. I give an almighty heave and the chest bangs noisily up the next three steps. I turn to see that there are just three to go. I've managed another one when the left-hand drawer shoots open and a load of old black and white photographs fly out and spill down the stairs.

Oh bugger! That's all I need.

I manage to heave the chest into my bedroom and put my clothes in the drawers. Then I gather up the photographs from the stairs. They're all of the *masseria* and the surrounding area. They're old and worn, but amazing. I pour myself a glass of rosata and call it a night on my labouring, then sit down outside the back door in the setting sun. As I sift through the pictures of how this place used to be, it starts to come alive in my mind. The noise and chatter of that first night at the Bellanuovos' is the soundtrack to the images playing in my head as I look at the big old olive tree reaching out its branches as if embracing the family, and imagine the happy times they must have had here.

The next morning I'm sitting outside the back door, with a coffee and some toasted bread and jam, staring at the quote Ryan left me. It's more than I have in savings just to fix the *trullo* roof. It'll leave me nothing to live off unless I can get some more work from Brandon. I have no idea how I'm going to pay for it and I certainly can't ask my mum or Ed for a loan.

Daphne has finished her breakfast and is lying in the sun in the courtyard, along with three little grey kittens who are playing round her and sometimes over her. But she doesn't seem to mind. *Mamma* cat is just out of sight, keeping an eye on her young, ready to pounce on predators.

I try and put the *trullo* out of my mind. I've done all I can to tidy up the mess in and around it and have now shut the door on it. There's no way I can afford to have it done. I'll have to ring Ryan and tell him later. Right now I'm going to tackle some brambles before it gets too hot. I've had a text message from Lou's agent friend, who has people in the area wanting a holiday property, a project to do up and rent out. I need to get this place looking the best I can.

I grab the old pair of shears from the barn, oil the joints and then head out the back door. I plan to get this patio looking fabulous. My large floppy hat protects me from the sun and from seeing anything else; especially Marco working on his *trullo* over the wall. But I know he's there, probably watching my every move. Honestly, I thought Mrs Davis in the downstairs flat knew all our business back in Tooting but it's not half as bad as living a field away from a Bellanuovo. It feels like he's right there the whole time. I stick my headphones in and shove my phone into my cut-off jeans pocket.

I attack the brambles with gusto, cutting and chopping, and it's making me feel a whole lot better until suddenly a bramble flicks up and whacks me in the face.

'Ouch!' I put one hand over my eye like a patch, pulling

out my headphones. I can hear the thumping and banging of rocks and boulders being moved. I daren't look over, I don't want to catch Marco's eye. In fact, I can't.

Daphne staggers to her feet from her sunbathing position and trots off round the side of the house to the courtyard. I listen again. It sounds like the banging is coming from the front of the house, *my* house.

I drop the shears and follow Daphne. Someone is working in the *trullo*. There's dust and rubble flying out the front door. 'Oh God, Ryan. I'm so sorry,' I shout. 'I thought we'd agreed.' I dip my head in through the *trullo* doorway. 'I said I'd ring you when I had the money sorted . . .' I stop, seeing a familiar back stacking stones by the front door. He turns to face me. It's Marco Bellanuovo.

'The roof needs fixing.' He shrugs and throws some more fallen plaster into a pile outside the door where I've just tidied and swept.

'I've got someone lined up to do it,' I blurt.

'Who? Your Australian friend? What does he know about *trulli*?'

'He's worked in Alberobello,' I say defensively.

'These roofs take years of understanding. My family have been caring for them all their lives. It isn't possible to learn about them in one summer.'

'Oh don't tell me, he's another one just like me!' I wish I could think before I speak, or act for that matter. I seem to lurch from one self-inflicted disaster to another. I buy a house I haven't seen, without internet access, lose all my work and now my only other source of income.

Another shrug and he gets back to piling up the stones and plaster.

'Look, I don't know . . .' I daren't say I don't know if I can pay him, 'how much you're charging.'

He stands up and dusts himself down, taking a swig of water from a big bottle.

'Let's just say I'm doing us both a favour.'

'I don't understand. I can't let you do it for nothing. I have to pay you. But I have to know how much.'

He takes another swig.

'The paintings. Your paintings. The ones I saw on the table the day you arrived . . .' He must be talking about my college work. 'You're a good artist.' He puts the lid on his water.

'Thanks. *Was* a good artist, and painting's not going to pay the bills.'

He wipes his hands on a rag.

'It's my grandmother's birthday at the end of October, just before the olive harvest. She's been very upset by . . . all this business.'

I bristle and want to shout that it's not my fault. But I don't.

'Perhaps you could do a painting of the *masseria* for her. To remember the old days.'

'And?'

'And that's it. In return, I will mend your *trullo* roof. You pay for the materials, I'll do the work.'

'You want me to do a painting . . .'

'For Nonna, *si*.' He nods and smiles, a wide, relaxed smile.

'For Nonna,' I repeat. 'And in return you'll mend the roof if I buy the materials.' I say it slowly, looking for the catch.

He nods again. '*Si*. It's a deal?' He holds out his hand, and slowly I hold out mine.

'Thank you. *Grazie*. That would be fine,' I say, still a little unbelieving. If this is true, it's the only way I can afford to have the roof done. 'I'll call Ryan and tell him I have help,' I say slowly, hoping it won't affect . . . well, things, whatever that might be, between us. I'd still like to have him as a friend, and who knows, maybe still have that dinner sometime.

'Ryan,' Marco says with a laugh. 'Okay, you call Ryan. I'll get on.' He looks up at the ceiling. 'And some coffee would be good too.'

I stop as I'm stepping out of the *trullo* and shake my head, but really I'm feeling relieved. I can actually get the roof fixed and then sell up and leave.

I go back into the house, put the kettle on and compose a text to Ryan. Then I pull out one of the old photographs of the *masseria* that I was looking at last night. I reach for my paintbrushes and run the bristles over my hands, then set up the easel up by the glass doors at the back of the dining room and put a canvas on it. I pin the photograph to the easel and get a faint memory of the excitement I used to feel when I was just about to start a new painting at college. A fresh canvas, a new beginning. I smile. I'm going to enjoy doing this.

I make the coffee and take it out to Marco, who has put the table and chairs under the big tree in the middle of the courtyard. There's so much work to be done here. The wall around the courtyard is lovely but crumbling in places; I wonder if the new owners will repair it or perhaps take it down completely. However, it feels like a small part of the wall between me and Marco has come down, and it feels good. A pair of dragonflies bob their way past me, dodging and sidestepping each other in the lazy heat of the last of the summer days.

I pour two cups and he comes out of the *trullo* wiping his hands.

'So how long do you think it will take you to do the roof?' I ask, sipping the hot black coffee.

'About two weeks. How long do you think it will take you to do the painting?' he asks back.

'Um, about two weeks,' I reply. 'Look, Marco this is very good of you. And I know you said you want the painting for your . . .'

'*Nonna*.'

'*Nonna*,' I confirm, 'but I still don't know why you're helping me. Don't get me wrong, I'm very grateful. But I mean, I've told you I'm putting it on the market.'

He smiles, and it grows into a gentle laugh. My mouth starts to tug at the corners, his laughter infectious.

'Well, I want the roof to be in good shape for when the house is mine again. When you sell it back to me, of course.' He knocks back his coffee, then picks up his small pickaxe and returns to work without another word.

I freeze with my cup halfway towards my mouth. Words fail me, actually fail me, and I shake my head and return to the house to start Nonna's painting.

Chapter Fifteen

'I see Ryan's making a start on the *trullo*, then. That was quick,' says Lou with a cheeky wink. We're having what is becoming a regular lunchtime meet-up. 'I wondered if you two might get on,' she grins.

'Actually,' I say, putting hot toasted bruschetta rubbed with garlic and drizzled with golden olive oil on to a warm serving plate, 'it's not Ryan.' I chew my top lip with my bottom teeth.

'Who is it then?' She pours the rosata from a plastic container from the *cantina* into a jug.

'It's Marco,' I say quickly, and grimace, embarrassed.

'What?' She stops pouring. 'Marco Bellanuovo?'

I nod, turning to look at Lou. After everything that's gone on, Marco is doing me a huge favour, even if he does think he's doing it for his own benefit.

'How did that come about?' Lou says, looking amazed.

'We did a deal.' I attempt a Mediterranean shrug and actually, I think I pull it off. 'He's doing the roof in return for a painting.' I toss the salad and put it on the tray with the plates and knives and forks.

'A painting? What painting?' Lou grabs the glasses from the old Formica top that I've cleaned within an inch of its life, so there's practically no pattern left on it at all.

'It's for his *nonna*, for her birthday. I think it's actually part of my penance for being here. He wants me to paint the *masseria* for her, a memento.' I pick up the tray and start making my way outside. 'I haven't painted anything in years. It's bound to turn out to be terrible.'

'Have you started it?' She follows behind me. 'I'd love to see it.'

'It's just by the door.' I nod to the easel and she goes over and peers at it. Suddenly it matters to me what she thinks. What if I can't do it any more? What if it was all a complete waste of time, years at art college, and I was never actually any good at it? My brother thought everything I painted was rubbish.

'It's fabulous!' she says, and I break into a broad smile. It feels good, very good indeed. 'I love it. So bold. Is it acrylics?'

'Uh-huh.' I nod, still smiling, and join her to look at the picture. The *masseria* is in the middle of the canvas; its walls are terracotta, not faded pink like they are now. I've painted in the olive grove around it, showing their green and silver leaves and the red poppies that grow in May across the deep red soil. I like to fill the whole canvas with colour. I used to like painting people too, but I'm not sure whether I still can.

'Are you doing anything like this for the card company you work for?'

I shake my head and shrug again, realising it's a habit I've picked up from Marco. My smile drops.

'I can't get any kind of answers from my boss. Seems

like I just slipped off his radar once it became hard to get hold of me. I haven't heard a thing from him and nothing has gone into my bank account recently. I'm living off the savings I had from the flat sale, and there's not much left now. And I've still got to pay for the materials for the *trullo*.' We sit down at the barrel table, which I've covered with a red and white cloth I bought in the market.

'Well, I've spoken to the estate agent I know and he has some buyers coming out in just over a week's time. He wants to show them this place,' says Lou, helping herself to salad.

'Oh, that's brilliant!' I breathe a sigh of relief. 'Hopefully the *trullo* will be finished and I can get a big push on and get the rest of the place cleared out and cleaned up.'

'It's looking fabulous out here.' Lou glances around at my hard work and effort. 'And in the courtyard.' She nods her head sideways.

'Oh, I found something I wanted to show you when I was cutting back the brambles there.' I put down the salad servers, grab my wine glass and lead Lou round into the courtyard. When we reach the corner where I've uncovered three lemon trees, and have the scratches to prove it, I point.

'Wow! Look at that mosaic.' Holding her glass carefully, Lou steps across the soft soil to study it. She rubs her hand over the smooth pieces of boldly coloured ceramics. 'It's beautiful.'

'It was behind a whole load of weeds and stuff. Marco will probably tell me I've cut down all sorts of important plants, but it's lovely, isn't it?'

'It looks like the *masseria*. I wonder if it was some sort of family crest.'

We both stare at it and then straighten up and look around.

'Oh, and I've got some pictures to show you.' I lead her back round to the table and bring out the photographs I found in the old chest of drawers. We slowly work our way through them as we eat and drink, recognising parts of the house and the land, deciding where we think the pictures were taken and discussing who's in them.

'That's by the *forno*, over there.' Lou points at Marco's *trullo* and the stone oven beside it.

'And that's the big tree in the courtyard,' I say.

'That must be Giovanni,' says Lou.

'And Anna-Maria.' I point at the slim, attractive young woman with a baby in her arms.

'That's Sophia!'

'No way!' We look at the stunning young woman .

'Wow! Time hasn't been kind to her,' says Lou, and I give her a gentle clip round the arm, but we both allow ourselves a little smile trying to match up this stunner with the very large, bad-tempered Sophia.

We turn to the next picture and my heart suddenly makes an unexpected and surprising lurch as I immediately recognise a young, good-looking Marco, with another man who is quite possibly his father. There's also a young man about the same age who looks like he could be Marco's brother, with his arm around Marco's shoulders. They're smiling and laughing.

We keep working our way through the pictures and

I'm getting a very different picture of the Bellanuovos and how family life used to be here. It looks like it was a home.

'The house looks amazing,' I say as we spread out the photos. And a painting that's been forming in my head at night starts to come into clearer focus.

'You've done so much here already,' says Lou, looking around, breaking into my thoughts.

'Thanks. I mean, I'd've loved to have really got stuck in here. There's so much more work to do, but I think it's the sensible thing to sell up. I'm never going to belong here. I know that now. I'm not a Bellanuovo,' and we both laugh.

'Where will you go?' Lou runs her finger round the edge of her glass.

'I might go and stay with my friend in Cornwall for a bit. See if that job's still going. Fingers crossed. If not, it's back to my mum's settee until I can sort out a flatshare.'

Lou pulls her mouth downwards.

'Well, I'll miss you, that's for sure,' and she raises her glass. 'And I'll miss your piccalilli! But here's to your first viewing. I'll ring and make the arrangements if you like.'

'That would be great.' I raise my glass too, though I can't help but feel a pang of disappointment that I couldn't make a go of it. But a bit like my relationship with Ed, I have to learn when to give up and walk away. It'll be an amazing place when it's finished, but it's not my home. I need to go, find somewhere of my own.

I decide to ring my mum once Lou's gone. I can't let my pride get in the way any more. I have to tell her I've made a mistake and that I'm coming back. I raise my eyes, hoping that the tears that are prickling under the surface don't spill, and force a smile.

Chapter Sixteen

Marco got up as soon as he woke. It was dark in the *trullo* but he kept the shutters open to see the sun as it started to rise. He jumped into the hot shower and made coffee before heading out to the *masseria*. He was keen to start work before Ruthie got up. He didn't want her to think he wasn't putting in the effort, and he wanted the roof finished on time.

He stopped in at his *mamma*'s house.

'Filippo!' he called in a half-whisper. But there was no answer. He went up to his brother's room. He could have done with his help finishing off this morning. But Filippo wasn't there either.

'*Ciao, bello!*' Anna-Maria came out of her room and kissed him on both cheeks. 'He's staying with friends in town,' she added, nodding at Filippo's door. 'Looking for jobs in the UK again, no doubt.' She rolled her eyes and shook her head.

'You have to let him live his own life,' he told her, and she shook her head again and headed downstairs. Marco followed.

'Coffee?' she asked, putting a hand out to touch his face.

'No, I have to get next door to finish the *trullo* roof.'

Anna-Maria pulled a face. 'How much longer?' she said, putting the kettle on. 'You know, that house will make a lovely home for you and Rosa.'

'Oh Mamma. Don't start that. Rosa is a good friend . . .'

'Yes, who you have known since school.'

'I have a job in Naples. Rosa lives here,' he said.

'And she and her family own the olive press and the land around it. This family could be a big name around here again if you were to marry. And her father is keen to retire. He would be delighted if you were to take over.'

'I think Rosa is quite capable of taking things over herself,' Marco said, looking at his watch. 'I have to go, Mamma. I have work to do.'

'Don't be late. I've invited Rosa and her family over for *aperitivos*. A chance to talk about the future. Think about it, Marco.'

Marco rolled his eyes and looked at his watch again. He wasn't thinking about Rosa; he was thinking about Ruthie. She'd be hard at work already. She hadn't stopped since he'd started on the *trullo*. In fact, she hadn't stopped since she'd got here. The place looked totally different. He was beginning to think he'd got her all wrong. She really did want to put this place back to how it was. But why? Why would you move to a different country, where you couldn't speak the language?

Whatever her reasons, she was throwing herself into it. She'd even taken on Nonno's goat!

He'd be sorry to see her go, he realised. Not just because she was very capable – and beautiful too, though he knew nothing could happen; she would go home eventually. But she had already made such a difference. She'd been good for the community, reminding them how the *masseria* used to be. It made him feel proud. He wanted to help her. Yes, she was feisty and a bit bossy, but he got the impression that was just a cover. It couldn't have been easy coming here all on her own, and she was still driving a hard bargain. She knew what she wanted. He'd been impressed by her, intrigued.

He realised that he and Filippo hadn't spent this much time together in ages either. He enjoyed working outside again instead of in an office or lecture theatre. He felt more alive than he had in months and he knew that was partly due to Ruthie Collins being here. Perhaps he should try and persuade her to stay after all.

Marco has been working his socks off these past couple of weeks, and there's no way I want him to think I'm working any less hard preparing for the viewers. I've been whitewashing all the rooms, cutting back the brambles and weeding in the courtyard and the veranda outside, jet-washing the white stones and planting red geraniums. I've even blacked the woodburning stove, though I still can't light it.

Marco works from seven in the morning, sometimes earlier, on the *trullo* roof, stopping for a few hours when the sun gets too hot, when he goes back and works in his own *trullo*. I use the time to carry on with the painting. Then he returns and works into the evening. Sometimes he brings Filippo with him. Filippo always makes me smile. He's a funny young man, playful, flirting and teasing. Marco is forever telling him to stop messing around and pulling him back into line. And he obviously loves being with his big brother.

The electrician comes back every so often, turning up at the most peculiar hours, late in the evening or early morning, fitting me around his other jobs as he works his way through the house. And every time he leaves, I give him another jar of piccalilli.

Now that two weeks have gone by, my hands are red raw from scrubbing, my hair is pebble-dashed with white paint and my arms are so scratched I look like I've been thrown to the lions. As I drift off to sleep each night, my mind fills with the painting I can't seem to shake the thought of. Last night I dreamt that the house was full of guests and family again, and there was laughter in every room. It's the sort of dream you don't want to wake up from. But Daphne put paid to that by kicking at her pen door to be let out early in the morning.

'So, are you nearly finished?' I ask Marco when he arrives. There's a nip in the air. Summer is on its way out and autumn is letting us know of its imminent arrival. 'I have viewers at five o'clock this evening,' I tell him, feeling nervous, which probably makes me sound more bossy than I mean to. 'Lou organised an estate agent to bring them over.'

'Not Ryan?' he says, not looking at me.

'No, not Ryan,' I say carefully, not sure why he's asked. 'I haven't seen Ryan for a while,' I realise and then wish I hadn't said it out loud. Marco's tight jawline seems to relax slightly. I look away quickly and gaze at the roof instead. It seems complete from the outside, but Marco hasn't let me see inside, insisting that I wait till it's done.

His little dog, Lucia, is at his feet, as she always is, looking up at him. All day she sits outside the *trullo* waiting for him, and only moves when he does. Daphne on the other hand has been patrolling the front of the house as if her life depends on it. I bend to pat Lucia, and although she lets me, she is still staring up at Marco.

'She's a very loyal dog,' I say, rubbing her ears.

'Yes, she hates it when I go away.' He smiles at her. 'I don't like to leave her, but the city is no place for her. And I am out all day long. She's better off here.' He straightens up. 'Just a few finishing touches. I'll call you when I'm done,' he says. 'It's almost ready,' he adds with a mischievous smile, and I'm sure he's just saying it to wind me up. I'm as nervous as I was the first day I arrived here.

I'm still in my paint-splattered three-quarter-length dungarees and I have some final sweeping-up to do before I attempt a shower. The shower is temperamental: sometimes hot, depending if I can get the fire to light, but mostly cold, and sometimes it doesn't work at all. Another thing I'd sort out if I was staying. I'd certainly have to get to grips with the wood-burning stove. But right now I just have to get the place looking its best.

I've weeded around the worn cobblestones at the front of the house and along the drive. I've tried my best to straighten the gates and have given them a lick of red paint. I've put pots either side of the front door and have more pots with geraniums in them for the front of the *trullo* when Marco's finished. I've covered the remaining junk in the barn with a tarpaulin and taken all the rubbish from the house to the dump.

I've added a few bits of furniture I've bought from the market, but have left the little church as it is, because it's so beautiful. I've just put a bunch of olive branches on the altar in there. I've swept everywhere, opened all the repainted shutters and mopped down the walls and floors.

The patio is now stripped of its brambles. I've tried to tidy up round the vegetable plot, but I have no idea what I'm doing there. If I was staying, of course, I'd repaint the outside of the house. And I'd do the walls around the courtyard too, but there really isn't time. I put some more olive branches in an old wine carafe on the plastic table in the cavernous dining room, then I stand back, brush down my hands and admire my work.

Not bad for a fortnight! The kitchen is bare and basic but clean. I've rehung the cupboard doors that were listing. But just taking all the junk away has brightened the house no end. I feel hot and as if I've got dust in every part of my body. I run my hands down my dungarees and look around again. One last thing . . . I hurry out to the covered patio and put out a bottle of wine, two glasses and a little dish of olives that Lou gave me from her own olive grove. I would've loved to have been serving up my own olives, but it wasn't to be. I look around for Daphne, who seems to have disappeared. I need to find her and coax her into her pen in the barn. Typical that she chooses now to disappear. Usually she wouldn't leave the front door.

I decide to shower and then look for Daphne. Upstairs

the basic bathroom is more like a wet room: white-tiled, with a shower on the wall. Not a big expensive shower head, just a hand-held one. There is a low white wall separating the shower area from the toilet and basin. I hope the basic facilities won't put my buyers off. I love the space this bathroom has, I think as I stroll across the room and turn on the shower. And the view from the window, which is ajar to stop any condensation, is amazing, over the tops of the olive trees as far as I can see. I put my hand under the shower. Today the water is cold, constant cold. But that's okay. I'm hot, and after the initial shock, the trickle cools me down.

I decide against more dungarees and instead put on the short lime-green dress I bought in the market. I put my two-euro sunglasses on my head and slip on the black ballet pumps I got in the supermarket, showing off the small star tattoo on my ankle. I go to add a scarf, but change my mind and leave it with the other ones Ed's mother bought me. Scarves never were me, no matter how hard I've tried. I look in the mirror. My little diamond nose stud glistens. My freckles have come out and my face is lightly tanned, even though I've spent most of my days inside, cleaning and painting. My hair dries quickly into soft, shiny curls and smells of the olive oil shampoo I bought in the supermarket. It'll be back to Head & Shoulders when I return to the UK. With a final look in the mirror, I go downstairs and look at the time. Just over an hour to go until the viewers arrive. Now all I have to do is get rid of Marco and find Daphne.

It looks busy at Anna-Maria's house. She's obviously

got guests coming. No doubt she'll be wanting Marco home.

Marco is just sweeping up as I go out the front to find Daphne. I sigh with relief. He stops and leans on the broom, cocks his head and raises an eyebrow in what looks like pleasant surprise.

'You look very . . . Italian,' he says finally. I blush, not knowing if it's a compliment.

'Thank you,' I say, and find myself smiling. He nods and smiles gently back. I blush some more and try and quickly move away from the subject.

'Have you finished?' I ask, suddenly sounding school-marmish again, but wanting to give him the painting and get him gone so I can be ready for the viewers.

He nods towards the *trullo*.

'Come and see.' He steps back and holds his arm out for me to step inside, still smiling. I go towards the door. I'm very aware of him as I stand in the doorway. He's hot and dusty, but I can still smell the citrusy aftershave he wears. I'd know that smell anywhere now.

'Come,' he encourages.

The first thing I notice as I bend down through the doorway into the *trullo* is how clean the floor is. Brushed and mopped and the room emptied and tidied of any debris. I breathe a huge sigh of relief and feel my shoulders relax. I look around at the clear space just crying out to be a wonderful little self-contained cottage. Then I let my eyes drift up to the ceiling. It's beautiful. The plaster's all gone and now it's just exposed stone; absolutely gorgeous cream stone.

'It's wonderful,' I breathe.

'If you want, we can plaster it on the inside, but I quite like it like this . . . natural,' he says, his arms folded casually across his chest.

I feel nervous. It must be the thought of the buyers coming. The *masseria* is looking lovely. It's like a blank canvas for someone else to paint their Puglian picture on. In mine, there would have been the *forno* puffing out smoke, holidaymakers staying in the *trullo*, and who knows, one day a wedding in the church and a celebration in the courtyard, with lanterns and fairy lights and the happy couple drinking Prosecco and eating olives from the grove. Maybe I'll paint it one day, just for the sake of it. I've enjoyed getting out my paints again.

'Thank you,' I say quietly.

'*Prego*,' he replies just as quietly, and I don't look at him. A small cluster of butterflies whizz round inside me, and my hand moves to cover my tummy . . .

I clear my throat. 'I have the painting for you.' This time I do turn. I'm determined not to end things badly. 'Why don't we have a drink? I'll bring it to the table under the tree.' I nod towards the old olive tree in the middle of the courtyard.

I bring out the tray with Nonna's duck poo aperitif, two glasses and a small bowl of Lou's olives and put it on the rusty round table, which wobbles on the uneven ground. Marco grabs it and pushes it round to stabilise it. I've got a bottle of rosé in the fridge but I felt it would be a good move to drink his grandmother's home-made stuff.

'Wait!' He holds up a hand and eyes the bottle. 'I have

something else, far better,' and he jumps up and heads over the wall to his *trullo*. I'm intrigued, and slightly relieved to be able to put off the duck poo moment.

I go back into the house and pick up the painting and the box of photos, which Lou has scanned for me on her computer and given me copies of.

Marco returns, carrying a bottle. 'Here,' he's only slightly out of breath, 'I think we can save Nonna's for . . . a really special occasion.' He looks at me seriously and I don't know whether he's joking or not. Then his face breaks into a smile, and so does mine. He pours the light yellow liquid into the glasses.

'How's the book coming on?' I ask, as he pours. Things are much easier between us since he's been spending so much time here.

'Slowly,' he says, handing me a glass. 'I've been working on two *trulli*.'

'Ah yes, sorry,' I say apologetically, taking the glass.

'Don't be. I enjoyed it,' he says, still smiling.

'Really?'

'I feel as if it's helped me reconnect with the land. I'll write better for it in the long run. *Salute*.' He raises his glass.

The sun catches in my eyes through the branches of the tree. I hold my hand up. All I can see is his silhouette. I can't see the expression on his face. Suddenly I feel slightly shy, so I take a sip of my drink. It's lemony, not too sweet, and warming as it slips down.

'That's gorgeous!' I say, realising too late that I sound surprised. He laughs. It's strange hearing him laugh. I haven't heard it before now. It's deep and rich and, frankly, quite sexy. But this is Marco Bellanuovo we're talking about; he is not a man I'm going to find sexy. Frustrating, infuriating, bolshie, but not sexy.

'Here.' I pick up the picture from beside my chair and hand it to him to stop myself thinking ridiculous thoughts. I mean, I'm sure someone finds him sexy: his girlfriend, the one I met the other night at supper, Rosa. He's still standing when he takes the picture from me, and I can't see his expression. He's not saying anything and I'm suddenly filled with nerves and feel light-headed and queasy. Oh God! He hates it! What if it is rubbish and I can't paint any more? I'll have to pay him for the work after all. Maybe he wasn't expecting it to be quite so bold and bright. Maybe he was hoping for a soft watercolour. I should have done a soft watercolour . . .

'Look, if you don't like it, I can redo it. I just wanted it to be how it was in the picture I had, big and proud . . . Look, really, I'll do it again.'

He sits down heavily on the seat next to me, and suddenly I can see his face. He's staring at the picture, holding it and just staring. I'm cringeing from my toes upwards, slowly dying inside.

'It's beautiful,' he finally says softly, still looking at it.

'Really?' I wonder if he's doing that joking thing again and is about to break into laughter and tell me it's awful. He turns to look at me, but no laugh follows.

'Really,' he says. 'Just beautiful.' There is a glistening in his eyes, which may be the sun catching them, or it may be that I've hit a nerve. 'I will give it to Nonna on her birthday.'

Relief floods through me. 'Here, I found these photographs whilst I was clearing out too. They're your grandfather's, or yours, or . . . well, the family's anyway. I hope you don't mind. I took some copies as a memento of the place.'

I hand him the tin. He puts down the painting and takes it and opens the lid. He runs his hand over the black and white pictures sliding and jostling inside.

'*Grazie*,' he says.

I take another sip of my drink. I can feel it lifting my spirits, and I sit back and look at the *masseria* as Marco glances through the photos.

'I'll study them more tonight, *grazie*,' he says finally, putting the lid back on and topping up our glasses. I should stop him – I have viewers coming – but it is so nice to actually be sitting here and being civilised. It would be churlish to say no. Anyway, it can't be that strong.

'This is lovely,' I say, as if I'm enjoying a quarter of sherbet lemons.

'It's made from the lemons here.' He points to the trees by the mosaic and crosses his long legs, leaning back in his chair and looking up at the big tree.

'Really? Wow! Maybe I'll . . .' And then I stop. I won't have a go at making any myself, because I won't be here. With any luck, I tell myself, I'll be in Cornwall eating fish and chips and hoping there is still room for me at the art gallery, where I'll be enticing rich clients to buy complicated bits of artwork.

'Ah yes, of course . . . you won't see the fruits of your labour, so to speak,' he says lightly.

'No. No I won't. I'll be back home,' I say, looking up at the tree too.

'Where is home for you, Ruthie?'

'Well, London. I was brought up in London, just me, my mum and my brother.'

'Whereabouts?'

'Clapham. But then I moved into a flat in Tooting with my partner. Ex-partner,' I correct myself. 'It was a former council flat but surrounded by glorious buildings. And of course it needed loads of work on it.'

'And is your partner—'

'*Ex*-partner,' I correct him and then am cross with myself. Why am I making a big deal of the fact that he's my ex? It's not like I'm looking for a new relationship. Well, that's not entirely true. I think Ryan and I could have had fun together. It's a shame I haven't heard from him. But I'm not looking for anything serious. I want to stand on my own two feet and not have to share my life or my home with anyone else.

'Does he enjoy doing up old houses?' Marco nods at the *masseria* and for a moment I wonder if he's talking about Ryan, then realise he means Ed. I laugh.

'No,' shaking my head and sipping at the glorious limoncello. 'I did the work on the flat. I think it all stemmed from working from home. I'd be designing cards and watching daytime TV.'

He looks blank.

'It's all DIY shows, doing up old properties. I did a couple of evening classes and then started on the flat.' I sip again, thinking I should stop talking now, but my mouth has other ideas. 'When we sold the flat, I knew I wouldn't be able to afford to buy a place on my own and I didn't fancy flat-sharing again, so . . .'

He says nothing but is listening. I sigh. I might as well tell him now that I'm leaving.

'I was selling our furniture on eBay, and that's when I saw it. This place. I thought it was everything I wanted.' I look wistfully back at the house.

'Don't beat yourself up. Lots of people do it.'

'I just thought I was different.'

He smiles and seems to agree, ridiculously making me blush again.

'You've done a great job of tidying it up. It has been neglected, I'm sorry to say. But with me away working and the rest of the family here not interested, and then my cousins living away and, well, with them not . . .' Seems like I'm not the only one whose tongue has been loosened. This time I top up the little glasses and look at him questioningly.

'They don't really speak. My father's side and my uncle's side. They're not alive, my father or my uncle, but still it goes on.'

Before I have a chance to ask more, he's changed the subject.

'See this tree.' He looks up at the big olive tree we're sitting under. 'This is the oldest tree in the whole Bellanuovo estate, when it was an estate. It's over two hundred years old.'

'Wow! That is old.'

'It has seen families come and go. My grandfather was

born here.' He nods to the *trullo*, with its new roof. 'All my family were born here and grew up here.' He nods in the direction of the *masseria* this time, then reaches up and snaps a branch from the olive tree.

'And now you have come and are going. You helped it get back on its feet, Ruthie Collins.'

I'm confused. One minute he doesn't want me here; the next he's thanking me like I came in and did a job and am leaving again.

'I hope you find what you're looking for,' he says. He's almost frowning at me. 'I'm sorry it wasn't here.'

'It's just I was offered a really good job at home. And what with my work drying up . . . Well, it seems the sensible thing to do. I wouldn't be going if it wasn't for, well, the money,' I say, lifting my chin. He laughs and I want to be offended, but it's hard when he's so laid-back.

'Come on, really?' he says, still smiling. Maybe it's the limoncello that makes me laugh too.

'What?' I say, trying to be on the defensive but failing.

'Well, a single woman, in a foreign country, running an olive grove, not to mention the work that still needs doing on the house.'

For a moment I'm gobsmacked. I'm not sure if he's joking or if he's serious. He's smiling, but still . . .

He shrugs. 'Look, I'm really impressed by the way you've thrown yourself into this, but I'm just saying I can understand why you'd realise it wasn't for you.'

'I told you, it's because of the job. That's the only reason I'm going.'

'So you have a job to go back to?'

'Well, not exactly, no. I'm hoping it might still be there.'

He shrugs and laughs some more and tops up the glasses. 'Okay. Maybe we should agree to differ.'

'No, no.' I can feel myself starting to build up to full-blown picket line with placards. Stubborn to the last, that's me. 'I really wanted to make a go of this place . . .'

'Be honest,' he goads, 'you wouldn't have made it to the first olive harvest.'

'Yes I would.'

He shakes his head. 'No you wouldn't.'

Suddenly Daphne appears and I jump up.

'Quick! Stop her going that way!' I shout. 'I need her in her pen before the buyers get here.'

Marco follows. We both crouch slightly and start herding the goat towards the pen. She tries to duck this way and that. My tongue is poking out of the corner of my mouth and Marco is smiling, clearly enjoying the chase. Finally we close in on her and she has no option but to run into the pen. Marco closes the gate and I bolt it, and as I do, our hands touch. Is it my imagination, or was there just a spark between us? My stomach suddenly flips over and back again. It can't be that I fancy him. He's Marco Bellanuovo, the bane of my life. Maybe it was static from the gate. There really couldn't be any attraction between us, could there? But today, he seems very different. Maybe now he knows I'm going, he's happier to be around me.

He dusts down his hands.

'Well, I must be going. The viewers will be here soon,'

I say, confused and feeling inexplicably nervous.

'Yes, and I have some sheep to see to.'

'I didn't know you had sheep,' I say. I'm surprised, as I know he hasn't been living here.

'A neighbour has been taking care of them for me. Luigi, the goat man. He cares for my olives too, with his son. You might have seen them around.'

'Ah yes.'

'I need to go and move them this afternoon. Keep them closer now that I'm staying around for a bit.'

'Right, well . . . good luck,' I say, suddenly tongue-tied.

'And you, Ruthie Collins.' He smiles at me, then pulls the olive branch from his top pocket and hands it to me. 'Good luck, and I hope you will forgive me.'

I put out a hand slowly and take the branch, not knowing what to say. Marco nods goodbye and turns towards the wall, jumping up and over without looking back and disappearing in the direction of his *trullo*.

I look down at the olive branch. Feeling a little light-headed, I decide there is just time for a really quick siesta before the viewers arrive, so I step into the cool of the *masseria*. My hand tingles and I rub it, still holding the branch, remembering the little static shock by the gate. Maybe I can forgive him after all, I think as I head upstairs.

Chapter Seventeen

I wake to the sound of horns honking and sheep baaing and my phone ringing from somewhere downstairs. My head is thick, like it's been stuffed with cotton wool while I was napping. I grab the clock on the old wooden crate that serves as my bedside table, nearly knocking it over in the process. Bugger! I've overslept! Am I dreaming these noises? My head starts banging like there's a skiffle band starting up in there. I screw up my eyes against the sunlight. There's more baaing and honking. Don't tell me Daphne's escaped. The afternoon aperitif was lovely, but boy, I'm paying for it now. That limoncello was way stronger than it tasted. And I should know better at my age! I'm not a teenager knocking back alcopops.

I throw myself off the bed and out on to the landing, pulling open the window overlooking the front drive. I blink, rub my eyes and look again, wondering if it's the limoncello giving me hallucinations. There are sheep all over my front drive, jumping and tumbling over the wall and running with a mixture of confusion and joy into the shade of the olive and almond trees.

Just inside the gates are two cars, surrounded by sheep. They're honking, making the sheep run, but not enough to clear a pathway through. One is a small Fiat, the other a brand-new bright red Alfa Romeo.

Shit! The viewers! The driver of the Fiat gets out, scattering sheep with his door. He's followed by the driver of the Alfa Romeo, who's wearing large sunglasses and a blue and pink polo shirt with the collar turned up. He's shouting at the Fiat driver, who is trying to placate him and holding his phone to his ear. I hear my phone ringing from downstairs again.

Shit! Double shit! I need to get down there and explain that this is just an accident. But how on earth will I do that? In between me and my prospective buyer is a sea of sheep. I'll never be able to reach him. I try and shout and wave, but he's too far away. Then I spot Marco. He's standing by the crumbling wall holding a long thumbstick. Thank God! At least now we're on speaking terms he can help. There's no way I can sort this one on my own. I need him to herd the sheep away from the cars, and quick.

My heart's racing. I can't let this chance get away. I feel like my winning lottery ticket has blown out of my hand and is fluttering along the ground in front of me. I need to chase it and jump on it. Whatever it takes. Even asking Marco Bellanuovo for help. I may be stubborn, but I'm not stupid. A little voice in my head begs to differ, sounding remarkably like Ed's.

'Marco!' I shout and wave. '*Aiutatemi!* Help me!' I wave again, but he doesn't seem to notice or hear me. 'The sheep!'

The agent turns and looks up at me, as do the Alfa driver and his passenger, a blonde woman in large dark glasses who sticks her head out of the window and looks to be mouthing something very rude. Taken aback, I call to Marco again.

'Marco! The sheep! Help!'

He looks up at me, smiles and waves back.

'*Buonasera!*' he calls back over the baaing, and then, quite unbelievably, goes back to watching the sheep jump, chase, stumble and leap around the front drive.

'Marco!' I shout again. The agent shrugs at the Alfa driver, who makes a dismissive gesture and then holds his hand on the horn. He's exchanging words with his passenger, who's telling him to get back in the car by the looks of it.

Oh no! I turn and run to the stairs, taking them in tiny fast steps. By the time I get to the front door and fling it open, there are more sheep outside, a whole bloomin' woolly blanket of them. Anna-Maria, Nonna, Marco's sister, Rosa's family and Luigi the goat man are all standing by the wall watching the car trying to reverse through them. Young Luigi and Rosa are standing together, slightly apart from their families, by the gateposts. Young Luigi is leaning towards Rosa, sharing the joke. It's the first time I've seen Rosa smile. They're pointing and laughing, all of them. This can't be happening. Surely they can see I need their help.

'Shoo, shoo!' I wave my arms at the sheep and then above my head as I run across the worn cobbles. 'Shoo!' Surely now Marco and his family will help, but they seem to be laughing even more. Even Nonna is showing off the gaps in her teeth. Only Marco isn't laughing; he's just standing there doing nothing. I dive into the woolly blanket, waving and barging them out of the way.

Now that I'm closer, I recognise the man standing in the open door of the Alfa Romeo, or at least I think I do. He looks like that rugby player turned TV chef who's been in all the papers recently, something about an affair. And he was on the front cover of *OK!* magazine. I bought it coming over here, and read the article about how he and his wife are having a second honeymoon. These are serious buyers. Cash buyers, no doubt. And by the looks of it, they are not happy, not happy at all.

The man is leaning against the car. Nonna lifts a hand and points, and they all turn and laugh as one of the sheep jumps in through the open door behind him, making the blonde woman scream. Maps, papers and cardigans fly about as the woman tries to get away from the sheep. The growing crowd of neighbours hoot with laughter. Anna-Maria has tears rolling down her cheeks. Now he's trying to get the sheep out of the car, but he chases it on to her lap instead. Oh good God! At last she opens the door on her side and tumbles out head first, shrieking. The sheep follows and leaps over her. She staggers to her feet, brushing droppings from her white jeans and screaming hysterically at her husband. Marco's dog is barking furiously, adding to the chaos that is unfolding before my eyes.

'Marco, please. I need to move these sheep. My viewers are here,' I say, hoping he'll appreciate the urgency. For a moment he looks at me and I think he understands. But he still doesn't move.

'Sorry, I can't help.'

I puff out my cheeks with rage. He is so bloody annoying! And childish! What's his problem? Why won't he help me? I stomp down the drive, shooing sheep to each side of me and trying to avoid the droppings that now litter the ground. The sheep jump away and then trot back as though they're in a maypole dance, skipping in and out in front of me. I can still hear the baaing, and the revving of engines, but most of all I can hear the Bellanuovos laughing at me.

A sinking feeling washes over me as realisation smacks me in the face. Of course Marco isn't helping me. I turn to look at him. He's not smiling. He's had his joke, it seems. He's not helping me because they're his sheep! He did this! I stop and glare at him, but I can't tell him exactly what I think of him while there's still a chance of getting my viewers down the drive and into the house.

There is now a crowd by the front gate. For a quiet lane, I've got quite an audience. The local businessman Franco Pugliese is here with his family, and some tourists have stopped and got out of their car to watch the commotion. Everyone is laughing at me and I have never felt more alone or homesick in my life.

'Please, wait!' I call to the reversing Alfa Romeo. I wave my hands madly above my head like my life depends on it, and frankly, it does. I'm not sure, but I think the driver gives me a single-fingered wave back as he speeds off in a cloud of dust and scattering locals. I turn to look at the agent, hoping he'll do something. But he shakes his head, gets back in his Fiat and reverses out behind the Alfa Romeo.

'I'll be in touch,' I call through his open window. 'Perhaps set up some more viewings for next week. I'll have all this sorted by then. I promise.'

He looks at me, shakes his head in annoyance and disbelief and then follows the Alfa, chucking up more clouds of dust.

'No, wait! Please, I can explain! It's the neighbour . . .' I trail off. 'He's a complete pillock!' That's when I realise there's no hope of them coming back. I mean, who's going to buy a house with a complete pillock for a neighbour? I did! I think. That little voice in my head again, telling me how stupid I've been.

The Bellanuovos and their guests and neighbours are still gathered, still enjoying the spectacle. Still reliving and retelling the tale of the sheep that got into the celebrity chef's car, and of his hysterical screaming partner. I'm not sure if it was his wife or his girlfriend in the end. What I do know is they're not coming back. And the agent won't be bringing any other of his well-heeled clients either.

I watch the tail lights of the little Fiat drive away, down the dip and up again along the lane back towards the main road and the town. When I can't see the lights any more, and every ounce of hope has left my body, I turn very, very slowly back towards the *masseria*. My fists are clenched into tight balls, my nostrils taut and flaring.

'How dare you!' I say slowly in a low voice that I don't recognise. 'What on earth were you doing letting your sheep on to my land like that? You knew I had viewers coming. You don't want me here as much as I don't want to be here. What the hell were you thinking?'

Everyone has stopped laughing and there's a hush that falls across the gathered audience, apart from the sheep, who just baa a little less.

Marco clears his throat.

'You may own the *masseria*, but I'm afraid you don't own the land in front of it.' He pulls a piece of paper from his back pocket and holds it up.

What? I really am in no mood for any of this nonsense. My heart is ripping in two and I just want to go inside, shut the door and get very, very drunk on Nonna's duck poo.

'Here. It was in the will. I was left the *trullo*, and this strip of land.'

I snatch the paperwork off him. It's all in Italian, but there is a plan, with a red line around his *trullo* and the area in front of the *masseria*. I don't doubt its authenticity. I didn't really check my plans. I was too busy hoping not to miss my flight home. I can hear that little voice again. I only have myself to blame. I knew I was taking a chance when they told me the road was blocked and I wouldn't be able to see the *masseria* that day. It was sign now or leave it. I signed. I know! Mad!

'You have ruined everything!' I wave my arms around and in the direction of the departing viewers, then hold both hands to my head. The paperwork flaps around.

'Officially, you're trespassing.'

'Oooph!' I let out an explosion of frustration.

'*Bravo!*' shouts Nonna.

'Nonna says you look like a real Italian now,' Filippo translates helpfully.

Nonna nods and smiles and goes back to her seat on the veranda. The gaggle of onlookers starts to break away, until it is just Marco and me and some much quieter, happily grazing sheep.

'Now what am I going to do?' I say, feeling really quite tearful.

'You said you'd stay if it wasn't for the job,' Marco says, reminding me of my earlier words.

'You said I wouldn't make it to the olive harvest.' I remind him of his.

'So then, stay until the olive harvest. Prove to yourself and your doubters.' He raises an eyebrow.

I say nothing. Did I tell him about Ed, Mum and all the others who thought I couldn't do it? That they all thought I'd give in as soon as it got tough?

'Tell you what, if you make it until the end of the olive harvest, I will give you this piece of land. Then you can sell the *masseria* and the land to whoever you want and go home.'

'What?'

'But if you decide to wimp out and leave early, you sell it to me at the price I offered.'

'Half what I paid for it!'

'Exactly. So you can stay and try and prove to everyone that you can do it, or you can go and sell to me.'

I let the information sink in. I can leave now and lose my money and, frankly my pride, or stay and get my money back, maybe more, and prove everyone wrong. Do I really have a choice?

'Where I come from, we call it a ransom strip. But anything to wipe the smile off your face,' I say and put out a hand.

His face does indeed break into a broad smile.

'We have a deal then?'

I nod, knowing that as soon as I shake, my dreams of a little flat and a job in Cornwall will disappear for good.

'Would you care for a drink, to settle the deal?' he asks, and I shake my head. I'm exhausted. I turn back towards the house.

Daphne, who has somehow let herself out, looks like the queen bee with her new gang to keep in line.

'No! Not my geraniums!' I shout at the sheep at my front door.

'You may own the drive, but you don't own this bit!' I call back to Marco.

I open the door and stamp in. Looks like this is where I'm staying for the time being, and I'm going to have to show them all I can do it. I slam the door shut.

Chapter Eighteen

The sheep were still all over the front drive in the morning. Trying to get the car out was going to be nigh on impossible. So instead I walked to market, balancing along the low wall between me and the Bellanuovos to get to the front gate and avoid walking through sheep and sheep droppings or on Marco's land. I don't want to give him any excuse to pull me up. This way he can't accuse me of trespassing again.

'He did what?'

'Honestly, there were sheep everywhere.'

'Oh no.' Lou looks concerned.

'I'm so sorry, what with you setting up the meeting,' I say, touching her hand.

'Don't worry. I'll explain that it wasn't your fault. You weren't to know your pillock of a neighbour was going to herd his sheep over your land,' she says, putting a forkful of food into her mouth. I'm grateful for her understanding.

'No, and I never realised they were so big!'

Lou can't help but laugh, nearly choking on her orecchiette, or little ears, as I've learnt it translates. Pasta covered in pomodoro sauce: rich red tomatoes cooked in garlic and olive oil, sitting in little pools in the pasta with a scattering of green basil. She takes a big sip of red wine and shakes her head disbelievingly.

I can see my own reflection in her sunglasses and laugh too. The September sunshine is warming our faces. It seems to be so much kinder than August's. Warmer, softer, instead of the harsh, intense heat we've had over the past couple of weeks.

'And then he bet you?' she asks, still incredulous.

I nod, 'Uh-huh,' and dig my fork into my pasta: broccoli, garlic and chilli, with cherry tomatoes, in shiny linguine. I take a big mouthful, letting some of it fall back into the bowl; juice collects in the corner of my mouth and I lick it away.

I have a new ankle bracelet that I bought in the market that catches in the sunlight and just sits below my tiny tattoo. I would never have worn an ankle bracelet in the UK; Ed would have told me I looked cheap. But I like it. It looks like olive branches linked together. Just as I like the new black and gold sunglasses I've bought. Bigger and with more bling than the last pair, and I don't feel a bit out of place wearing them.

'So what are you going to do?'

I shrug. 'Stay, I guess,' and give a little sigh, thinking about the email I'll have to send to Beth.

'What will you do for work?'

I shake my head and shrug again. I've just tried to email Brandon again but he hasn't replied. He doesn't these days.

'I have no idea,' I say with a hint of panic in my voice.

'You've got to look to what you've got. At least you've got the *trullo* now.'

'But that won't be any use until May. The holidaymakers are all leaving.' We both look around at the relatively quiet bar. The usual people are there: Franco Pugliese and his sidekick; Luigi and some of his friends; the old men I saw that first day at the ironmonger's. They're still nodding and talking about me and the sheep, no doubt. It's so much quieter than when I first arrived. This is it. Holidays are over. For those left behind, it's real life.

'You know you have your olives,' Lou says, picking at a bowl of olives in front of us.

'I know, but I haven't really given them much thought. It was the house I wanted to do up. And the harvest isn't till . . . When is the harvest exactly?'

I throw my hands up and we both laugh. I shake my head.

'This is great. I don't even know how long my bet is.'

'November . . . ish. It all depends on the weather. You want to leave it as late as possible so they turn from green to black, but not too late. Leave it too late and the frost will have them.'

'Oh God,' I sigh, taking it all in. This isn't what I signed up for. Yes, I knew the place had an olive grove, but I was thinking about the house, what I could do there.

'And then what?'

'You take them to the press and either sell them there, for them to use in their lower-grade oil, or get them pressed and keep the oil and sell it yourself: Puglian extra-virgin olive oil!'

'But I won't get any money until the oil is sold, right?'

Lou nods, dipping her finger into the bowl and licking it. My heart sinks. Then she says, quietly and thoughtfully, 'Unless you sell it beforehand.'

'What do you mean?' I frown. 'How can I sell what I haven't got?'

'Look,' she's warming to an idea, 'why did you come here?'

She's put me on the spot and I feel a bit on my guard. She's the very last person I expected to chip in with criticism.

'Because . . . I fell in love with Italy, with everything about it. Because I loved the house.'

'Because you fell in love with the *idea* of Italy,' Lou says, straight to the point as usual.

I feel slightly affronted and take a big slug of water.

'Oh, I'm not having a go.' She puts her hands up and I feel slightly better. 'I'm just saying that's why you wanted to come here, and that's what you should be selling.'

'I'm not with you.'

'All I'm saying is, you sell the dream . . . in a bottle.' She's grinning at me like a Cheshire cat and I still don't get what she's talking about. 'I've heard about it done with wine. You sell your harvest before it's harvested.'

'How?'

'You're the creative one! Get your computer out.'

I do as she says and open my laptop. Lou starts typing into the search engine.

'Bingo!' She shows me a wine maker's page. 'There! "Rent a vine". That's what you do!' She sits back and folds her arms like her work is done.

'What? You buy a tree for the year and you get the oil from that tree at harvest time?' I'm suddenly feeling a flutter of excitement.

'Exactly!'

'Oh my God! That's brilliant!' I say, wide-eyed and feeling positive for the first time in ages.

I start searching other rent-a-tree schemes while Lou goes to the ladies'. It looks great, but I have no idea if I'll be able to do it. Suddenly a new message pings into my inbox. It's from Brandon.

Sorry love, I just haven't got anything for you. You know how it works. The jobs come in and I get someone on to them. I can't wait for you to get in touch. I've taken on another couple of designers who I can get in contact with when I need them. Hope Italy works out for you. Brandon.

So that's it. There really is no more work. I can't believe it. I've worked for Brandon for years, and now he's dropping me, just like that! I need that job! No notice, no pay-off. Nothing. I feel like I've been abandoned in the middle of the Gobi Desert with no idea which way to start walking.

I hold my head in my hands. If I hadn't left, I wouldn't be in this mess . . . any of this mess. All my plans have been ripped up and tossed to the wind. I shake my head from side to side in my hands. When I look up, I see Lou, back from the ladies'. I look at her concerned face and take a deep breath.

'Looks like this rent-a-tree scheme really is my only option now.'

'Prosecco?' Lou doesn't ask twice and waves to the girl behind the bar.

'Why not?' I say. I feel like a runaway fairground ride that's come off the rails and is heading for who knows where. I'm hurtling towards either a great adventure or a huge big crash.

'*Duo Prosecco, per favore,*' Lou says. You'd never think she was Welsh when you hear her speak Italian. I wonder if that'll ever be me, and then remind myself I'm only here till the harvest. We sip the Prosecco and it tastes fabulous.

'I bet you have loads of London friends who'd be up for a few bottles. That'd show Ed you're serious too.'

She's right, of course. If I could pull this off, it would show Ed and my mum that I'm not just a hot headed-fool. And that bit of the plan really does appeal.

'I could do the labels and a newsletter too.' I sit looking at the computer, planning the design already. Lou is gathering her stuff.

'I must go. I have to get back to work.' She finishes her drink.

'Okay, I'll stay and start work on a Facebook page, maybe look at putting it on Gumtree too.' I start tapping away on the keyboard, then stop and look at Lou. I realise there's just one small problem.

'I have no idea how to look after the trees or anything like that.' My heart sinks again. 'It's never going to work.'

'But I know someone who does.' She waves in the direction of the bar, and I turn to see Ryan, who's just walked in. A little wave of excitement shimmies through me. He walks over and kisses us both on the cheek, and I get a flutter of butterflies in my tummy.

'Hey!' he says, smiling, showing his lovely white teeth; his shaggy, sun-bleached curls bounce as he nods his head towards me. 'Heard you had a few problems with some sheep the other day.' He points to the old men at the bar and the smiling barmaid wiping coffee cups with a tea towel.

'Oh, nothing I couldn't sort out.' I find myself joining in good-naturedly, and Lou raises her eyebrows with a cheeky smile.

'I told you, if you ever need a hand, call me,' Ryan says, giving me another card.

'Actually,' I look at Lou, who nods. 'You know a thing or two about olives, don't you?'

'Yep, got a few customers out your way. I look after their trees and land and in return I get their oil. Look after some of the Bellanuovo land, actually.'

'Marco's land?'

'His cousins' actually.'

I'm surprised. I would have thought Luigi would have looked after them.

'Did you want me to do the same for you?'

'No, I don't want you to take the oil. Sit down. I'll explain,' I say a little excitedly. I'm not sure whether my excitement is down to the rent-a-tree idea, or the fact that Ryan and I are finally having a drink together. I gesture to the chair.

'What was it you were saying about it never going to work? Looks like it will now.' Lou pulls her bag on to her shoulder and slips out with a *ciao* and a kiss for her husband. I clear my throat and my thoughts and look back at Ryan.

'I think I might need you to help me with the harvest and all that,' I say, having no idea what 'all that' might entail.

'Sure, no worries. Whatever it is, I'm your man. Another?' He points to my empty Prosecco glass, and I know I shouldn't but he smiles and orders it anyway and I don't resist. Because if I am to make this work, I'm going to need some expert help, and it looks like Ryan is just the man for the job. If he knows what to do with the olives, I can go ahead and finish designing my Facebook page and get this started today.

'Cheers,' he says.

'*Salute*,' I reply. I feel like I'm stepping on to the first bricks of the road home and I may just have found a travelling companion.

Chapter Nineteen

It's getting colder, and this morning I try again to light the wood-burning stove that's going to give me hot water and some heat. I fail, again. It's like my worst enemy; in fact I've renamed it Marco. Talking of which . . . there is something I need to do. I stand up and leave the smouldering fire, picking up Nonna's painting from the table, wrapping it in my painting shirt and tucking it under my arm. I have to head next door and deliver it.

I swallow and take a deep breath. My heart is racing and I have no idea why. Maybe it's because I know that as soon as I knock at the door, the dogs will career around the corner at me. I'm still getting used to being around dogs. It's not that I don't like them. I loved Dudley. I'm just not used to them as a gang. We never had pets when I was growing up. I did have a goldfish from the fair that came through Clapham Common every year, but it died. In fact, I'm pretty sure my brother may have done something to it. I specifically told him not to overfeed it, but I swear he was sprinkling titbits into the bowl all night long. I spent ages building it an underwater home with little toys I'd collected and weeds I bought from the pet shop. But the next morning it was floating on its back. I didn't get another one.

I put my hand up to the big, dark wood door and then stop myself. I can hear a voice. It's Anna-Maria. I can't really make out what she's saying, but she's talking about Marco and *l'inglese*. I'm guessing that's me. I still can't tune into her fast way of speaking: something to do with *stupido* and the *masseria*, I think. I wonder if she's cross about the bet. A slightly mischievous side of me can't help but give a little smile. Sounds like it's caused even more ructions in the Bellanuovo household. I can't help wondering why he made it. If he wanted me just to go, he had his chance. He could've kept quiet about the strip of land, like my solicitor did to me. But Marco doesn't strike me as the dishonourable type, no matter how infuriating he is. He shifts up a notch or two in my estimation.

There is still more arguing coming from behind the door, and actually, I realise, I don't want to hear what they're saying, even if I could understand them. Let's face it, they're not going to be suggesting they invite me round for supper again any time soon.

I knock loudly and firmly. The talking stops and the dogs start barking, and I brace myself for their arrival, clutching the paint-splattered shirt closer to me. It used to be Ed's, but I used it to paint in when we were still students. It's got a strangely reassuring feel about it right now.

The door flies open and I jump. Anna-Maria is standing there. She doesn't smile. Nonna is sitting inside, a large white handkerchief in her hand, in contrast to her black outfit. Filippo is there too, and the rest of them. Yep, looks like I've interrupted a family meeting.

'Is Marco here, please?' I say in Italian, and Anna-Maria insists on replying in very poor English.

'He very . . . how do you say? Nonna?' Nonna shrugs and blows her nose loudly.

'He's out,' says Filippo with a smile and a raised hand.

'He's out. At the press, with Rosa,' Anna-Maria says with a smile that looks like it took effort. 'I can help?' She holds out her hand and gestures to the shirt under my arm. I hold it tighter and she eyes me suspiciously.

'No, it's fine. I . . . *Grazie*.' I turn to go.

'They are very close, him and Rosa. The *masseria* will be a lovely family home for them.' This is more English than I've ever heard Anna-Maria speak before. I don't turn back. I don't need to. I'm being warned off. But that's just fine, because I really have no desire to jump on Marco, or him on me: that much is obvious. Suddenly an image of Marco flashes in front of my eyes. Only he's not outside his *trullo*, he's in my bedroom; the windows are open, there's a soft breeze. He's smiling, one of his rare smiles. I shake my head and carry on walking. Like I say, ridiculous! The image is replaced by him and Rosa, and three happy children running round my dining room table. She is cooking; he's writing and smiling at his family playing. I don't know which image is more shocking or frustrating.

I can feel Anna-Maria's eyes on me. I don't want to climb over the wall whilst she's still watching. I hold my head a little higher and set out on the road into town.

I stick to the grassy verge and the low, uneven stone walls as I walk. Dotted in amongst the small square houses are the *trulli*, most of them standing idle, left abandoned whilst families move into modern houses in town. I pass a small house with a veranda covered by a vine. The washing is out in the early-morning sunshine. An elderly couple stop what they're doing and look at me. It's Luigi, the goat man, I realise, turning over his vegetable plot. He's wearing dark trousers, braces and a flat cap. His wife, just as short and stout as him, in black, is hanging out large sheets on the line. They stop and stare as I pass. I raise a hand. They nod back. I can't help but glance at the wonderful vegetables he's got growing. I wish my vegetable plot looked like that.

'*Ciao*,' I say, but it's a bit half-hearted, as is their response. They probably think I'm the mad *inglese* too. I walk on, the sun starting to beat on my neck, my spirits sagging.

At the *forno*, Sophia doesn't raise a smile either, or even speak as I buy my focaccia. At the café, I sit outside and open up my laptop. I might as well have three heads. They are all staring at me. I'm still the novelty round here. But I carry on. I need to find out if my rent-a-tree idea has taken off.

One taker. It's Beth, and much as I'm grateful to her, my heart sinks even lower.

There's another email from Ed asking if I've come to my senses yet. Honestly, I don't know why he's so bothered. He's with Annabel now. For someone supposedly so loved up, he's spending an unhealthy amount of time worrying about what I'm doing. It's like he can't bear the fact I've moved on or might be happy. Maybe if he'd been this interested in me before, things might have gone differently between us. I don't reply to his email; instead I attach a link to my 'rent an olive tree' Facebook page. I might be feeling like I'm drowning in quicksand but I'm not going to let him know that. Feeling reckless, I press send. There, Ed, that's what I'm up to. What about you? And I try and tell myself that that's made me feel better and that I'm not beaten yet, even if I feel it.

I close the computer and leave the café and decide to have a walk in the last of the warm sunshine, hoping it'll lift my spirits. It doesn't. But as I near the single-storey concrete building that's the school I can hear happy, excited chatter that gives me a little lift. I can see children sitting under a big bamboo-covered area with drawing boards, sketching. Lou is walking amongst them slowly, encouraging and pointing to their work.

I stop and take out the bottle of water from my bag and take a sip. I think I'm feeling a little envious of Lou. I must have spent too much time on my own in that house, with only Anna-Maria's unwelcoming glares and the watchful eye of Marco for company.

Lou looks up, sees me and waves. I wave back. She waves again and then beckons me over. I don't need asking twice. I'm delighted to see a happy face.

'*Ciao*,' she says and kisses both my cheeks

'*Ciao*,' I reply. 'Wow! This looks great,' I say, looking at the children. Lou introduces me and explains that I'm an artist. I try to correct her but she brushes my excuses away.

'And this is my son, Giac.' She puts a hand on the boy's shoulder and rubs his smartly cut mousy hair. He ducks away from his mother's fussing and I can't help but feel that pang, the same pang I felt when I thought about Marco and Rosa and the children they will one day have. It hasn't happened to me, and by the looks of it, it won't. I have to throw myself into getting my life back on track, and that means getting the olives to harvest. I look up at Lou and see there are tears in her eyes.

'Lou, is everything okay?' I'm suddenly cross with myself for being so self-obsessed. See, I've definitely spent too much time on my own.

Lou sniffs and turns away from her son, who looks up, worried.

'It's the bar. It's going to close. Antonio just can't keep it going.'

'Oh Lou,' I say, and without thinking put an arm around her shoulders as she blows into a tissue. 'It's definite then?'

'Landlord came to see us last night. He's putting the rent up, like doubling it. There's no way we can afford it now.'

'That's terrible! Isn't there anything you can do?'

Lou shakes her head and gives a derisory laugh.

'It's how things work round here.' She blows into her tissue and I rest my hand on her shoulder. 'I wish my dad was here. It's hard at times like this, being so far away, y'know? I know we've got Antonio's family, but when the shit hits the fan, you just want to be at home.'

I nod but say nothing. My throat closes up. I know what she means, which is why I'm determined to get through the next few months and get home. I'll start over again in the new year and this will all be a distant memory.

'Can I do anything?' I finally manage to say. She blows her nose one final time and then slips her dark glasses back down. Her phone rings with the Welsh national anthem.

'Oh, that's my dad calling now!' She looks at the phone she's pulled from her pocket. 'Actually, could you just keep an eye here for a moment. I could really do with taking this. I know he's worried about me. I won't be long.' She holds the phone to her ear.

'Um, sure . . .' I say, feeling really *un*sure. I know nothing about teaching or kids, and frankly my Italian doesn't seem to be up to much either. I put down my shopping and lean the painting against the big grey wall, obviously part of a new extension.

'Hi, Dad, just hang on,' and I notice Lou's accent has suddenly got a lot thicker. 'Just help them with their paintings and it'll be a good chance for you to practise your Italian. Children are far less judgemental than adults.' She smiles at me.

'Of course, take your call. I'll be fine,' I say breezily.

'Um . . . Giac,' I say, '*posso?*' I hope he'll understand I'm asking to look at his painting. He tears his gaze from his mum, who is walking across the yard, one hand to her ear, the phone pushed against the other side of her head.

'*Sì, certamente,*' he says clearly, and sits back for me to see his painting.

'*Bueno,*' I say, not embarrassed to try out my Italian on him, and he smiles. I point to the trees he's painting opposite and tell him to put in more . . . more detail, I'm trying to say, and use my hands rolling over each other to explain.

'*Di piu?*' he replies.

'*Si!*' I answer, clapping my hands with delight.

Surprisingly nearly half an hour goes by and I'm loving being in amongst the children and their art. When the lunch bell sounds, the children start to pack up and then stop and look at me.

'*Si, si!*' I reply, and then '*Grazie, mille grazie.*' They thank me politely and pick up their drawing boards. Lou is walking towards me switching off her phone and looking a little happier.

She touches the heads of the last few children as they push their chairs straight and go inside.

'Time for some lunch?' she asks.

'Why not?' I say, feeling really lifted.

''Fraid I'm on lunch duty, but the food's good.'

She's right. We have *verdure grigliate* to start – griddled vegetables, in olive oil. Red and yellow peppers, courgettes, and aubergine with deep charred lines across its white flesh, plated up in a soft mound, ready for the children to help themselves. There's garlic in there as well, and fresh dill. It glistens with the olive oil and vinegar it's been marinated in. Then from deep metal trays we have baked orecchiette pasta in tomato sauce layered with stringy, melting mozzarella cheese and topped with grated parmesan. To finish there's fresh fruit – bowls of orange slices and strawberries – and a small slice of simple lemon sponge cake. I watch the children enjoying their food and chatting, topping each other's glasses up from the jugs of water on the table. 'This is amazing,' I tell Lou.

She nods and smiles, looking a little brighter.

'All the pasta is organic and the olive oil has to be extra virgin in schools. It's a rule.'

'Really?' I can't believe it. 'It's a long way from the white-bread sandwich and packet of crisps I used to take to school,' and we both laugh.

'So, what's under the shirt? Is it Nonna's picture?' she asks, wiping her hands.

'Yes, I went round to give it to Marco but he was out, with Rosa. I suspect Anna-Maria thinks I have designs on her son.'

'Oh heaven forbid . . . You wouldn't want to stand in the way of Anna-Maria and her future daughter-in-law!' She laughs and I feel a strange shiver, as if someone's walked over my grave.

'Can I?' She nods to the painting.

'Of course,' and I hand it to her, shirt and all. She unwraps the painting and holds it up. I wait with trepidation.

'It's brilliant!' she says. 'Wow! The *masseria* looks amazing! She'll love it.' She's still staring at it.

'Look, children,' and before I can stop her, she turns it to show the children, who all nod and clap and point and exclaim.

'I've just had a thought.' Lou suddenly puts her hand on my arm, as if she's discovered the meaning of life.

'What?' I laugh.

'You could do a painting here.' She throws out a hand to the big hall.

'Well, I could, yes,'

'Not just a painting . . . a mural, on the wall outside. A painting of the *masseria*, or the town, or the olive trees, whatever you fancied. You could do it while the children have art. It would be like a painting and history lesson combined for these kids. Before long there'll be none of the Bellanuovo estate left. Families split up, go to live in towns where the work is. This town was built around that estate. It was the oldest and the best for miles.'

'Oh, I don't know.' I suddenly feel very daunted by such a big task.

'Look, there's a *festa* in the town at the end of October, just before the olive harvest. We could unveil it then.'

'Around Nonna's birthday, I think.' I remember Marco saying.

'Then she'll love it, and she'll have this as a keepsake. You did like being here this morning, didn't you? Please say you'll do it. It would be so good for the children to have a real artist working here. And so good for them to remember the town's recent history. A legacy if you like. This town was built on olive oil; it would be a shame if the children were to forget.'

'I did love this morning.' I smile tentatively. 'But it's been so long since I've done any real painting, and I really don't think I could do people or faces.'

'Then you'll do it!' Lou claps her hands together.

Have I just agreed to something else I'm not going to be able to pull off? Let's hope I can come up with something that will make everybody happy. Just something simple, symbolic. A large olive tree, for example. But even that makes me nervous. Get this wrong and my mistake will be on show for all to see for a very long time.

'What if it's terrible?' I worry.

'Then we'll paint over it with large buckets of white paint,' she laughs. 'I'll check with the head teacher, but I'm sure she'll be delighted.'

I walk back to the *masseria* up the familiar long lane and nod to Luigi and his wife as I did on the way there. Once again they stand and stare at the mad *inglese*.

I decide to have one more attempt at dropping off the picture to Marco and march purposefully up the shiny steps to Anna-Maria's house. This time there's no shouting. And the dogs are less enthusiastic than before. As I wait, I glance over to the *masseria* and notice that the sheep have gone.

Anna-Maria opens the door. The disappointment on her face is obvious and her smile falls.

'*Ciao*,' I say with an effort. 'Is Marco here, *per favore*?'

'*Non*,' she says shortly and shakes her head. His car's there and she notices me looking at it. I get the distinct impression Anna-Maria is deliberately making this hard for me. 'He's out.'

I nod. I'm not going to argue and I won't leave the painting. As I turn, I come face to face with Marco, who is walking up the steps towards me, smiling.

'*Buongiorno*,' he nods.

'I've come to pay what I owe you.' I look at him meaningfully, feeling Anna-Maria and Nonna's eyes on my back. Nonna points, asking Anna-Maria what I'm carrying. Anna-Maria shrugs and peers and I know that any moment she's going to ask me what it is.

'Perhaps we could walk to the *trullo*,' says Marco, standing back and gesturing.

I don't really want to have a conversation with him, but I can't give him the picture in front of the two women so I do as he suggests.

At the *trullo* I can see it has really come on. I have no idea how he's done this and worked on my *trullo* at the same time.

'Thank you for bringing the picture. I wasn't sure if I was still entitled to it after . . . well, the sheep.'

'It's what we agreed,' I say tightly, unable to stop myself taking in the beautiful room and archways again.

'Thank you. And I can assure you, I too am as good as my word. The land will be yours if you make it to the olive harvest.'

I nod. 'Well, I have it all planned.' I let out a big breath, as if convincing myself.

He raises an eyebrow. 'Really? That's good. What plans?'

'Plans for the oil. Customers, y'know,' I say more confidently than I feel. 'In fact, I've just been confirming a new client.' I wave my laptop and wish I could stop talking. It's nerves making me witter on. I'm certainly not going to let Marco in on my worries about the lack of interest in rent-a-tree.

'Good,' he says again, and it's like we're doing a dance, each of us trying to avoid saying anything that might give away our plans to the other. 'Can I get you something to drink?' he offers, pointing at a small whirring fridge.

'No thank you. I'd better let you get on. I don't want your mother to think I'm keeping you from Rosa.' I blurt it out without even thinking and wish I hadn't. What is it with my runaway mouth? I blush. 'I mean, not that I'm . . . I'm not . . .'

'Rosa? No, I've seen Rosa already today. I have been to provisionally book my olives into the press. The later the better. Right now I have to spend some time with my book.'

'The one you're writing?' I notice a small table and chair at a window set deep into the wall overlooking the *masseria*. 'What's it about? The book?'

He smiles. 'What else? Olives.'

I can't help but smile too.

'Just like you teach at the college?'

'Yes, tasting, growing, the history.'

'And now you're writing a book about it? How you grow the olives here?'

He shakes his head. 'Sadly I haven't spent as much time with my olive trees as I should've done. But I have some time now and being back here has made me want to get my hands dirty again.'

'I bet Rosa's pleased to have you back.' There I go again. Why am I so interested in this man's love life? Just leave the picture and go! I tell myself.

'Rosa and I were at school together. We go a long way back. She has a very good nose.'

I suppose that's a compliment of sorts, but I look a bit confused.

'For oil tasting,' he finishes, and I get the impression he's teasing me.

'Here, your painting.' I hold it out to him, paint-splattered shirt and all. 'I hope your *nonna* likes it.'

'*Grazie*,' he says and takes off the shirt. 'I saw you at the school today,' he adds as he turns the painting towards him.

'Yes, I'm going to be helping out there with the children's art lessons.' I'm keen to show him I'm making my own friends and life in the area.

'*Bene, bene*,' he smiles. 'So look, about the harvest, the olives. If you need any help . . .'

'No, I'm fine,' I say quickly.

'The painting is fabulous, thank you,' he says. 'I still have a bit to finish up on the *trullo* roof. I'll get it done, though,' he insists.

'No rush,' I say, backing out of the door, desperate to get back to the *masseria* before I ask any more stupid questions about him and Rosa, like when the wedding is, or how many children they're hoping to have.

'Who did you say you had helping you out, Ruthie?'

'A friend. It's all sorted.'

'You need to make sure they understand what they're doing . . .'

'Yup, got it,' I say. I am fine. I do have help and that's all he needs to know. I'll show him I can do this. I just wish I felt as confident as I sound.

Marco is still looking at the picture and smiling, clearly delighted with it. He puts it on the table by his laptop, then steps back and stares.

'Thank you, Ruthie,' he says and it looks as if things are finally going to be a bit more civilised between us.

'Thank you for moving the sheep,' I return.

'Ah, no problem. They are grazing on my brother's land on the other side of the *masseria* now.'

I turn to go and notice a van pulling up at the *masseria*.

'You have a guest.' Marco juts his chin.

'Oh, he's not a guest,' I say as Ryan gets out of the van and shakes his curly hair. 'He's my olive contractor.' As I look back at Marco, I notice that his face has turned to thunder.

Chapter Twenty

'*Ciao!* I mean, hey! Sorry, force of habit,' Ryan calls as I walk up the drive. Daphne immediately leaves her grazing and gallops over to him, sniffing him and snorting.

'Heeey!' he says, trying to dodge her enquiring nose, prodding this way and that. He holds two bottles of yellow liquid in the air out of her way and snakes his hips this way and that. He's wearing a washed-out T-shirt and combat shorts. His blond curls shake as he does his goat-swerving dance.

'Just tickle her between the ears,' I call, trying to hide the laugh that's bubbling in my throat. Ryan tentatively scratches Daphne between the ears. She stops prodding him and raises her nose with pleasure.

'Urgh!' Ryan sidesteps Daphne and makes a run for it to the front door. 'Hey,' he says again, composing himself and kissing me on each cheek. His shaggy curls bounce around his face. I think it's his hair that makes him attractive. It seems to match his personality, bubbly and happy. But despite being pleased to see him, I'm feeling a bit on the back foot, and I'm not sure if it's Ryan's friendly greeting that's made me flustered or the fact that Marco seemed so cross about him helping me out. Well, if I'm going to win this bet, I'm going to need help. I'm not foolish enough to think I know anything about olive trees. Tiling and power tools are one thing; the great outdoors is a mystery to me, so Marco will just have to put up with it, because it really isn't any of his business who I ask to help with my olives.

'Come in,' I gesture and Ryan follows me quickly inside as Daphne approaches.

'Shut the d—' I start, but he already has. It's dark inside and cool. The doors are open at the back of the dining room. 'Go through, I'll bring us some coffee.'

'Ah, not for me, thanks. I'm good with water. Here . . .' he holds out the two bottles of yellow olive oil to me. 'From Bellanouvo olives,' he says.

'Thank you. That's really kind,' I smile as I take the bottles and put them down in the kitchen.

He shoves his hands into his pockets and looks around. He's avoiding Daphne and it makes me smile again.

'I'm glad you agreed to this. I mean, after I didn't use you to do the *trullo* roof. Thanks for coming over. I'm really grateful,' I say, passing him a glass of water.

'Really?' His eyes brighten and a cheeky smile spreads across his face.

'I mean, I'm grateful you could help with the olives.' This time I laugh. He's funny and it feels really good to laugh.

'Right, let's go and look at the trees,' I say, sipping my own water. I step outside. The sun is bright, but I pull a light cardigan around me. There's a feeling in the air, like everything is about to change.

'Down here.' We walk across the brushed concrete and past the overgrown vegetable plot. 'My job for later.' I point at the pile of weeds and choking brambles.

He guffaws. 'Look like that's your job for the next month!'

My heart dips. I was really fired up about getting stuck in, but he's right, it's going to be a massive job.

'I don't quite know where to start,' I say, half to myself.

"Fraid it's not my area of expertise. I'm just an olive man. And I live in the town. If I want good food, I go to a restaurant. All this self-sufficiency stuff isn't for me!' He shakes his blond curls again; blond curls that are much more mousy at the roots than their very yellowy tips would suggest.

'Yes,' I sigh with a hint of regret, 'I used to live in the town.'

'Really? What, round here? Martina Franca? Ceglie?'

'No. London,' I say flatly, still staring at the overgrown plot that's supposed to provide me with delicious, nutritious food now my income is down to zilch.

'Now that is a town!' Ryan nods, impressed. 'Love London. Lived there for a while. Might start looking at doing some business over there,' he adds. I feel a sudden, completely unexpected pang of homesickness, and tears prick my eyes.

'Really?' I pull my sunglasses down from my head.

'Yeah. I have contacts in America, which is where I do most of my business, but I'm thinking London would be great to tap into.'

I suddenly have an image of Ryan and me meeting up

in London, going for a drink in town, a walk in Hyde Park. The twist of homesickness in my stomach tightens even more. I try and distract myself and walk briskly towards the first of the trees, high-stepping over the long grass.

'What do you . . .' I'm about to ask him what business he would be doing in London when I see Luigi jump down from Marco's side of the wall, remarkably sprightly for someone so rotund, and walk right across the back of the house.

'*Buongiorno.*' He raises a hand and nods as he passes behind us, making his way towards the sheep in the field on the other side of my wall. He's wearing green working trousers, a shirt, a green jumper with elbow patches and a flat cap.

'*Buongiorno,*' Ryan replies loudly and waves a hand back. I, on the other hand, just stand with my mouth waggling up and down as he passes the back of my barn and courtyard, then puts a hand on the far wall and nimbly jumps over it.

Ryan turns back and starts inspecting the trees. I'm still staring at Luigi as he makes his way across the field. The sheep have begun to make their way over to him, baaing loudly.

'Did you see that?' I finally manage to say, outraged.

'See what?' Ryan asks, turning back to me.

'That! Luigi! He just walked straight across my land, without a by-your-leave! He can't do that!'

Ryan laughs and puts his hands on his hips. 'Yes he can.'

'What d'you mean?'

'Italy's right to roam. You can walk almost anywhere, if there are no fences or walls.' He shrugs. 'He can walk pretty much all over here,' he adds, looking at the tumbledown walls.

'You . . . you . . . mean . . . Just say for example I didn't own my driveway, I'd still be able to use it?'

'Can't see why not.' He shrugs again. 'As long as there's no fencing to keep you out.' He turns back to study the trees more closely.

'Bloody Marco!' I say, and grind my teeth together. I've been trying not to use the drive in case I'm accused of trespassing, and now I find out I'm perfectly entitled to. Why couldn't Marco have told me that?

'Wassat?' Ryan says, clearly thinking about something else.

'Nothing.' I shake off my frustration and smile. 'Come on, let me show you the rest of the trees.'

Just at that moment, Daphne comes dashing up to join us.

'Whoa!' Ryan skips around me to stand on my other side, resting his hands on my shoulders.

'She's fine, honest.' I rub her head and she falls into step beside me. 'See?' I turn and smile at Ryan, who, I notice, still has his arm around my shoulder. Am I imagining it, or does he leave his hand there just a little longer than necessary? I look at the hand as he slowly slides it away, and realise I quite enjoyed it being there. I already feel I can count him as someone who's there for me if I need him, and that makes me feel a whole lot better. Lou was right, we would make a good pair. This is me moving on. I feel the little shimmy of excitement again.

'They go down to the wall at the end there.' I make an effort to return to the subject of the olive trees, and point to the crumbling wall in the distance.

'I look after the land on the other side of that pile of stones. One of Marco's cousins owns it. He lives away. Up north. Like the rest of the family.'

'How come they don't get one of the family to look after it? There's lots of them here,' I say, remembering the night before the funeral.

'Well, from what I gather,' Ryan lowers his voice, 'Marco's away and—'

'*Buongiorno.*' The voice behind us makes me jump. Ryan and I turn together to see Marco taking the same path as Luigi before him. He stops and raises a hand.

'*Buongiorno,*' Ryan replies again. I, on the other hand, find myself just scowling.

'Everything okay?' asks Marco.

'Fine, thank you,' I reply crisply, infuriated by his cheek. 'Just sorting out my olives,' I add, childishly emphasising the 'my'.

'Do you need any help?' he offers, and I frown again.

'No thank you,' I say, politely but firmly. 'Ryan is telling me everything I need to know.'

Marco raises a hand and walks slowly across my field towards Luigi. I turn my back, hoping that if I ignore him he'll go away.

'So, tell me what I need to do, Ryan.' Marco's family history will have to wait until another day.

'Not much really. Looks like these olives are the only thing round here that's been well cared for.' He tucks his hands into his pockets, which drags at his shorts, revealing the elastic round the top of his boxers. He turns and looks back at the house. I follow his gaze and see Marco with Luigi looking in our direction, pointing to the trees. I stiffen, and I'm not sure if it's because of Ryan's comment about the house or Marco's interest in my olives.

'Do we need to rotovate this or anything?' I wave a hand at the long grass.

'No,' he laughs. 'I'll bring some weedkiller.'

'Is that okay to use?' I say, surprised.

'Yeah, no problem, as long as we hang an empty bottle from the tree to let people know we've put it down. You get some types who don't want us using it, but it's the way forward. These guys have to move with the times. You should see the olive groves in Australia. It's a real up-and-coming market. Straight lines so you can just drive the tractor along and shake and strip the trees. None of this hand-picking, taking forever.'

'Is that what you'll do here?'

'Yeah, I'll bring in the tractor down there.' He points to the side of the house. 'Then we'll grip the trees and shake the branches for all they're worth, and bingo! We'll be done in half the time it would take hand-pickers. We'll get a slot at the press booked nice and early. Get it over and done with before it becomes too busy.'

'Great.' I smile. That's exactly what I wanted to hear. Ryan looks around again.

'Couldn't live out here on my own,' he says, giving a

fake shiver, his hands still deep in his pockets and his combats now halfway down his hips.

'Oh, I'm not on my own,' I say, thinking about the stream of people who seem to know my business. 'It never stops around here.' Lou drops in on her lunch breaks, and then of course there's Marco, who seems to pop up every few minutes, supposedly finishing the roof. And the electrician and Luigi and Anna-Maria and Nonna; not to mention Daphne and *mamma* cat and her tribe.

'So you don't think I need to do much at all?' I say, bringing the conversation back to the olives and finding myself wondering if Marco has gone or if he's still watching with his critical eye. Ryan shakes his head.

'They were well pruned after last year's harvest. That's the hardest part, the pruning. Everyone's got a different way of doing it. But mostly they work in three-year cycles. Cut back hard the first year and don't get much oil, not as hard the second year, and then lightly prune the third year for a good crop. Lots of farms have their olives in three sections so you have a good crop every year.'

'And mine?'

'You look like you're in for a good crop this year.'

'And you'll come in and organise the picking?'

'Yeah, leave all that to me. I'll harvest them and then bring back the oil to you. We'll book the slot at the press for a few weeks' time. We'll try and get it done by the beginning of November at the latest.'

'We're going to book now? Will it be too early?'

'Might as well. This town will talk of nothing else from now until the end of November, maybe even the beginning of December, but we'll get yours out the way. Don't worry. The oil will be fine, especially if you're selling it abroad. Most of my clients don't know the difference between good oil and . . . well, just oil. It all tastes the same to them. You can get harvested early and put your house back on the market.'

'Great!'

'And then we can talk about meeting up in London.' He smiles widely and I feel myself smiling back.

We turn to walk back to the house and Ryan swaps sides to avoid Daphne again, brushing past me and bumping into me like a playful puppy, and I can't help but laugh again, especially because I can feel Marco's eyes on us.

'Oh, here.' I dash inside to the kitchen and come back to find Ryan in the dining room. 'Thanks for the oil. Have some piccalilli,' I say, handing him one of my jars. I still have mountains of the stuff.

'Cool. What's piccalilli?' he asks, looking puzzled at the yellow and green mixture in the jar, holding it up to inspect it.

'It's an English thing,' I say, and he looks impressed. He undoes the lid, sniffs it and grimaces.

'Interesting . . .' he says. He's obviously trying to be kind.

By the time Ryan leaves by the front door, Marco is on the roof of my *trullo*, painting the topknot. Ryan disappears in a cloud of dust, stopping only to open and shut the gates and then driving off down the lane with a friendly toot.

'So your friend Ryan is teaching you about olives,' Marco says finally from his position up high.

'Yes.' I cross my arms. 'Yes, he is.'

'He's taught you what you need to do?'

'Yes,' I say even more firmly.

'So you know you must get the grass cut. Keeping the grass down is the most important thing at this time of year for the olive trees.'

'Actually, he said he'd deal with that. Everything's looking fine. I don't have to do anything. He's gone to book the slot at the press.'

'What? *Merda!* You must keep the grass down. It's important! How else will you lay the nets when the harvest comes?' He shakes his head and waves an angry paintbrush in the direction of the grove. 'I presume he told you about the nets. Picking by hand is a skill. He'll need to lay nets.'

'Oh, he's not picking by hand. He's using a machine,' I say. Marco goes a furious shade of deep red and I turn and go back into the house.

If I wanted to prove to Marco I can do things my own way, I think I just did. His irate expression flashes back into my mind and I decide to hide out in the veg patch. Those prickles have got to be easier to handle than Marco in this mood. Judging by the look on his face, I don't think he'll speak to me for days. Which is exactly what I wanted . . . isn't it? So why then am I suddenly feeling like I've found a penny and lost a pound?

Chapter Twenty-one

'Good God! What have you done to your hands?' Lou says as she swings into the seat opposite me, kissing me on both cheeks before she sits down. We're meeting in Mia's pizzeria. It's market day, but it's quiet. The sun is hiding behind the clouds. There are shoppers at the stalls, locals. But no one is buying brightly coloured scarves or sunglasses today. There are still plenty of bra stalls and tablecloths, but apart from that it's mostly food. Up the road, outside Franco Pugliese's bar, a group of short, fat, mahogany-skinned men in jumpers and flat caps – Luigi's friends – are standing and talking. Luigi waved a greeting to me as I passed. I can't understand a word he says, but I nodded and smiled. There are still men on the *bocce* pitch, and playing cards at the tables in the pine-covered playground.

I push my little laptop to one side. It's the only place I can get Wi-Fi in the town now. If only Antonio's bar had been able to stay open.

'Ah, started to get to grips with the veg plot,' I offer up by way of explanation, looking at the scratches. In fact I ache like mad and I've hardly made an impression on it. But needs must. If I can get through the bramble hedge that's grown up round it, who knows what might be in there.

Lou looks tired and stressed.

'How's your Antonio? Found any work yet?'

She shakes her head. 'No, nothing. He seems so depressed.'

'You're not thinking of moving away, are you, going back to the UK?'

She shrugs. 'Maybe. I mean, Antonio could go and work with my dad, labouring. It's just a little building firm, but Dad wants to start taking things easier, look towards retirement. And he'd get to see more of Giac if we were there.'

'But you love it here.'

'I know, but I love my dad too. He's on his own. It's hard. He's hardly seen Giac. And like I say, he wants to start taking things a bit easier.'

In a way, I'm grateful my mum has Colin. I mean, I may not have relished sharing the flat with him, or like the way Mum runs round after him, making him tea and cooking and washing for him without a word of thanks. And I really didn't like using the tiny bathroom after him in the mornings. But at least she's not on her own. She's happy. They have their own life and I'm not part of it. Now I need to work out where I belong. I get that wave of homesickness again. The only problem is, I have no idea where I'm homesick for.

Mia, the pizzeria owner, a beautiful-looking woman in her fifties, with long dark hair, big gold earrings and a figure-hugging polo shirt tucked into her jeans, comes over with olives, mozzarella balls and little tomatoes and tells us to take our time. We both thank her.

'Any news about the rent-a-tree website?' Lou asks when she's gone.

'Well I've set up the Facebook page. I took loads of photos and put them on there and explained how it works. I've pushed the idea that people can pay for a tree as a gift. The gift that keeps on giving. You rent it for a year, and come the harvest I send out the olive oil from that tree to the recipient.' I put one of the tomatoes in my mouth and it cracks and explodes with flavour. Why does food never taste like this back home? I vow to make a conscious effort to buy better food when I get back, not always the value stuff. In fact, I may even put my name down for that allotment. When I know where I'm going to be.

'And how many bottles will they get?'

'I think three half-litre ones. Ryan says that should be about right.'

Lou raises her eyebrows and smiles knowingly. I say nothing, but blush.

'And what's the take-up been like?'

'Nothing so far,' I sigh. 'I don't know what I'm doing wrong. I've set it up, invited people to like the page, advertised on Gumtree, but so far, nothing. Apart from my friend Beth, of course.'

'I could buy one!' Lou suddenly says brightly.

'Don't be daft. You live here!' I laugh.

'I could buy it for my dad,' she argues.

'You can give him your own oil. You still have the trees at your *trullo*.'

And we both smile, hiding our own sadness. Lou

wants to stay but will have to leave; I want to leave but have to stay.

'Show me your Facebook page, I want to see it,' she says, pointing to the computer. 'Perhaps I could share it with my friends.'

I reach for the computer and sign into Facebook, sighing. I don't know what I'm going to do if I can't get this off the ground. I look at the screen and then refresh it, just in case it's a mistake. Then I take a moment to absorb what I'm seeing.

'Ruthie? Everything okay?'

I stare again and blink.

'There are orders, lots of orders!' I say.

'Let's see!' Lou pulls the screen round to her.

'But how?' I search the page frantically to try and work out what's going on.

'Look there. Whoever that is has liked and shared your page and it seems to have gone from there. Who's that?'

I look at the name on the screen.

'It's Ed. I sent him the link just to try and make him jealous. I was feeling really fed up.'

'Well, whatever the reason, it's done the trick. That's fantastic! Looks like all his City mates want a taste of Puglia.' Lou waves at Mia and orders two pizzas. 'Oh, and I have some more good news. The headmistress has given the thumbs-up to the living history project. She'd love you to come and paint the mural.'

'I'm looking forward to it.' And, I realise, I am. All I have to do is work out what on earth I'm going to paint!

After lunch, when Lou has gone back to work, I reply

to all the orders, check my PayPal account and breathe a huge sigh of relief. Thank you, Ed! Looks like all his corporate mates have come up trumps for me after all.

I walk back to the *masseria* via the ironmonger's and treat myself to a new pair of secateurs and some heavy-duty gloves, ready to carry on with the veg plot. Back home, I go to the big barn to find a bucket and rake I know I've seen. There's still a lot of stuff that needs sorting in here, including a huge plastic barrel the size of a deep paddling pool that may have been used to transport an olive tree. If only the old olive press wasn't here, it would be a great space. It could even become a function room or an art gallery. But, I remind myself, I can't think too far ahead. I just have to get the place looking as good as it can by the end of the harvest and then find myself a flatshare back in London once I've sold.

I find a pair of old wellingtons and put them on. They make me flap like a penguin when I walk, but better than my falling-apart deck shoes. Pulling on my new thick gloves and my market sunglasses, I feel like Buzz Lightyear, ready for anything. As I make my way to the side of the house and the vegetable garden, I swear I can hear gentle laughter in the rustling of the trees.

I spend the next few days cutting and sawing at the brambles round the area. I work until my hands hurt and my back aches. By the end of the week, it's looking good. Finally I can see what's there, and there is plenty. I buy bamboo canes from the ironmonger's and stake the tomatoes, and in the evening I use the hosepipe and water everything. I feel like the plants are coming back to life. But I'm not. I'm exhausted. I ache all over. I've never felt so in need of a bath. I pile the brambles and leaves and rubbish from the veg plot together with my rake. It's like trying to herd jelly uphill, as the brambles flick out and snake around, refusing to be tamed. Eventually I manage it. I run my thick gloves, which no longer look bright green and new, across my forehead. I just want a bath and a glass of wine. And if I was really going all out for a luxurious evening, a good book too. Then I have an idea. A mad idea!

Downing tools, I run back to the barn and drag out the big plastic barrel. I roll it like a giant cheese round the back of the house on to the patio, then I run the hosepipe from the outside tap into the barrel and turn it on. An al fresco bath! The sun is beginning to set, deep red, like a fiery ball in the sky. I pour a large glass of rosata and grab some shower gel and shampoo from upstairs. Then with a quick look around to check I'm alone, I strip down to my underwear, step up on to one of the wooden crates I use as stools, and climb over the edge and into the water. It's warm! Actually warm from where the hosepipe has sat in the sun all day. I sit down, then stretch back and close my eyes. Bliss! The water level rises, and as it does, I slip off my underwear and toss it on to the ground, enjoying the water around every bit of my body, waving my legs to and fro in a star shape.

Suddenly I hear footsteps. Oh good God! The last thing I need is for Marco to see me naked in a barrel. I sink as low as I can in the water, covering my chest with my arms.

'*Buonanotte*,' calls Luigi as he walks past, back to Marco's field, with a smile on his face. Oh God! Now he thinks the mad Englishwoman is madder than ever. '*Buonanotte*, Luigi,' I say, giggling into the foam and giving thanks that at least it wasn't Marco.

The barrel is nearly full and I'm going to have to get out to turn the tap off. Water starts to tumble over the top, cascading down like a waterfall, but it's such a nice feeling – like a jacuzzi – that I lie back, letting it slosh around, covering my ears. This is heaven! I dip under the water, running my hands through my hair to rinse off the shampoo, then come back up through the bubbles, eyes shut, feeling the freshness of the air.

As I resurface, I hear barking and shouting. What on earth's going on? I sit up as far as I can and turn towards the vegetable plot. Marco's dog is tearing around in it, barking. It seems to be chasing something. Suddenly the dog turns in my direction, barking for all it's worth. There is more shouting, and I see Luigi and Marco running after the dog, who's chasing what looks like a wild boar. It runs right in front of the barrel, spraying water and squealing. The dog is seeing it off with all its might.

'*Scusi. Buonanotte*,' calls Luigi as he passes. Marco is behind him, calling the dog and whistling. He stops and turns to me.

I can't speak or move.

'*Scusi*,' he says, slightly out of breath. 'You seem to have wild boar in your veg patch.'

I sink under the water again, hoping that by the time I reappear he'll be gone.

Chapter Twenty-two

The next morning I wake to the sound of banging. I jump up and look out of the window. Luigi and Marco are hammering in stakes around the vegetable plot and attaching green gauze between them. I pull on my clothes, zipping up my hoodie. It's starting to feel cold.

'Marco?' I call, and he stops work for a moment, letting the sledgehammer fall to his side. 'What are you doing?'

'Helping to fix the mess my dog made,' he says, and lifts the sledgehammer again.

Luigi nods, smiles and wishes me good morning, his big round face gleaming like a conker, then goes back to banging in another stake.

'You don't have to do this!' I look at the broken bamboo canes and the trampled vegetables, feeling like a deflating balloon. I planned to get to work straight away this morning, but Marco has beaten me to it.

'It was my dog that made this mess,' he argues.

'But only because she was chasing off the boar,' I reply.

'I should put it right,' he says, and returns to work.

I gather up trampled chilli and pepper branches, cauliflowers and courgettes. I put them all into a bucket and then tread down the mounds of earth like I'm at a polo match treading in divots. Only I'm not. I'm wearing old clothes and a pair of size 9 wellies that could well have belonged to Marco's grandfather.

When Marco and Luigi have finished, I go into the house with the bucket of vegetables and return with coffee, water and jars of piccalilli for them both. It's the least I can do. Luigi is intrigued and studies the jar with his big, dirty hands.

'Where is the goat?' Marco asks.

'In the barn. I've just let her out of her pen and fed her,' I say, sipping my thick black coffee.

'She must stay out at night. That's why she's here. She'll see off the boar.' Marco finishes his coffee in one mouthful and starts tidying his tools. 'It's her job. She's . . . how do you say . . . a guard goat!' and he gives a little smile, as if he's made a great joke. I smile too.

'Look, perhaps I can stay and help a bit more,' he says as Luigi heads off for his lunch. 'There's a lot to do, and if you don't know what you're doing . . .'

'I'm fine really,' I insist quickly. He's already done too much, and I feel I have to find a way to repay him.

Marco returned to the *trullo* feeling like a boiling kettle about to blow its lid. He was frustrated. He wanted to do more. He'd loved being out there and there was so much more that needed doing. He set down his tools by the door, where Lucia sat lifting her chin to the sun. He patted her and bent to go into the house. He had plenty to be doing here, but right now, despite himself, he wished he could be next door helping Ruthie. She was a worker, no doubt about it, and he'd enjoyed toiling side by side with her. It had been a good couple of hours building the fence and repairing the vegetable garden.

He looked at the jar in his hand, unscrewed the lid and sniffed the contents. Then he put his little finger in and tasted it.

Hmmm. He nodded in approval. It was strange but quite tasty. He put the jar in his kitchen. Maybe he'd do some work on the book. It had been ages since he'd actually opened the document and written anything. He sat down at his little table and looked out over the olive trees; Ruthie Collins' olive trees. He hadn't doubted she would throw herself into the bet. She seemed the sort of woman who did everything wholeheartedly. He liked that . . . he liked that very much.

He slid his glasses on and opened his computer, but he wasn't really concentrating; he was gazing out of the window and wondering what it would be like to go back to work at the college after spending so much time back here on the land. He'd liked that too, very much, and wished he hadn't. He wished he could help Ruthie more, show her what she needed to do, but he knew she wouldn't take his interference. He could only wait until she needed him. And who knew how long that would take. Maybe never . . .

He slid his glasses further up his nose and tried to put Ruthie Collins and the land to the back of his mind.

I head to the back door, slip off my muddy boots and go into the kitchen to start making another big batch of piccalilli. Whilst it's bubbling away, I decide I might as well get rid of the big pile of weeds. I'll burn them like I've seen so many of the farmers doing around the area. I have no idea how else to get rid of them. And it would be great to take some more pictures of the olive grove as we get closer to the harvest. I'll put them on the website to let people know how their trees are coming on. That way they'll really feel a part of the process. The more pictures I take of life at the *masseria*, the more real it will be for them.

I grab my camera and put it on charge. Then I go out to the weed pile and stuff scrunched-up paper underneath it. I hope I'm better at lighting this bonfire than I am at getting the wood-burning stove to work. Perhaps a small garden fire will make the photos look even better. There's a real sense of autumn in the olive grove, with a gentle, soft breeze in the air, like a blanket wrapping itself around me.

I strike a match and put it to the paper. The wind suddenly picks up and a big orange flame shoots up the side of the bonfire, making me jump back, nearly falling over Daphne.

Jeez! I wasn't expecting that. I'm better at this firelighting thing than I thought. Or maybe the rubbish is drier than I realised. Either way, the fire's taken much more quickly than I was expecting. In fact, this isn't what I was expecting at all. Shit! Another flame shoots skywards, sending my heart racing in panic. But I'm rooted to the spot, mesmerised by the fire taking hold so quickly in front of me.

Suddenly I'm knocked sideways. There's a shout and then an arc of water falling on to the flames, hissing and fizzing. But as fast as the flames are dampened, they flare up somewhere else on the pile. On command, I run and get the washing-up bowl full of water, and keep running back and forth to the barrel of water where I had my bath. The fire hisses, fizzes and spits, and at last the flames start to die.

The hosepipe is still pouring out water. The bonfire is still hissing and smoking. Slowly I turn round. Marco's chest is rising and falling and he takes deep breaths. Exhausted and sweating, he rests a hand on my shoulder and bends over to catch his breath.

'Marco, I'm sorry. I didn't realise. Ryan said I didn't need to worry about anything.'

Marco says nothing.

'Look, I'm sorry,' I repeat. 'I thought I could just burn the garden rubbish. I had no idea.'

'You could've caused a huge fire!' He suddenly erupts as he stands up. 'Uncut grass is the biggest threat to olive trees. You could've killed off hundreds of years of history . . . if not yourself,' he roars, pointing at the line of scorched grass making its way towards the big tree.

'You haven't been near these trees in years. You've been working away. Why do you care all of a sudden? And you certainly wouldn't care about me!' I blurt out.

We both stand furious, breathing heavily, our faces cross and hot, up close to each other. It must be the panic and the fear. For a moment neither of us says anything, the air heavy with unspoken words. Does he have feelings?

Could he care? I find myself thinking. But why would he? I'm the one who's standing in the way of his family getting their house back.

I can feel his hot breath on my face. See the sweat forming beads on his brow and the dark streaks of dirt on his cheeks. For a split second it feels like we're both moving closer, as if drawn magnetically. Briefly I wonder if his lips are going to meet mine. His angry blue eyes are flashing and darting from my eyes to my lips and back again, and I know mine are doing the same. Both of us are still breathing heavily, nostrils flaring with each deep inhalation. His chest is rising and lowering. Now my eyes aren't darting around his face; they're just looking at his lips, and I'm wondering, just a little bit closer . . .

Suddenly there's a shout and we catapult apart like we've actually been burnt. It's Anna-Maria, waving a tea towel and asking if everything's okay. Nonna is with her.

'*Va bene*,' Marco shouts back. 'It's fine.'

Anna-Maria and Nonna return to the house with shaking heads and waving tea towels. Neither of us knows quite what to say as we turn back to each other. He looks at the ground and I inspect my wellies.

'Look, Marco,' I say at the same time as he says, 'Ruthie, I . . .'

We both stop. He gestures to me to speak. His breathing is slower now, as is mine, but my heart is still beating at double speed. Daphne is nudging at my hand, looking for reassurance.

'Marco, I'm sorry. Please, will you tell me what I need to do,' I say, feeling like I've just eaten a huge slice of humble pie. I'm not used to asking for help.

'No,' replies Marco, and our moment of truce is gone. The barriers drop like the iron gates on a castle and I shut myself in again, furious that I've let down my guard even a little bit.

'Fine!' I say, taking a couple of steps backwards and turning to go. He catches my elbow and I spin round, furious at his touch.

'I won't tell you what to do . . . I'll show you!' he says, and marches off towards my big shed.

I watch him go. Anna-Maria is calling to him again but gives up and goes back inside with a flick of her tea towel. I could tell Marco I don't need his help after all. I'll find Ryan, ask him what I should be doing. Or I could just follow Marco.

Despite the fire dying down and the danger and the argument abating, my heart is still racing in my chest, thundering like a horse on the gallops. Taking a deep breath, I follow Marco to the shed.

Chapter Twenty-three

'You need to cut the grass. It has grown too tall. It is a fire hazard,' he says, repeating what I now already know.

'It's fine. I can do it,' I say. 'Really, if I need your help, I'll let you know.'

He shakes his head. 'You will,' he says. 'I have to get something from Rosa at the press. I'll be back.' He lets go of the old strimmer he's holding, letting it fall against the old stone press, and stalks away from the shed.

As soon as he's disappeared down the road in a cloud of beige dust, I go up on to the *trullo* roof via its tiny stone steps to ring Lou. My phone toots into life, showing me I have messages. They're from Ed, of course, one asking if I can remember the name of a particular restaurant in Fowey. Presumably he wants to take Annabel there. The other wanting to know if I took an electricity reading on the day I left the flat. I ignore both messages. I have Marco to contend with right now. I'll show him I can do this, but I'll do it my way.

'Lou, can I ask a favour? Do you have a lawnmower you could lend me?'

I drive to Lou's apartment in town. Antonio gets the lawnmower from the shed at the back of the bar, once used to cut the little grass verge out the front. Giac immediately wants to show me his new paintings. It makes me smile. Antonio can't help but smile either as he helps me load the lawnmower into the back of my Ford Ka. He's talking to me constantly and I pick up the occasional word.

'*Si, olivio*,' I reply, assuming he's asking if I'm cutting the olive grove. Again he smiles, with a look on his face that asks if I'm joking. Eventually we have to resort to leaving the boot open and the lawnmower sticking out the back. He assures me it'll be fine.

'You haven't got far to go,' Lou points out. 'Oh,' she adds quickly. 'The mural. Okay to start a week Monday?'

I nod, smile and kiss them both and hurry back to the *masseria*. I want to get stuck into this before Marco gets back.

Stones fly out like missiles from the blade and I can barely get the lawnmower to move in the thick soil. I even try rocking it from side to side. It whines and wails and then judders to a stop. I stop too, totally exhausted, wipe my brow and look back at my progress. I've managed to cut a rectangle the size of a yoga mat.

Suddenly I see Marco's car arriving back in much the same cloud of dust that he left in and I turn back to the lawnmower and pull at the handle. The wire stretches out, and then whips back but it doesn't start. There's a smell of petrol.

'Come on . . .' I grit my teeth. I can hear Marco getting out of his car. I pull again with much more force and this time it starts, groaning into life like a marathon runner after they've hit the wall.

I swing it round and start on a new patch of long grass, hoping to make better inroads. I know he's watching me, but I'm not going to turn around. My arms ache, and my back, but I won't look at him, and I definitely won't look at how much I've still got to do. I push harder into the thick clumps, feeling my eyes prickle with salty sweat. I'm getting nowhere. The lawnmower starts its high-pitched whining again and then cuts out. I stand stock still, my body vibrating from holding the juddering handle. I bend to try and start it again, but this time nothing happens. Then I hear a high-pitched buzzing: *crack*, *crack*, *whizz*, *crunch*. I turn. Marco isn't standing at the wall laughing at me as I thought. He's wearing goggles and leather gloves and is strimming round the base of the trees. He's done more in that short space of time than I have with my lawnmower, which now looks as if it's found its final resting place, abandoned at an angle in the middle of a large clump of long grass.

Marco stops strimming and lifts his goggles.

'There are goggles for you in the shed. And new gloves. It's hard on the hands. This should have been done weeks ago. Your olive man should've told you.'

Without a word I walk towards the shed, my hands throbbing, to where the old strimmer is waiting for me, charged with petrol and with goggles hanging from the handle. I put on the soft leather gloves and carry the strimmer to the olive grove. It starts much more easily than the lawnmower. It spits and fires out grass in all directions, pieces ricocheting off my goggles, making me flinch. It feels like I'm in a snowstorm of grass.

Suddenly there are two arms around me. I jump and tense. Marco is standing right behind me, his arms all the way around either side of me. The strimmer chokes and cuts out.

'No, like this,' he says, and slowly swings the strimmer back and forth, like a metronome. I'm tense and trying not to touch him; I can't do it.

'Relax. Stop fighting me.' He tightens his arms around me. I am very aware that I must be hot, sweaty and frankly stinky.

'Go with the flow,' he says close to my ear, and just for a moment I shut my eyes and relax. I find myself swinging from side to side with him, my shoulders dropping back and resting on his chest.

'You have it.' He suddenly releases me and I take a step or two back before righting myself.

'Yes, right, I have it.' I adjust my goggles.

'We will leave some flowers around the edges for the bees,' he tells me.

I fire up the strimmer again quickly and begin to sway from side to side. I turn to look at him. He smiles and gives me the thumbs-up, and I find myself smiling and giving him the thumbs-up back.

We work all day in the olive grove, and the next, breaking only for lunch and some time in the shade.

'You see, these olives are coratina olives. They ripen later than other varieties,' he says as we sit in the shade of my bamboo awning eating bread, cheese, olives, tomatoes and piccalilli. 'They deal well with different conditions and environments. They are very popular here in Puglia.

The oil is very fruity and pungent,' he tells me.

Each day I find out a little more about the olives on my land. Marco tells me about the olive oil process, the acidity levels that make an oil, and extra-virgin oil. But he never talks about himself, or his life here with his family in the *masseria*.

After lunch we go back to work, and in the evenings he returns to his *trullo* and I bottle up a new batch of piccalilli, even though I already have tons of the stuff. I'm going to have to find a way to get rid of some of it. Then I make more sketches for the mural.

I think I'll go for something simple and bold. A big olive tree filling the wall. I get out the pile of black and white photographs that Lou copied for me. Photographs of the *masseria*, the estate and the family. But instead of sketching an olive tree, I find myself pencilling out the picture that has been forming in my head every night as I go to sleep, making little sketches on the back of the electrician's bill. I know I'd never be able to do it. It would be too big a project for me. I haven't done proper painting in years and I'd never be able to get the faces right. Painting faces was always hard for me. Besides, I'm not sure it's what the town would want.

I put away the photographs and go back to sketching out the olive tree before hauling myself into bed.

But by day three I can't go on.

Chapter Twenty-four

The sun comes up, creeping in through my shutters, but instead of throwing back the covers and going to the window to watch the mist rise off the olive trees, I don't move. Every bone in my body aches. I *can't* move. I can't do this any more. I pull the covers over my head and ignore Luigi's cockerel doing its best to wake me, and the dogs next door barking for their breakfast, and the little birds being cheerful and chirpy. Don't they ever get fed up of the daily grind? I wonder, getting up, singing songs, finding worms, watching out for cats. It must be exhausting.

I gather the covers even tighter over my head and find that big fat tears are rolling down my cheeks, making wet puddles on the pillows. I pull the duvet to my nose, breathing it in, trying to find any remaining smell from home. I inhale deeply, sucking it up. I want to be at home, back in the flat Ed and I shared. I want to hear the buses rumbling down the street, the metal shutters of the shops opening, and car alarms and sirens bursting into life. I want to go home! I ache in my joints but I ache inside too, in my stomach, in my chest, a physical pain that won't go away.

I should've just stayed on Mum's couch and got myself

a flatshare like other people did. What made me think I could do things so differently? I'm not different. People split with their partners all the time and just get on with it. Why couldn't I just accept it and carry on with life in London? Or go to Cornwall?

My thoughts turn to Beth and Theo and the weekends I used to spend with them: on the beach, walking the dog, wind blowing in our hair, trouser legs rolled up, scarves and coats keeping out the cold. I hear a wail of despair and realise it's coming from me. If only I could press a bloody button that would take me home again.

Just then I hear a knock at my front door and I catch my breath and hold it. It can't be the electrician; he works at the ironmonger's at the weekend. The knock comes again and still I hold my breath, hoping that whoever it is will go away. Usually I'd be up by now, but I just can't do it. I want the world to go away. I turn my face into the pillow and pull it around my ears.

When I eventually release the pillow, the knocking has stopped and I start to breathe again. They've gone. Thank God. And hopefully Marco will see I'm not working today. It's the weekend, I remind myself. Take the day off! I intend to, I reply. I can't bear to get up. If I get up, I'll have to do more strimming, and then there's the veg patch to work on, and I can't even have a warm shower without trying to light that fire! I definitely can't attempt to go into battle with that this morning.

My stomach rumbles but I ignore it. I was so shattered last night, I just fell into bed. I couldn't even wait to boil the water for my slut's pasta, which has become a regular supper, when I'm not too tired to cook. Pasta with chillies from the veg patch, anchovies, garlic and olive oil. It's cheap and gorgeous. Or if I am too tired, it's Sophia's focaccia or whatever leftover bread I have, with cheese and piccalilli. Even the thought of that doesn't stir me from my bed, nor does a trip into town to buy one of Sophia's pastries, a cornetto, hot off the wooden paddles from the oven. The only thing I want is a bacon sandwich, on white bread, with butter and ketchup. Or maybe a fried egg on toast, its yellow yolk running into the bread, white again, mingling with the ketchup on the side of my plate. I want strong builder's tea with sugar in it, and then shepherd's pie for lunch, one of my mum's microwaveable ones. I want my mum, I realise. I miss her. And Ed. Good old dependable, stuck-in-his-ways Ed. I was so sure when we split up that it was the right thing to do, that we'd come to the end of the road. But what if it wasn't the end of the road? What if it was just a pothole, a sodding great crater that knocked us off course for a while? Maybe we could have found our way back if I'd just stuck at it. A part of me would like everything just to go back to how it was.

Suddenly there's a shout under my window.

'Ruthie!'

Oh good God, it's Marco. It must have been him knocking. Does that man never give up? Doesn't he ever have a day off?

'Ruthie!' he calls again. A little smattering of stones hits my shutters, and some land on the wooden floor just inside the window, making me jump.

'Go away!' I mouth, turning into my pillow.

'Ruthie!' Another shower of stones comes in through the window.

'I'm in bed,' I shout back with all the strength I can muster, but it comes out as a rasping whisper. 'I can't work today.'

I don't know if he heard me or not, but he doesn't call again. I pull the duvet up around my shoulders and try and find the patch that still smells of home, then let myself drift back into sleep. I have vivid dreams, about Ed up a ladder fixing the *trullo* roof, Lucia the dog turning over the veg patch and my mother cooking shepherd pies, loads of them. Then I dream I'm trying to catch a plane but it's left without me. I'm chasing it down the runway, but I can't keep up. The black tarmac keeps disappearing from under my feet as I run. Then the familiar image of the painting I have in my head takes over. The characters coming to life, telling me why I should paint them. I push them away, telling them to leave me alone.

Throughout my dreams I can hear this buzzing noise, like a giant mosquito, and in my waking moments I realise it's the sound of a strimmer. No matter how guilty I feel, I can't get out of bed to tell him to stop. I just can't.

The next morning, I still feel like I've been hit by a bus. I don't have an ounce of energy. My shutters stay shut. There's a knock at the door and this time I just ignore it and roll over and close my eyes on my soggy pillows.

I'm not sure if I'm dreaming or not when a bright light suddenly fills my world and Marco is standing in front of me with a tray. I hold my hand over my eyes against the light and pull myself up on to my elbow. I must be dreaming. He wouldn't really have the cheek to come into my house, into my bedroom! Would he?

'I brought you something to eat. You need to help the body refuel,' he says, as if talking to one of his students about the science of food. 'Only a fool would work in this way and not feed the body in the right way.'

I'm wrong. He really is in my house and in my bedroom. I can't believe it, but I just don't have the energy to tell him. Instead I whisper hoarsely, 'I, um, how did you get in?' My mouth is as dry as the desert.

'Spare key,' he says flatly. 'My grandfather kept it under the big stone by the front door.'

I'm too stunned even to be outraged that Marco knew all along where there was a spare key and has let himself into my house. The food on the tray smells amazing: hot rolls and coffee. My mouth starts to water but I can't eat; I just want to go back to sleep. The most random fact ever occurs to me. I realise I must look a right mess! Once again I retreat under my covers.

'I'm sorry, I just need to sleep.'

'Eat something,' he instructs and puts the tray down next to the bed. 'Oh, and by the way, Luigi has sent you two chickens.'

Definitely a dream!

'Chickens? What for?'

'To thank you for the piccalilli. He loves it and so does his wife. He'd like some more. Get some rest and eat!'

*

The coffee goes cold and the rolls stay untouched. I just want to go home. He can have the *masseria*. I've had enough. As the sun goes down on another day and the whirring strimmer stops, I slip back into sleep. I know I've lost. I can't do it. I've no more fight left in me. They were right all along, those who said I couldn't do it. I can't.

Chapter Twenty-five

The next morning there isn't even a knock at the door, or if there was I was too deeply asleep to hear it. I'm woken by the shutters flying back, letting in the bright light. I try to sit upright, my arm protecting my eyes. It's that dream again. Marco's standing in my bedroom in front of the window. Only this time there's no tray.

'It's time to get up, Ruthie,' he says.

'I can't. Have it, have it all. I don't care.' I attempt to collapse on to my pillows, but before I can, he's pulled back the covers and is handing me my dressing gown from the back of the door.

'Really, Marco, it's over. I can't do this. There's too much to do! I can't.'

'The olives won't wait for you. They need your attention now. You have to do it.' He thrusts the dressing gown at me again. 'Get dressed. Coffee's downstairs. I've put the chickens in the old henhouse. This is the life you wanted. You can't just lie down and hope it will all disappear. Life isn't like that, Ruthie. We can't run away and hide from our problems. Problems have a habit of popping up wherever we go.'

'Why do you care? It doesn't matter if I don't make it.

You'll get your house and you and Rosa can have your happy family.' I feel drunk with exhaustion.

'Just get up. Meet me downstairs.'

Oh God! This man is so infuriating! I sigh deeply. I don't have the energy to argue. And I didn't even know I had a henhouse.

Marco marches out of the room and downstairs. I sit upright on the edge of the bed.

He's right, of course. What exactly am I hoping to go home to? Nothing's changed. Ed is still living in Canary Wharf with Annabel. Colin is still with my mum and I'd still be on the lumpy sofa. The only thing that's different is that I don't even have a job with Brandon any more. I don't have anything to go back to. I contemplate just falling into bed again, but I can hear Marco down in the kitchen. I know that if I do that, he'll be up here again, telling me to get up. I have to go downstairs to get him out of my house! I stand up, kicking yesterday's tray, and cold coffee splashes over my foot.

Downstairs, the fire is lit.

'There's hot water if you want a shower,' he says, putting a cafetière on the table. I'm gobsmacked, but I'm too done in to ask how he did it. I sit down and accept the coffee he hands me.

'We should finish the strimming today. Then we'll make small bonfires . . . controlled ones! They'll keep the insects away too.'

'Really, Marco, you don't have to help me. I'm fine. I can do it,' I say, sipping weakly at the coffee. I feel it travelling through my body, lifting my energy.

'I have some walls to repair and logs to cut, but I'll be here. I must take the strimmer back to Rosa today.'

'Rosa?'

'Yes, I borrowed it.'

He puts rolls and jam in front of me, and ham and olives.

'You need to eat. You have an olive grove to look after as well as yourself,' he says.

'And two chickens,' I add, surreally.

'Today we must start sweeping.'

'Sweeping?'

'Yes, sweeping and weeding. I'll show you how to sweep and then I'll start on the brambles along the wall.' He drains his coffee and takes the mug to the kitchen.

'Are you ready, Ruthie? Your olives won't wait.'

I sigh deeply, and although my body is still protesting and wishing it was back under my duvet, I pick up a roll, fill it with ham and follow him out. It's cooler, a nip in the air. There's a smell of autumn. Whilst I've been asleep, summer has gone.

'We must get done before the colder weather comes. You need to be prepared.'

I nod, taking in the seriousness in his voice.

'Okay, so when you have finished strimming, you must sweep. You use this,' he holds up a rake, 'and you sweep under the trees so it's clean. You must keep it like this. You don't want your nets to get caught and rip when you lay them under the trees at harvest.'

I think about telling him that I won't need nets, as Ryan's going to be organising it all. But he seems to be ignoring that fact and I don't want to fan any flames of fury there.

'So we clear up all the fallen twigs and make little piles around the olive grove.' He stops and looks at me, then repeats, 'Little piles.'

'Yes,' I say, shaking my head like a teenager being told off by a parent.

'And then we will light the little fires. The smoke will seep up through the trees and keep the olive flies at bay. The *vermi*. It's said that the olive fly thinks the tree is on fire and so evacuates.' He smiles, and I feel a smile tug at the corner of my mouth too, but even those muscles are exhausted.

'Is that true?'

'Maybe.' He smiles again. 'Most of us run when we lose our home.' He looks at me and I feel slightly uncomfortable for a moment.

'So, to work.' He breaks into my thoughts, and I stand stiffly from the tree stump I'm sitting on. Work is exactly what I intend to do. Although I do feel an awful lot weaker than before and maybe I won't push myself quite as hard as I have been.

'Oh, and another thing.' He stops me in my tracks. 'When the sweeping is done, you must keep doing it, every day if you need to. When the first few olives start to fall, we will take them to the press.'

'Really?' I'm surprised that they're worth pressing.

'The press owner will pay you for them. They'll use them for low-grade oil. It will bring you in a little money. Not much, but a little.'

By press owner, he means Rosa.

'Oh really, it's fine, I don't want any special favours.' I put up a pathetic hand to argue. I don't want to feel like a charity case.

'It's how we do things here. The press owner will pay for the sweepings,' he repeats.

Slightly embarrassed but grateful, I drop my head. I know that I couldn't do this without him right now.

'*Grazie.*'

'*Prego,*' he replies, and smiles like a tutor praising an attentive student. I pull my fleece round me and begin to sweep.

'No, no, like this.' Once again he puts his arms around me and shows me how to make big sweeps under the tree, and I find my stomach fizzing up like cola bubbling up and frothing over the top of the glass. He lets me go but still there is a fizzing in my stomach, and I wonder if it's just a result of days without food.

The sun starts to come up and the heat is much more pleasant, warm but not punishing.

At lunchtime, Marco produces soup, onion, tomato and pancetta, with crusty bread, and we sit on the terrace at the back of the house with a bottle of sparkling water. Afterwards he picks prickly pears and figs from the trees for us to share.

That evening, when the heat has gone from the day, he lights the little fires. I go to find us a cold beer each, and when I return, he has filled the barrel bath for me.

'*Prego,*' he says, and points to it. 'It will be good for your bones.' And my bones very much agree, only this time I put my swimming costume on and he turns his back as I sink into the deliciously warm water. When I get out, he hands me a towel and averts his eyes.

When I go back into the house the fire is lit again and I wonder how the hell he does that so easily. I clearly need to practise.

'Ruthie, you must eat with us tonight.'

'Oh no, really I couldn't.'

'I insist. You must keep the body fuelled,' he tells me again. 'Or you will not be able to manage your work.'

Slightly embarrassed at my recent slump, I agree and thank him.

'This way I can keep an eye on you.'

And I blush all the way upstairs to get changed.

Chapter Twenty-six

I'm not looking forward to another evening with the Bellanuovo family at all. I could just have said no, but to be honest, if it hadn't been for Marco these last few days, well, who knows how much lower I could have got. It would be rude to turn him down, no matter how difficult I'm going to find this. And actually, I surprise myself by thinking, I'm quite looking forward to spending time with him again.

I think back to that first supper when the family were all there. All of them telling me it was a mistake, a mistake that I thought I'd bought it and definitely a mistake that a single woman from England could even think about living here on her own. I look out of the window at the rows of olive trees and the henna-red ground beneath them. There are tufts of grass with flowers in patches, unlike the field beyond, which Ryan looks after, where there isn't a weed or a tuft of grass to be seen. That's how my land would look if I let him use the weedkiller on it. Thank goodness he won't have to now. I think about Marco's face when I told him Ryan was going to be looking after my trees. He knew what Ryan intended to do. The olive grove looks fabulous now. The veg patch is orderly and thriving. I look in the mirror again. Tanned and freckled. Some might say I am thriving too, despite my recent blip. I'm certainly beginning to feel it this evening.

I dress simply, in a plain mustard-yellow maxi dress that Lou made me buy in the market, with grey leggings, a long necklace, again from the market, and a few more strings of beads for good measure. I put on my leather boots and stick my sunglasses on my head, then pull on my leather flying jacket. Not bad if I say so myself.

'*Buonasera*,' I say to the mirror beside the open window in the bathroom, and smile.

'*Buonasera!*' Young Luigi is passing through the olive grove and he calls back. I laugh.

'*Buonasera, Luigi.*' I lean out of the window and wave.

'Hey, Signorina Piccalilli.' Old Luigi waves back.

With a final look in the mirror, I take a deep breath, scoop up a jar of piccalilli and leave the house. I pat Daphne on the way out, lock up the chickens and put down some more food for *mamma* cat and her playful kittens. Then I make my way down the drive towards Anna-Maria's front door.

'*Buonasera*, Anna-Maria,' I say as she opens the door and I hand her the jar. She nods and puts out her free hand for me to shake, then offers each cheek for me to kiss, formally and tightly. I greet Nonna in the same way; she smiles and nods. Filippo is there, trying to send a text by waving his phone around in the air.

'*Buonasera.*' He greets me more warmly. 'So how are things at the *masseria*? I hear Marco has been working you hard. Too hard.'

Anna-Maria gives him a warning look, and he shrugs and smiles.

Marco's sister is cooking. She turns and kisses me on both cheeks, not warmly but as naturally as if she were breathing, eating or sleeping. She stirs the steaming pot at the same time and calls to her husband, who is watching football on television, to turn it down. Not so different from our house when I was growing up. The place is stifling hot, with radiators pumping out heat, and I take off my jacket and stuff it through the handles of my bag.

Anna-Maria looks at the piccalilli I've given her suspiciously, then she puts it on the side in the kitchen and opens some wine.

For a moment I'm not sure what to do with myself. Marco is nowhere to be seen and I shuffle uncomfortably. His sister shouts to someone to offer me an *aperitivo*. I remember from last time and ask for a *piccolo* one. Filippo chats away, asking me what phone I've got and about some of the London football clubs.

'He's only asking so he can go and lay bets on them later,' Anna-Maria tells me as she brings in plates of vegetables in oil, mozzarella balls, deep-fried potato croquettes, tiny tomatoes and a pot of strong-smelling ricotta, tempura-batter-fried courgettes, roasted peppers and salami.

'Hey!' Filippo quips back.

'It is a fool's game, Filippo.' Marco is behind me. I can smell him, sense him and hear him. Suddenly there is a whoosh of butterflies flying through my belly. Like a murmuration of starlings, they swoop and dive and I have no idea why this man has this effect on me. Is it nerves?

'*Buonasera*, Ruthie. Please sit.' He gestures to the table. Anna-Maria berates him for being late and asks where he has been. He kisses her fondly and placates her.

Rosa and her family join us for dinner. During the meal, the talk is of whether the olive groves should be rotavated or not. Is it good for the trees or should they be left alone? I listen and Filippo translates for me.

'Sometimes a little intervention makes them happier and so more productive,' Marco says. I wonder if he's talking about me and we smile at each other. Anna-Maria sees the smile and scowls. Marco pulls a face with the corner of his mouth, like we've been caught eating sweets in church, and I smile some more. These muscles at least are coming back to life.

They all agree that weedkiller is bad for the land, but Rosa argues that olive farming has changed: the youngsters no longer want to spend their days climbing ladders to reach hard-to-get olives from older trees. People live away from the groves and therefore don't have the time. It has all changed. People are buying oil for quantity not quality. Spain makes it in huge amounts but Puglia makes the best, they all loudly agree. It is people buying up land and not understanding it, Rosa says, and I wonder if it's a dig. But we must move with the times, she adds. Marco hotly disagrees, saying that the traditional methods are still the best. He asks about her watering system and then they move on to pruning methods and everyone disagrees all over again. The image of the painting in my head comes rushing back in, all of them at the table discussing life, family and food.

All the way through the meal Rosa seems distracted, glancing out of the windows at the back of the house just like she did on the first night I met her, as if looking for something, or maybe someone. But Marco is right here, and has been all night. She even takes some air on the back patio in between courses, arriving back at the table flushed and flustered. I wonder if she's a secret smoker.

By the end of the meal I'm tired and ready to go. Rosa and her family stand up to leave. Nonna has fallen asleep in her chair, glass of limoncello in her hand. Anna-Maria bids the visitors goodbye and prepares to take Nonna up to bed. She gives me a stern look as I thank her and say good night.

'Marco will see you to your door,' she says, and Filippo translates. I get the impression she means he's to go no further.

I unlock the front door and Marco leans past me to push it open. He holds the door for me to go in first. I dip my head so as not to look at him as I brush past. But I can feel his breath and smell his lemony aftershave.

Inside the house I turn to say good night and thank him for the meal and his hard work, but he is already at the woodburner, opening the door, putting on an extra log. Obviously not a man who listens to his mother, then.

'Don't forget to put a log on before you go to bed and turn it down low. A slow burn will be much better than a roaring fire now.' I wonder if he's talking about the fire or matters of the heart. Marco seems to have advice on lots of things. He stands in the glow of the fire, his face lit up. He's a very attractive man when he's not being cross, I think. I need to get a grip on myself. He is spoken for – well, if Anna-Maria has her way he will be; and he is also the man who wants to take my house from me. He should be the very last person I consider attractive. And then of course there's Ryan. Ryan who makes me laugh and who wants to help me get my olives in so I can go home, to London.

'For a good night's sleep you take a spoonful of olive oil,' Marco is instructing. He wants me to sleep to be fit for work. But I'm not going to drink olive oil.

I don't want to turn on the big lights. It's late and I'll be going to bed in a moment, so I go to the table and light the big storm candle there.

'Where is your oil?' he asks.

'What?' I follow him as he heads to the kitchen.

'It coats the larynx and stops you snoring,' he calls back over his shoulder.

'I don't think I snore.' I frown, following him up the two steps to the kitchen.

'It has many beneficial properties, olive oil. One spoonful before bed can help fight all sorts of troubles,' he says, turning to look at me.

'Here.' I lunge for a bottle of oil that I've already opened, hoping he'll just say what he wants to say and then leave. I have to be up early.

He picks up a spoon from the work surface and turns back to me. The woodburner is throwing up big dancing flames, as red as my cheeks. His blue eyes light up like sky-blue topaz in the firelight. My breathing quickens. My nerve endings seem to be standing to attention, jittery, like my overstimulated senses. Maybe it's the limoncello, because I didn't have the coffee for just this reason.

He takes the oil from me. I'm standing in front of him. He's big and broad, and my eyes just about reach his chest. He looks down and I look up. My chest is rising and falling like waves washing in and out. He holds the spoon to the tilted bottle without taking his eyes off me. The butterflies in my stomach are dancing like the flames in the fire.

He stops when the spoon is full. I have no idea how. Instinct, I suppose. Then he lifts it to my lips. It glistens in the candlelight.

'You first.' I push the spoon towards him. He cocks his head and gives me a disappointed look. He doesn't look at it, just smiles broadly, opens his mouth so I can see his white teeth, his pink tongue curled in laughter, and tips the spoonful into his mouth. He closes his lips around it and drags the spoon out slowly, making sure every last bit is gone. His lips are glistening, wet with oil.

Suddenly his eyes darken and he pulls back. His mouth turns down at the corners, his nose wrinkles in disgust.

'What the hell?'

I step back, reeling from his reaction. What is his problem now? I grip the back of a chair.

'*Merda!*' He glares at the bottle. 'Where on earth did you get this shit? It's nothing more than lamp oil!'

'Lamp oil?' I say, confused. 'No, it's Bellanuovo oil.'

'This is not Bellanuovo oil! I know Bellanuovo oil and

this . . . I wouldn't use it to fry chips in! Where did you get it?' He looks at me like I've stolen sweets from his younger brother.

'I . . . I . . .' What do I say? If I tell him Ryan gave it to me, everything he already thinks will be confirmed and life will be ten times harder when Ryan comes to harvest the olives. I still need Ryan. I can't have Marco scaring him off.

'It was here. I thought it was Bellanuovo oil,' I say and hope he believes me. For a moment he says nothing, his eyes flashing, and I wonder if he's going to realise I'm lying to him. My heart starts thundering again.

'My grandfather's oil?' He shakes his head and looks like I've kicked his dog. An expression of pain tears across his face. Then he throws the spoon with a clatter on to the table.

'You cannot be an olive farmer if you do not know the difference between a good oil and a bad one!' he finally announces and slams the bottle down too.

'I'm not going to be an olive farmer, though, am I?' I glare back. 'I'm going home!'

'You still have to make it to harvest first. There is many a trip along the way and much to learn!' And with that he storms out.

I bolt the door firmly behind him, turn off all the lights and head straight up to bed as the fire in the stove flickers and fades. As I lie there holding my pillow to my hot, angry cheeks, I try my best to push Marco Bellanuovo out of my mind, but his image is as stubborn as he is.

Chapter Twenty-seven

When I come downstairs the following morning, the fire has gone out. I crouch shivering in front of the woodburner, a blanket wrapped around my shoulders, and try to get it going again with scrunched-up paper and the sticks that Marco left in the basket. Once again I try to forget his dark, angry face last night.

At least I start work on the mural at the school today. I give up on the fire and go and get dressed. Layers, lots of layers. That way as the day warms up I can take some off, then put them on again when it's colder.

I wrap a thick scarf around my neck and hear Marco's voice in my head telling me to eat to keep my strength up. I certainly don't want another episode of him having to drag me out of bed. In fact the further I am away from Marco right now, I think, the better.

I drive to the edge of town down our long, twisty lane, bouncing off the little potholes and brushing the grassy verges, and park in the school car park, just down from Sophia's *forno*. There's a breeze rustling through the trees and white clouds tumble across the sky like excited fluffy puppies. I turn to look at the school and the big wall that is to be my canvas.

Children are arriving, smartly dressed with manners to match, all kissing their mothers goodbye and greeting their friends and teachers eagerly.

'Hey!' Lou spots me and waves enthusiastically. She kisses me on both cheeks.

'How's things?' I ask, wanting to know how she and Antonio are doing.

'So, so,' she says, bobbing her head to either side. Then she quickly changes the subject. 'Have you booked your slot? When are you going to start picking?'

'Sorry?'

'Sorry, force of habit.' She waves a hand. 'It's all anyone talks about at this time of year. The olives. Have you booked your slot?'

'No. Ryan's doing it. Soon, I think.' It occurs to me that I haven't seen Ryan for a while. Perhaps that dinner won't happen after all. But I have been otherwise engaged. 'Ryan thinks I should get them done quickly,' I say, and then add something I didn't even realise I was thinking, 'but I'm beginning to think I should wait until they're really ready.'

'I thought you just wanted to get them harvested and go.'

'Yes, but . . .' I find myself trying to let my brain catch up with my mouth, 'the coratina is a late-harvesting olive. I want the oil to be the best it can be.'

'That's what everyone wants round here. You're starting to talk like a local.'

'Am I?' I'm suddenly flustered. 'I just want to show Ed's friends that . . . well, I did the best I could.'

'Well, then wait. Wait for as long as you can.'

'How will I know when's the right time?'

'Well I know someone who will know.' She raises an eyebrow at me.

'There's no way I'm asking him!'

Lou laughs. 'You'd better let Ryan know your plans too. Come on, come in and have coffee and then we can get you started.'

She leads the way from the gates, following the blue footprints painted on the grey concrete, to the front door of the school. The glass panels on either side are covered in balloon shapes and rainbows cut out of colourful paper. There is the sound of happy chatter and laughter from both sides of the entrance hall. Lou leads me through into the staff room, where I'm greeted by the headmistress, a woman in a smart red skirt, thick gold-rimmed glasses and red lipstick. She shakes my hand warmly and welcomes me, telling me how much they're looking forward to seeing my artwork on the wall; how it will brighten the school and the town.

I hope so. I'm holding a folder with the sketch I've made of the big olive tree. There are photographs in there too, the ones Lou scanned for me, as well as a sketch of the painting that keeps coming back to me when I lie in bed at night. Part of me feels I need to keep things simple, to think of this as a big greetings card design and do something that will please everybody. On the other hand, if I can get the painting I have in my head right, it could be perfect. But it's risky, and might do more harm than good. So for once, I'm going to listen to my head, and try and lock away the picture in my heart.

After hot, strong coffee from the machine, Lou introduces me to her class. They stare, smiling and expectant, from their small chairs, giving me their full attention. Lou speaks clearly and slowly and I can understand every word she says. She tells them how I'm here as part of a living history project, an art project that will tell the history of the town and of all the families who have lived here. It is a town built on its olive oil, like a good meal, she says: olive oil is the foundation of any meal, and the olives are the foundations of the town we live in.

As she sets the class to work, Lou tells me how the children living in the high-rise blocks around the foot of the old town spend more and more time on Xboxes and mobile phones and are losing touch with the land.

'I want my boy to be part of the land too, otherwise he could be living anywhere. It's about their identity, who they are.'

Outside, as the day begins to warm up, I peel off my scarf and fleece and stare at the big concrete wall. I get the same feeling I had when I saw the *masseria* for the first time . . . where on earth to start?

But start I must. Like every journey, I remind myself, it starts with the first step, and I slide on my painting overall, pick up my brush and choose one of the many tins of paint at my feet. I open it up, stir it and then begin the simple, straightforward olive tree design.

At break time the children clatter round to see my progress, which is disappointingly slow by the looks on their faces. At lunchtime, another fantastic three-course meal, comprising tomato salad, risotto and cheesecake, the children's enthusiasm and chatter is infectious, and I am smiling from ear to ear. The beauty of children is that they're living for today. Isn't that what I've been doing for the last few months, instead of plotting out the future like I did with Ed, with pensions and ten-year plans? This is why I did this, to live for today.

I stand and look at the olive tree. I take a deep breath, pick up my biggest brush and paint over it. Then I start again, going with my gut instinct, the picture I have in my heart. What is there to lose? I'll be gone soon anyway. If I don't try and paint the picture I really want to do now, I don't think I ever will. I've spent years creating simple designs for Brandon, hoping to please lots of people. But I can't carry on being scared of what others might think. I have to do what's right for me.

By afternoon break, there are marks and blobs all over the wall. This time not as many children have come round to see. By the end of the day, the novelty of my presence has worn off and they meet their parents happily chattering about their friends and what they learnt in class.

Lou helps me to hang large sheets over the wall to protect it overnight.

'So have you thought about asking Marco about the best time to pick the olives?' She takes up the conversation where we left off this morning.

'I don't think so. He's not speaking to me,' I tell her as I stand on one of the children's chairs to drape the sheets.

'Why not?'

'Oh, it was all to do with some olive oil. I thought it

was Bellanuovo oil. He stormed off. Like I say, all over some oil.'

'Out here, it's always to do with land, or oil.' Lou nods and waves as she spots her husband walking towards the school to meet her and her son. 'But trust me, you should say something. These things have a habit of growing and growing until there's no way back. It's best to sort it out quickly.'

Chapter Twenty-eight

After more sweeping round the olive trees that evening and weeding in the veg patch, I feed Daphne and the hens, Kirsty and Phil. I've taken poetic licence with Phil, pretending it's short for Philomena. But then everyone round here thinks I'm mad naming chickens. Nothing new there, then. They don't look like chickens from back home. In fact Kirsty looks more like a small dinosaur and Phil is very round and golden. Daphne is doing a great job guarding them and the veg plot at night; in fact just guarding in general.

I decide Lou's right, I need to sort things out with Marco. I'm going to ask him to come and eat with me, thank him for everything he did when I was unwell, and ask him about the olives. It's me offering the olive branch this time.

I shower quickly in cold water, using a kettle of warm water for the important parts, and dress in a simple soft grey woollen jumper, faded three-quarter-length jeans I got in the market and a short cardigan. I blow-dry my curly hair and look in the mirror I've put up in my bedroom. Waves of hair are beginning to curl around my face. I've always kept it short and practical until now, but I like this new softness.

My face is really quite brown now, with the freckles that I've always hated spreading across my nose and cheeks and up the side of my face, touching the corner of my eyebrow. I put my hand to them. I don't know why I hated them so much; looking at them now, I quite like them.

Suddenly I hear a car in the drive. My heart skitters and tumbles over itself like a Labrador puppy at feeding time. Marco! At least now I don't have to go over to his house to ask him to join me for dinner.

I run down the stairs and open the front door with a smile.

'Hey! Wow! You look great. You been working out?'

It's Ryan.

'Something like that,' I say, but instead of leaping for joy at the sight of Ryan's friendly face, my heart dips and collapses into a disappointed heap.

'Looks like you've been doing some work around here.' He swings around, taking it all in.

'You could say that.' I'm wondering if I have to invite him in. Of course I should! I smooth down my hair by running my hand over it and smile. I look around for Marco's car. It's still there, next door.

'Come in, come in.' I step back and he walks into the house. The fire is making a tiny attempt to stay in, gently flickering against the cooling evening. Across the olive trees at the back of the house there are little plumes of smoke from *trulli* chimneys. Everyone is starting to prepare for autumn and the harvest to come.

'Wow, you have been busy,' Ryan says, looking at the olive grove. 'Really, you didn't have to.'

'I wanted to,' I say quickly.

He steps out through the back doors just as Luigi and Young Luigi are passing by the back of the house on their way home.

'*Buonasera*, Signorina Piccalilli,' Luigi says and waves.

'*Buonasera*, Luigi.' I wave back.

Marco is right behind them.

'*Buonasera*,' he says and stops. At first he looks at me and I can see he's realised I've made an effort to dress for dinner. He nods appreciatively, then he looks at Ryan.

'*Ciao*,' says Ryan, reaching forward to shake Marco's hand.

'*Buonasera*,' Marco replies stiffly.

'They're looking good, these trees.' Ryan slips his hands into his back pockets and his combats slide down again.

'That's because they are well cared for,' Marco says bluntly, surprising me. Was that a compliment? 'Have you come to check on the crop? You'll find it in order.' He nods to me.

'I can see,' Ryan says cheerfully. 'Actually I brought the weedkiller and I've booked a slot at the press for next week.' He beams.

'Next week?' Marco practically spits. 'That's far too early.'

'But I thought you wanted to get it done.' He turns to me. 'The faster it's done, the faster you get home, you said, Ruthie. Back to London.' He gives me an impish grin.

I blush, realising how things have changed for me. I'm not in any rush right now but I can't say that. I don't want to think about leaving right now.

I clear my throat and take a deep breath. It's time to stand up for what I want. Just like with the painting, I can't always worry about pleasing other people. I have to do what my heart is telling me. 'I want to put off the harvest, for as long as possible.' I give a little cough and can't look at Marco.

'Well, it's a busy time,' I hear Ryan say, and suddenly my new-found confidence leaves me.

'But you'll still be able to do it, right?' I look up at him with a mild whiff of panic.

For a moment he doesn't say anything, looking from me to Marco, and then suddenly he breaks into a big grin.

'Yeah, course! I'll get your harvest in, promise.'

I look at Marco. His face is set. He's looking beyond me to the lit fire in the house, and the table laid with a candle, a bottle of Prosecco and a bowl of nuts and olives. He looks back at me.

'I can see you have plans,' he says stiffly. 'You've worked hard. You should take time to relax.'

'Yeah, we could go into town. I know a great little restaurant that does fantastic fish and chips. Cheap and cheerful,' says Ryan. But instead of my heart doing a happy dance, it dips a little more. This is what I wanted, me and Ryan, dinner, plans to meet in London. But not tonight, tonight I wanted to just put things right with Marco.

'Oh I don't know. I thought I'd stay here. Have a quiet evening.' Now that's come out all wrong. Just when I thought I had a grip on this think-before-you-speak malarkey!

'I see. Well, whatever. I hope you enjoy,' Marco says tightly. I'm furious that he's misunderstood.

'No, I mean . . . going into town would be lovely, but I was just planning something different . . .' I'm digging a deeper and deeper hole for myself.

'You should go. Like I say, you need to take time to enjoy life too. I must go, I have work to do.' He gives another tight smile. 'And eat. Don't forget to eat,' he adds seriously. 'Have a good evening. Enjoy your date,' he says like a father to his daughter, making my hackles rise.

It's not exactly a date! I want to correct him. But Marco has marched off to his *trullo* and my plans for a reconciliation dinner have gone with him. He now thinks I've got dressed up for Ryan and am going on a date with him. And by the grin on Ryan's face, so does Ryan. A few weeks ago, this would have been just what I wanted. A dinner date with this good-looking, friendly Aussie. But now, for some reason, I'm not so sure.

'Wait! Marco!' I have to say something. I run after him and catch his arm. 'I wanted to say thank you,' I try and explain.

'Be careful, Ruthie. Make sure you can trust your olive man. He can't let you down.' And then he turns and jumps the wall back to his *trullo*.

I turn back to the *masseria*. Of course Ryan isn't going to let me down. Marco's just saying that because . . . because . . . Why would he say that? Not jealousy, that's for sure. Is he just trying to unnerve me? It is a bet, I remind myself. Whatever he means, I do need to make sure that I keep Ryan on my side. I need him.

'So, shall we go?' Ryan says, pointing towards his van. I nod and smile politely.

I close the vent on the fire, like I watched Marco do, and hope it will stay in, then pick up my jacket and wind my scarf round my neck.

'Look after things, Daphne,' I tell the goat as she sits in the last of the sun's rays on the front step. This wasn't how I planned the evening at all, but then I don't know what I expected really. I need to make the most of it.

I need Ryan to help with the olive harvest so I can go home. And he's so good-looking and lovely. He and I could be just right for each other. But Marco's words of warning are ringing in my ears. More than anything, I realise, I need to show Marco I can get something right. Do something right, make a right decision. I want to show Ed and my mum too that something good has come of my time here. That I can move on.

The next morning, Marco's car has gone. I drive into town to work on the mural. I can't help but wonder where he is but I know it's not my business, so instead I think about the night before. It was fun. Ryan was good company and his stories were funny. Never a dull moment, no awkward silences like me and Ed ended up having. Admittedly I didn't do much talking. But I listened.

The little fish and chip restaurant was sweet. A small cellar place, with curved cream ceilings. We had simple home-cooked antipasti to start – rice balls, that smelly ricotta cheese with tomatoes, mozzarella knots and grilled peppers – and Ryan told me about when he first moved out here. Then we had *fritto misto* – mixed, lightly fried fish and, yes, chips. Over a jug of red wine, Ryan told me stories of his travels before he came to Italy.

Afterwards we walked back through the town. Ryan made several attempts to put his arm round me or hold my hand. It should've have felt like the perfect time and place, with just about the perfect person, to start a romance. But something was making me hold back. Marco's annoying warning words kept coming back to me, no matter how hard I tried to forget him and enjoy my evening with Ryan.

I didn't invite Ryan back for coffee, though, explaining instead that I had to be up early to work on the mural. I was shattered, trying not to yawn on the way back in the van as Ryan told me about life back in Australia. I didn't want to seem rude, but by then I was even finding laughing hard work and my mind kept slipping back to my painting. That's what I need to focus on, not Ryan or anyone else for that matter.

And for the next couple of weeks that's what I do. I get up, go to school, paint, come home, sweep around the trees, weed the veg plot and fall exhausted into bed. I dream about the mural, the *masseria*, the trees, and the one tree in particular where I gave Marco the painting and he gave me the olive branch. I lose myself in the mural, living and breathing it, sketching the faces that keep haunting me; the ones that seem to live in the walls, the fields and the fabric of this place. Faces that all have a story of their own to tell.

*

One morning when I wake there is condensation on the window panes and a chill in the air. I go downstairs and get down on my knees to light the woodburner. I open it to find there is still a spark glowing in the grate. I quickly scrunch up newspaper and throw on twigs.

Suddenly the little fire sparks into life. I actually give a cheer, and then hold my hands to my mouth as the sparks turn to big orange flames. I know there will be hot water later. No more washing up in cold water. I want to tell Marco I've managed the fire, but he's still not here.

That evening, after a day at the school, the fire is still in and I eat toast and jam in front of it. Then I pull on my fleece over my dungarees, add a bandanna around my neck for good measure and walk out to the olive trees.

As I'm sweeping, I look across to Marco's *trullo*. I feel disappointed. I know it's ridiculous. It's time for me to stand on my own two feet now. It's like someone's taken the stabilisers off my bike and I must now ride alone.

As I'm sweeping, something drops behind me. There is a breeze in the air, rustling through the trees. I turn to see olives falling to the floor where I've swept. There is a scattering all around me.

'Hey!' I shout. 'They're falling! They're falling. The sweepings!'

I look to Marco's *trullo* again, but I'm on my own. All I have is his instructions: *You must keep this very clean. Clear away the bonfire ashes. And when you have enough olives, take them to the press.*

The harvest is coming, I tell myself. It's nearly time. But instead of feeling elated, for some unknown reason I feel incredibly sad.

Chapter Twenty-nine

Driving back along the twisting, potholed lane I feel a strange mixture of joy and sadness. I've finished the painting. Well, I say finished, I could carry on tweaking for ever. But tomorrow it will be unveiled and I've done all I can for today. I'm feeling so buzzed that I've done it, my painting, the one I never thought I would be brave enough to do, but sad too, because it's over and I don't know when I'll get the chance to paint again, if ever.

I raise a hand and give a toot to Luigi and Young Luigi as they move the sheep out of the road into a field so that I can pass. Luigi is dressed for winter. But his smile is wide and genuine despite there being so many black holes where his teeth once were. Mrs Luigi waves as I pass their little *lamia*. She's not here as much these days, preferring to stay in their apartment in town. It's been two and a half weeks since Marco left, according to Filippo to go back to his job at the college, and in that time autumn has well and truly settled in.

I see the familiar white car of Rocco the electrician coming towards me, and we wave as we squeeze past each other, stone walls on one side and kissing wing mirrors on the other. I've taken to telling him where the key is so he can come and go when he can. And I leave jars of piccalilli out for him when I know he's coming.

The sun is deep and low and red in the sky. There's a nip in the air. It's a beautiful autumnal evening and more than anything I'd like to throw some more wood on the fire and sit down and watch *Coronation Street*, but I have trees to sweep. Marco told me that with just a little kindness, 'the tree will repay you handsomely up top', meaning the more I do, the bigger my harvest. As I swing round the corner, I can see the *masseria* through the trees and Marco's *trullo* behind it, and if I'm not mistaken, Marco's car! My heart suddenly and unexpectedly lurches into my mouth and starts thrumming loudly, playing a hip-hop beat in my ears. He's back! Suddenly everything I have tried to stop myself feeling comes rushing at me at once. Oh God! I realise. I've missed him. I've really missed him.

I reach the drive, my hands shaking, and stop the car. I get out, my legs not really working in unison, and lift and open the sagging gates. Once I've driven through, I pull in and shut them again. It's part of my daily routine now, just like climbing the stairs to my mum's flat when the lift was broken. And I need to keep acting normal.

As I drive towards the house, I see him straight away. He's standing outside his *trullo*, underneath one of the olive trees, the last of the setting sun forming an orange glow around him, and my heart's suddenly pumping to a techno beat. He's got a table out and is concentrating on something; looks like he's working. I stop the car and just look at him for a moment, unable to believe that it's Marco

Bellanuovo who's making my heart race like this. His broad, muscular shoulders are creating ripples under his long-sleeved white T-shirt and his tanned hands are holding what looks like a bottle at arm's length. I have no idea why he's making me feel like this, or if he feels the same about me. I don't know how long he's here for. Is he just back to collect the rest of his belongings? I swallow, only to discover there is a lump the size of a tennis ball in my throat.

I pull up and get out, scratching Daphne's head by way of a hello and trying to act as normal as possible.

'*Buongiorno*,' I call, much more high-pitched than I was expecting it to come out. He turns round as if I've taken him by surprise and smiles widely. That's a good start.

'*Ciao*.' He waves a hand, almost shyly.

For a moment neither of us knows what to say and I'm guessing he doesn't want me to disturb his work. But as I turn to go into the house, my heart crashing around in my chest, he walks purposefully towards me, jumps the wall and stands in front of me.

'You've been away,' I say, with a mouth as dry as the desert, trying to sound as if I've hardly noticed when actually I've counted every day, I realise.

'I've been waiting for you,' he says, shyly again, no hint of arrogance at all. It's all very different, very strange.

We're both nervous and not sure where we stand with each other. Well, he did storm out of my house the last time I saw him, claiming I was some kind of oil adulterer. You'd think I'd been running a brothel, he was so disgusted.

'I had to go back to Naples, organise some more leave,' he explains, and I hear a voice in my head shouting, 'Whoopee!' and feel my heart doing little jumps of joy. 'Just until after the harvest . . . until Christmas. Then they want me back,' he explains.

Christmas. I'll be gone by then, I suddenly realise. No more sweeping or weeding. It'll be *Mrs Brown's Boys* Christmas special and a box of Celebrations on Mum's settee. I try and push the thought out of my head.

'So you're back. In time for Nonna's birthday, I suppose.' I suddenly realise that's why he's here. Not because of me, of course not! It's Nonna's birthday and I suddenly feel both silly and very nervous about the unveiling of the mural tomorrow.

'Of course,' he says. 'The whole family is looking forward to it.' He smiles and I feel even more nervous.

'So what's all this?' I try and distract myself, nodding at the table of bottles and cups. 'Sorry, I mean, it's none of my business. Actually, I have sweeping to do.' I realise I need to get a grip, get control of these feelings. I turn back towards the house.

'No, Ruthie, wait.' He steps towards me and catches me by the elbow. My breathing quickens. 'I'm sorry. I must have seemed very rude when I left here last time.'

'No, it's fine.' I try to be light-hearted and turn away again. I cannot work out why I feel like this around this man. He makes me so tongue-tied and nervous.

'No, I want to explain,' he says, catching my other elbow and turning me to him. And as much as I don't want to, I can't help myself. I slowly look up at him, his face lit by the orange and red rays of the sun. He has a very beautiful face when he's not scowling at me.

'It's just . . . the oil.' The flash of pain shoots across his face again, though not so deeply this time.

'I know, I know, *merda*!' I remember and raise my arms dramatically, then drop them, trying to make a joke of it. It works; he laughs.

'*Merda*,' he nods. 'Lamp oil. It . . .' He stops suddenly. 'There's history,' he says eventually. 'I don't . . . I can't talk about it really.'

'It's fine,' I say. But it's not. Maybe if he explained how he felt, he wouldn't feel so frustrated and angry. And I wouldn't feel like I do now. Lost and wondering if he feels the same way I do about him.

'Look.' He holds his hand out to the table. There are bottles and little tulip-shaped glasses. It must be research for his book.

'You've started writing?' I smile, feeling pleased for him but disappointed that he doesn't want to share whatever upset him the other night. It's confusing the hell out of me. When he left, you could barely have called us friends. Just neighbours trying to get along. A neighbour who seems to turn my whole mind and soul upside down every time I see him.

'What? Writing? Sadly, no. But this is for you.' He nods his head and holds out an arm, pointing in the direction of the table. 'If you are to be an olive farmer, you need to know about olive oil.'

'But I . . .' I start to remind him that I'll be watching *Coronation Street* with my Celebrations by Christmas, but he's leading me towards the table on the other side of the wall, under the tree, just by the old *forno*, the outdoor oven. He steps around the other side of the table. A slight wind lifts the corner of the tablecloth.

'Like I say, it's time you learnt a good olive oil from—'

'*Merda!*' I say, and we both laugh, the awkwardness gone.

'You must train your palette,' he says, and I can tell he feels on safe ground talking about oil, keeping away from the past and his feelings. He starts to pour some oil into the tiny tulip glasses.

'I brought these from my laboratory at the college. Here.' He hands me one. 'First you must warm it. Cup it in your hands. In the labs in the college we use baby-bottle warmers to bring it to twenty-eight degrees. Optimum temperature.' He swills the oil in the glass in his hands and I copy. 'Now then, first the nose.' He raises a finger, and I can't help but smile as he slips into teacher mode. He lifts the glass to his nose and sniffs. 'What can you smell?'

I sniff again.

'Well . . . it smells like oil, fruity oil,' I say hopefully.

'Good, now sip it and let it sit on your tongue,' he instructs. He's standing next to me, close, and I can feel butterflies in the pit of my stomach. The drumming of my heart, playing out in my ears, has been turned up a notch too.

'How does it feel?' he asks.

It's not easy to answer with a mouthful of oil sitting on your tongue. I want to say 'oily', but I don't think that'll get me any Brownie points.

'Syrupy,' I try and say, but the oil slides down my throat, coating it as it goes.

'Try again, and this time you must do this.' He smiles and takes a big slug of oil, then pulls back his lips and makes a loud hissing noise at the back of his mouth, like a horse with chewing gum stuck in its teeth. I burst out laughing and step back.

'You must,' he says sternly, as my giggles take hold and multiply. 'You must move it to all areas of the mouth. Now try again.'

The sucking thing is hard to do. I look like a complete amateur next to him, which of course I am.

'Again,' he instructs, and I try really hard but the giggles get the better of me. He doesn't berate me as I'm expecting, but to my relief laughs too. His face is soft and smiling and very beautiful. He looks at me as I try to compose myself, but the wings of the butterflies flapping in my stomach are making it very hard to concentrate.

'Try this one,' he says, and I warm it in my hands, sip it and try and do the sucking thing through my teeth, but the giggles stop me again. Or maybe it's the fact – and I can't believe this is happening – that this man seems to render me helpless just by being so close to me. My heart ups its techno beat and bangs loudly in my ears as every nerve in my body stands to attention. A fire is beginning to burn down below.

'Let the oil sit on your tongue and you will find the flavours work like a balloon, first at the tip of your tongue and then expanding to touch the sides,' he explains. I watch his mouth, his lips and his white teeth and his pink tongue, as he speaks, and I feel a tingle that starts in my toes and travels like electricity all the way up to the tops of my ears, lighting up every nerve ending on its way. 'Then it tapers away before sliding down your throat.' He holds up his hands and creates the shape in front of his lips, and I am captivated, under his spell, gone, hook, line and sinker. If he'd told me to stand on my head and juggle the bottles with my feet, I'd've probably tried that too.

Frankly, right now, the taste of the oil is the last thing on my mind, but I don't want it to stop. I want to carry on doing this for ever. But all of a sudden, I get a real hit from the flavour.

'Oh wow! Peppery!' I say, holding my fingers to my lips and looking at the glass.

'This is a blend I've been working on.'

'Where? Here?'

'At work, in the labs. It is a good everyday oil. You should get the taste of tomatoes, apple and then pepper.'

'It's delicious!' I look from the glass to him. His lips are glistening with oil and more than anything I want to kiss them, and I feel a pulse start thrumming between my legs where the fire was burning. A feeling I haven't felt in . . . I'm not sure how long.

'The Tuscan oils, they're verdant, peppery, slightly bitter. In Umbria they are often fruitier and softer. Then you have Sicilian oil, a fruity oil, leafy. The flavour varies from east to west, just like wines.'

The sun is setting and he lights the lanterns hanging from the tree, little jars with tea lights in them. I'm loving how alive he is talking about the oils.

'Are you cold? I can light a fire,' he says, and points to the *forno*.

I nod, and he lights it. I watch the little flames and just for a moment remember the awful day I nearly set fire to the whole grove, the day when I felt something reignite inside me. I've come a long way since then, I think.

'Drink some water to clear your palate. In the lab,' he carries on, 'we use green apples, Granny Smiths, I think, to cleanse the palate.'

I shiver.

'You're still cold. Here.' He puts his jumper around my shoulders and I can smell the lemony scent of his aftershave. The butterflies take off in my stomach, swooping and beating to match my heart.

'Now,' he says, as I'm sipping away at the water and he's pouring another oil. 'Try this one.' He holds it up to the lamplight like he's raising the Olympic flame. It's deep green and thick and looks like molten glass.

I take the glass he's offering me and he picks one up for himself. We swirl the oil, and the murmuration in my stomach follows, dipping and rising again like waves. Then he puts his glass to his glistening lips and I follow, our eyes locked on to each other's now. We tip them back in unison.

The thick oil touches the tip of my tongue. I curl it back and then draw back my lips and take in some long sucks of air. The oil fills out in my mouth just as Marco explained, and it's like a taste explosion.

'Oh wow!' I say as it tapers away and down my throat. 'It tastes of freshly cut grass and green tomatoes. It's so fruity.' It's strong, powerful and pungent. There's a sweetness to it. It tastes of woody herbs, and an aftertaste like walnuts and a sort of bitterness. His eyes are dancing as I nearly explode with excitement at this new-found flavour.

'And that,' he says, his smile widening, his lips glistening, 'is Bellanuovo oil.'

'It's . . . perfect,' I manage to say, my eyes darting between his soft mouth and his excited blue eyes. My face is moving closer to his and there doesn't seem to be anything to stop the draw between us.

The glasses clatter on to the table as his lips touch mine, oily but delicious, gently, so gentle and soft, but then his tongue finds its way into my mouth, like the balloon, on the tip of my tongue first and then deeper as our bodies move closer and the rhythmic motion of our mouths dips and rises and the butterflies spin in circles in my stomach and set off explosions in my groin as I melt into his kiss.

Suddenly there's a loud bang. What the hell? Shit! I fall away from him, trying to catch my breath and get a hold on my disorientated senses and my racing heart.

Chapter Thirty

Marco catches my arm and laughs.

'It's the *festa*, in town.' He points. 'Fireworks. It used to be a celebration to mark the start of the olive harvest. Now,' he shrugs, 'it's a just a *festa*. Would you like to go?'

My heart starts to slow down to a gentle canter.

I smile and nod, feeling ridiculous and too light-headed from the kiss to speak. And then I stop myself.

'Rosa!' I say out loud, and suddenly feel like a bucket of cold water has been poured over my dancing butterflies.

'Rosa? What about Rosa?' Marco frowns.

'You should be with her.' I step back into the table, making the glasses rattle. He smiles and catches my elbow.

'Rosa is a good friend.'

'Yes, a good friend you're going to marry. Your mother told me.' He laughs. 'I really should get an early night,' I say, flustered. 'It's a big day tomorrow.'

'As much as my *mamma* would like it, I'm not going to marry Rosa.' Marco still has hold of me, and in a way I'm thankful, because my knees haven't fully recovered from that kiss.

'You're not going to marry her?' I don't know whether to be pleased or cross.

'My *mamma* would like me to be with her so that the Bellanuovos can be part of a big olive estate again. But Rosa no more has eyes for me than I do for her. We are just friends. She is a fine businesswoman and is about to take over the press from her father. But she doesn't need me there to do that. Like someone else I know, she is more than capable of managing on her own.' He raises an eyebrow and I really want to believe him, despite his mother's words banging in my head. I want to believe he's free. So for now, that's what I'll do.

'So? The *festa*?' he asks again.

And I smile and nod.

We make our way through the narrow cobbled streets, past the school, where my painting is under wraps until tomorrow. I look at the sheets covering it and shiver with nerves. Marco pulls me closer to him. There are wooden stands bedecked with fairy lights where the market usually is. We walk up towards the old town. The side streets are lit up, with lanterns strung from one side of the street to the other. They show off the whitewashed walls, the steps and the low doorways. The pizzeria is in full swing, and everywhere we go Marco is stopped and spoken to by neighbours. He introduces me as his neighbour from Masseria Bellanuovo. When he slides his arm around my waist, the butterflies go into overdrive with their swooping and zooming. We stop when we meet Rocco the electrician and his wife and daughter, and Luigi with his grand-daughter on his shoulders. Both his sons are with him, the elder, who I've never met before, with his wife and daughter. Young Luigi looks shy and awkward as usual.

We see Lou with her husband and son. Giac waves and calls my name. They seem to have put their worries aside for the night too. I spot one of Marco's cousins, who must be here for Nonna's birthday, but he and Marco pretend not to see each other. I wish Marco would talk about it. The shops are all lit up, brilliant white lights showing off the wares in their windows against the dark autumn night, and it feels like Christmas in Oxford Street but far nicer. Everyone is dressed up smartly and they stop to talk to the neighbours they pass on their *passeggiata* through town.

'Hey!' I hear a shout and turn to see Ryan jogging through the crowds towards me. My heart dips a little and I suddenly feel awkward, even though nothing ever really happened between us.

He's smiling broadly and kisses me on each cheek. I feel self-conscious and step away from Marco, whose hand is now only loosely on my shoulder, but if Ryan has noticed, he doesn't show it.

'You saved me a journey. I was coming to see you,' he says, and I cringe, hoping he doesn't want another date. I'm about to say something but he continues: 'Your olives. Thought we'd get them booked in now. Get them done soon,' he says firmly, nodding for me to agree.

'Oh, I . . .' I look at Marco, who drops his arm and steps back, as if letting me know I'm on my own here.

'You do want me to do them still?' Ryan frowns at me.

'Yes, yes,' I say. 'But, erm . . .' I take a deep breath. 'Not yet.' I don't look at Marco. This is my decision. 'I'll ring you when I'm ready.'

'I have other customers, Ruthie. I've already started on the other Bellanuovo land,' Ryan insists.

Marco says nothing.

'I don't want you to leave it too late and not get a slot at the press.'

I take another moment to think. He's right, of course. What if I miss it? But a voice inside me is telling me loud and clear what I should do, and I think I need to listen.

'Soon, I promise. But I want to wait just a little longer. Please.' I can hear my voice but I don't recognise it. Me, impulsive, rush-at-things Collins. 'I want them to be the best they can be. These things take time. We must wait.'

'Well, okay . . .' Ryan sucks air through his teeth and then looks at Marco, who is still standing a little way away from me, head down. 'Don't leave it until it's too late, though. It'll be your loss.' This time he's frowning, distant. The cheekiness is gone and in its place is something far edgier.

'I'll ring you as soon as I'm ready,' I say.

With a dark look, he turns and disappears into the crowd, and I breathe a sigh of relief. I'm guessing we don't need to have the conversation about a second date. For a moment I wonder if I've done the right thing telling him to wait on the olives. He's already doing the other Bellanuovo oil. What if I've got it wrong? I look up at Marco.

'You have to trust your own instincts to be a good olive oil producer,' he says, with no trace of humour. 'Do you believe your olives need more time?'

I think, and then I nod.

'As long as I can leave it.'

'Then you've done the right thing.' He smiles gently and we carry on walking, jostling through the slow-moving crowds up to the big square by the church. Something about that encounter has unnerved me, though. Ryan's dark face when I told him I wanted to wait. Marco does his best to cheer me up as we move through the crowds.

As we reach the top of the hill and arrive at the church, the crowd comes to a standstill. I look up at the church steps, the same steps where I saw Marco and his family the day after I arrived. The faces that have come back to haunt me as I painted at the school.

Suddenly there is a flash and a bang as more fireworks fill the night sky, bigger and brighter than the ones before. Big wooden stands have been erected looking out over the valley below. People cheer and clap at the colourful crackles and bangs lighting up their excited faces. The air is filled with their infectious happiness. As I smile and look around, I catch sight of a single pair of eyes not smiling; staring, glaring eyes boring into mine. It's Anna-Maria, Marco's *mamma*, and she doesn't look happy at all.

When the fireworks are over, I look round for Anna-Maria but she's nowhere to be seen. Marco and I walk back through the town, moving with the crowds, but I'm looking out for his mother all the way.

'Get an early night,' Marco says, seeing me to my door. 'You have a big day tomorrow.' And suddenly I'm terrified. I have lived and breathed this painting for the last few weeks, and now that it's finished, I'm torn between being

thrilled with it and convinced I've made an awful mistake.
At first, as I plotted it, I followed the picture I'd sketched
out, but it soon began to take on a life of its own, filling in
faces and spaces as if it was a story demanding to be told.
Some nights Lou would bring me food and drink when all
the children had left. Other nights, as it got dark, she had
to tell me to go home and start again in the morning.
When I finished, I actually cried. I'd done it. I'd painted
the picture that was in my heart. I'd painted their faces
and their lives as I saw them. Now all I have to do is live
with the consequences.

'I'll pick you up and drive you to town in the morning.
I'll bring the painting you did for Nonna and give it to her
at the unveiling. It will be fine, you'll see,' Marco says,
sensing my nerves. But I know I won't get a wink of sleep.
I have a feeling that none of it will be fine. He leans in and
kisses me gently, brushing my lips, then leaves me at the
door and disappears over the wall to his own little *trullo*. I
watch him go. I touch my lips. It may be the last time he
ever kisses me. After tomorrow, I doubt he will ever want
to see me again.

I squint into the dark, watching him disappear into the
shadows. It's then that I realise Phil and Kirsty's pen is
open and both the hens are missing. My heart squeezes
and I look around in despair. None of this is going to be
fine at all.

Chapter Thirty-one

The next morning I go straight downstairs and outside to find Daphne in the barn. Hiding behind her are Kirsty and Phil.

'Oh thank God!' I say as I chuck down handfuls of grain for them. I give Daphne an extra scoop of feed for looking after them so well.

I could have sworn I shut the henhouse last night. Or did I? I was all over the place when we left to go into town for the *festa*. I remember going to get a jumper from upstairs and turning off the light. Then I checked on Daphne. If I did shut them in, would someone really open up the henhouse? Am I being ridiculous, paranoid? Or did someone do it deliberately?

My mind flits back to today. The big day. The unveiling of the mural. I feel sick with nerves. To be honest, I didn't realise it was going to be like this. A big event. I thought it was just something I was going to do for the school kids, but Lou and the headmistress want to make an occasion of it, and I can't say no. Lou has been so good to me.

Luigi walks past and waves and wishes me luck. I thank him and tell him I hope to see him there.

'Of course!' he replies in English.

I'm stunned.

'Luigi, you speak English?'

'Of course,' he replies and carries on his way, smiling and waving.

Marco arrives, his hair slightly damp. He smells wonderful, with a hint of the lemony aftershave he wears.

'Good morning.' He kisses both my cheeks and I want to tell him to forget the unveiling and take me upstairs. But of course I don't.

'Parking is going to be a nightmare in town. Just after church is always busy,' he says.

'What about Anna-Maria and Nonna?' I'm suddenly nervous all over again.

'Filippo is taking them to Mass and then on to the unveiling. Nonna is wearing a brand-new dress for her birthday treat.'

'Oh lovely, something colourful?' I feel pleased for her.

'No, black,' says Marco seriously and then breaks into a smile. 'But I know she will be delighted with her picture, and with the mural.'

My knees actually start to shake.

'About the mural,' I begin. 'It's not quite the same as the little picture I did for Nonna.'

'I'm sure it will be just as good. Now go and get ready,' Marco instructs, and turns back to the pathway that has been worn into the ground between his *trullo* and the *masseria*.

'Marco, I'm sure I shut the hens away last night,' I call after him. 'Can you remember?'

'No, you didn't,' he replies.

I'm relieved. So I forgot, with all the kissing and the excitement. I'm overthinking things.

'I did, though.' He smiles at me. 'Why do you ask?'

My mind starts racing again. I'm like a ship being battered on the rocks and out to sea again. What on earth is going on? Is he telling the truth? Did he shut away the chickens, or did he in fact let them out? Is this all some kind of elaborate game to get me to leave? Am I a fool for falling for him? Did our kiss mean anything to him? I have no idea.

I run inside and get changed with shaking hands and my head whirling.

'Ruthie, you seem . . . different this morning. Have I upset you?' he asks as we fly into town, brushing hedgerows and hitting potholes. I hold my breath as we pass other cars.

'No, no, just a lot on my mind, that's all.' I try and change the subject. 'So, will all the family be here today?' I ask, twisting a tissue round my fingers.

He nods, and my heart sinks.

'My cousins are back from up north.'

The tissue in my hands rips apart as we pass Sophia's *forno*, closed up for the day. My stomach tightens further. As much as I would like to ask him about his cousins, I can't speak.

People are milling around everywhere. There is a smattering of tourists, probably second-home owners, or people looking for a late break. You can spot them by their long shorts, whereas the locals are in padded anoraks, winter coats and scarves. Despite the fact that the sun is still putting in an appearance, to the townspeople it is obviously winter. There are no men in the park playing *bocce* and cards today. The children's swings are abandoned.

Marco swerves into a small space between two cars, barely a space at all really. He mounts the kerb and cuts the engine. I think we've parked. We're right opposite the school. The nerves come in waves, each one making me queasy. What if they hate it? It'll be whitewashed over, like my time here, and I'll return to real life like none of this ever happened. I feel all the colour drain from my face.

We get out of the car. There are flags flying from the top of the school building. Lou is there with her husband. They have covered upturned barrels with red and white checked tablecloths, and there is a large bucket full of bottles of Prosecco. A table is laid with upturned glasses and another with bowls of olives, small round savoury biscuits and nuts. Lou sees me and waves. I go to wave back but I can't. I'm now paralysed with fear.

'It's no good, I can't do it. You don't need me here,' I say to no one in particular and turn to walk away from the school, back towards the lane and the *masseria*. Marco catches my arm and wheels me round.

'We'll do it together,' he says, leading me back towards the school.

'But you don't understand what I've done.' Panic is rising in my voice.

He cocks his head and looks puzzled.

'You have done a painting, for the community.'

And now I'm terrified that Marco will hate me. I

should've gone with the simple olive tree design; that's what everyone is expecting. What I've done instead is so personal. I need to explain. I take a deep breath.

'Look, I don't know why your family fell out. I just think it's sad,' I say quickly.

'My family?' Marco looks confused.

'You have such knowledge. You could be running the estate again if you could just get the family to come together.'.

He shakes his head. 'I don't understand what you're talking about. What has my family got to do with your mural?'

'Your *mamma* wants you to be an olive oil estate again. You want the *masseria* to stay in the family. What you need is for your family to remember what it was like to be whole.' The words are pouring out of my mouth and I wish they weren't. I wish I wasn't falling for this man. I wish I knew that he felt the same, and that he didn't want the house at any cost. I wish he would realise that his life should be back on the land, not in a laboratory somewhere.

'It will never happen,' he says lightly. 'There is too much history.' He shakes his head and my chest tightens.

'History,' I repeat.

'Yes, like the project you have worked on. History.'

Franco Pugliese chinks his glass of Prosecco to get everyone's attention. He smiles, and I cringe and want to run.

'The thing is, Marco,' I say quietly, but I don't get to finish. Rosa is standing with Anna-Maria and Nonna. Anna-Maria gives me daggers. To my left is Sophia with her family. She doesn't smile either. They're all here for Nonna's birthday. Nonna is sitting in a chair by the mural, and I wonder if she's going to have a heart attack when she sees it.

Franco is giving the painting a huge build-up. My toes curl, my cheeks burn and I want the ground to open up and swallow me. There's no going back now . . .

And then the sheets are pulled down. All around me there are little gasps. No one speaks. I look to my left and right. Both families seem as stunned as each other.

In the middle of the painting is the old olive tree. Around it I have painted the family, the two families, as one: in the olive grove, at a table, smiling, sharing a harvest supper together, just like in the photographs. There are tall sticks leaning against the tree, wooden ladders and nets. The adults are together at the table, children up the trees, dogs and helpers.

No one speaks. Instead they whisper. Some turn away. I can't read their faces at all. I'm sure they hate it. I know I shouldn't have done it. I take a few steps back whilst the people around me stare at the painting. I want to fade away and disappear.

'How were your chickens this morning?' says Anna-Maria quietly in my ear as I move backwards. I turn, stunned. 'It would be terrible to think of anything happening to them, or that lovely vegetable garden you have worked so hard at. The wild boar is very persistent.' She smiles the smile of a victor, and I'm dumbfounded. 'Like I say, that house will make a wonderful home for Rosa and Marco . . . once you are gone. I have friends who can help make that happen.' She nods towards Franco. 'We wouldn't want your olive harvest going up in smoke again, would we?'

'So it was you! You were trying to warn me off. Well don't bother!' I say loudly. 'I wouldn't want to be a part of your family if it was the last one on earth.'

Heads turn to look at me. I've made some mistakes in my time, but this is the biggest yet, and suddenly my mouth is rushing ahead, not bothering to wait for my brain to catch up. I'm embarrassed, hurt and feeling more of an outsider than ever before. I have absolutely nothing left to lose. Marco can have the *masseria*. After this, there is no way I can stay until the harvest. 'You're all so busy trying to keep newcomers out, you don't realise what you've lost along the way. You used to be a big oil producer, a name. But there will never be a Bellanuovo name again until you can remember the past as it used to be, before you stopped speaking to each other.' There's a sharp intake of breath, and I realise that Sophia is listening too. 'Look, this is your family's business, not mine,' I say to the two women. 'I just drew what I saw in the photos; I don't want to cause any upset. None of you seem to realise how lucky you are to have a family.'

I think about my mum and Lance. We're not much of a family, but we are a family all the same, and I need to remember that too, I realise. They should be part of my future.

'The Bellanuovo name isn't about the house, it's about the family. You don't need the *masseria* to get the name back; you just need to work together. But you're all too stubborn to see it.' I look from Sophia to Anna-Maria, both standing with their arms folded across their chests, like they were that day on the church steps. Nothing has changed and nothing will change.

Anna-Maria guffaws and turns away, and Sophia mirrors her.

'Well if you'll excuse me,' I say, 'I have to pack.'

I spin on my heel to march off, and as I do, I hear Nonna say in Italian, 'Reminds me of someone else I knew when she was a young bride.' She looks up at Anna-Maria, whose face is like stone.

Filippo leans in to me and begins to translate. 'She says it—'

'I know.' I turn a watery smile on lovely Filippo. 'I understood.'

His face lights up. 'You understood!'

Finally, just as I'm about to leave, I've started to pick up the local dialect. It doesn't matter what Nonna said; all that matters is that I could understand it. But now it's time for me to go. I turn away.

'It's a shame you're leaving us now,' Filippo says, stopping me in my tracks. I can't look at Marco.

'Yes, it is,' I reply.

'Let her go,' I hear Anna-Maria say sharply.

Chapter Thirty-two

I walk out of the schoolyard, tears streaming down my face, feeling more alone than I have ever felt before. Not only am I the foolish Englishwoman who thought she could buy the big house and do it up on her own. I have now alienated the people who did talk to me.

Suddenly I hear footsteps behind me. Instinctively I know it's Marco.

'Look, you don't have to come after me. I'll be gone soon. The mural will be painted over and there'll be no trace that I was ever here.'

He steps in front of me, walking backwards, and stops me in my tracks. More than anything I want him to take me in his arms and kiss me like he did under the olive tree. But I know that can't happen now. We are from different worlds. He wouldn't fit into mine back in London and I certainly don't fit into his.

'What you have done, no one else has dared to do,' he says, wide-eyed.

I groan.

'Come, walk with me,' he instructs.

'You should get back. You'll be missed,' I point out. 'I just want to go home.'

'I may have a *mamma* I adore, but I am not a child, Ruthie. I know my own mind.'

I don't think his mother would agree. She will certainly never accept me.

He turns me away from the school and we walk up through the streets where the *festa* was last night, past the area where the market will be tomorrow, past the flour mill, which is closed today, and the empty flower stalls. Past Lou and Antonio's closed-up bar and the place where I stopped the funeral procession getting to the church. Past the restaurant where I had fish and chips with Ryan and up into the old town. At the top of the hill, we stop and gaze out over the patchwork quilt of olive trees below.

'You are right. This family is nothing in parts. Our problem is not about the house; it's about being divided.' We lean against the barrier overlooking the valley. 'My father and uncle stopped speaking. It was my father's fault. The Bellanuovo oil was becoming well known. Things were going well, but he got greedy and wanted to make lots of money. He started producing fake oil and selling it overseas, to the Americans and the British. They didn't realise what they were buying. It was labelled as Italian and extra virgin, and that was all they needed to hear. But it was . . . *merda*!' and we both manage a little smile. 'After that, well, my uncle never spoke to my father again and the land was divided up. It's worthless.'

'And the debts?'

'Gambling. My grandfather, he tried to keep things going as best he could, but he couldn't manage. He had a passion for football. West Ham! He ran up debts and couldn't pay them. If you die with a debt on your house, the debt gets passed on to the family or the new owners. He didn't want to leave us any more grief.'

'But it hasn't worked,' I say bluntly.

'No, it hasn't. Maybe today that will change.' He sounds hopeful.

We turn and start to wind our way back to the school.

'Marco, the oil you tasted in the *masseria*. It wasn't your father's, or your grandfather's. It was given to me. I was told it was Bellanuovo oil, but . . .'

He silences me by kissing me again, and my whole body wants to just give in to him, but I know I have to be strong for both our sakes. It takes all my willpower to pull away. He looks at me.

'I don't want you to leave, Ruthie. You have come to mean a lot to me,' he says, but I don't want to hear it. I know he means it now, but I don't want to get in any deeper than I am already. It will hurt too much when I have to leave.

'I must get back to the *masseria*. I don't want anyone to see me. I've done enough damage for one day. They'll cover it up and paint over it on Monday. Could you run me home? Or I could walk if you need to stay.'

'Ruthie, wait! Look!' He points towards the school.

'Really, I don't want to!' I insist.

'Just look!' He spins me round. I can hear the noise, the chatter, and then – I'm not imagining it – laughter. Are they laughing at *me*? Or could it be . . . I look at the people in the schoolyard. They are studying the mural, picking out faces, talking excitedly, laughing not *at* me, but with me.

'Marco!' It's Marco's cousin, beckoning him over. 'There is a scene of you and me when we used to play in the olive grove. Remember when Nonno would shout for us and we would hide inside the roots of the tree at the back?' And I understand every word his cousin says.

A wide smile spreads across Marco's face. He takes my hand and pulls me towards the painting.

'Do you remember how I got this scar?' he asks his cousin, pointing to his chin. 'You pushed me out of a tree!' They both laugh.

'That's my dog!' Marco's sister says. 'She used to eat the sweepings.'

'And look, the old press!'

'When it was a still a cold press.' Someone else joins in. 'There's my *papa*!' says one of the cousins.

'And mine,' says Filippo, and suddenly everything goes a little quiet, like no one's mentioned him for a very long time.

Marco puts his arm around his brother, and then his cousin does the same.

'It was just human nature. He thought he was doing the right thing for his family. But he made a mistake. He loved this place,' Marco tells Filippo, and it seems Filippo needs to hear about his father.

'That's where we all grew up,' says another cousin, looking at the painting.

I turn to look for Nonna. She's crying, clutching a big hankie, just like the day I first met her. She beckons me over, and I bend down. I'm expecting her to tell me all the terrible things she wants to happen to me.

'*Fantastico!*' she announces loudly, nearly deafening me, and kisses me wetly on the cheek. Everyone cheers and claps enthusiastically.

'It's wonderful.' I turn to see Sophia smiling at me, her eyes bright and shiny. 'Thank you.'

I'm stunned, tears smarting at my eyes. I manage to say quietly, '*Prego.*'

Then Marco hands Nonna the painting I did for her, and she hugs and kisses me all over again and flaps her white hankie around her face, and everyone claps and cheers some more.

More fireworks are sent up into the schoolyard with huge bangs and flashes by Lou's husband, Antonio. Marco stands beside me, and his fingers reach out to touch mine, sending fireworks of my own throughout my body. How can I leave now?

Chapter Thirty-three

That evening, all the family return to Anna-Maria's, and Marco insists I come too, despite it being a family affair. Sophia makes the dough and pizzas are cooked on the *forno* by Marco's *trullo*. A fire pit is lit and seats and tables are gathered beside it. The air is full of the smell of woodsmoke, warm and comforting. Little bats fly between the trees overhead. Lanterns are lit and the fire gives off a wonderful heat. When it gets colder, the older members of the family move inside and I go to leave.

'Wait, Ruthie,' Marco calls after me as I try to make a quiet exit into the darkness and over the wall. It has been years since this family has been together. I don't want to intrude. Besides, Anna-Maria is still giving me daggers.

'Wait. Let me walk you back,' Marco says. He smells of the fire pit, hot and smoky. His cheeks are red and rosy from the heat, the night air and the Primitivo.

'I'll be fine,' I smile, and the butterflies dance in my stomach as he wraps his arms around me.

'Marco!' There is a familiar shout from behind us, making my whole body lurch. I turn. It's Anna-Maria. I sigh. I don't want to argue with her now. But she's not looking at me. She's looking at Marco. And standing beside her is Sophia and her son – the one from the photo. He is the image of Marco. They could be brothers. They're all smiling.

'Marco,' she calls again, and the three of them walk towards him. I dip back into the shadows of the olive tree, but Sophia turns to speak to me.

'Ruthie,' she says, and I'm surprised she even knows my name. 'I want to thank you again for what you did today.'

I blush. 'I just painted what I saw,' I say, my throat dry from the smoke of the fire. 'The family as it was.'

'Thank you,' Sophia says, 'for reminding us.' Then she turns to Marco. 'We have been talking, as a family.' She points to her son and to Anna-Maria. 'Ruthie was right. This family needs to work together again. It's been too long. We have let the past come between us and we must not let it ruin our future.'

'*Si, si*,' Marco agrees.

'We want to bring the estate back together. Pool all the land and the olives and make one single olive oil again.'

Anna-Maria is beaming broadly, as is Sophia's son.

Marco looks shocked for a moment, then his face breaks into a huge smile, like a child who's been given the best Christmas present ever.

'There is much we could do to put our stamp on the market,' he starts, jabbering like the words are falling over themselves to get out.

'But Marco, the thing is, it won't run itself, this estate.' Anna-Maria finally speaks, and Marco stops, like the rug has been pulled from under him.

'We all work away. How will we manage it? It will be a

full-time job if we can bring all the land back together, and who knows, even bring back our own press,' Sophia's son joins in.

Marco says nothing. He looks like all his dreams have come at once and then been snatched away again. He puts one hand to his mouth and his other arm across his body, and I want to reach out to him but I know I can't.

'Marco,' says Sophia quietly. 'You are the only one who has the skills and the knowledge to do this. Will you run the estate?'

The two women fall silent and I feel I shouldn't be here. There is a huge elephant standing between them, but it's not me. They have been joined now by Filippo and the rest of the family. The fire crackles and spits behind them.

Marco finally speaks. 'After what my father – our father – did, how can you ever trust me not to do the same? He was greedy. He ruined this estate and this family. My own father. I feel responsible.' His voice is dry and quiet. He has spent so many years not talking about how he felt; now the words are trying to come out but still it's hard for him. Sophia pats his shoulder.

'You are not your father, Marco. Remember the mural today. That is history. It's just part of the past.'

Marco looks at Sophia and Anna-Maria standing side by side, sisters-in-laws coming together finally.

'I don't know. I would be worried about letting everyone down. I would have to give up my job. It's a big risk. I'm not sure we should try and go back.' He shakes his head.

'Let's talk about it,' says Sophia's son.

Marco looks at me.

'Go,' I tell him encouragingly and turn to leave.

'Wait!' he says. 'There was talk in town today and I have heard the weather forecast. There is a big frost coming in. You must start to pick. Get your contractor to come as soon as possible. You must get your olives in.'

I tell him I will and say good night.

And so my time here is coming to an end. I have to get my harvest in and then I can put the house on the market and leave. Marco, on the other hand, looks to be on the verge of a new beginning.

Ryan, I need to start the harvest. Please come as soon as you can, I type into my phone. Then, using the torch, I climb up the tiny stone steps to the *trullo* roof and turn to look out over the olive trees. The mist is rolling through the branches like gymnastics ribbons and the party next door is in full swing. I take a deep breath and press send.

Chapter Thirty-four

The following morning, despite the early hour, I text the olive press to book a slot. They work practically twenty-four hours a day at this time of year. And I text Ryan again to tell him.

It's a cold, dark November morning, but the fire in the dining room erupts into life when I open the door on it. I throw on another log and then pull on my fleece and a cream hat with a bobble in each corner and a black heart on the front. You'd never believe we were sitting outside last night. Like a season passing, it all seems to be a faint memory.

I open the back doors on to the grove. It's six o'clock and pitch black. The mist has thickened. Daphne is there to greet me as always. I feel my throat tighten, like there's a ball stuck in there. I hope her new owners will be kind to her and know that she likes to be tickled on the head and that she doesn't like carrots. I'll also have to return Kirsty and Phil to Luigi when I leave.

Outside the back door is a tiny olive branch Marco planted up in a pot from when we were strimming, telling me that one day it would grow into a tree. I look over and his car is gone. He's up earlier than me!

I lay up the table outside with water and coffee cups and little *biscotti* for the workers. I put paninis in a basket and set them on a tray with butter and jam for later. I want Ryan and his team to work hard; this army is going to march on its stomach.

As it begins to get light outside, I'm still waiting. I look at my watch. I take the steps up the *trullo* to the roof and look at my phone. It pings into life. A text from the press confirms my slot. Time is crucial now. I have to make the press. If I lose my slot, the olives will be ruined.

The sky is getting lighter; like a big ball of peach and red flame, the sun is starting to rise. Then my phone pings again, letting me know the message I'm waiting for has arrived. Only it's not the one I wanted.

Sorry Ruthie, called away on another job. It was too big to turn down. Back in about a week. Will come then. Rx

He's not coming! Oh my God! After all this, he's not coming!

I hold the phone to my chest. My cheeks are red and flushed and my eyes prickle but no tears come. I'm furious. Furious with myself for relying on him. Furious that I made the wrong decision. There's only one thing I can do.

I go as quickly and carefully as I can down the steps, determination and humiliation driving me. In the barn I find big plastic buckets and the long poles I first saw when *mamma* cat scared me in there. They're leaning against the back wall, behind the old stone press, along with the old wooden ladder. I get the orange nets that were wrapped up in the corner and tuck them under my arm.

I take everything round to the back of the house and

put it down under the nearest tree. I look over at Marco's *trullo*. There's still no sign of him, and I realise my heart is twisting thinking about where he might be. Perhaps he has decided to return to his job in Naples, finding it too difficult to come back here and take up where his father left off after all.

With a heart as heavy as a medicine ball, I take the short cut over the wall to Anna-Maria's. The dogs wake up and come and greet me, but they barely bark. I bend to touch their heads, giving an extra pat to Marco's little dog, Lucia. I stop and take a deep breath and remind myself that this is no time for cold feet. I've come too far. Anna-Maria can think what she likes of me. In a week, one way or another, I'll be gone and all this will be a mad, distant memory.

I take the steps two at a time. There's a light on, thankfully, despite the ridiculously early hour. I take a deep breath, hoping it will bring courage, and knock on the door. I wait a while, then knock again, and eventually it opens.

It's Nonna. She smiles at me and gestures for me to come in.

'*Prego*,' she says, and still I get a tiny thrill, despite my desperation, that I can understand her.

'I'm looking for Marco,' I tell her, and she nods in understanding. 'It's really important I get in touch with him,' I add. She nods again. And then Anna-Maria is by her side in a fleecy zebra-print dressing gown and pink rollers. She's not wearing make-up, which is a little startling, but she is wearing all her gold jewellery.

'How can we help you?' she says in English, refusing to switch to Italian, keeping me a tourist. I shouldn't have come, I realise. She's like a firewall between me and her son.

'Anna-Maria, I know you are keen for me to leave, and the sooner I get my harvest in and bottled, the sooner I'll be gone.' I feel like someone's suddenly kicked me in the stomach and my words catch infuriatingly in my throat. 'I really need to get in touch with Marco. Please. Can you contact him for me?'

She looks at me for a moment, and Nonna looks at her and then pulls out her own mobile phone from her dressing gown pocket. My heart lifts a little and I smile. Thank God. Finally she's going to help me.

'No. Marco is busy. Busy sorting out his future. I can't get hold of him, sorry,' she says sharply, and tells Nonna to put her phone away. Nonna scowls and calls her a rude name, I think, throwing her hands up in disgust and shuffling away.

Now I know the tears are in danger of falling, and I turn and run down the steps. I don't stop running until I am back at the *masseria*, where I pull my hat down over my ears, run my sleeve across my dribbling nose and pick up a long stick and a bucket. I have to get these olives to the press one way or another. I can't let the doubters win. I'm not going down without a bloody good fight!

By midday my fingers are red and sore from stripping the olives from the branches like Marco showed me when we were strimming. The sun is out but it's cold.

At least it isn't raining. Rain would slow things up even more. I wonder how many days I've got before the frost comes.

I stop to drink water, lots of water, and eat a panini, even though I don't really have time to. I can't afford for my body to give up on me now. It's just me, like it's always been. Only this time, if I don't make the olive press, I'll be left with practically nothing after I've paid back my olive oil customers.

I keep picking. Daphne stays with me every step of the way. As I work, I replay everything that Ed and Mum said to me when I left. I replay Marco's incredulity when he learnt that I planned to live here, his and Anna-Maria's. I replay that damn kiss, when something in me woke up, when I felt something I had never felt before and will now never feel again. I'm so angry that I let myself fall in love with Marco, I realise.

I bang at the trees with the long stick. My shoulders ache like I've never known before. Then I pull down the branches, sliding my fingers along them, and more little black olives hit the orange nets laid out on the ground. I climb up into the higher boughs and strip those branches too, and when I really can't reach the topmost ones, I get the ladder and disappear into the leafy loft of the tree. Finally I climb down, pick up the net and pour my pickings into the plastic bucket. I turn to look at my work.

'Three down. One hundred and twenty to go!' I say to absolutely no one with a hint of hysteria in my voice. I move on to the next tree.

*

By six in the evening it's got much colder. Like a marathon runner, I'm eating and drinking water at regular intervals, and I try to swing my arms to loosen the stiffness in them as often as I can. I experiment with picking in gloves but can't get the fruit off the trees. I'm exhausted and just want to collapse into bed, but I have to keep going. I put my headphones in and get Dolly Parton pumping out '9 to 5' to get me going again.

By midnight, I've found my head torch, but I've slowed down considerably. More than once I trip over the net while I'm taking it to the plastic barrel, causing me to lose the olives all over the ground. Daphne has chosen to lie under one of the trees. Thankfully one of the ones I've already done. She's keeping an eye on me and I'm so grateful that she's there.

There's a screech from a fox and then the bark of the dogs next door, and I jump. My hands shake and my heart thunders, so I turn the iPod up louder and sing along tunelessly.

By three in the morning, silent tears are running down my cheeks and I am rocking backwards and forwards to stop myself falling asleep next to Daphne on the nets. I feel like I've been hit by a bus, and my hands are so cold it's as though they've been cut with razor blades. Robbie Williams is playing, pumping through me, and I'm trying to jump up and down and shimmy my backside to 'Let Me Entertain You' when suddenly there's a tap on my shoulder. The first scream catches in my throat, but the second comes out at full volume as I swing round, hitting my attacker with my olive stick, my earphones flying out of my ears.

Chapter Thirty-five

'*Che cazzo?* What the hell!' He holds up his hand to the bright light shining into his eyes from my head torch.

'Marco?' I take a sharp intake of breath and put my swollen, stinging hand to my mouth.

'You hit me!' he says, clutching his head.

'I'm so sorry!' I say. 'It was Robbie's fault.'

'Robbie? Who is Robbie? I thought it was Ryan.'

'Ryan? No, Robbie. Robbie Williams.' I shake an earphone, realising that I'm sounding drunk.

'Where's Ryan?' He holds his hand up against the light, then says, '*Scusi*,' and reaches towards me. For a moment I wonder if he's going to scoop me up and kiss me like in *An Officer and a Gentleman*. I lean slightly forward and then it all goes dark as he switches off my head torch. I feel disappointed and crushed, like the olives under my feet.

'Where's the contractor?' he asks again, impatiently.

'Ummm . . .' My brain isn't really functioning as it should. 'He, um . . .' It's not easy to find the words to say, 'You were right.'

'He couldn't come,' I manage eventually in a small voice, and the fox screeches again. 'He was a pillock and completely let me down!'

Marco takes hold of my shoulders.

'Don't tell me you are attempting this on your own?' Marco says crossly. 'I told you! I know his type.'

'He said he'd be here!' I'm now scratchier than I've ever felt, and this is no time for 'I told you so'.

'He's been selling the Bellanuovo oil, watering it down with cheaper oil and selling it on,' Marco says.

I clear my throat.

'Like the stuff he left here. The lamp oil?' I ask.

He nods. 'It was him, wasn't it, who gave you the oil?' His voice is quiet but steely.

I nod too. I don't know if he can see me.

'You should have told me. Why didn't you?' Marco asks.

'Because I thought that . . . he might not turn up for the harvest and then I wouldn't get the harvest in and I wouldn't get to sell up and leave.' The last word sticks in my mouth. Because that's what this is all about: me going home.

'And so he's gone on a bigger job?'

I nod again.

'How far have you got?' Marco juts a chin at the trees.

'I think I'm nearly at thirteen.'

'You will never make your slot at the *frantoio* at this rate! The harvest will perish!' He throws his hands up and then turns and stalks off to his car, getting in and driving off, his headlights lighting up the trees in the pitch-black night.

I can't believe it! He didn't even offer to help! How wrong could I have been? My hands ache and my shoulders are sore, but now my heart feels like it's ripping in two as well. Now I know I really am on my own.

New determination sets in as I sniff and rub my nose with the corner of my sleeve. I look a mess and feel a mess. No wonder he didn't want to sweep me off my feet. That kind of love is just for the movies. It's impulsive, and what I've come to realise is that impulsiveness always lets you down.

Chapter Thirty-six

By five o'clock I am a snivelling, dribbling wreck sitting on the cold November ground. I am crying, great deep sobs, gulping and coughing as I pick the olives from the lower branches of the tree. I'm doing that rocking thing again, back and forwards, and more than anything now I want to go home. I want to go to Starbucks for coffee and buy one for the guy living rough on the corner. I'm beginning to realise what life outside must be like for them. I want to go back to buying my fruit and veg in the market. I'd even put up with Colin walking around in his vest and belching. Belching would be absolutely fine right now.

My eyes can't stay open and suddenly I stop. This is madness. Marco is right. Ed was right. My mum and Anna-Maria were right. I am never going to get this done in time for my slot. I was a fool to try. I'm beaten. Marco can have the place. It's just a house. But it's not the house I'm grieving for, it's my broken heart. When Ed and I finally split up, we just sort of fizzled out. There was nothing there any more. We'd become a habit. We were different people. We'd never really had each other's hearts to break in the first place. But Marco, I realise, has mine, and the pain is more excruciating than the aches in my shoulders, my hands and my neck right now. I lie down amongst the olives on the orange netting, curl up and cry myself into a very deep sleep.

The sound of clanking and voices cuts through my dreams. Italian voices and shouts, talk about olives. It's like I've slipped finally into madness, where I'm perpetually harvesting olives. Someone shakes my shoulder.

'Ruthie.'

I swear it's Marco's voice, come back to taunt me. 'Ruthie,' I hear again, and a wet tongue licks my face, catapulting me awake. It's Daphne. But beside Daphne is Marco . . . I think, or am I dreaming it?

'Ruthie, wake up. Look.' Marco points. I raise myself on my elbow and squint into the rising sun. I look at the buckets of olives around me. The fallen olives on the ground next to my stick.

'Look,' he says again. Against the big ball of red starting to creep up over the horizon are people, lots of people, with ladders, buckets and sticks. I sit up and try and let my eyes adjust.

'It's time to get your harvest to the press,' he says, pulling me to my feet.

I stand and stare in amazement. Maybe it's a dream or a mirage. Maybe this isn't happening at all. They're all here: Luigi and his wife, Rocco and his wife and kids, Lou and her husband, and the vegetable stallholder I bought strawberries from when Sophia and Anna-Maria looked like they were going to fight to the death. More surprisingly, Sophia herself is here; she nods and waves.

And so are Marco's cousins, wrapped up against the cold morning, laughing and joking as though they are revisiting their youth. For me it would've been the funfair on Clapham Common with my brother. For the Bellanuovos, it's coming back here for the olive harvest.

'They're here to laugh at me. They didn't think I could do it, just like Ed didn't,' I say to Marco, and turn away.

'No,' he says firmly. 'They're here to help you. They *know* you can do it.' He turns me back to face them.

I begin to smile. They're not laughing. He's right. They are here because they want to help. They think I can do it. Dream or no dream, it's a lovely sight.

'Hey!' I hear Marco call crossly, and turn to see Nonna, her small wiry frame dressed as always in black, pulling on a hat. She's still in her slippers.

'Go back to the house, Nonna,' he tells her.

'What, and miss out on all the fun?' she snaps back. 'I've been doing this longer than you were alive. Thank God someone's brought the old place back to life.' She looks around at the misty scene and smiles widely. '*Buongiorno*, Ruthie.' She nods at me and then sets to work next to Luigi and his wife at the lower branches.

Even Franco Pugliese is there with his wife. And, to my great surprise, Rosa's parents.

They are all chatting, laughing and picking at my olive trees; setting up ladders, moving the nets from tree to tree, working in teams. Everyone is there except one person. I scan around again. Everyone except Anna-Maria, but then I really wouldn't have expected her to be. I can't believe they have turned out like this.

'You! You did this, didn't you?' I turn to Marco and search his big blue eyes. 'I thought you'd gone to find Ryan.'

'Don't worry. Ryan won't be coming back this way.' He looks to Franco, who raises a hand.

'He's on a big job,' I say wearily.

'He thinks he's on a big job,' Marco smiles. 'By the time he gets there and realises there's no work for him, we'll be done here. No one will employ him now they know what he's been up to.'

I look around and frown. I'm confused.

'Why? Why would you do this for me? If I win this bet, you lose. You lose the house. Why would you do that?'

He smiles, and my heart flips over and back again. There's an ache lower down, below my belly, that's nothing to do with the olive picking.

'Because you are an amazing woman, Ruthie Collins, and I think I must love you,' he says, looking straight at me. The butterflies in my tummy tumble and loop the loop.

'Damn! Now I know it's a dream!'

'It's not a dream, really. I think I love you and have done from the moment you arrived. Well no, maybe not from then. But when I saw how hard you worked here, your determination, I began to fall for you. And I realised I loved you the day I saw you with the lawnmower in the olive grove.'

I stare at him in utter disbelief. The pickers seem to have stopped too, and I can feel all eyes on me. There are things I need to say, that I wouldn't normally, but it's okay because this isn't real. I'm not really standing in an olive grove on a misty November morning with the man of my dreams telling me he loves me. And like all good dreams, I know you have to wake up.

'But you can't. Stop messing with me. What about Rosa?' I turn to look, cringeing with embarrassment. 'Her parents,' I say in what I hope is a whisper. Rosa's parents are there, picking and chatting as if nothing is happening.

'I've told you, Rosa and I have known each other since school.'

'Exactly, you're childhood sweethearts. I can't come in between that!'

'Rosa doesn't want to marry me and I don't want to marry her. She has eyes for someone else. As do I.' He takes hold of my elbows and draws me closer. 'My mother had high hopes for Rosa and me, but it just made both of us unhappy. It was easier when I was away. In life, I have learned, you have to follow your heart, whatever strange places it may lead.' He laughs, lifting me up on to my tiptoes, and kisses me all over again, just as I've been hoping he'd do ever since that first kiss after the olive tasting. It's delicious, but I am very aware that I have been out here all night and need a shower and to clean my teeth. I pull away, knowing that, just like in a dream, once you die and go to heaven, you wake up. He looks at me. He's still here.

'It's not a dream, then?' I mumble.

'It's not a dream. I want you, Ruthie Collins, you mad Englishwoman!'

And the pickers all clap and chant, '*Bacio! Bacio! Bacio!*'

'They want us to kiss again.' He smiles and moves his lips to mine and runs his finger down my cheek, and I shiver with delicious excitement. I stop him, though, not because I don't want him to – my lips are positively aching to feel his again – but because I have to know.

'Your mother?'

'My mother just needs time . . . and her family around her.'

'She wants me gone, Marco. She will never let you be with me. She'll never accept me.'

'I have left my job. I plan to return here, to run the estate. We're all agreed.' He nods at his family. 'She will be happy. But I want to make you happy too.'

'So you're going to do it. You're going to run the Bellanuovo estate again! That's *fantastico*!' I say, and he laughs.

'We have to try.' He gestures to his cousins and the fields beyond. 'You're right. It was never about the house. It was about the family name. We needed to be the Bellanuovo family again. You made us realise that this place is part of all our childhoods.' He looks out over the grove full of family, friends and neighbours, and I know I could never take this away from him.

'Now, let's get your olives to harvest. Or would you rather rest?' He suddenly looks concerned. Right now, I would love to go to bed, I realise, though not to sleep. But that's not for now. That's for later, and the prospect thrills me. I will enjoy every moment of the waiting, and even more so finally going to bed tonight. A knowing smile passes between us as he strokes my cheek again, and all my aches and pains seem to disappear.

'No way! I have an appointment at the press.' And I have never felt more awake and alive.

Chapter Thirty-seven

'Who's that with Nonna?' I ask Lou. Nonna is chatting and giggling with a short, dark-haired man. Lou laughs.

'That's my dad!'

'What?'

'Remember I told you how we were thinking of going to live in Wales, helping him with the business so he could start to take things easier? Well, he decided that life was too short. What was the point of us going over there when he could come out here and help us do up the *trullo*? And see more of Giac! So he's selling up, the house and the business, and is coming out to join us.'

'Lou, that's fantastic!' I nearly knock her out with my olive stick as I try and hug her. Tears well up in her eyes.

'I know. It's brilliant. We're going to restore the *trullo* just like you've done here. It's you that convinced us we should do it.'

'What? Because all holidaymakers want is old falling-down properties?'

'Something like that!' she laughs. 'We're going to do *agriturismo*. B and B to you and me. Dad's going to help Antonio and put some money from the sale of his business into it. He wants to see his grandchildren grow up.'

'Hang on, did you say grandchildren?' I look down at her belly and she squeals in delight and nods her head and hugs me so tightly I think I might fall over. And I hug her back, truly delighted for them.

We pick all morning, and then the olives that are ready are loaded into Luigi's trailer on the back of the tractor. The fruit and veg man from the market has brought his Ape van, and Sophia takes some too, in the back of her Fiat 500.

Cars, mopeds and vans are reversed and there is a lot of wheel-spinning. By the looks of it, a convoy is ready to set off to the *frantoio*. It's very different from the funeral cortège that left Anna-Maria's house when I first arrived. There is smiling, shouting and the beeping of horns.

'Ready?' Marco asks me.

'I'll get my car,' I say, then realise it's totally boxed in by the wall.

'No, you get to ride with the olives,' Marco says. He climbs on to the crossbar between the tractor and the trailer and holds out his hand. He pulls me up and shows me where to stand, then puts his arms around me and holds me tightly to him.

'*Pronto?*' He looks around.

'*Pronto!*' we all shout back. 'Ready!'

The tractor lurches forward and I cling tightly to the trailer and to Marco. There is a cacophony of horns again, and I feel my heart bursting with pride and happiness as we travel down the drive.

There is a dip in my delight as we pass Anna-Maria's

villa. She is standing on the front steps, under the red and white awning, wiping her hands with a tea towel. She doesn't smile. I find myself pulling away from Marco and dropping my eyes. Nonna passes us on the back of a Vespa and shouts excitedly to her. Like I say, Anna-Maria is never going to accept me into her family, that much is clear.

We wind our way down the lane and take a right-hand turn off the main road towards the press. Then we bump and sway along the tight and tiny lane through fields of Bellanuovo olives. Very soon all this land will be one again and the walls will be knocked down. The olives tumble and fall in the trailer, like excited schoolchildren on a day trip.

I look at my watch. We're only just going to make it, but we've got the wind behind us and the gods on our side.

Just then the tractor comes to a sudden halt, catapulting us forward so that I nearly end up head first in the olives with my feet waggling out. Marco catches me and I regain my balance.

Luigi is jumping out of the cab and shouting. I turn to see him waving his arms, waddling very quickly on his short legs towards the flock of sheep that have wandered into the road. Young Luigi jumps out of the car behind and waves his big worker's hands too, and between them father and son move the sheep into a field by the side of the road. They pat each other on the back and the tractor starts up again.

Almost immediately the convoy is stopped in its tracks by a little car coming in the other direction.

'UK car! Holidaymaker!' Marco shouts, and rolls his eyes playfully. I strain around the cab of the tractor as Luigi shouts that the car will have to reverse up. All I can see is a large map being wrestled with in the front seat. It reminds me briefly of home – Ed always liked a map – and for a moment I wonder if they're viewers looking for the *masseria*. I feel a stab of regret go right through me.

'We're not going to make it,' I shout over the tractor noise. Just then the whole convoy begins to beep its horns. My heart starts to swell again as I look round from the tractor to the line of cars and bikes behind us. Nonna is even shaking her fist. With squealing accelerator the car starts to reverse from side to side up the lane, bouncing off walls and hedgerows. Again I'm reminded of Ed; he was a terrible driver. But Ed is a very long way away, and I'm beginning to believe that finally that part of my life is over and done with.

The convey lurches off again, quickly getting up a head of steam. Luigi barely slows down as we approach the olive press. It's nearly lunchtime and I just hope the gates are still open. They are! Luigi gives us a quick glance as he takes the corner at speed, the wheels of the trailer lifting. Marco and I shout, 'Whoa!' and cling on to each other for dear life, because that's how I feel about him, like he's now my life here in Puglia.

We hurtle down the long drive towards the big metal sheds at the end, where Rosa is standing, just pulling the door to on the press.

'She's closing for lunch! I've missed my spot!' I wail in horror.

She stands up straight when she sees us approaching and folds her arms. The cars and mopeds all screech to a halt and the occupants jump out, apart from Nonna, who has to be lifted off the back of the Vespa and nearly topples Lou's dad over in the process.

They are surrounding Rosa now, arms waving, trying to persuade her to reopen. But she shakes her head, shrugs and explains that they know the rules. They must be there on time or the slot goes. Her staff have gone for lunch.

'She doesn't have another slot for three days,' I wail. 'The olives will be ruined! Too acidic. I won't be able to sell it as top-quality oil, and I'll have to reimburse all the customers who have paid me!'

Marco turns and raises an eyebrow, and nods his head, impressed. And much as I would like to enjoy the moment, I can't help but feel despair. All my hard work, and theirs – I look around – for nothing! Even Rosa's father is trying to get her to bend the rules, but they just start arguing about who is in charge now.

Marco jumps down from the tractor. If she says yes to him, I will be thrilled but my heart will break at the same time. I'll know for sure that she's in love with him and there's no way I can step in there. There's lots of hand movements and talking . . . and then she shakes her head. I don't know whether to laugh or cry.

Then Young Luigi emerges from the back of the crowd, and everyone stops shouting and arguing. He slips his hat off and holds it in front of his chest. He blushes under that deep olive skin and then lifts his big eyes to Rosa, who looks like the Angel Gabriel himself has come to talk to her. Her face is lit up, glowing, waiting on his words.

'Signorina Rosa,' he stutters quietly, 'this woman has worked so hard to pick the olives. If you turn her away, they will die. She has done it out of love. Sometimes love can be a painful thing.' He's looking right at her now and she is searching his eyes. 'She hasn't always found the right path, the right words or the right way, but she has kept the love in her heart,' and I'm beginning to think it isn't me he's talking about any more. I look up at Marco, who smiles back knowingly. 'Just like I have kept love in my heart. If you understand any of what I'm saying, please reopen the press.'

Rosa speaks with difficulty. 'My machine operator has gone into town for lunch,' she says.

'I will help, we all can.' Young Luigi gestures to the crowd, who cheer, and he shyly tilts his head once more. 'You just have to say the word.' He looks back at her, and they're definitely not talking about the olives now.

Beaming, Rosa grapples with the keys and swings back the huge concertina doors. The gathered crowd cheer some more and surge forward, grabbing grey crates to unload the olives into, whilst others go straight to the weighing scales and the machine powers up. Now I just need to know I have enough olives to make my own pressing. I hold my breath.

Chapter Thirty-eight

When the scales tip round, Rosa lifts a hand. Yes! That means I get my own pressing! Young Luigi dives straight in to grab a couple of crates, exchanging smiles and looks with Rosa on the way. Marco's arm slides around my shoulders and he kisses the top of my head. I think I've joined Rosa in believing the Angel Gabriel has visited.

Everyone surges from the weighing scales towards the big machine, tipping the olives from the crates into the steel collecting bin, which is like a huge hungry mouth. I pour my crate in and they cheer and clap again, then the machine starts. As a group, we follow the olives on their journey. Young Luigi is standing side by side with Rosa and her father, who is obviously impressed by his enthusiasm for the machines. From the washer, the olives travel up a spiral tube. The group chat amongst themselves, about this year's harvest and the quality of the oil. There is an air of expectation as the olives go on to be ground into paste and then the oil is separated from the water. Finally, there is a shout. A large metal canister appears from somewhere, and from the little pipe at the end of the long room full of blue and silver machinery, deep green olive oil starts to trickle out. More cheers and I'm nudged and pushed forward.

'There it is! Your oil,' Marco whispers in my ear.

'Bellanuovo oil,' I correct him with a smile.

Someone holds the canister under the flow and starts to fill it. Then Marco is handed something by Rosa. He leans forward, then turns back to me with a small white paper cup.

'Taste it,' he says, holding the cup to my lips. Our eyes lock again, like magnets drawn back to each other. I put my hand to the cup and his doesn't leave it. An electric shock ricochets through my body. The rim touches my mouth, and it's like Marco is putting his own lips to mine. As he tilts the cup, the thick, syrupy oil reaches my lips. I hold his gaze; the butterflies do the haka in my stomach and a fire is blazing down below.

I let the thick liquid touch the tip of my tongue first, then slowly seep into the sides and back of my mouth. It's peppery and fruity, then it slides warmingly down my throat and I close my eyes. There is a hush in the room. At last I open my eyes, smile and raise my little cup like an Olympic champion.

Everyone claps, and then the shouts of '*Bacio, bacio!*' start up again. Marco and I both laugh and blush, then to the delight of our audience he kisses me gently on my fruit-flavoured lips, before pulling away and licking his own.

But still the clapping goes on, and we turn to see Rosa and Young Luigi kissing deeply and fully, like they've waited a lifetime to do it. I can't help but get caught up in the feeling of love and happiness and join in the applause.

'Here we believe that good things take time. Like our

food, slow-cooking is the special ingredient that makes an amazing recipe. All good things take time to grow.' Marco looks from the oil pouring out of the pipe back to me. Prosecco appears from somewhere and is poured. The glasses fizz up and mine fizzes over. Everyone is toasting the harvest, *my* harvest. Glasses are chinked and good health and thanks. I am giddy with relief, happiness and something that feels a lot like falling in love. Perhaps it's something else I haven't felt before too: a feeling of belonging.

Chapter Thirty-nine

Travelling back to the *masseria*, the neighbours peel off one by one, returning home as the late-afternoon sun begins to dip in the sky. They all promise to be back in the morning to pick the last of the olives and finish the harvest.

Luigi has a smile like the Cheshire cat when he drops us off at the *masseria*. Young Luigi has stayed on at the press to help Rosa out with a machine that needs stripping down.

We unload the big steel drums full of oil from the back of the tractor and lug them into the barn. Then Luigi starts off down the lane. As soon as he is out of sight, we turn and practically run inside. Daphne looks positively affronted as we shut the door in her face.

Inside, our lips fall on each other's and stay there, like they've found home and can never be separated. We pull at each other's clothes, hungry to touch skin, our hands exploring. We move upstairs like playful pups, and I hardly notice my aches and pains as layers of clothing are stripped from me, leaving a trail all the way to my bedroom.

'Wait!' I say as we land on the bed and the bedclothes bounce up to wrap around us. I pull away and run to the little bathroom, panting with excitement and anticipation.

I clean my teeth and quickly shower. The water is hot and the flames in the grate are burning as furiously as the fire in my groin. I go back to the bedroom, where Marco has his shirt off. His chest is broad and muscular and his skin dark and soft. He kisses me and excuses himself to the bathroom. I lie down on the bed, a towel wrapped around me. I'm so tired I can barely keep my eyes open, and I decide to rest for a minute or two, just until Marco comes back.

When I open my eyes again, I'm not sure what time it is. I reach for my phone. It's five o'clock, just before dawn. It's still dark, but the birds are beginning to sing. There are voices outside the window. I catch my breath and go to sit up, but I can't. Marco is lying beside me, on top of the covers, his arm wrapped across me. Oh God! I'm mortified. I'm in my pyjamas, the fleecy ones with the bunny on the front; the ones no one is supposed to see. Marco must have put me to bed and then lain down on top of the covers and pulled my dressing gown and coat over himself.

He begins to stir. His hands start to move across my body, and I catch my breath. His face is next to mine and he begins to kiss me, and his body moves closer. I can feel him wanting me. Explosions are crashing about in the pit of my stomach; like New Year's Eve celebrations, Christmas, birthdays and the excitement of my first olive pressing all at once. He moves on top of me and slides his hand under my pyjamas, running the back of his fingers down the inside of my arm and my side, just beside my breast. I shiver and nearly explode there and then.

'Hey, *ciao, buongiorno,*' I hear from below the window, and it's like someone's chucked a bucket of cold water over us. Our neighbours are back. We look at each other. Is there a chance we could carry on? Then we both laugh. We can't. They have turned out on Marco's request, and there's no way I can let them pick the rest of the olives while I stay in bed. With any luck we should get the final ones to the press today.

Marco rolls off me, rubs his face with his hands and gives a low laugh. 'Don't worry.' He turns on his side to look at me, tucking his arm under his head. 'Like I told you, here we believe the best dishes take time to cook. We will enjoy ourselves even more when we finish the harvest tonight.' He kisses me again and stands up, fastening the top button on his jeans and doing up his belt. Shy but happy, I slide out from under the covers and pull on my dressing gown from the pile that was covering Marco. Then we try and relocate all our clothes from last night, giggling like teenagers as we do.

Once dressed, Marco goes out to greet everyone while I put the kettle on for coffee. A happy little part of me keeps whispering, 'Tonight, tonight.' I put more wood on the fire in the woodburner and it blazes up, flames flickering and dancing.

Chapter Forty

With the exception of Anna-Maria, everybody is here again. In fact, there seem to be more people who have come to help, and I feel tears of gratitude welling up in my eyes. The ironmonger, teachers from the school, and even Luigi's friends who I saw on that first day. I brush the tears away, pretending it's the early-morning mist, then stamp my feet and bang my hands together and say good morning to everyone, shaking hands and kissing those I know better, like Lou and Antonio, on both cheeks.

'Make sure you take it easy today,' I tell Lou.

'No worries, I've brought my own chair,' and she pulls out her folding chair and sets it down in the middle of the grove. Antonio insists she puts a blanket over her knees. Giac climbs on to her lap and hugs her.

I smile and go to make the coffee and lay out bottles of water and little biscuits from Sophia's *forno*, whilst the pickers get their ladders sorted and nets laid ready to begin just before the sun starts to rise in the fiery red and purple sky.

With the olives picked, we load up the tractor and trailer and the Ape and Sophia's Fiat. Just like yesterday, we start moving with lots of shouting. Marco opens the gates at the end of the drive and after a great deal of manoeuvring we're ready to go.

Marco pulls me up on to the tractor trailer again and we stand side by side, proudly taking the last of the olives to harvest. After this it will just be the sweepings. Then I need to get the oil bottled, ready to go to my customers in the UK. I'll label them with the labels I've had made: a miniature of the painting I did for Nonna. I still haven't found a courier to take them yet, and that's my job first thing tomorrow.

'Hey, stop!' Marco calls to Luigi. The tractor stops with a judder, nearly sending me head first into the olives again. Marco jumps down and runs back to the barn, and comes striding back out with one of the bottles I bought from the ironmonger's.

'For the first bottle of Bellanuovo oil,' he says, waving it at me.

I can't help smiling and thinking I couldn't get any happier if I tried.

The tractor starts up again and the convoy is off, just like yesterday. Only it's colder, a lot colder. I pull my hat down and my scarf tighter around my neck. Marco draws me closer to him and I put my head against his chest, breathing in his smell. We turn off the main road and are met by the same herd of sheep taking their lunchtime stroll across the lane. Once again Luigi and Young Luigi get out and shoo them into the field. Off we go again, and blow me, minutes later Luigi is slamming on the brakes as the same little British car from yesterday comes hurtling towards us. This time I do end up head first in the olives, and there's the sound of breaking glass as the bottle smashes on the road. As Marco helps me out of the trailer, I hear shouting. The little car has actually hit the front of Luigi's tractor.

I get back on the crossbar. I can hear Marco speaking in English.

'You need to back up. That's it. Left hand down and then straight back.'

I brush myself down – no harm done – and smile as Marco and Luigi deal patiently with the driver, who is blatantly like a fish out of water.

'This is ridiculous! There's no way I can reverse all the way back there!' I hear him say in a clear London accent. My blood turns to ice and I feel like someone's popped all my birthday balloons at once.

'Ed?' I say, turning slowly.

'Ruthie? Thank God!' He marches up to the trailer. 'This idiot hit me, did you see? These roads are lethal. I've been driving round and round for two days!'

'Ed?' I say again, cutting him off. 'What on earth are you doing here?' I look down at his familiar face.

'More to the point, Ruthie, what are you doing up there? That's highly dangerous. Health and safety would have had a field day if this accident had been any worse.'

'Ed!' I stop him again. 'What are you doing here?' I repeat.

At first he says nothing, and then, more calmly, 'Looking for you, of course.'

'Who is this, Ruthie?' Marco faces Ed, scowling. Young

Luigi is behind him, arms folded and frowning too. My mouth is dry. The convoy are all out of their cars, craning their necks to see what's going on.

'This is Ed, my ex—' I begin, and Ed finishes quickly: 'Partner.'

I never did like that word. It sounds so . . . businesslike.

Marco's frown turns to a full-blown thunder cloud, but Franco is calling that we need to get a move on or we'll miss the slot, and she won't hold it twice.

Having swept away the broken glass from my Bellanuovo bottle, I reverse Ed's car back, disentangling it from the front of Luigi's tractor. Marco gets on to the back of the tractor and it moves off. He gives a single arm wave telling me to follow on, but it feels like he's gesturing to a stranger.

I put the car in first and follow at the back of the convoy.

'These roads are madness, I tell you. Bit like the rest of this place, by the looks of it,' says Ed as he watches the convoy pass: Filippo driving Marco's car and revving the engine and waving, Franco in his Rolls Royce, Young Luigi in the Ape and Nonna on the back of the Vespa also scowling at Ed. My stomach is in knots as I think about Marco's face. I have to get to him and explain that I don't know why Ed's here and that it changes nothing. Does it? I snatch a sideways glance at Ed's familiar profile. Suddenly my old life is here with me. The old life I wanted back so badly.

'Why are you here, Ed?' I say, following Nonna, who is

holding on to Lou's dad on the Vespa with one hand.

'I told you, Ruthie. I came to find you. Annabel lent me her car. To give you this.' He turns to the back seat and points to a box of records. My records. And there next to them is the record player. It seems smaller than I remember.

'You were right. It was childish of me to take them. I didn't need them or want them. We both collected them. I want you to have them, and the record player.'

I glance at the box as we pull up at the press. Marco is already off the trailer and loading up grey crates with the olives. My heart lurches looking at him.

'You came all the way to southern Italy to give me a box of vintage records and a record player?' I ask incredulously. The sight of the records brings it all back: our home, our life together. The places we hunted for them, on eBay and at car boot sales. They were good times, I remember, happy times. When we split, the records were the only thing we argued over. In the end, I gave in. Now here he is giving them to me and I really don't want them.

'Yes, like I say. I've been driving round for two days trying to find you, and not a moment too soon by the looks of it!'

Chapter Forty-one

To say that this pressing is a much more sober affair compared to yesterday's is an understatement. In fact it has the mood of a wake as Marco stands back, scowling intermittently at Ed. Ed scowls at my neighbours. The neighbours whisper and stare at the newcomer.

The oil is finally extracted, but there's no Bellanuovo bottle to put it in and so we make do with more metal urns. There's a murmur of congratulations and general goodwill when the oil comes out, but it's a far cry from the hubbub of yesterday. There's no *bacio*. I'm not sure there ever will be again, looking at Marco's face.

On the journey home, I travel next to Marco on the tractor crossbar, but he doesn't have his arm around me. He is holding on to the trailer and his knuckles are white. Luigi picks up speed and my now much longer hair whips around my face. I want to tell Marco how Ed's just come to give me the records and the player. But it may have to wait until we get back and everyone has gone. That's it. Don't rush it. Good things take time here in Puglia, I tell myself. I can explain about Ed as soon as he goes back to his hotel and the pickers take their ladders and nets and leave.

*

Marco couldn't believe it. But he should do, he told himself. He had tried so hard not to fall for this woman. She had arrived in his world unannounced and he had been determined she wouldn't stay there. But little by little he had grown to admire her: her determination, her attitude and the way she had grown more beautiful with every day. He had believed her when she said it was over with her ex. But he had been lied to before, by the man he thought was his hero, his own father. He couldn't take being let down again, giving his heart and having it shattered. What he had hoped was going to be was clearly never destined to happen. Why else would a man come all this way to find his ex if he wasn't still in love with her? This Ed had everything Ruthie wanted: her life back home. That was what she wanted, wasn't it? She wanted to go home. Marco had been a fool to think he could compete.

Chapter Forty-two

When we pull into the *masseria* drive, Ed is still following the convoy. I jump down from the tractor, but not quickly enough judging by the cold shoulder I'm getting from Marco. I can see through to the courtyard. Checked tablecloths have been laid over the old stone press in the barn, with plates piled high and buckets of knives and forks. There are baskets of bread and bowls of shiny black and green olives, little *aperitivo* biscuits and gherkins. There are short stubby glasses, and terracotta jugs that I presume contain red wine. Under the biggest, oldest tree in the middle of the courtyard is a long table, maybe two joined together. It too is covered in a red and white tablecloth. In the olive grove, just beyond the veranda, the fire pit that Marco built after I'd scorched the area with my bonfire has been lit and is sending up little ribbons of smoke. I catch my breath. Just like my painting, I think.

Who did all this? Is this something to do with Ed turning up here?

Suddenly I spot Anna-Maria coming down the drive carrying a large terracotta dish with big oven gloves. It's steaming hot.

'Marco,' she calls. 'Go and get the other dishes and

bring them to the barn. You too, Filippo.' Their sister is following behind with bowls of green veg.

I'm too stunned to speak. Anna-Maria finally reaches me, and the smell from her dish makes my stomach roar.

'Pickers need feeding,' she says, this time in Italian. '*Caccatoria.*' She lifts the dish a little closer to my face.

'Hunter's stew.' I smile in reply. 'Thank you, Anna-Maria, for all of this.'

Suddenly it's like her mask has been snatched off. Her face is softer. She puts the hot dish down on the cloth-covered stone and instructs everyone to come and help themselves.

'I have seen how my son looks at you. He looks like a man in love.'

I blush but say nothing.

'Someone recently said something that made me think. They said that you reminded them of me when I first came here. I was new, young and an outsider. But I remember I wasn't going to let them drive me away.' She stops, and there is a tear in her eye. 'I see that in you.'

I feel a little choked too and look at my feet and then back at her, for once lost for words.

'You've worked really hard. You deserve to be here. And you have brought my family back together. It may not be in this house, but you have restored the good name of Bellanuovo oil. My son is coming home thanks to you.'

And this time I let out a little hiccup. Maybe it's exhaustion. But I have to find Marco and explain about Ed. I have to tell him that I love him and I love being here. I don't want to leave.

'Er, could someone give me a hand here, please, *per favore?*' The English tones cut through the Italian chatter as our neighbours pour drinks and hand round bowls and plates of antipasti. They all stop and stare.

'Who is that?' Anna-Maria scowls as we look at Ed being pinned against the wall by Daphne, who is stamping her foot, snorting and demanding an ID check. There is a ripple of laughter round the courtyard.

'That's Ed. My ex. From England,' I say briefly, and Anna-Maria's face turns as thunderous as her son's.

Chapter Forty-three

After dinner, during which Marco sits as far away from me as possible, his face set and staring into space, with occasional murderous looks towards Ed, some of the group move towards the fire pit, while I go inside to make coffee. I stop and put another log on the roaring fire in the stove.

'Wow! That was some meal!' Ed follows me, rubbing his stomach, which is bulging from his thin frame.

'You made me jump,' I say crossly. I wish he'd just go away. I have no idea what he's doing here. He's turned up out of the blue, expecting me to welcome him in, and actually he's just in the way. I really need to talk to Marco. Why won't he just go? He's delivered the record player, which I'm supposed to be grateful for, and now he looks like he's settling in for the night.

I look around the kitchen. There are neat piles of plates and glasses waiting to be washed up everywhere, and I fill the sink with hot water and noisily dump in some of the plates. I may be cross at Ed turning up like this, but having him here reminds me of how far I've come, how grateful I am to have hot water, good neighbours and really good food on the table. Back in the flat we had on-demand hot water and heating, Sky TV and microwave suppers whenever our busy lives meant we didn't have time to cook. Out here, there is always time. There has to be. Everything good comes with time. Marco's words come back to me and a knife twists in my stomach. The butterflies have closed up their wings and gone to sleep. And it's all Ed's fault!

'Everything all right, Ruthie? You look different. Tired.' Ed puts a hand on my shoulder and I freeze, furious. 'And your hair is longer. Don't expect they have a decent hairdresser for miles,' he says with a laugh. That's it! I turn to him.

'Why have you come, Ed? Really?' I say through gritted teeth. I look at his familiar face. The face I wanted to see when I thought I couldn't do this. The face of the person I have hidden behind for so many years. Familiar but strange at the same time. Like he's from another lifetime.

'I told you, I came to give you the record collection.'

'You're a dreadful liar, always were.' I shake my head.

That's one thing about Ed. He couldn't cheat. When he and Annabel started getting close, I could tell straight away. I don't think Ed knew what had hit him. But she scooped him up, moved him in with her, took care of him and finally declared her love.

'I . . . er . . .' He takes a moment to find the right words. 'I . . . well . . . this place. Once I'd liked your page on Facebook and all my friends started ordering oil, I saw the pictures you'd posted of you and your . . . boyfriend. He looks . . . nice. He not here tonight?' He makes a half-hearted attempt to look towards where voices are still chattering away on the chilly night breeze.

'My boyfriend?' Then the penny drops. 'Oh, you mean Ryan! Ryan's not my . . .' then I realise I don't need to explain anything to Ed any more. 'Ryan won't be around . . . not for a long time.' I think about Franco, and know Ryan has been warned off. 'In fact, I doubt he'll be coming back at all.'

'Oh, I'm sorry.' Ed seems to brighten. 'So . . .' He looks around. 'You're here on your own?'

'Hardly,' I reply, listening to the gathering outside as I make the coffee and lay it up on a tray.

'Oh?'

'I have neighbours.'

The smell of the coffee fills the kitchen as it begins to bubble and steam.

'It's just, well, I've been thinking. Maybe I was too . . . judgemental. Telling you that you should come home, give it up. Saying you couldn't do it and shouldn't try. Everyone I speak to talks about how brave you are to live your dream, to have a go. I wish I was more like you, Ruthie.'

I can't believe it. Suddenly Ed thinks I'm brave. I'm taken aback, but right now the only person I want to talk to is Marco. I want Ed to go.

'Well let's hope they like the oil when they get it. I'll be bottling tomorrow and then shipping it home.' The emphasis being on 'home', hoping he'll take the hint.

'Do you think we were too hasty, too rash, Ruthie?' he suddenly blurts out. 'I mean, you know, if you wanted to give it another go, I'd give it a try.' He grabs hold of my hands and turns me towards him, and I hope to God

Marco doesn't walk in now and get the wrong idea. My eyes flit to the door, and then I pull away and stand back. Here is Ed, offering me everything I wanted, everything I dreamed of when I first arrived here: my old life back in London.

'Ed, why did you really come?'

'I told you . . .' he starts, then his shoulders slump. 'I miss you, Ruthie. I realise I should've been more . . . adventurous. I envy you.'

'Ha! You have a great job; you live in a flat in Canary Wharf with a partner who clearly adores you. Why would you envy me?'

'Because you're not scared.'

'Yes I am!' I'm angry now. 'I was scared the day we agreed to split up. Scared at how clinical you were about dividing everything. Scared about being thirty, single and homeless. And scared shitless that I'd made the biggest mistake of my life by coming here!'

And now I'm scared of making another rash decision. Do I want my old life back with Ed? Back in London, back home? Or do I, ridiculously, want to stay here with a man I've only just got close to? I feel like someone's put a vice on my skull and is tightening it, and with every turn I'm getting more confused.

'I could stay, Ruthie. I could stay with you and we could do it together.'

My anger seeps away.

'I've done the scary bit, Ed. I'm not frightened any more. I know I can go anywhere and do anything now. But this isn't all as rosy as it looks. You can't run away from your problems; they follow you wherever you go. I've found that out.'

He hangs his head.

'Annabel thought I might still want to be with you. I wanted to be sure. I'm getting older and I'm wondering if I've made the right choices in life. I need to find out if I've got any regrets.'

'And have you?'

He takes a moment.

'No.' Then he brightens, 'We had fun, didn't we?'

'Yes.' I smile through the tears that seem to be forming. 'I suppose we did in the beginning. But that was a long time ago. Before we got brave.'

'Before *you* did,' he corrects.

'Before we realised we weren't meant to be together.'

Falling in love is the most painful thing you can do. You definitely need to be brave for that, I think.

'Annabel wants us to get married. She proposed.'

'And what did you say?'

'I said I didn't know, that I had to come and deliver these things to you.'

I realise that this is my now-or-never moment. If I want Ed and my old life back, I have to say so now.

'Do you want to marry her?' I take hold of his wrists. He takes a deep breath and looks up at me.

'Yes, I think I do.'

'Then go for it, Ed. Running back to me isn't the answer. You can't stay scared all your life.'

He lifts his head and nods.

'A man with no future goes back to his past,' he says.

'Go home, Ed. Go back to Annabel. Life out here isn't all sunshine and good food, you know.' I'm quoting Marco again, and now I'm desperate to go and find him. 'We did the right thing. We are different people, but that's not to say we can't be friends.'

Ed throws his arms around me and hugs me, and I can't help but hug him back, as friends, as two people who have shared a past but who need to move on. Right now I have to go and find my future. I pat him on the back to let him know we're fine and good and all done. Still he hugs me, and I realise there are a lot of unspoken words in that hug, like sorry and goodbye.

'I didn't realise I was interrupting.' Marco's voice cuts through the sorrys and goodbyes like a sword. We pull apart, and I watch in horror as he slaps down an envelope on the table, then turns and stalks out.

'Marco!' I call after him in despair, but he just keeps walking. I go cold.

'What about you, Ruthie? What are you going to do?' Ed asks, and I really don't have the strength to tell him that that is the million-dollar question. I look at the envelope on the table and I know exactly what's in it. It's the deeds to the land. I could sell up now; I could go home.

Chapter Forty-four

Outside, everyone has moved to the fire pit in the olive grove. People are smoking and chatting and starting up the ongoing debate over pruning. The fire is pumping out little plumes of smoke and the seasoned olive logs, from Marco's log pile, are glowing. There are jam jars with tea lights hanging from the trees, which seem to be reaching round us like a great big hug. It's cold, smoky and Marco is nowhere to be seen.

'Once the olives have rested for the winter, we start to prune,' Nonna is telling Lou's dad, and Filippo is translating. 'Everyone thinks they have the best pruning method.' She raises her hands and laughs. Anna-Maria is talking to Rosa and Young Luigi and touching their cheeks, like she's basking in the love they're giving off. She looks at me as I arrive with a large tray of coffee and put it on the table under the tree, the same table Marco used to teach me how to taste olive oil.

'Olive oil is the foundation of good cooking and good cooking is the foundation of family life,' Nonna is saying.

Anna-Maria smiles a small smile at me and then, seeing Ed following closely on my heels, turns the smile upside down and scowls. The moon is bright and throws an iridescent light over us. I look around for Marco again.

'Thank God that tall fella's gone. He gave me the creeps,' Ed says, helping himself to coffee and giving Anna-Maria a wide berth. I look over to Marco's *trullo*, where the lights have gone on and the door is firmly shut.

That night, once everyone has headed for home, with waves, kisses and good wishes and the last of my jars of piccalilli to say thank you, I make up the spare bed for Ed. Ed, my first house guest. Who'd've thought that? Not me, that's for sure.

I lie awake listening to him snoring away, sleeping off the Primitivo and the limoncello he's put away. A shaft of moonlight stretches in through the slats in the shutters. I get out of bed, pull a blanket round my shoulders, pad over to the window and open them. It's cold; I shut the window but let the light flood into my bedroom. I look out over the olive grove. The fire pit is still glowing and slowly smouldering. There are piles of fallen branches and leaves across the grove. The nets have been rolled up and pushed into the boughs of the trees. If I strain my neck, I can just see the light on in Marco's *trullo*. Looks like he's not sleeping either. I long to go over there, explain Ed's appearance and what he saw. I long to be in his arms like I was this morning, when anything and everything seemed possible.

I look down at the envelope on the wooden crate that is my bedside table. I pick it up and take it to the window. Slowly I open it and pull out the A4 sheets. As I thought, it's the deeds to the land at the front of the house. He's kept his word. I'm free to sell up and move home. Then I put my hand in and pull out something else. It's an olive branch. It's over, finished.

I let my head rest against the cold glass of the window. If only he knew, that's the very last thing I want right now.

Chapter Forty-five

The next morning I'm up early again, mainly because I didn't get a wink of sleep. All I could see was Marco's furious face as he stormed out of the kitchen, like it was on replay on a DVD. And then there were the deeds. The fire is blazing in the woodburner and eating up wood at an unstoppable speed, like it's found a whole new lease of life. Outside there is a harsh frost. Everything is white. Marco was right, but then he's right about a lot of things, I've come to realise, apart from affairs of the heart. There, he has no idea what I'm thinking or what I want.

I wash and put on plenty of layers, then as quietly as I can, so as not to wake Ed, I slip out into the yard.

Daphne is there, and I let out the chickens and check the veg patch. Then I go to the barn, which yesterday was filled with people and laughter and chatter, just like in the picture I painted; just like it should be. *Mamma* cat and her little ones are snuggled into the box I've lined with blankets, but when they see me, they get out and miaow for food, rubbing against my legs.

After feeding Daphne, the chickens and the cats, I bring out my box of sterilised bottles and begin filling them with the deep green oil from the big steel drums.

When I've finished, I go to the house to find the labels I've made. I pull them out of the envelope and spread them across the table. They're a copy of the brightly coloured painting I did of the *masseria*, and in the top left-hand corner is an olive branch. Underneath the painting it just says *Masseria Bellanuovo*.

Just then Ed comes bumping down the stairs with his very large overnight bag. He looks at me, and I have a feeling that if I say he could stay, he would. But I know that's not right.

'You're going, then?' I ask. He nods.

I feel like I'm standing on the top of a very high diving board. Someone behind me is offering me a hand, a way back down, but I'm still wondering whether to jump.

'Ruthie? Will you be all right?'

'I'll be fine. In fact, I may well be coming back to the UK myself . . . a bit sooner than I was expecting.'

'Really?' Ed pulls a surprised face. 'I thought this was the dream, everything you wanted.' He gestures around him.

'So did I. But I told you, Ed, problems don't disappear with a bit of good food and sunshine!' I try and laugh, but it catches in my throat. I know what I've got to do and it's going to hurt like hell. But I can't stay if Marco really doesn't want me here. I couldn't bear to live so close to him, knowing things could have been so different.

'Hey, these are great. Are they the ones for the guys in the office?'

I nod. 'Wanna help me put them on before you go?'

'Sure,' he says, clearly happy to put off his journey for just a little longer.

He pulls up the zipper on his fleece and follows me to the barn, and we stand side by side over the old press, labelling the bottles. Ed moans about the cold, the quiet, the lack of local shops. I don't think he realises he's moaning; he's just slipped back into his comfortable ways, like an old pair of slippers. This life would never suit him. But I have come to realise I love it . . . Too late I've come to realise I love it.

We finish the first lot of bottling, the ones that need to go to the UK and I haven't forgotten I still need to find a reliable courier. The *masseria* has never felt quieter. It came alive over the past couple of days. How it should be, I think, looking round at the empty *trullo* that I wanted filled with holidaymakers. I look at the courtyard that yesterday was full of olive pickers and neighbours, laughter and talk. The smell of the bonfire still lingers in the air. Who knows when the place will be used like that again. It would be amazing to see this barn working as a press once more, a traditional press like Marco described, pressing Bellanuovo oil. I rub my hand over the stone.

'Penny for them,' says Ed.

'Oh, I was just thinking about home.'

'Me too!' Ed smiles. 'Now if you want, I can give you a lift back. Give us time to talk things over. It'll be fun!'

'You definitely have a distorted memory about some things, Ed. Remember the last time you and I drove through Europe. You had heat rash and an allergic reaction to the sun cream.'

'And you thought you were Jenson Button!' he laughs.

It's a long way from where Ed and I were when I left. We haven't shared a joke in . . . I don't know how long. It feels nice. But I know for sure now that it's not love.

'There's something I have to do,' I tell him, putting the last of the bottles into the boxes and stacking them just outside the barn door.

'Okay, I'm going to get my stuff into the car. Think about it. You could come with me if you want.' He gives a hopeful shrug and shoves his hands into his fleece, looking like he's desperate to get back to London.

'I'll think about it.' I close my eyes and breathe in the fresh smell of the late morning. I could be swapping this for smog in the blink of an eye.

I run into the house and grab the envelope, then take a deep breath and hop over to Marco's *trullo*. This isn't acting on impulse. I've had three and a half months to come to this decision, and it's the right one. I bang on the door.

Marco throws it open with as much force as I've knocked on it.

'*Buongiorno*.' He nods brusquely and then looks beyond me to see who else is there.

'I've come to give you these.' I hold out the envelope towards him. He scowls.

'They are the deeds to the land. You won them fair and square.' He tries to push them back to me and I sigh.

'Marco, I may have made it to the harvest, and I may feel more at home here than I have ever felt anywhere else . . .'

He nods and goes to say something.

'But I realise the *masseria* was never mine to own. It's Masseria Bellanuovo. It's your family's. Not mine.'

For once he doesn't say anything. He is lost for words.

'So here, have the deeds back. And . . . write that cheque out again. I'll take what you offered. I'll sell the *masseria* back to you.'

'But . . .'

'Don't argue, Marco. Take it. You belong there.' I find myself choking.

'You're leaving, then?'

'I think I should.' I can't tell him I can't bear to stay if he doesn't want me, and judging by the look on his face last night when he delivered the deeds, he doesn't. 'But do something for me.'

'Of course.' His eyes are sparkling with tears.

'The press, bring it back. Put in the traditional press you talked about. Oh, and I had another idea. Olive-picking holidays, for people who think a little bit of dolce vita can solve all their problems!' and we both laugh through the tears that are pouring down our cheeks. I turn to leave.

'And one last thing. Courses, residential courses. You could still teach oil-tasting, when you're not harvesting. You have the space, and you could use Lou and Antonio's *trullo* as well once it's up and running.'

He's smiling and brushing away a tear.

'I have never met anyone like you before, Ruthie Collins. You aren't scared of anything.'

Yes I am, I think. Terrified of never falling in love like this again!

'Listen to your heart, Ruthie. You deserve to be happy, more than anyone I know. Do what your heart is telling you to do.'

I can't speak. I spin and run back across the field and over the wall to the *masseria*. I have to get away from Marco, now! Before he hears the sound of my heart ripping in two.

Chapter Forty-six

Ed is loading his big bag into his car.

'Take the records and the player, Ed. I really don't want them. I don't have any use for them,' I tell him, and he shoves the box back into his boot. He turns back to me, almost too nervous to ask.

'So, you decided?'

I nod. 'I have.'

'I've room in the car.' He points to the passenger seat with a hopeful smile.

I could do it. I could just get in the car with Ed and go. Leave all this behind. Return to my life in London. I could come to my senses and listen to my head. Maybe go and stay with Beth for a while and think about what to do next. But my heart knows what it wants. I may be impetuous sometimes but I know I'm doing the right thing. I've had time to think about this and consider it. I'm not acting in the moment. I've wanted this for a long time, I realise. I take a deep breath,

'I'm not coming, Ed.'

'What?' He bangs his head as he pulls away from the boot. 'You're staying here?' He looks incredulous.

'Sadly, no. I can't. But I'm going to find somewhere

else to live. Closer to town maybe.'

'What will you do for work?'

I shrug. 'I'll find something. I might even start teaching, art classes, what do you think?'

At first he looks horrified. And then he smiles.

'You always were the impulsive one, Ruthie.'

'Only this time I'm not acting on impulse. I've had months to decide. This place is home now. I can't go back.'

He steps towards me and hugs me.

'Go back to Annabel. Go and get married. Don't be scared!' I tell him.

He gets into his car and starts the engine. Then, with a beep of the horn, he sticks his hand out of the window and waves. I glance back at the *masseria* and see that Marco is standing on the front step, looking like he's always belonged. I turn back and watch Ed's tail lights moving up the drive and stopping at the gates. In my hand is the olive branch, the one Marco left in the envelope. I look down at it. Am I doing the right thing? Can I really stay here knowing that Marco doesn't want to be with me?

'Ed, stop!' I shout suddenly, and run down the drive waving my arms and the branch.

'Changed your mind?' Ed looks confused but smiles, holding his mobile as it pings into life with message after message.

'Ruthie!'

There's a shout from behind me, and Marco is running towards me. He's standing right in front of me now, and I'm willing him to find the words to tell me how he's feeling. He's looking at me and I'm looking at him. My heart is thundering, banging away like the funeral band the day of his grandfather's funeral.

'Don't!' he says finally.

'Don't what?' I search his face. He has to tell me how he feels. I can't guess this. He can't run away from his feelings for ever.

'Don't do it!' Every word is hard for him.

'What?' I need him to say it.

Suddenly Daphne butts him from behind and he grabs my elbows. Our faces are up close.

'Don't leave.' And suddenly the words begin to come to him. 'You belong here as much as I do. I don't want this place if it means having it without you. I offered you half what you paid for it. I will only buy half, if you will share the other half with me!' he finally manages to say. For a man who can talk endlessly about olives, those words took a long time coming. But as I've learnt, anything good here takes time, and when it comes, it's worth it.

'What do you say? Will you stay? With me?' His eyes search mine.

For once, I'm lost for words. I can't speak. Instead I just nod and then let my lips do the talking as I reach up and he bends to meet me. Ed's phone is pinging with more messages. I know this time I'm not acting on impulse. It's destiny. However this turns out, I have to take the chance. I couldn't bear not to try. I have to jump off the diving board.

'Sooo,' Ed interrupts us as we pull apart, smiling like loons. 'It's Annabel. She's wants me to come home. I'm going to get married, Ruthie.' He waves the phone.

'That's great!' I beam. 'I'm staying put too, here, home.'

Ed frowns. 'So why exactly did you run after me?'

'Oh, I was thinking you could deliver the bottles to your colleagues, seeing as you're going home.' I shrug cheekily.

Marco steps back and looks mildly affronted.

'You mean . . . you weren't leaving?'

'No, I couldn't leave. I still have so much to learn about pruning!' I tease.

'Yes, you do!' He laughs too and kisses me all over again.

We wave Ed off and then walk back to the *masseria* hand in hand. The sun has come out, autumnal and bright.

'Marco!' Anna-Maria calls. 'Will you be here for dinner? You too, Ruthie?'

Marco looks at me.

'Not tonight, Mamma.' Then he drops his voice. 'Family is all very well and good, but there are times when being alone is better.' We nudge each other and grab a kiss that turns into a longer one.

As the sun starts to dip in the sky, Marco lights the fire pit again, and the tea lights in the olive tree. He lays a sheepskin rug from the *trullo* beside the fire and then kisses me deeply, like I've never been kissed before. We make love, slowly and gently, under the olive tree, and as the wood smokes and crackles in the fire pit, little sparks fly up and bigger sparks explode inside me. I look up at the flickering candles as our bodies finally fit together and know that I never want this night to end.

Later, wrapped in jumpers and blankets, we eat potatoes cooked in the fire and sausages fried over the flames. And that night, as soft snowflakes start to fall in the olive grove and we make love all over again in Marco's little *trullo*, I know I've finally come home for good.

Epilogue

I close the door on the *trullo* and walk carefully across the stepping stones Marco has laid, in my light blue ballet shoes and sheer floral dress, pulling my pashmina around me.

Everything is ready. The wind is lifting the white ribbons that I've spent all morning tying to olive trees around the terrace at the back of the *masseria*. It's now tiled in cream stone, with stone seating like an amphitheatre along one side. Out here there are speakers neatly disguised by two white rose bushes. Fairy lights lead the way into the courtyard, where more lights are strung and more white ribbons lift gently in the breeze. The intense heat has gone out of the day and the breeze is very welcome.

The honeymoon *trullo* is covered in more fairy lights, working their way all the way up the conical roof. Inside I do a final check, putting olive branches in a jar on the table and adjusting the cushions on the lavender-coloured bedclothes. Then, with a final nod of satisfaction, I turn and shut the door. It's all ready for its first newlyweds tonight.

I skip over the cobbles to where Daphne is gently

grazing in her pen. She too is wearing a white ribbon around her neck and seems thrilled with her elevated position as wedding guest.

In the house there is a buzz. Every room upstairs is full. In fact, they are all fully booked right up until the harvest. Loads of Ed's work colleagues are due to come as working students, and we have guests staying at Lou and Antonio's too. After that, Mum, Colin and my brother are coming to stay again. Marco and I have moved into his *trullo* and are planning another extension there.

'Marco!' I call.

'*Si*,' he calls back. I follow the sound of his voice, and as I step into the room I catch my breath.

'It's beautiful!' I say, standing in the doorway of the little church. There is a big bunch of olive branches on the altar. Nonna and Anna-Maria have made new red and gold curtains for the back wall and I have replicated the mural from the school down the side of the room.

'Our first wedding!' I squeal.

'My grandfather would be so proud,' he says. 'He knew what he was doing when he got you to move here.' He slides his arm around me and kisses me.

On cue, Nonna arrives in the church and immediately covers her nose with her big hankie and blows loudly. Lou's dad is by her side, guiding her to a seat at the front.

I need to go and meet the bride and groom. I sidle reluctantly from Marco's grasp.

Out at the front of the house there are more ribbons, and my heart soars as I see Young Luigi and Rosa arriving with their family and friends in convoy behind them.

Rocco is doing car-parking duty and his daughter is handing out posies of lavender. The young waitress from Antonio's café is handing round glasses of Prosecco.

After the ceremony, we eat at long tables. Marco's sister has made the food and we've brought in some of his cousin's teenage children to wait on tables. It's a family business after all. It's not just producing, marketing and selling the olive oil that we're all pulling together on. It's this place too.

Then, as darkness falls, the dancing begins. Traditional dancers waving scarves in the warm summer evening appear from behind the trees, twisting and turning, their long hair flying behind them as they tell stories of love and love lost. The dancers are barefoot, and the little bells around their waists and ankles tinkle as they dance on mats laid out on the terrace. They encourage the guests to join them, and I hand round Ed's mother's scarves. Finally the guests call for '*Bacio, bacio, bacio!*' and the bride and groom kiss like their lives depend on it.

'And who will be the next wedding?' Anna-Maria raises an eyebrow as we dance amongst the twisted scarves, and I throw back my head and laugh. But when I look back at Marco, he isn't laughing.

'Well?' he says. 'Will you marry me?'

'I'll tell you what,' I say, trying to hide the smile that is bursting to be set free, 'if you can make it to the end of the olive harvest, then yes, of course I'll marry you!'

'I think I could manage that. But I'll need a good assistant, one who's willing to learn.'

'Looks like I'm your woman then! Although you have a

lot on, what with the book you're finally writing, and getting the courses ready for next year. And we have a lot more takers on the rent-a-tree scheme, I thought you could be my assistant!'

He picks me up and spins me around and I am as happy as if all my olive harvests have come at once, as a light breeze shimmers through the olive grove and the white ribbons flutter in approval.

Luigi beams a wide toothless smile as he dances with Mrs Luigi, twisting her around in the scarves as she channels her inner Isadora Duncan.

My electrician is there with his wife, as is the ironmonger and the fruit and veg seller, Franco and his family, and the headmistress from the school. Lou is there nursing her swollen belly, and Antonio and Giac move to the music. Marco's cousins dance with Filippo and the rest of the family, clapping along as Nonna shows Lou's dad her moves.

Sophia and Anna-Maria have taken to the dance floor, smiling and laughing together like old friends, like sisters-in-law. Anna-Maria looks round at me and nods.

'*Grazie*,' she smiles.

'*Prego*,' I mouth back. Because sometimes in life, a bit of sun and dolce vita is exactly what you need.

Suddenly Daphne is on the dance floor.

'Who let the goat out!'

But Daphne isn't going to miss out on a party like this, and we all dance around her, because the goat lives here, it's her home. As it is mine.

Acknowledgments

Thank you, Rich, for introducing me to the world of olive oil and for helping me to find out all I needed to know on a fab research trip. Lynda, it couldn't have happened if you hadn't introduced me to Puglia and olive trees. Thanks to Pete and Jen for lovely pizzas by the *forno*, and for help on moving to Italy, local knowledge and Ed and Layla's beautiful wedding.

Thank you as always to my lovely agent Hannah Ferguson, my editor Emily Griffin and all at Headline for their faith and guidance. And as always to my friends at the Romantic Novelists Association for their encouragement. To Katie for her continued support and friendship, and to the Thomas family at home for being there, always.

Read on for an extract from Jo's debut novel
and runaway ebook bestseller,
available now in paperback and ebook.

The Oyster Catcher

**Dooleybridge, County Galway. Population: 482
(or thereabouts). The last place Fiona Clutterbuck
expects to end up, alone, on her wedding night.**

But after the words 'I do' have barely left her mouth,
that's exactly where she is – with only her sequined shoes
and a crashed camper van for company.

One thing is certain: Fi can't go back. So when the
opportunity arises to work for Sean Thornton, the local oyster
farmer, she jumps at the chance. Now Fi must navigate
suspicious locals, jealous rivals and a wild, unpredictable
boss if she's to find a new life, and love, on the Irish coast.
And nothing – not even a chronic fear of water –
is going to hold her back.

**Join Fi on her romantic, unpredictable adventure as she
learns the rules of the ocean – and picks up a few pearls
of Irish wisdom along the way . . .**

headline
review

Chapter One

A bracing blast of sea air hits me head on. It's clean, fresh and smells of salt. I'm standing on the steps of the Garda station. Mind you, it's more of a shabby Portakabin than a police station, really. The wind blows my hair and I hold my face up to it, letting any tears that may have escaped mingle with the damp air. With my eyes shut and my face in the wind I realise two things. One, I'm in a place called Dooleybridge; and two, I am absolutely stranded wearing the only dress I have – the one I'd just got married in.

I open my eyes and shiver, pulling my arms tightly around me, trying to warm myself up and protect myself from the nightmare I'm in. Only forty-eight hours ago I was saying the words 'I do' and thought I had everything I wanted in life: a job, a home and a husband. It was all mapped out. Now I have no husband, not even a fiancé. I've left my job, my home and my life, in a stolen camper van that I'm apparently under caution for stealing, parking illegally and driving recklessly.

In a state of shock I walk back to where I'd last seen the camper. Well, where it'd come to a crunching halt after crashing into the harbour wall. Looking at the wall now, I don't know how I didn't see it. But I was very distracted at the time, to say the least. I remember the road getting bumpier and hitting some big pot holes. I could hardly see through the tears. I remember the final bend, not knowing whether to swing left or right. It all happened so fast. My heart was racing and suddenly the van was as out of control as the rest of my life. I couldn't stop. Today was supposed to be the first day of my married life. Now it couldn't be further from how I'd imagined.

I roll my shoulders back and rub my neck. A doctor visited me in the Garda station but said my injuries were nothing a hot bath and some TLC wouldn't cure. Maybe he's right, but I'm a long way from either of those things right now. A very long way indeed. And now the camper van has been reclaimed by the hire company and towed away, I have no idea what I'm going to do.

There are some scuff marks on the harbour wall and the remains of one of the headlights, but other than that I can't see any trace that the camper was there at all. I bend down to pick up the light and look around to see if anyone's watching me, but no one's there. Not like earlier when I had been escorted to the Garda station by a uniformed officer. With blue lights flashing we'd travelled all of 200 metres from the crashed camper to the station. You'd think he'd caught one of Ireland's most wanted criminals. I could feel eyes on me from everywhere – the doorway of the pub and the windows of the houses – as the sirens sang out and the lights lit up the buildings either side of the road. My cheeks had burned and my stomach twisted as I was escorted, in my wedding dress, from 'the scene of the crime'.

Oh, that's the other thing I realise as I look at the abandoned headlight in my hand: there's absolutely no way I can go home, no way at all.

I turn round and walk back towards the road; when I say walk, it's more of a hobble. My shoes are killing me and they're splashing water up the back of my feet and calves. But then it isn't really gold mule weather. It's cold and wet and I couldn't feel any more miserable than I already do. I head back up the hill, across the road just below the Garda station, and stand outside the pub. I pull a piece of paper from my pocket and look at my shaky handwriting. I must be mad even thinking about this. I'd jotted down the details of a job advertised in the paper I'd been looking through as I tried to distract myself from the wreckage of my life while the Garda filled in his report. I have no idea what made me copy it down. Maybe it's just my survival instinct kicking in, sink or swim.

I take a deep breath that hurts my chest and makes me cough. I look at the paper again. I have no other choice. I put my head down and step into a tiled doorway, touching the cold brass panel on the door, and with all the determination I can muster, I push it open.

The door crashes against the wall as I fall in, making me and everyone else jump. As I land I realise it's not the throng I was expecting but a handful of people. All eyes are on me. A hot rash travels up my chest and into my cheeks, making them burn, and inside I cringe. I feel as though I've walked on to the set of a spaghetti western and the piano player has stopped playing.

'Sorry,' I mouth, and shut the door very gently behind me. My stomach's churning like a washing machine on spin cycle. I look round the open-plan pub. At one end is a small fireplace and, despite it supposedly being summer, there's a fire in the grate giving out a brave, cheery, orange glow in contrast to the chilly atmosphere. There's an unfamiliar smell in the air, earthy yet sweet. In the grate there are lumps of what look like burning earth. Back home I'd just flick on the central heating, but home is a very long way away right now. There's wood panelling all across the front of the bar, above it, below it and round the walls. When I say wood panelling, it's tongue and groove pine that's been stained dark. It's the sort of place you'd expect to be full of cigarette smoke but isn't. In the corner by the fire there's a small group of people, all of them as old as Betty from Betty's Buns. Or The Coffee House as it's now known.

Betty's my employer – or should that be my ex-employer? She refuses to take retirement and sits on a stall at the end of the counter, looking like Buddha. She's never been able to give up the reins on the till. She did once ask me to take over as manager but I turned it down. I'm not one for the limelight. I'm happy back in the kitchen. Kimberly, who works the counter, tried for the job, but Sandra from TGI Friday's got it and Kimberly took up jogging and eating fruit.

The group by the fire is still staring at me, just like Betty keeping her beady eye on her till. There are two drinkers at the bar, one in an old tweed cap and jacket with holes in the elbows, the other in a thin zip-up shell suit and a baseball cap. They've turned to stare at me too. With burning cheeks and the rash still creeping up my chest, I take a step forward and then another. It feels like a game of grandmother's footsteps as their eyes follow me too. The barmaid's wiping glasses and smiles at me. I feel ridiculously grateful to see a friendly face. It's not her short spiky hair that makes her stand out, nor her big plastic Dayglo earrings. It's the fact she's probably in her early twenties, I'd say, unlike any of her customers.

A couple of dogs come barking at me from behind the bar. I step back. One is black with stubby legs, a long body and a white stripe down its front. The other is fat and looks a bit like a husky crossed with a pot-bellied pig. I'm not what you'd call brave really. I've always thought it was better to try and skirt conflict rather than face it head on. I look for someone or something to hide behind but the barmaid steps in.

'Hey, settle down,' she snaps. She might be small but she's got a mighty bark. Unsurprisingly the dogs return behind the bar, tails between their legs. I think I'd've done the same if she'd told me to.

'Now then, what can I get you?' She wipes her hands on a tea towel and smiles again.

'Um . . .' I go to speak but nothing comes out. I clear my dry throat and try again. 'I'm looking for . . .' I look down at the piece of paper in my hand, the back of the parking ticket I was handed for parking a camper van illegally. It was the only paper I had. I still can't believe I'm even contemplating this, but I'm just not sure what else I can do. I look back at the barmaid, feeling as confused as she seems. '. . . Sean Thornton?' I say as firmly as I can. 'I'm looking for Sean Thornton.'

The barmaid cocks her head to one side and frowns. She reaches up on tip-toes and leans over the bar. Unashamedly her eyes travel upwards, taking in my shoes and the torn hem of my dress. I tug at it. Bits of hanging cotton, like tassels, catch round my fingers. Some come away and I shake my hand to flick them off. The rash starts to creep up my chest again.

Finally the barmaid nods over to the opposite side of

the bar from where everyone else is sitting. There's a man on his own. He looks up at me.

'Over there,' she nods again, keeping her eyes on me, as if I've got two heads which may start spinning in opposite directions at any minute.

'Thank you.' I turn to look at the man in the worn wax jacket. He looks terrifying. He's got a table to himself and I'm not surprised. He's scowling, tapping a pen on a notebook and making the white cup and saucer next to him rattle. He looks up at me and raises an eyebrow then beckons me with a single flick of the wrist. I'm rooted to the spot as he impatiently calls me over again. What I should do is leave very quickly. But my feet won't move. He does not look like the sort of person you'd pull up a chair with for a friendly chat.

'Oh, looks like someone's beaten you to it,' says the barmaid as we watch the younger of the two men from the bar, the one in the shell suit, go over and speak to Sean Thornton. 'Can I get you something while you wait?' she says a little more cheerily. I feel my spirits plummet even lower, and I hadn't thought that was remotely possible, as I look over at the man in the shell suit, sitting on a small green velour-covered stool opposite Sean Thornton.

'Do you do tea?' I sigh rather more loudly than I'd intended to. The group in the corner is still watching me.

'Tea? Sure.' The barmaid picks up a pen and pad. 'Anything to eat?'

I shake my head, thinking about the few euros I've got left after paying the damages at the Garda station. 'For reckless driving,' he'd said. He was probably right too. My stomach suddenly rumbles loudly, like a lion's roar.

My hand shoots up to cover both it and my blushes at the same time.

'Soup and a sandwich,' the barmaid tells me rather than asks, with a raised eyebrow.

'Fine,' I quickly agree.

The barmaid flicks on the kettle with a flourish. I can't help but feel she's still keeping an eye on me. Now that she's moved to the back of the bar, I can see she's wearing purple leather-look shorts with tights underneath and a red T-shirt saying 'Drama Queen' in sparkles. In contrast I look down at my big grey sweatshirt and nude-coloured tatty dress.

'On holiday, are you?' she shouts over the noisy kettle, cutting into my thoughts.

'Um, well, not exactly. Well, sort of.' I can't answer this without going into a long explanation and that's the last thing I want to do right now. 'Excuse me,' I try and change the subject quickly. 'Could you tell me where the loo is?' To my surprise she put her hands on her hips and shakes her head. The kettle is still warming up noisily.

'Daloo?' She shakes her peroxide head again and then to my bigger surprise says, 'No, can't say I've ever heard of it.' She looks genuinely puzzled. For a moment I freeze and then the penny drops. OK, very funny. It's that Irish humour. I try and join in the joke and laugh good-naturedly.

'Hey, John Joe,' the barmaid calls over to the group huddled by the fire. Oh dear God, please don't tell me this is happening, that it's some sort of prank they pull on holiday-makers looking for the toilet.

'Any ideas where Daloo is?'

An elderly man in a holey jumper shakes his head.

'What about you, Evelyn? You've got kids living all over the place, any idea where Daloo is?'

Evelyn's in an oversized anorak. She turns down her mouth and shakes her head.

'Frank? Any ideas?'

Frank scratches the black spiral curls poking out from under his woollen hat.

'Grandad? What about you? If anyone knows about this place it's you.'

Someone nudges Grandad awake and he splutters.

'Daloo! She's looking for Daloo!' Evelyn shouts at him. He shakes his head and goes back to sleep, resting his elbows on the arms of his wheelchair and letting his head fall forwards.

If there really is a God, would he just let the floor open up now and let me fall through it? I look up to the ceiling and shut my eyes in hope. Nothing. Just like my mother, He's never been around when I've needed Him either.

'I think . . .' a voice pipes up next to me and makes me jump. My eyes ping open. Sean Thornton is standing beside me. The man in the shell suit is back at the bar, picking up his pint and shaking his head. 'I think,' he repeats slowly and quietly, 'that the lady is looking for the bathroom.' He puts down his cup and saucer on the bar. 'Through there to the left,' he points, and gratefully I put my head down and scuttle in that direction.

I grab hold of the porcelain sink and splash water over my face and then attempt to dry it with a stiff paper towel, which just inflicts pain. I look into the mottled mirror. The person staring back scares me. I hardly recognise myself. My eyes are swollen, my face blotchy and red, and

I look as if I've aged ten years. A far cry from the blushing bride that left home yesterday.

'Sean told me to put your food over there,' the barmaid says a little sulkily as I return from the loo, like someone who's been told off. She goes back to polishing the glasses.

On a table tucked round the other side of the bar a bowl of steaming orange soup and a huge doorstep sandwich is waiting for me. My stomach roars again in expectation.

'Thought you might like to eat somewhere a little more private.' Sean Thornton nods to the group on the other side of the pub.

'Thank you,' I say and go to sit down.

'No problem. I'd like to say they mean well, but . . . I can't,' he says, throwing a look first at the locals on the other side of the bar and then at the two standing next to it. They pull down their hats and turn in towards each other. I realise I need to seize my opportunity.

'Actually, are you Sean Thornton?' I pick up the red paper napkin by my bowl and twist it in my hands. I try and smile but it probably looks more like a grimace.

'I am,' he says evenly and stares right back at me, making me feel nervous. There's no humour in his eyes.

'Good.' My throat is drying again. 'In that case,' I say really quickly, with what feels like a tennis ball in my throat, 'I've come about the job.'

Escape to the vineyards of France in Jo's latest romantic novel, available in ebook and paperback.

Late Summer in the Vineyard

Emmy Bridges wouldn't say that life has exactly gone to plan so far.

Whilst everyone around her is getting engaged, married and promoted, Emmy is less than enamoured with her job and still lives at home in Bristol with her dad.

But all that is set to change . . .

When her bosses propose sending Emmy to the South of France to learn about wine, she knows this could be the big break she needs. But with three other colleagues in tow, a dream job up for grabs and a wine merchant who is paying her rather more attention than she'd like, Emmy will have her work cut out if she's going to make the most of this fresh new start.

But life – like the local wine – is better when you trust your instincts. Now it's up to Emmy to plant new roots of her own.

headline
review

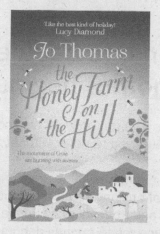

When one book ends, another begins...

Bookends is a vibrant new reading community to help you ensure you're never without a good book.

You'll find monthly reading recommendations, previews of brilliant new books, and exclusive features on and from your favourite authors. We'll also introduce you to exciting debuts and remind you of past classics.

There'll be a regular blog, reading group guides, competitions and much more!

Visit our website to see which great books we're recommending this month.

welcometobookends.co.uk

f /welcometobookends

🐦 @teambookends